COUNTDOWN

By

Kristen Moran

ISBN 0-9615528-0-8

Library of Congress 85-73211

Manufactured by Apollo Books, 107 Lafayette St., Winona, MN 55987

PRINTED IN THE UNITED STATES OF AMERICA

To Joe,

for sharing the thrill

of it all

PREFACE

On September 22, 1979, a U.S. reconnaissance satellite, orbiting somewhere over the South Atlantic and Indian Oceans between South Africa and Antarctica, registered the detonation of a nuclear device.

To this day that explosion has never been explained.

Nearly everyone in the world, however—from politicians to men on the street, from diplomats to scientists—has expressed an opinion on the subject. The United States and various other members of the world community charged South Africa with entering the ranks of nations possessing and testing nuclear weapons. The South African Government vehemently rejected that claim, even though its involvement in nuclear activities is well-known, and ventured its own theory: that a Soviet submarine, known to be patrolling the area, exploded. The Russians hedged that question in a typically Soviet fashion, but it is generally conceded that while a nuclear sub can melt down, it is physically impossible for it to explode.

One of the more common, albeit uninformed, opinions advanced was that the satellite simply picked up the flash of an ordinary lightning bolt. The only thing wrong with the idea was that there was not one flash, but two, occurring in rapid succession, as there always are in nuclear explosions. For the "ordinary lightning bolt" hypothesis to have been true, it would have to have been a quite extraordinary double-bolt of lightning.

While few authorities accepted the lightning bolt theory, some scientists have suggested that it might not be far off,

1

that the explosion might have been the result of some strange, unidentified natural phenomenon, but others maintained the satellite simply malfunctioned.

Each of these claims has been subject to hot international debate, and yet none has ever been definitively proven. In all probability, one of these theories is the correct explanation.

But maybe not....

PROLOGUE

JULY 22, 1979

A man, deep in thought, walked along a Cairo sidewalk towards an intersection. He was an ordinary-looking man, a man whose only distinctive quality was that he possessed no distinction whatsoever. That, his command of languages and his lack of any obvious ethnicity, allowed him to move anonymously anywhere in the world, something that did not go unnoticed by either the leaders of the terrorist organization to which he belonged or the international peace-keepers who tried unsuccessfully to contain him.

The man reached the corner and stepped into the street without looking. In all but one time in a million, he would have crossed that street safely, as most of us cross most of the streets of our lives. But this one time, the car moved a little too fast, the man, too slow, and a connection was made.

Death is a unique experience—obviously, because it only occurs once in a lifetime—but also because it strikes every man differently. The cliché that there are no atheists in foxholes is not an accurate one. Many men find that the ideals they have lived by, good or bad, are strengthened in the end. The fact that there was a purpose to their lives gives them a sense of peace in death.

But other men, as they face impending death, just spill their guts.

Beyond pain, beyond dignity, the dying man looked up into the crowd that was forming around him in the street and searched for the uniform of authority. Ten minutes ago he would not have considered revealing what he knew, but then,

3

he had not been dying. The accident changed his entire perspective. He knew that the warm, sticky substance oozing out of him was all that was left of his life. It was going fast and so was he. But he had to hold on until he found someone who would listen to what he had to say. He had to make amends for what he had done and what he had planned to do.

Instead of the focused attention he required, however, the man saw only mild interest in the faces above him. The greatest tragedy in his life was nothing more than a minor spot of entertainment in theirs. One man did try to perform a little rudimentary first-aid, but most of them just stared at him, without really looking. They were already thinking of the ways they would embellish this story later when they told it to friends, before forgetting it forever.

"The police!" the man shouted. Not once, but many times, in several different languages. In his confusion he couldn't remember what country he happened to be traveling in at the moment.

No one appeared to stir, but someone, somewhere, must have made the call because the sound of approaching sirens could soon be heard.

A small, wiry man with an odd appearance and the unlikely name of Rahmire Jones happened to be passing that intersection at the time of the ambulance's arrival. He was a dark-complexioned young man, with huge, anxious eyes in a small ferret face that was ridiculously crowned by an unruly mop of reddish-blond hair. People often gave Rahmire a second glance, but only because his appearance was somewhat unusual; he was convinced, however, that it was because he was a freak. He was shy and pitifully self-conscious.

Rahmire saw the crowd gathered in the intersection and joined it out of curiosity. Most of the people in front of him were taller, and because he was too timid to push his way through, he never saw the man in the center of the crowd who was being treated by the ambulance drivers. The police arrived and parted the crowd, pushing Rahmire back even

4

farther. He was about to give up and move on, when a garbled, incoherent, but still familiar voice, rang out.

"In Israel!" the dying man said. "It will...happen...in Israel. Within...the next...six months."

Rahmire did not know because he couldn't see them, but at the mention of Israel, both he and the police officers became instantly alert, though for different reasons. While the Egyptian Government officially opposes terrorism, some of the individual officers who carry out that policy actually favor it, some despise it, and others are indifferent to it, but they all know one thing: thwarting a major terrorist offensive can result in significant career advancements.

"What will happen?" one of the officers asked.

"From...South Africa...South Africa."

"What is from South Africa?"

"South Africa...Israel...South...Africa," the dying man muttered before passing out.

The policemen looked at each other and shook their heads. They couldn't make any sense out of it. Only one person in that whole crowd understood what any of it meant, and that was Rahmire Jones.

The dying man regained consciousness again just as he was being lifted into the ambulance.

"Watch...out for...the...American reporter," he warned.

One of the drivers looked to the police officers to see if they wanted to hear any more of the man's statement, but the policemen just waved for the ambulance door to be shut. The dying man refused to be silenced just yet, however. His hand clutched at one of the drivers, signaling him to stop. Then, with a surprising show of strength, he lifted his head and made direct eye contact with one of the officers.

"Ask Ali," he said with great deliberation.

Ali! the policeman thought disgustedly. That part of the world was filled with Alis. Where did he start? But he knew that fate had given him the responsibility to allow that poor man to go to his rest.

"I will," he said with all the sincerity he could muster.

5

With that, the dying man lowered his head and the gurney was pushed into the ambulance. A moment later, with his conscience cleared, the man died, although no one knew it until they reached the hospital.

"Why don't you ask Ali?" the second policeman asked, a little envious that the man hadn't chosen him to receive his dying declaration.

The first officer responded with an obscene gesture.

The intersection started returning to normal. The ambulance sped off, the policemen returned to their car, the crowd dispersed. Soon, Rahmire Jones was the only one left standing there.

A total Palestinian in his soul, if not his heritage, Rahmire lived for only one thing: the reclamation of his homeland. In his naiveté, he believed that only there would the problem of his uncommon origin be solved; only there would he really fit in. He knew the dying man might have destroyed the dream he felt sure was finally within his grasp. Only he didn't know what to do about it. He just knew he had to do something.

Armageddon couldn't be abandoned that easily.

PART ONE:

THE SPARK

CHAPTER ONE

SEPTEMBER 6, 1979

A car backfired in the street outside London's Heathrow Airport. Amidst the din produced by heavy traffic it was not terribly noticeable, but the miniature explosion was different enough from the norm to cause some people to turn and look at the offending vehicle, a few to start suddenly and one elderly lady to clasp her chest in a gasp. Alison Hayden happened to be passing the woman on her way to the terminal entrance. She paused and placed a reassuring hand on the woman's arm.

"It's all right. Nothing's happened," Ali said, then muttered to herself as she turned away, "Nor is it likely to."

Most excitement you'll see for a while, she thought as she pushed open the door to the terminal, quite secure in her certainty that she was right. They weren't holding the presses, she was sure, to immortalize that comment in the latest edition of *Famous Last Words*.

She pressed through the door and paused to savor the sight before her, a wry little smile lifting one corner of her proud, irreverent mouth. The object of that smile was a crowded terminal. It was jammed, packed to the rafters with a motley assortment of visitors of every possible international persuasion, each of whom seemed convinced that his was to be the last flight ever available to mankind, which, therefore, demanded that he fight to the death to keep his place on it. The pushing and shoving, the impatient, irritable tempers, and the non-stop barrage of unfamiliar languages should have made the terminal an unbearable place for Ali to enter, particularly since she was leaving behind one of the most beautiful days London had seen that year, but it did not. After more than a month of relative inactivity while vacationing in her native San Francisco, she was back in the harness again, and she loved it. Like a laboratory animal suddenly returned to its natural environment, she thrived on the sights, the sounds, the smells of her world.

Alison Laurel Hayden was a thoroughbred. Her face combined the flawless skin and classic bone structure of a photographic model, with the strong, firm chin of a fighter. Her body's long, lean lines altered only by slightly too-full breasts made for an elegant, thoroughly female form which moved with the brusque, impatient energy of a racehorse at the starting gate. A body built for speed, with the strength to go the distance. She looked a little younger than her thirty-three years, but took charge like someone who'd been around a lot longer, a result, no doubt, of her unusual background. She was a daughter of one of San Francisco's oldest and wealthiest families and also the best foreign correspondent employed by *The San Francisco Star* newspaper. She was one of the few people who didn't find that combination strange; she had always known that the pretty, little debutante she had been raised to be was a lot tougher than anyone gave her credit for. Her eyes were sea-green, alert and intelligent; her hair, a rich reddish-brown, cut to her shoulders in a way that took advantage of her natural curl. Infinitely more familiar with the names of Palestinian terrorists than Paris or New York fashion designers, her knowledge of clothes was virtually nil, although very few people realized that. She was one of those rare women who can throw on any old rag, which best described most of her wardrobe, and make it look chic, a woman oblivious to fashion but with a style all her own.

When someone bumped into her, she realized that she was still standing in the doorway. No more time for reverie, she thought. She was on her way to an assignment, even if it wasn't one that thrilled her.

10

"South Africa!" she had said when her editor, Sam Elliott, first proposed it. "Whatever for? Nothing ever happens there, apart from apartheid, and that will never change."

Elliott had said that was not true. Other things did happen there occasionally, such as the story she had covered there about a year and a half before. Now he needed an update on that piece, and she was the logical person to do it. And since she was going, he added, she might as well do a "South Africa Today"-type piece for the paper's Sunday Supplement.

"Look at it this way," he had said, "South Africa's practically on the way to your regular post in Cairo."

Ali had snorted at that geographical fiction and reminded him that she would need a photographer for the Supplement assignment. Elliott told her he had secured the services of one of the best young photo-journalists in the world: Evan Michael Todd.

"What a waste," she had muttered.

Waste or not, she was on her way to the place where nothing happened. Whether the celebrated photographer was going to condescend to join her was still up to debate. As she made her way to the ticket counter, she searched the male faces around her, repeating Elliott's description in her mind: a little taller than average, brown hair, brown eyes, a slightly stocky build. She had joked at the time that she was sure to recognize him easily since that description wouldn't fit more than half the men in Heathrow, only as it turned out, it didn't fit any of them.

She glanced at her watch. She was running late, as usual, but she took the time during check-in to make sure Evan Michael Todd had secured the seat next to hers. The clerk assured her that he had. At least he did that, she thought irritably.

Though they had never met, Ali knew about as much about Evan Todd as most people in the media. In spite of his reclusive nature, his story was well-known. He had been born in New York City thirty years before, to a wimp of a mother

11

and a drunken brute of a father who liked to take his temper out on victims too helpless to fight back. It was a terrible life for Evan and his sisters, and the court was forever taking the children out of that family and shoving them into foster homes that weren't much better.

He became a withdrawn child, who found it hard to love and impossible to trust, until he had the good fortune to be placed with foster parents who really cared about the children they took in. One Christmas those people gave him a simple box camera, which changed his whole life.

From the start, he displayed an uncommon gift that was to grow as the years passed. Photography saved Evan's life; it gave him a means of escape when he needed it and, later, a career, but, more importantly, it gave him a way of dealing with the world. The lens did more than protect him from the cruelties he had good reason to know the world possessed, it filtered them out, letting only the goodness in. And through that same lens, he was able to express the benevolence he still felt for his fellow men but was not able to show in any other way. His photographs showed none of the bitterness he would have been justified in feeling.

One year, early in this career, he happened to stop off in London, liked it, and stayed. And his reputation continued to grow until he was regarded as one of the world's best photo-journalists. For all his brilliance, however, he was also reputed to be a moody, sometimes even tempermental, person to work with.

Elliott had told Ali to ignore those rumors when she had mentioned them. The temperment was just a cover for shyness, he had insisted; Evan Todd was really a very gentle man.

Ali had accepted his assessment at the time, but was now beginning to doubt it. In the two days she had spent in London she had tried repeatedly to talk to him, but he never deigned to return any of the many messages she left with his answering service, including the one in which she had asked him to meet her at the ticket counter. She was not at all sure she was going to like working with the great Evan Michael

Todd. But she was grateful to him for one reason—he had insisted on flying first class. Since they were working together, the same travel arrangements had been approved for her, a rare luxury she was always eager to enjoy.

Since it was quite close to take-off time, the gate was nearly empty when Ali passed through it. But there was one other late passenger approaching the plane's tunnel, a cute little blond girl with a German accent who had coaxed an airline employee into toting her small carry-on bag for her. Ali smiled in cynical amusement and was suddenly aware of the weight of her own bag. She wasn't jealous of the girl and her ability to use men, however, she felt sorry for her. Women like her only seemed aware of what they gained from living their lives through men, she thought, but never of what they lost.

Once in the first class cabin, she saw Evan Todd standing near their assigned seats. Relieved that he had shown up, most of her anger faded. Perhaps he had not received her messages. She recognized him, not so much from Elliott's description, as the camera gear he was stowing in the overhead compartment.

"Are you Ali?" he asked shyly as she approached her seat, nearly dropping a camera that had probably cost enough to feed a family of four for a month. "I'm Evan. I can't tell you how glad I am to finally meet you. Sam told me so much about you."

Sam. How funny that sounded. Everyone on the paper, from the lowliest employee to the publisher, had always called Sam Elliott by his last name. She had never even heard anyone who knew him preface it with a Mr. Ali had always assumed that to be his preference, but if he told Evan to call him Sam, perhaps he didn't like it as much as his staff believed.

"South Africa. This is my first time," Evan continued. "And I can't wait."

"What are you going to do instead?" Ali asked seriously as she took her seat.

"What am I.... Oh, I get, it. A joke, right? Funny. I guess there's nothing I can do but wait. But I am excited. Do you have any ideas how we should go about this?"

"Well, I thought—"

"I want to shoot it all. The people, the land. Everything. I want—Oh, I'm talking too much, aren't I?" he said, suddenly retreating into timidity. "I do that sometimes when I'm excited. Sorry. But I really am excited. I have so many plans. I want...."

As Evan's voice rambled on in growing excitement once again, she studied him. Elliott's description fit, more or less. At least his hair and eyes were the right color. He was a little taller than she was expecting, however, and thinner. Much thinner actually. She remembered Elliott's saying he weight-trained and was a little stocky, and she thought that he had obviously found a way to remove his extra musculature when it was not in use. He was also a young-looking thirty, but she dismissed that along with the rest of her obviously erroneous anticipations. Physical descriptions were always just approximations, she thought, and, for a journalist, Elliott was sometimes a notoriously inexact observer of his fellowman. One discrepancy from the description did seem to be glaring, however. Elliott had called him a gentle soul, and she couldn't see any sign of that, but surmised that was probably just as subject to interpretation.

It was actually funny, she thought. Here she'd spent days dreading the idea of having to take care of the quiet man-child she was expecting, and now she wished he were there. Instead, she found herself seated with a man who was simply immature, who gushed with the open warmth of a puppy and sported the young, slim body and inexhaustibly shallow smile of a male model. After five minutes of his chatter she wished she could turn the page.

Fortunately, after only a little more time than that, he seemed to have run out of things to say and turned his attention to studying their fellow passengers. For lack of anything else to do, Ali did the same. She noticed a black man sitting across the aisle from them and a few seats up. He

14

wasn't wearing a suit the way the traveling businessmen were, he was wearing a good leather blazer. Probably his concession to casualness, she thought, for she noticed he also wore a tie, and pegged him as a person to whom being casual did not come easily.

Her study of him was interrupted by a loud giggle, which came from the blond girl from the gate who was seated directly across the aisle from them. Shifting her gaze, she watched the girl, whom she and everyone else in the cabin who possessed anywhere near normal hearing now knew to be called Trudi Schmidt, go to work on the elderly man sitting next to her. Young, Ali thought, not as young as she looks, but still young enough to be a professional innocent. She heard Trudi tell the man about the modeling career that had taken her from her native West Berlin to London, Paris and New York, and now Johannesburg. A model! Ali thought. Whoever heard of a five foot model? But then they were always models, she thought, or actresses, only they never spent any time before the cameras because they were always too busy between the sheets.

She noticed the old man was interested, but to what was being said between the lines. He was no fool, Ali thought, but she noticed that someone else was. Evan was obviously very attracted to the girl and seemed to be trying to figure out how to approach her. He didn't seem to realize that as long as he had the price, meeting her was the simplest thing in the world.

Ali watched his obvious discomfort for a moment and thought that she would have realized when Elliott referred to Todd as gentle, what he was really implying was simplicity. Problem solved, she thought, case closed.

Then the plane's engines ignited and Ali felt a little jolt of excitement go through her. Over the years she had become indifferent to the time she spent in the air, but she had never managed to become blasé about that first burst of raw power or the process that immediately followed it. It was always like the first time. She leaned back in her seat and enjoyed the sensation of the quickening rhythm the jet's tires beat

15

against the breaks in the runway as it accelerated to take-off. She loved that sense of vicarious activity a take-off always gave her. She was moving, going places, she thought. Or was it something else? Her mood changed when she remembered a conversation she'd had with her mother when she was in San Francisco.

"You're running, Ali," her mother had said. "You always have. You have such high expectations that you've never been able to stay in one place and commit yourself to anything that you might fail at or that might disappoint you."

Ali argued angrily that she had committed herself pretty damn well to her job and had built up quite a successful career as a journalist. Her mother had countered with a reminder that she had simply fallen into that job, that she had been intending to be a novelist but found writing newspaper pieces less risky emotionally.

"People change, Mother," Ali had said.

"The tragedy in life, darling, is that they usually don't."

It isn't true, Ali thought. At least it isn't the whole truth. She had argued to herself at the time that parents never understand their children's choices, but the thoughts kept coming back, and each time her protestations became more feeble. She closed her eyes against the memory, and with the ease of a frequent traveler forced herself to fall asleep. But one last thought flickered through her mind as she released it to unconsciousness: by forgetting about it, rather than facing it, wasn't she proving her mother right?

Evan started to say something to Ali until he noticed she had fallen asleep. He turned away and continued to gaze longingly at Trudi.

Another man seated nearby also watched her, but with much less admiration. That man was Rahmire Jones. The sound of her silly, girlish laugh grated on Rahmire's nerves. He knew that other men enjoyed women like her, but since he had no use for them himself, he couldn't justify their existence. The idea that neither Trudi's existence nor anyone else's needed his justification did not occur to him.

16

Rahmire felt very uncomfortable traveling first class; it wasn't Spartan enough for his taste. That had been the only seat available on the flight he decided to take, however, and he was too impatient to wait for a later one. He had known he wouldn't belong there, but now he felt even more painfully out of place than he expected. The fact that none of his fellow passengers even gave him a second glance proved it. That should have thrilled him, since he thought people usually stared at him, but, instead, it made him feel overlooked and out of his league.

But Rahmire was an easy man to ignore, despite his unusual appearance. His small personality just did not assert itself. The fact that he was frequently discounted was the second worst problem he had to face in life. Ironically, his greatest problem also served as his mother's greatest pride: the fact that her son was the result of a sanctified union.

The product of a Palestinian mother and a Welsh father, a professional mercenary soldier, that marriage had always been a source of shame to Rahmire; whereas, the knowledge that her child was conceived in wedlock had always allowed his mother to rise above the abuse she took for falling in love out of her own kind, although it was anyone's guess how many "legal" wives the man, whom they hadn't seen in years, actually had. Rahmire, however, would gladly have taken the life of a bastard over one forced to carry so alien a name.

It wasn't only the name that bothered him; he could have changed that. It was that he was branded with his father's physical traits. He accepted none of the man's ideas and was very vocal about that, but he was still never sure that he'd been fully accepted by his peers. He always felt he had to work twice as hard as anyone else, to be twice as loyal to prove himself, and he was never sure that proof was believed.

But now he had a chance to settle the matter of his hybrid origin once and for all. He believed he was given a gift from Allah that day in Cairo when he saw his comrade dying in the street, the opportunity to personally salvage the greatest operation his organization had ever attempted to

17

mount. He did feel a little nagging guilt from time to time because he had not reported the incident to his superiors, but he knew if he had they would have called it off or sent someone else to oversee it, and who knows when he would have gotten another chance? He honestly did not believe that anyone else could do a better job because no one else had a greater need to.

He heard the stewardess's movements in the galley behind his seat as she prepared the equipment for serving their dinner and walked back to join her.

"May I help you with that?" he inquired stiffly.

The stewardess looked up, surprised. Men occasionally used that line to start a conversation with her when they really didn't want to help at all. But she could see Rahmire was different; he was really serious.

She smiled pleasantly. "No, but you can stay here and talk to me if you'd like."

Suddenly Trudi's laugh rang out again. She spoke in a fairly loud voice, as if she were advertising herself to all of the other men in the cabin just in case things didn't work out with the old man seated next to her.

"I hate women like that," Rahmire said with feeling.

"I'm not crazy about them myself," the stewardess said candidly. "You can always pick out the working girls, can't you?"

"Working girls...?" Rahmire asked. He had never heard the expression.

The stewardess didn't understand his question. "At any rate, I can always tell. I've seen enough of them."

"I don't think women like that should be allowed to live," Rahmire said with sudden vehemence.

The depth of his anger scared the stewardess, and she gave a second look to the passenger she dismissed as harmless before.

"Fortunately, that is not your decision to make," she said curtly. "Now, why don't you return to your seat, sir? We'll be serving dinner shortly."

Rahmire shrugged. He didn't know what he did to upset her, but knew he did something. He didn't really care. She didn't matter any more than anyone else did. He returned to his seat and contented himself with studying the faces of his fellow passengers. Some of them he would have to remember.

The flight continued to pass uneventfully, but it was very long. Fortunately, it was a British, not a South African plane. South African planes were not permitted to refuel in or even fly over the airspace of the other African nations. The wide swing out over the Atlantic that ruling necessitated made their flights even longer than this one. But for these passengers, this flight was long enough.

Terry Mantizima, the tall, slender black man in the leather jacket, was one of the few people in that cabin who did not study his fellow passengers, even briefly; his mind was totally occupied with thoughts of himself and his future. The hours of waiting weighed heavily on him. He started feeling restless in his seat after a while, so he went up the little winding staircase to the first class lounge. He sat at an empty table, and in a moment a pretty stewardess approached him.

"What would you like, sir?"

Sir. How long would it be before he heard that one again? If he ever heard it.

He gave his order to the girl and let his thoughts drift back to the questions that were never far away. Why was he doing it? he wondered yet again. Why was he going to South Africa? Was he really planning to leave everything he'd built behind in Boston and settle in a place where re-creating it would be impossible? That sounded absurd, but there he was on a plane bound for that dismal destination. Of course, it was just a trip, he reminded himself, but he knew he hadn't yet booked his return flight and knew he wouldn't until he found the answers he was looking for.

19

He had always believed his life to be his own, and his own happiness to be the purpose of that life. Was he abandoning that view now? Did he believe his life belonged to the rest of Black South Africa? If he did, what purpose would that serve for either him or them? Would his acceptance of suffering in any way lessen the suffering of his brothers? He couldn't see how. Did he believe his life belonged to his ancestors, the ancient men and women born on the African land when it was new, but who lost it to the White Man? Were they alive today, what would they ask him to do? Would they want him to spend his life fighting to reclaim their land or would they be proud of his new life and want him to return to it? He didn't know.

He had always believed he struck the greatest possible blow against South Africa when he withdrew his mind and his talents from it. Would he now be returning his sanction to it along with his body? How could he continue to make the same statement? Somehow, he couldn't see himself in the role of a freedom fighter. He couldn't see himself living like his brother-in-law, Entato Siqusno. Entato worked as a cleaning man in an exclusive White apartment house by day, six long days a week, and spent his seventh day publishing a small underground newspaper that didn't begin to pay for itself. He knew Entato derived a sense of victory out of that, but would he? And did it accomplish anything?

He didn't know. He just didn't know. But he would find out, one way or the other. Unanswered questions had always been a heavy part of his emotional baggage, and he just couldn't carry them around any longer. He would find the answers he needed when he passed through whatever was awaiting him on the ground. He really believed that. He had to believe it.

The flight did not feel as long to Ali because she had slept through most of it. When she awoke from her after-dinner nap she felt thoroughly rested, but very stiff. She stretched a little in her seat and noticed that Evan was not in his. She was grateful for his absence. She didn't think she was going to like having to spend the next few weeks with him and hoped he was one of those photographers who liked to go off on his own. Perhaps she might suggest that to him if the opportunity to do so ever arose. She stepped out into the aisle and was about to walk around the cabin to work out the kinks when she saw the stairs to the lounge and decided they could be worked out just as well over a drink.

The first class lounge was crowded when she reached it. Evan was seated on the other side with that blond girl, Trudi Schmidt. So he made it, Ali thought. Unfortunately, the only empty table was right next to them. She wasn't sure she wanted to be too close to that conversation. Then she saw the black man she'd noticed in the cabin sitting alone at a table near the stairs.

"Is this seat taken?" she asked him.

"No, it isn't. Won't you join me?" he said, rising a little as she sat down.

South African, Ali thought of him. Couldn't be anything else. His speech reflected that unique combination heard nowhere else: the gutteral sound of his native tongue—Xhosan, she guessed—and the crisp, formal, almost British-sounding English that laced most South African speech. But there was a softening to it. He'd been away for a while, she decided.

"I'm Terry Mantizima," he said, extending his hand.

"Ali Hayden," she responded, extending her own.

Ever the people-watcher, she took the opportunity to search his dark eyes while their hands were clasped. He was an interesting-looking man. She'd thought that in the cabin. Intelligent, too, and good-looking, but more importantly, he was also intriguing in some indefinable way. There was a mystery about him that she suddenly wanted to solve. She could be wrong about that, of course; sometimes the simplest people hid behind the most complex of faces. But she did not think she was wrong. Not this time. There was too great a feeling of

21

excitement about him. The air around him positively bristled with his complex personal charge. Not that he was aware of it himself, she thought. People like him never were. They never grasped that the by-product of their quietly going about their own private pursuits actually moved the world forward.

She wondered what he was thinking about her and whether she had affected him in the same way. Probably not, she decided. He had scarcely thought of her. The shell surrounding him seemed too complete to let anyone else in. Then she noticed something that caused her to reassess that judgment. Perhaps she had made a little chip in that armor after all. At any rate, he had held her hand longer than a conventional handshake required, or even allowed.

When he realized he was still holding her hand he ended the handshake, but he did not seem embarrassed by having maintained it so long.

"Will this be your first time in South Africa?" Mantizima asked pleasantly.

"Don't feel you have to talk to me just because I sat at your table," Ali said.

"What if I think you might be an interesting person to talk to?"

So he found her interesting, too, Ali thought. She felt herself flushing slightly, though she could not imagine why.

"Then talk."

They both laughed at that exchange. Any stiffness that might have existed between them, a result of just having met dissolved, but the excitement they seemed to generate did not.

Evan noticed Ali just then and motioned for her to join him and Trudi. Ali smiled but shook her head.

"Your friend had better have a lot of money if he plans to buy that one," Mantizima said. "Unless I'm wrong about her."

"I don't think you are, but he isn't my friend, just a temporary co-worker. And I don't think the poor fool knows it's going to cost him anything."

"Some men do seem drawn to that type like lemmings. One experience usually cures them, and it gives them quite an education," Mantizima said philosophically, "but it does cost them."

His comments interested her. Not the statements themselves, but the manner in which they were presented. The detachment of them pegged him as more of an observer than a participant, which is what she was. She sensed he was a kindred spirit in more than that obvious way, in a sense she could not define. And since she was more interested in pursuing that thought than a discussion of the men who were attracted to call girls, she directed the conversation in his direction.

"What do you do?" she asked.

Mantizima reached into his pocket and pulled out a business card that he passed across the table.

"Mantizima Electronics. Terrence Mantizima, President," she read aloud, then looked at him with surprise. "Mantizima Electronics? Should have made the connection. I have one of your M-2 computers in my office. It's great."

He smiled, pleased at the compliment, but not surprised.

"And I've read about you in business magazines," Ali continued. "Let's see. Born in South Africa, educated in the States. One of M.I.T.'s geniuses, if I remember correctly. And now, one of the leaders in the computer field."

"Thirty-five years were required to live all of that, but you seem to have covered it quite well in a matter of seconds."

Ali continued to stare at him, this time with concern. How could he do it? she wondered. How could he allow himself to set foot in South Africa when it would mean trading the respect he's earned for the abuse he was bound to encounter there?

"Is this your first time back? I know you lived in the States for a long time," Ali said.

"Yes, this will be my first visit and, again, yes, I did live there for quite some time."

She noticed but did not comment on the fact that he used the past tense.

"Wife, kids?" Ali asked.

"No. No one. Nothing." Only a life.

Mantizima abruptly changed the subject, asking Ali about her work, and when she told him about the assignment that was sending her to South Africa. She gave him the background on the piece.

About a year and a half before, diamonds had been found in a remote area northeast of Johannesburg, not known for being a diamond area. The find created a sensation. Prospectors from all over South Africa, as well as a sundry assortment of creatures that had crawled out from under rocks throughout the world, flocked to the site, but as Ali predicted, since she had researched the area very well when she covered the story, diamonds, beyond the initial few, were never found. Gold, however, was.

"You know what it's like in South Africa," Ali said. "Scratch the earth anywhere and you find something valuable. The site's been bought by a gold mining company. I'm meeting with one of its executives tomorrow. Maybe you know it—the Haagen-Aykroyd Mining Company."

Ali thought she saw a flash of recognition in his eyes, and even something that seemed to resemble pain, but it was gone in an instant.

"No, I've never heard of the company," Mantizima answered. "How could I? As you said, I have been away a long time. Why don't you tell me about some of your other assignments."

She was sure he was lying, though she couldn't imagine why, but decided not to press the issue. She spoke, instead, about the subject he suggested. They talked, freely and easily, as if they had known each other for years. She told him about her trip back to San Francisco, her work in Cairo and various other assignments. She amused him with anecdotes about famous people she had met in the course of her work. He suspected she had embellished some of those stories for the sake of entertainment, but they were so well-told, it didn't matter. When pressed, he told her about his business and his life in Boston, but nothing about the reasons why he had left them behind.

The time passed quickly. When the stewardess passed out their landing cards, Ali checked White and Mantizima, Black. She thought about what that designation meant for him down there and wondered if he'd been away so long he might have forgotten. Then she saw that they had checked the same citizenship.

"You're an American," Ali said.

"Do you always look over people's shoulders?" Mantizima laughed.

"Always. Snooping's the only way to learn anything," she said, then added, "Remember, I'm a reporter."

"And you think that justifies it?" he asked pleasantly, with mock indignation.

"It explains it," Ali said. "I never justify anything."

Mantizima laughed with genuine enjoyment. Then the stewardess told everyone the plane had begun its approach and asked them to return to their seats.

"I've enjoyed this," he said, rising.

"Me, too."

They shook hands and, once again, she was aware of the magnitude of his presence. She remembered that the mystery he presented was still unsolved and struggled to find a way to keep some kind of connection between them.

25

"Do you think I could interview you sometime?" she asked. "I'd really like to include you in a piece I'm doing."

A shadow seemed to cross his face for a moment. She was sure he was going to refuse; he seemed much too private a man to want a reporter picking through his life. But he surprised her.

"Of course," he said. He took his business card from her hand and wrote something on the back. "That is my mother's name and number and the number and address of the clinic where she works. She's a nurse. You can leave a message with her if you're unable to reach me."

"Thanks," Ali said. "You know, I'm surprised they agreed to give you a visa. The South Africans, I mean. They didn't have to since you're not a citizen anymore."

"Oh, it's not too surprising that they agreed to it. I told them I wanted to see my mother."

The stewardess reminded them again to return to their seats, so Ali couldn't pursue the subject any further. But she noted and filed away in her mind the fact that he *told* the South African Tourist Department that was the reason whey he wanted to come back, but that it wasn't necessarily the real reason.

CHAPTER TWO

"Have a pleasant holiday, sir."

The stewardess had spoken to Terry Mantizima as he prepared to exit the plane, and he answered her with a warm smile of gratitude. She could not know how much her wishes meant to him. She hadn't singled him out for some special sincere message; she said the same sort of thing to everyone who passed her, as her job required. And that was why he appreciated it. Because she didn't have reason to single him out, because he was no different from any other paying customer. That impersonal courtesy would probably be his final touch with a civilized world, and it was going to have to last him for what might be a long time.

Well, he told himself as he stepped out of the plane, you asked for it.

He chose the shortest Customs line, but soon discovered that to be a mistake. A woman a couple of places ahead of him was attempting to haggle with the Customs clerk about the amount of duty he said she owed and a supervisor had to be called over to settle the matter. By then, however, it was too late for him to shift to another line; the coach passengers had disembarked from the plane, adding to the lines, so that they all were long.

He sighed impatiently and nervously shifted his weight from one foot to another. Why did he care about the delay? he asked himself. He wasn't in a hurry. What did a few minutes matter? Then he realized he was tense about his first confrontation with South African officialdom.

He needn't have been.

27

"American?" the surprised clerk asked in a slight Afrikaans accent.

"That's right," Mantizima answered, a shade more defensively than he intended.

"That's a surprise. Well, no matter. We're glad to have you back for a while. In our minds, you're still one of us."

He was surprised and genuinely touched by the man's warmth. He had forgotten how friendly the Afrikaner could be. The outside world sees them only as bigoted brutes, missing their earthy charm and effusive warmth. He thanked the man and gathered up his bags.

Then he saw something that reminded him not to view South Africa in partial context again. There were two signs over the exit.

One was a colorful banner that proclaimed in South Africa's unique and peculiar combination of Afrikaans and English, "Welkom to Jo'burg."

The other was a small plate that designated that door to be used by "Whites Only."

He wouldn't make that mistake again. Yes, he was one of them, but only if he remembered his place.

He made his way to the exit reserved for Blacks, then wandered around the outside of the airport until he found a bus that could take him to the train station. The American reporter he'd met on the plane, Ali Hayden, had offered to take him home in her cab, but he refused. She offered it tentatively, as if she were afraid of embarrassing him, and her impulse was right. He had been embarrassed, for himself and for her, and he wouldn't have put either of them through the indignity of knowing he couldn't have gotten a cab on his own. He questioned that decision when, unaccustomed to standing in a moving vehicle, he was thrown across a crowded bus. That was another mistake he wouldn't make again. From now on, he refused nothing.

It was nearly rush-hour when he reached the station and he knew the train would be very crowded. Trains usually were at that time of the day, no matter where in the world they happened to be found. But that was South Africa, with a unique situation that made it immeasurably worse. It took an enormous amount of manpower to make a big city such as Johannesburg run, but when the work-day ended White South Africa did not choose to share its space with the people who helped keep it going during the day. It was illegal for any non-White, apart from house servants, to remain in a White sector after dark, so each evening hundreds of thousands of Blacks were packed into inadequate train cars and shipped back to the place where they slept.

Mantizima pushed his way into an overcrowded car. He didn't ride the subway often in Boston, but he did it enough to know that it made no sense to wait because there would never be a less crowded car. A very private man, he felt uncomfortable with other people's bodies pressed to his. He always did, but especially now because he could sense that the other people in that car were staring at him. He didn't think there was enough room in that car for anyone to stand out, but he knew he did. It couldn't have been anything physical, he thought. Most of the people there were laborers, and he was very well-dressed, but there were a few other men in business attire, so that couldn't have been it. There must have been something in his attitude, something which told them, despite what the Customs clerk had said, that he really wasn't one of them.

He felt like a foreigner in his own native land, which, in fact, he was.

The crowd poured out of the train at the station in Soweto, the Black township outside of Johannesburg. Mantizima was still a good distance from his mother's house, but decided to walk it, despite his heavy bags. He could have caught a bus that would have brought him closer, but he couldn't face any more crowding at the moment. Besides, walking was a good way to become reacquainted.

He was walking through the poorer section that made up most of Soweto, with its little concrete block bungalows, some of which were impeccably maintained and others which had been relinquished to despair, when he heard the sound of a car pulling up behind him. From the corner of his eye he could see it was a police car.

Hell! he thought, gritting his teeth. Does the hassling begin already? But then he heard a voice that tickled his memory.

"Terry?" the voice asked. "Terry Mantizima?"

He turned and saw a black man in a police uniform whose face was slightly familiar.

"Kenny?" he asked. "Is that you?"

"It sure is."

The two men embraced briefly.

"Kenny Zembezi, a policeman," Mantizima laughed. "I never would have believed it."

Zembezi had been the class clown in high school when Mantizima knew him and was always in trouble because of his antics.

"We all grow up sometime."

"Most of us do," Mantizima said, still laughing. "But I never expected it of you."

Then the laughter faded and Mantizima looked at his old friend.

"A policeman?" he asked, this time seriously.

Black policemen were usually hated and distrusted by members of their own race. They were often thought to be lackeys of White South Africa, traitors who enforced repressive measures against their own people. Others, however, believed they were simply men who had found a way to survive.

"Yes," Zembezi said without embarrassment. "A policeman."

Mantizima didn't know what he thought about Zembezi's job; he hadn't had time to think about it. But because he was a man in conflict, he liked knowing that someone had made peace with what had to have been a difficult choice. He smiled in understanding.

"Why are we standing here? Put your bags in the back seat. I'm driving you home. I want to hear about everything you've done since you left," Zembezi said, then added in a wistful tone, "I really want to know what it's like out there."

He said it as if he were asking to be told a fairy tale about another universe, which to him, it was.

The phone rang on relentlessly, hounding her with its irritating sound, but Trudi Schmidt didn't move a muscle to answer it.

Nothing changes, she thought sadly as she looked around her. The walls were different, the view outside the window was, but everything else remained the same. She had checked into a unit in one of the smart apartment hotels in Jo'burg's trendy Hillbrow district, and within an hour of settling in the phone had started to ring. Three times it had now rung, and still she couldn't bring herself to pick it up.

What did you expect? she asked herself, finally coming to grips with the reality she had managed to hide beneath the false enthusiasm she'd always managed to generate when she moved to a new locale. This is what you do. It's what you are.

She felt particularly disgusted with herself today, more so than usual because of the way she had acted on the plane. It was ironic, but she almost felt worse about what she had to do to get work then she did about the work itself. She was so embarrassed by it. The necessity of soliciting clients when she moved to a new place forced her to behave in such a cheap manner, like a barker at some tawdry strip show, or a street-corner hooker to whom she had always tried to believe herself superior. But what could she do, she had to eat.

There was a pocket calculator on the table next to her. She had been trying to figure out how long she could live if she stopped working right now. She did make a great deal of money, but her lifestyle cost a lot. Still, she had managed to put some aside, enough perhaps to see her through two years, maybe three. But what would happen then?

She rose and crossed the living room and went into the bedroom where she stared at her reflection in the mirror. What did she see? A pretty girl, but not a beautiful one. A petite little blond, who at twenty-four still had the look and body of

31

a precocious sixteen-year-old. How long would it last? How long could she continue to peddle innocent sexuality as her stock-in-trade? How long would it be before her flesh drooped, before the phrases she uttered actually began to sound as hollow as they were, before the lines etched on her soul showed on her face? How long? And who the hell cared?

At that moment she might have looked sixteen, but she felt a hundred. All of the years ahead of her stretched out like a prison sentence. At her young age she felt like a person doomed to immortality, a person forced to live through day-after-day, year-after-year, without ever knowing the peace of the end.

She hadn't always felt like that. Overall, she'd been a happy child. She remembered herself as having been frightened by her stern, repressive parents, but not enough to dampen her natural cheerfulness, because they did not play a large part in the drama of her early life. She was a child who lived in her mind, in her imagination, dazzled by dreams of the stardom she hoped to achieve someday. She lived in a world of her own creation that she was certain no one else could enter. Until someone did.

At thirteen she was raped. It was then that her parents moved from being shadowy figures in the background of her life to center stage. For the first time, she needed them, she turned to them, and they weren't there. How different would it have been, she wondered, if they could have held her and comforted her, if they had treated her as if she were the victim rather than the violator? Would she have found herself accepting money from men for an act she never had a chance to learn to enjoy before she was even out of her teens? Would she have felt the need to keep running to the four corners of the earth in an effort to escape from the things she now knew she carried within her?

Maybe, she thought bitterly, but maybe not. How could she say for sure? She never knew whether she had drifted into that life because she had wanted to hurt them or because she wanted to prove them right. Maybe they were two sides of the same coin, but she didn't care enough to pursue the thought.

She sighed and returned to the living room, where she finished her wine in a single gulp. It tasted sour.

Accept it, she told herself, all you know how to do is spread your legs. That's all you're good for. She felt her parents' verbal lashings beating in her mind. She was an evil person, they had said, or the rape would never have occurred. She would never be anything but. She would always fail at anything decent she tried because she was so totally depraved. It was better, they warned, for all concerned if she never even tried.

She believed it completely. How could she deny it? The evidence was insurmountable. A contradictory thought did flash through her mind, however. If she were really as awful as they said, would she feel that badly about it? She dismissed that reprieve, however, because it could not stack up against the last ten years of her life.

There really wasn't any choice about it, she decided. She had thought briefly about returning to West Berlin, but she could no longer maintain the charade that where she lived mattered. She was out of places to run to and out of the energy needed to even try. No, she would stay there and continue on as she always had until.... Until what? She didn't know and was too tired to care.

The phone rang again. Wearily, she answered it. It was the old man from the plane.

"Of course I remember you, *Liebchen*," she said in a throaty voice that sounded harsh because the seductiveness it required wouldn't come out. "What time would you like to come over?"

"Scotch and water," Ali said to the bartender, then, remembering what she had learned the last time she was there, that South Africans like to drown their liquor in tall, icy glasses, she added hastily, "in a short glass with just a splash of water."

The black bartender in a crisp, white jacket just nodded impassively. He didn't make any of the comments she had come to expect from white South Africans, about how curious American habits were. Why should he care how white people wanted their drinks?

She absently glanced around the bar. She felt restless. Sleeping on the plane cured her of the jetlag Evan told her he felt when they parted in front of the doors to their rooms, but it made her wide-awake at a time when she ought to be thinking about going to bed. She felt anxious to get started working again, but there was nothing to do until the next morning.

Then she happened to catch the eye of a man standing at the other end of the bar. There was something—she grasped for the word—charismatic about him, she thought as he held her glance, but then decided she must have imagined that trait because, in the next second, it was gone. What had appeared to be an unusual, though perhaps not totally admirable, person was suddenly nothing more than a garden-variety lounge lizard who was well on the way to getting drunk. She saw him start walking towards her. He was younger than she was, probably not more than late twenties, and very good-looking in a T.V. star sort of way. But she thought, judging from the start of what was probably his standard approach, that he lacked an actor's creativity. She didn't know why because they did not resemble each other physically, apart from coloring, but he reminded her of Evan. She looked away quickly, hoping he would get the hint and not join her.

He didn't get it.

"I'm Neil Logan," he said in an accent that out-Etonned Eton.

She glanced at his school tie and wondered irrelevently why English-speaking South Africans always clung so tenaciously to British ways while claiming that they don't want to be taken for English.

"Yes, you would be," Ali said, turning away.

"I could tell you were an American," he said cheerily, "before you even spoke. Do you know how?"

34

"From my drink."

"Yes," he said, crestfallen. "How did you know? Do you mind if I sit next to you?"

Well, he's persistent, she thought as he took the seat next to her without waiting for her response, but she had always considered persistence *per se* to be highly overrated as a virtue. People could be persistent about the stupidest things.

"Look, you're wasting your time," Ali said. "I'm not in the mood for this and I'm much too old for you."

"What's a few years?"

"Plenty, when one of the parties is still in grade school."

For an instant Logan's face blackened angrily, but then he recovered and smiled warmly. Oh, good grief! Ali thought, he's not going to tell me he likes a woman with spunk. He did. He also told her he wasn't trying to pick her up, he just liked to talk to Americans and get their impressions of South Africa.

"South Africans always ask outsiders that," she said. "Why should you care what we think? What do you think of it?"

He started to tell her.

"Forget I asked," Ali said, turning away. "I really didn't want to know."

She looked grimly at the bartender, who had to be hearing their conversation but ignored it. In any other country, she thought, she would ask for the bartender's assistance in getting rid of an annoying man, but there that was out of the question. The bartender wouldn't say anything in her behalf—he wouldn't be permitted to—and even if he did, it wouldn't mean anything to Logan. To people like him, the bartender was a nonentity.

Logan went on to tell her he really did just want to talk to her and that if she agreed to have dinner with him, he would give her cab fare so she could come back to the hotel alone.

Rising, she gulped the last of her drink down and tossed a few rand on the bar. Then she looked at Logan and just shook her head in disbelief.

"Perhaps another time," he shouted as she walked towards the door.

He stood at the bar, watching her intently, but without malice, until he saw that she had entered the lobby elevator. A subtle change seemed to come over his face. He was a different sort of man now, stronger, more ruthless in his determination, not the tipsy fool he'd appeared to be moments before. He became the man Ali had taken him to be in that first brief moment of their encounter. He walked out of the bar and found a telephone.

"Sorry, old chap," he said into the receiver after someone answered on the other end. "She wasn't interested in me."

He snorted in disbelief; there weren't many women he could say that about. Of course, if he'd played it his way, he thought, he probably would not be reporting failure. But his boss ordered him to play the fool; he hadn't wanted Logan to arouse her suspicions.

"I wouldn't underestimate her, were I you," Logan said in closing. "You've got your work cut out for you."

With his responsibility over, Logan, now sporting an amused, satisfied expression, sauntered back in the direction of the bar. There were plenty of other lovelies there, he thought, that duty had forced him to ignore. Now that it had been discharged, however.... He straightened his tie and entered.

Ali was annoyed at being driven out of the bar, but she forgot about it as soon as she reached her room. She busied herself for a while preparing for the next day and then surprised herself by falling deeply asleep.

A thought must have been lingering somewhere in her unconscious mind because it forced itself to the surface a couple of hours later, bringing her out of a sound sleep.

Why was that man *so* insistent on picking her up? The kind of men who hang around bars in search of easy conquests usually had such fragile egos a few sharp remarks generally sent them scurrying off with their tail between their legs. Only this one, who was so obviously of that type, didn't run. She had an uneasy feeling about his persistence. Why, with so many other single women in that bar, had he pounced on her?

She chuckled at her paranoia. He had probably struck out with everyone else and saw her as his last chance of the night. Besides, she had only been in South Africa for a few hours. Why would anyone have any suspicious interest in her?

CHAPTER THREE

SEPTEMBER 7, 1979

Ali glanced around uneasily. Something in the outer office of the Director of Public Relations for the Haagen-Aykroyd Mining Company did not feel right to her, but she could not have said what it was. Everything, from the thick wool carpet underfoot to the classic executive secretary hammering away at a typewriter behind a rich, mahogany desk, looked perfect. Exactly as it should. Still, she couldn't deny that she had that funny feeling in her stomach that she always felt when something didn't sit right.

Struggling for an explanation for it, she remembered all the vacant nameplates on the doors she had passed in this corridor, suggesting that much of the wing was unoccupied. But they wouldn't put a PR man who had to meet with countless people every day on an unoccupied floor. Maybe it wasn't always vacant, she thought, maybe they'd had to let all of those people go. Sure, that was it, they were not doing well and were struggling to hide it. She scratched that idea as soon as it occurred to her. In a world in which both the international monetary system and the definitive form of ornamentation required the same substance, gold miners were never going to go out of business. Besides, the whole building positively reeked of great wealth and tradition, the quiet kind of wealth that never needed to be flaunted because it had been possessed so long it had become a tradition itself.

You're just getting restless, she told herself. Eager to get to work and tired of cooling your heels in some pompous executive's outer office. That's all it was, she assured herself, just a little impatience.

She turned her attention to the end table next to the leather couch she occupied. There were three magazines, two of which were popular South African news magazines. Since she didn't like her news censored, she picked up the third, a trade magazine on mineral mining, just to kill time.

As soon as she did it, however, the secretary stopped typing and threw her a startled glance. Ali met her eyes. After a moment, they exchanged brief, correct smiles and the girl returned to her work. The incident had only lasted a second, but it had happened. Something had happened. Ali wondered why she felt as uncomfortable as she did when a police car was driving behind her, even when she knew she wasn't doing anything wrong. She glanced at the door to the corridor and thought that most people feeling that uneasy would make an excuse to leave. But reporters weren't like other people. They always rushed in where angels feared to tread, which is why angels never got the really good stories.

Her pulse quickened when the buzzer on the secretary's desk sounded, signaling permission for her to enter the inner office. Her feeling was right from the start. Something was going on there, she thought as she rose from the couch, and she swore that she would find it.

She marched into the office with a great sense of purpose, but she stopped only a few feet into it when she saw Rune Aykroyd, the Director of Public Relations, standing behind his desk. He was not what she expected.

This man didn't belong here, in an office, certainly not in Public Relations, she thought, outraged in his behalf. He should be in the mines, digging with his bare hands. He was a big, well-built man and she found herself thinking of museum statues of Greek gods. He could have modeled for one of those statues, she thought, but not for some god of the heavens; it would have had to have been one of this world, of the earth of which he seemed so much a part. The planes of his face appeared to have been chiseled from rock and his eyes were as hard and impenetrable as uncut diamonds. He was not good-looking in the conventional sense, but there was a great feeling of power about him that made ordinary attractiveness seem inconsequential.

For a woman who had always prided herself on being more interested in the essence of a person than the casing in which that was wrapped, she was unusually aware of his bodily presence. A presence that reduced everything to the most basic level, where nothing existed but the fact that he was a man and she, a woman. She lived exclusively on that level for a moment, but because people are more than their sexuality, she gradually began to view him in a larger context. The power that attracted her was only one part of him. There was also a second force within him, perhaps greater, that was struggling at that very moment to dampen the first. And it appeared to be winning. There was a fire in him—she could feel the heat across the room—but it wasn't raging any longer, though she was sure it must have been at one time. Now, it was only the heat of burning embers that were slowly dying out.

Why? Disappointment with his life? She knew from his name that he was part of the Aykroyd family. Surely they could have found something better for him than this. Was he a nephew or cousin who just didn't fit in? No, she decided, that wasn't it. Oh, he wouldn't fit into conventional society, there was no question about that, but this man would destroy whichever part of himself was offensive to that mob with the power to emotionally blackball anyone who was not one of them, and he would be accepted by them purely because of the effort.

Maybe it was that effort that was destroying him. She thought him to be in his middle to late thirties, certainly no more than forty; but she was certain, though there were no reasons to suggest it, that this man would never die of old age. The life force was so great within him, but something else was missing. Perhaps the need to keep it going. He just wouldn't fight as hard as one had to to live that long.

He had done something to her. She could not deny it. He had taken her on a brief, but wildly breathless roller coaster ride, but now the ride was over. She was back on terra firma again. She could not ignore the fact that, at some time in his life, the part of him that attracted her, was the part he had deliberately set out to destroy.

She crossed the remainder of the room and impersonally extended her hand.

"Mr. Aykroyd," she said, "Alison Hayden—*San Francisco Star*. Thank you for seeing me."

He murmured something correct, in a slight Afrikaans accent, about always being willing to help the press, and they were seated. While Ali set up her tape recorder on his desk, he studied her as she had him. Only for him, that roller coaster ride was just beginning, but the recklessness of it, which had been so exciting to her, frightened the hell out of him.

Why did it always have to be this way? he thought as he gazed at her beautiful face. Why couldn't that face belong to one of those elegant, young matrons he frequently met at his mother's parties. But he knew that to be an old and useless speculation. Had he met her in that setting, she would not have interested him. In fact, he had learned from her dossier that she could easily have been one of those society matrons. She came from the same sort of socially prominent family that he did. But the thing in her that caused her to reject that kind of life was the very thing that attracted him.

He didn't know it, but he sighed softly. The ironic curse of his life still caused him considerable pain. The women who were right for him left him cold. They seemed dead to him, and he felt nothing for them. The only women he had ever cared about were always wrong for him. Some of those women had been, on the surface, good, law-abiding people, albeit reckless from his viewpoint, while others were outright criminals. But there was something about them that was always the same. They were always exciting, independent and full of life. It was almost as if he thought that by possessing them he could vicariously share that vitality. He had learned from experience, however, that that intimacy was dangerous for him and the desire had to be fought with everything he had. Their thinking, their very being, gave him ideas that threatened the commitments that formed the foundation of his life. At this stage in his life, but for occasional visits to whores, he was practically celibate. Most of the time he managed to convince himself it was a choice he could live with; then he met someone like her and the desire was out of control again. He knew this woman, damn her, was going to prompt him to pay one of those visits he hated. Not to satisfy the desire, but to kill it.

Forbidden love was nothing new to him. As a man he'd experienced it many times, and, as a boy, his greatest friendship was one that had to be hidden. Perhaps it was because he was young, perhaps it was because the friendship was a secret, but, for whatever reason, that boyhood friend was the only person with whom he had ever really been himself. There had been no barriers between them; they freely shared all their deepest thoughts and dreams. But even then he had been required to betray that boy, as he fully intended to betray what he felt for this woman.

Duty to his country required that. That duty was everything to him; he put nothing and no one above it. His whole life was devoted to upholding the doctrine of the country that had given him birth, and he gave it his finest effort because, God forgive him, he had never been able to make himself believe a word of it.

Ali turned her tape recorder on and was about to start the interview when Aykroyd began discussing the mining business without her prompting. He discussed it, not specifically in terms of the site she had come to cover, but in general terms. His speech surprised her again because he talked about mining like a miner. He spoke from genuine knowledge, not with the empty razzle-dazzle PR men usually throw around. Then she realized he was doing to her what she often did in interviews, particularly when she had reason to believe the person was hiding something. He was softening her up, putting her off-guard, until he was ready to go in for the kill. Once she was sure of what he was doing, although she could not imagine why, she cut him off and took control.

"If a diamond pipe was never found on that site," she asked, "where would the diamonds in that stream have come from?"

"Any number of places."

She waited, expecting him to continue, but he did not.

After several moments, she asked, "Would you care to venture a guess?"

"No, I think not."

Well, this is off to a flying start! she thought. She couldn't understand why he was being so hostile to her, and he was hostile, there was no other word for it. She knew that South Africans were often defensive with foreign reporters, but they weren't discussing anything political, nothing to offend him. She almost believed he was intentionally trying to make her angry. And he was succeeding! But she suppressed that anger and asked him about the gold strike.

"Well, as you probably remember," Aykroyd answered, "the prospectors dug up the surface of that area pretty well...."

He paused expectantly. She got the feeling that he thought she would react to that statement, but she had no idea why he thought she would care about those old diggings.

"Of course, they never found diamonds," he continued, "but they did find a gold vein, which was a surprise. Gold mining in South Africa is different than in most other parts of the world. The reef is usually deep in the earth, often as much as a mile, or even two, below the surface, and is usually of such a low concentration that the gold can't be seen with the naked eye."

It occurred to Ali as she listened that Aykroyd was watching her as closely as she was him, Of course, she knew he was attracted to her. But this was something very different than the late twentieth century mating ritual; this, she was sure, was professional in nature. But why would a South African mining executive have such an intent interest in an American reporter?

"In this case, however, the vein began just below the surface and the gold was of a higher concentration than they usually are. Of course, that part of the reef wasn't large enough to be profitably mined, but it was an indication of what might exist below. We performed several tests and found it to be worthy of development."

We're like two boxers, she thought. Dancing around, sizing each other up, waiting to see who will take the first punch.

"What other minerals were found in the surface ore?" Ali asked.

It was just a routine question, but she realized from the subtle change that occurred on his face that he believed he succeeded in getting her to accept some bait he had been extending. But bait for what?

"The usual," he said, much too casually. "Silver, a little chromium...uranium. You know what we've called the mine, don't you? *Schmokkeling Reef.*"

"Uh...Smuggling Reef?"

"That's right. Very good. I didn't know you understood any Afrikaans. We named it that because a great deal of ore was smuggled out, even after we bought it."

"That's...interesting," Ali said while she thought, what the hell is going on here?

He continued, explaining the enormous investment needed to develop a new mine, but Ali was not listening. She struggled, instead, to bring some order to the confusion in her mind. At first, it was not easy—nothing made any sense—but gradually, as she looked around the office, she found substance to support her gut feeling. Once she was in control again, she resolved to keep that edge by being the one to take that first punch.

She asked suddenly, "How long have you been in this office?"

He paused before speaking, just for a moment, but it was a moment too long. "Two years. I was in another office before that."

"Two years! I admire your stamina, but I question what you are doing to your health. Until very recently the dust in this room must have been enough to kill you."

He did not respond.

"I live in Cairo, you know?" Ali continued.

"Yes...uh, no, no I didn't know. How could I?"

"The question is: why should you? Anyway, I do. Hot, dry place, terribly dusty, so I really know a lot about cleaning it. When it builds up, as it will have when I get back to my apartment, you can't wipe it away with big, broad strokes or you get little lines of it where the cloth wasn't pressed right to the furniture. Like those," she said, pointing to the lines of dust on his desk. "Of course, as I said, we have a terrible dust problem in Cairo, but you don't do you? You'd almost think this office hadn't been occupied for a long time."

"I am very sorry that our hygiene level does not meet your exacting standards, Miss Hayden."

"Don't apologize," Ali said, matching his sarcasm. "This office is perfect for you. Just perfect. The definitive office for a person in your position."

Her eyes moved very deliberately from the framed mining charts on the walls to the colorful company brochure placed at an angle on the desk, to the pile of papers before him and the sharpened, but unused, pencils, to the empty waste basket.

"Ever seen a movie being made?" she asked suddenly.

"No," he answered tightly.

Good! she thought. Got him on the run.

"I have once, in Hollywood. Fascinating business. They have production people that can come into an empty office and positively breathe life into it. They scatter around all the little touches the character would have in his office. And it's amazing. When they're finished it looks like the definitive office for that person, only somehow it doesn't feel it, if you know what I mean."

"I don't. I'm afraid I don't have any idea what you are talking about."

45

"Of course you don't."

The fact that Akroyd didn't demand some explanation for her ridiculous verbal sparring proved to Ali's satisfaction that her comments had hit the mark. She was certain that something was not kosher there and was more determined than ever to dig it out. But not yet, she decided, not till she was really ready.

Aykroyd seemed to sense that he was being let off the hook for a while and, not surprisingly, was eager to get out of that office. He suggested that they visit the company's research department.

As they walked out, they were both quite satisfied with what they accomplished during the course of that interview, but their emotional reactions to it were quite different. Ali was very pleased with herself and could not wait for the next installment; whereas, Aykroyd looked like a man hating the fact that his worst suspicions were confirmed.

He showed her some of the experimental work being done by the research department and introduced her to the supervisor of one division, a geophysicist named Wade Petri.

In dress and manner Petri appeared to be successfully middle-aged, but his face had the young, anxious look of a child desperately trying to be taken for an adult; averaging that out, she figured he was probably around thirty. Everything about Petri was acceptable—it was the only word that applied—and she could imagine that theme being carried out throughout the rest of his life: the right house, not too big, but still impressive, the pretty, young wife with socially important connections, and the 2.7 children. This was a greedy man who never in his life really wanted anything, but who grasped at everything other people told him he should want. With the attitude of a director casting a play, she thought, this should have been the PR man. This man I would never have questioned.

Aykroyd told her about Petri's ideas and credentials, then mentioned that the Haagen-Aykroyd Company hired him away from top-secret government research.

"I felt the opportunities for challenge were greater in this arena," Petri said in a stiff Afrikaans accent.

"Not to mention that you don't get that house on the hill on government pay," said Ali.

The bluntness of her remark extracted an honest reaction from both men. Petri fumbled for something proper to say before trailing off to silence and Aykroyd burst out laughing.

"Why did you say that to him?" he asked as they walked away, for the first time, quite naturally, almost as he would to a friend or an ally.

She shrugged. "Just testing the waters, I guess. But I needn't have. You can always pick out the ones who buy the party line. You can always pick out people of any persuasion."

"Can you?" he asked as if he really wanted to believe that. He hastily glanced at his watch. "It is nearly 11:15," he said impersonally. "Didn't you say you were supposed to meet your photographer downstairs at 11:00?"

They rode the elevator down in silence and found Evan Todd waiting in the lobby. Ali introduced the men, then arranged to meet the next morning so they could accompany Aykroyd on a visit to the mine.

"Perhaps, Miss Hayden," Aykroyd said, "you would do me the honor of taking dinner with me tomorrow night. And you, too, of course, Mr. Todd," he added in a way that made it clear Evan's presence wasn't really necessary.

"Sorry. I'm going to be very busy," Ali said sharply, hoping he understood that she wasn't busy at all.

"Of course. If you should find that you have some free time after all, please call me."

Aykroyd nodded his good-by and walked off in the direction of the elevator. Ali looked after him for a moment, trying to pull it all together.

"What do you think of him?" she asked Evan.

"He looks okay to me. Why do you ask?"

"No reason," she answered absently.

"Why didn't you agree to go out with him?"

"Because I don't like him."

"That figures," Evan laughed. "You're too much alike."

She was about to protest the absurdity of that when it occurred to her that he was probably right. In a lot of ways she and Aykroyd were alike, but they had used the raw material in radically different ways. She found it strange, however, that Evan had been able to see that. People did say that out of the mouths of babes and fools...but she had never bought it. She found herself wondering how this simple man could produce such incisive perceptions.

But she couldn't afford to waste time pondering the psyche of someone like Evan. She apologized to him for making him wait, then begged out of the afternoon's work they planned to do together.

She rushed back to her hotel room and started telephoning. She called everyone she knew in South Africa, everyone who might possibly hold some key to the mystery that was Rune Aykroyd. She called reporter friends in other countries that she knew had once served there and learned the names of their sources, and in some cases the blackmail needed to get those sources to talk. She worked at it for hours, but when she finished she smiled wryly to herself.

"Round two, Mr. Aykroyd," she said aloud. "And this time we're gonna play hardball."

CHAPTER FOUR

SEPTEMBER 8, 1979

The atmosphere in the official Haagen-Aykroyd car was subdued when it drove out to the mine the next day. Very subdued. Evan sat in the back seat and seemed to be content with staring out the windows, so he contributed nothing to further conversation. But for his occasional imitation of a tour guide, Aykroyd also said little, and Ali didn't respond unless she was asked a direct question.

Ali was wrapped up in her elation from her success of the day before. Those telephone calls provided her with information needed to nail Aykroyd, and what she didn't know she could make good guesses about. She really couldn't wait to lower the boom, but was determined to hold out until the time was right.

She did allow herself to steal triumphant glances at him from time to time when she was sure he wouldn't notice. Yesterday he had worn a traditional business suit, but today he wore one of those safari suits so popular with men in South Africa, the ones with short pants and knee socks. Ridiculous outfit for a grown man to wear, she'd always thought. They maintained those shorts were cool to wear, she knew, but she honestly couldn't say the extra yard of fabric on her legs was hot. Still, he had good legs, she noticed during one of her glances. Not that they were going to do him any good where she was concerned.

It occurred to her as they drove that it was Saturday and she feared that they might not get to see the mine in full production. She needn't have worried. When they arrived the day-shift was in full swing. She told herself that she should have remembered that South African employers don't treat their employees the way those in other western countries do. At least, not all of their employees.

Ali had been to that site only a year and a half before, and then it had been completely untouched, except by prospectors. Now, as she looked at the working mine, she was amazed at the speed and efficiency with which the Haagen-Aykroyd people developed their land. Buildings had risen up out of the rocks. Pre-fab, to be sure, but sturdy, functional buildings designed to last a long time. Aykroyd told them the initial shafts were dug and the mine elevators and electrical lights were installed, and a foreman said that the first quantity of ore reached the processing plant just two days before.

"But they won't be blasting today," Aykroyd assured them, knowing outsiders usually found it unsettling. "You need not worry about that."

"Oh, hell," Evan exclaimed. "I was hoping we would be here when they did it."

Ali considered that to be a bizarre interest, but assumed he did not know what he was talking about. Of course, she had been born and raised in California, where earthquakes were indigenous to life; while they did not frighten her as they did many newcomers to that state, she had never found the sensation of the earth rumbling beneath her feet to be a pleasant one.

Aykroyd excused himself for a moment and went to speak to a supervisor. Evan took that opportunity to begin taking pictures of the compound, leaving Ali alone where they stopped. She glanced around and saw Wade Petri, the geophysicist she had met the day before, walking in her direction. Here on a Saturday, she thought, such diligence, good for the brownie points. She derived a nasty thrill from thinking about how she would zing him today. She was reasonably sure he had not noticed her yet, but then thought he must have, because he paused near a miner sneaking a cigarette, then abruptly walked off in a different direction. I must be a pretty threatening character, she thought with some pleasure, as Aykroyd returned and continued the tour.

When they reached the main building in the compound, Aykroyd assigned an off-duty foreman to be Evan's guide. They went off without Aykroyd or Ali ever noticing they were gone. Then he guided Ali out through the door.

The first thing that struck her about the mine was the safety level. Signs were everywhere, as were the people whose job it was to see that those instructions were carried out. *"Rook Verboode"* proclaimed one huge banner, and those words were preceded by "No Smoking" in English and followed by several repetitions of the same thought in a few native languages. And that was another thing that struck her, the multitude of different languages. She not only saw it in the signs, but heard it in the voices of the workers, and commented on it to Aykroyd.

"There are a number of different native languages spoken here, that is true. But not all of these people are from South Africa. They come here for the work from countries all over Africa, bringing with them their languages and their customs," Aykroyd told her, then added, "You know, that's something you foreign journalists never realize. You are always talking about how bad our Bantu has it. If it's really that bad, how do you explain all of these other blacks who fight to work here?"

"They have to eat, don't they? If their own countries aren't developed enough to provide them with jobs, they have to go where the jobs are. That doesn't mean they like it. Sometimes you have to do things you hate just to survive. But there's more to life than that."

"Is there?" Aykroyd asked. "What is it?"

"Hopes and dreams, for a start," Ali said. "There's independence and human dignity. Triumphs and accomplishments."

"I wouldn't know about that. To me, survival, if you can manage it, is the greatest accomplishment you can hope for."

She looked at him, hearing without really understanding. She knew that he was speaking like that, despite his best efforts at control, speaking not so much for her benefit, but from some longstanding pain of his own. She didn't interrupt for fear that that would shut off this trickle of hidden thoughts. Yet she knew that despite what she thought of him, she would consider those comments as off-the-record. She would never use them against him. She was not one of those reporters who needed to violate the most private recesses of a person's soul when there was no point to it other than the sheer sake of it.

"Look at them," he continued, pointing to a cluster of black workers. "Don't you envy them, at least a little bit? I do."

"You can't mean that."

"But I do. Whatever you think of it, you have to admit the reality of their situation is that all their choices are made for them. There's nothing left for them to decide, other than whether they want to live with it or not. They don't ever have to make choices they can't live with."

She shuddered inwardly at this man's thoughts, at the futility in which he must have imprisoned himself long ago. Then she glanced up at his face and saw that the thing that had happened was over; he was in control again.

"I'm sorry," he said, stiff with embarrassment. "I don't usually...what is that phrase you Americans use? Spill my guts?"

She merely nodded so as not to contribute to his embarrassment. He glanced at the elevator at the main entrance to the mine as they passed it and spoke rapidly to cover his uneasiness.

"There's the lift. Would you like to go down?"

"No, thanks. I went down into a coal mine once and those shafts weren't nearly as deep as these must be. Never want to do anything like that again. It was the only time in my life I ever experienced claustrophobia."

52

"I suppose I can understand that. I know it happens to some people. But I have never felt it myself. I love it down there. I sometimes wish that I could do the job myself."

"Don't you feel that it's all going to cave in on you?" Ali asked.

"That's not the way to look at it," he said with sudden eagerness. "The way I see it, it's man against nature, and nature has all the advantages on her side. She has all the strength. All man has is his feeble body and his mind. Every day these men go down into the bowels of the earth and they challenge nature to try to destroy them, and with all the might she has on her side, most of the time she is no match for the human mind. On those rare occasions when the miners don't come out alive, it is usually because of human error, because of their own self-imposed defeat rather than the earth's victory.... Yes, I envy them. I wish I could be a miner."

"Why don't you?" she asked.

"Because life has another purpose for me."

Now! Ali said to herself. Do it now. There would never be a better time, she knew, but for some reason, the words would not come.

The lunch bell went off just then, relieving her of the decision. The workers poured out of the mine and the buildings, and Ali and Aykroyd followed them to the workers' cafeteria.

Standing at the entrance of the cafeteria, looking out at the sea of black faces seated at long tables, Aykroyd pointed out the good, wholesome lunch that was being provided for them. Ali mentioned that while the food did look good and satisfying, it was rather primitive.

"That's what they like. They wouldn't want anything better."

The standard stock phrase. He'd said it so often, he thought he ought to believe it. Why didn't he? Everyone else did. He looked at the face of his companion, at the tight, grim line she'd made of her normally sensuous mouth, and knew there was no doubt about what she thought of him. Well, that couldn't be helped, he told himself.

He pointed out the tubs of murky brown liquid they were drinking with their lunch. "That's Bantu beer," he said. "Would you like to try some?"

"I tried it last year. Wasn't bad, but I can't say I feel any need to try it again."

"It's an acquired taste."

Somehow, she was sure, it was not one he'd acquired himself.

"It's very low in alcohol," he continued. "If we didn't provide them with this, they would drink something harder. Some of them would be drunk all the time."

"Which proves we are definitely superior to them," Ali said when she'd heard enough. "Because no white man has ever been known to get drunk."

She started walking through the aisles between the tables just to get away from him, but he followed behind her, extolling the quality of the housing that had been provided for these men.

Well-built, you mean, she thought of the dormitories he described. But that was not her definition of quality. It wasn't a quality life when grown men were made to sleep together like school children. When they were forced to live hundreds, perhaps thousands, of miles away from their families, families they might only get to see a few times in a decade, but for whom they spent all the days of their lives providing.

She could not understand a single word of the languages they used, but she sensed that some of those men were talking about her. They seemed to know she was an American journalist, and they probably wondered what she was going to write about them. She had often been told, by white South Africans, that the Bantu is a simple creature, irresponsible and child-like. But the eyes that met hers weren't those of carefree children. They were those of individuals who had paid to be considered men, paid with more than their share of suffering.

Some of the eyes that connected with hers were young and still full of hope; others pleaded with her to do something for them, but absolved her in advance for what she probably wouldn't be able to accomplish. Still others were angry, hurt by past hopes of the sort she represented, which had always been dashed. But the worst of those eyes she'd had to meet were the ones that were empty, the ones beyond apathy, the living dead for whom no future existed. Those were the hardest for her to bear. She wanted to tell them that there is always hope. She wanted to tell them about Terry Mantizima, the man she'd met on the plane a couple of days before, and the life he had made for himself. She knew, however, that saying those things would accomplish nothing. Once the light in a man is extinguished, it never burns again.

"Let's get out of here," she said to Aykroyd as she passed him on the way to the door.

He followed her out without comment and kept pace with her as she walked out of the main compound. She planted herself on a rock near the entrance. Now, she was ready. It must have been obvious to him.

"What do you want to talk about now?" he asked, assuming she had something in mind.

"You."

"Me? I can't imagine why. I'm not very interesting."

"On the contrary, Mr. Aykroyd, I think you are very interesting. Did a little checking on you yesterday. I found out that, while you are Karel Aykroyd's son and a major shareholder in this company, you're not an employee. And I can't think of even one legitimate reason why you should have posed as one.... You're a cop, aren't you?"

He thought about what he was going to say for a a moment, then shrugged disarmingly. "Guilty as charged, Miss Hayden. I wanted to tell you yesterday. I would have, had it been my decision. I don't like subterfuge."

"Why?"

"I don't know. I suppose it was decided that for some reason you needed protection. I know my superiors chose this over in the hopes of preventing you from using the 'Police State' label that foreign journalists love to apply to us."

She smiled, but not pleasantly. "Nice try. But I know you are not an ordinary policeman. Not a local one, at any rate. And you're not with Security Branch either. That much I was able to confirm. That only leaves BOSS, the rather telling acronym for the Bureau of State Security, South Africa's chilling answer to our C.I.A." Ali gave him a chance to respond before going on; he didn't take it. "I was pretty sure of it yesterday, but you confirmed it today. You lied your way into a corner, Mr. Aykroyd, and you were pretty foolish to do it to me. You're not bad, my friend, but I'm very good."

He looked away. He had been careless. His lies were full of holes, his cover make-shift and inept. And he'd underestimated her. He would not make that mistake again.

"Now all I want to know," she continued, "is, why me?"

He sighed deeply and appeared to be a man caught in a difficult situation that was not of his making. "You realize," he said cautiously, "that I can neither confirm nor deny your suspicions. Officially, that is. But unofficially, if we accept your guess as the truth for the moment, although just for the moment, perhaps I can provide an explanation."

"I'm waiting."

He had to think fast, too fast for safety. He had to come up with some plausible explanation right now, and he had to make her believe it.

"Several months ago a West German reporter assigned to Jo'burg had been sending back very unfavorable reports, and some of my countrymen decided to put an end to that. I'm not justifying what they did, but they had a legitimate reason to be angry. However, that reporter almost died. You must have heard about it. It was in all the papers. It created quite a messy international incident. I think my government would like to avoid a repetition of that, and particularly with a citizen of the United States. You must realize there are a number of people in your country who would like to see the economic ties with South Africa severed. Were anything to happen to you, or Mr. Todd for that matter, though I think a photographer makes a far less threatening target, that might be all the ammunition those people needed. I'm sure you can understand our position."

"Why BOSS? This has nothing to do with intelligence. Why wasn't Security Branch given this assignment? Seems to be more in their line."

"I see you know something about the divisions within our internal police network," he said, filing that piece of information away for later. "But not as much as you think. For your information, the Bureau of State Security, unlike your C.I.A., is concerned with both internal and external security, and since this matter has both domestic and international implications, BOSS was the logical choice for handling. Still accepting your hypothesis as given, of course."

"Of course," she said absently.

She was assimilating the information he'd just given her; he could see it in her eyes. He'd told her too much, he thought. More than was safe. But it was nothing she couldn't learn herself if she chose to. Still, he should have been more careful, let her do the talking, but she had an infuriating habit of always being right. He just had to show her that it didn't always work as well as she thought.

"Why me? Surely every foreign reporter in South Africa isn't being given this treatment. You can't possibly have the manpower for it."

"As to why," he continued, "I wouldn't know. You'd have to ask my superiors. I suppose it could be a new policy, being applied to reporters as they enter South Africa, but I don't know that. Believe me, this was not my idea. I happen to think my talents are better spent on work a little more taxing than babysitting!"

Damn! he thought. That was too much anger; it was overkill. He wished he could take it back, but the damage was probably done. He was wrong, however; the touch of anger was just right. It explained his hostility of the day before and sealed away the last of her doubts.

"Babysitting? Well, you've certainly put me in my place, haven't you? No, don't apologize, that's what it is, although, believe me, I don't want it and I wouldn't have asked for it. But I am sorry you've been saddled with me. If you knew what I thought yesterday...well, to tell you the truth, I'm not exactly sure what I thought, but it wasn't.... Friends?" she asked abruptly, extending her hand.

"Yes...friends."

As they clasped hands, she felt a chill go through her whole body. She was certain, though she couldn't guess why, since he had done everything in his power to bring about that truce, that he hated the whole idea of it.

"I think she believed it. I hope so. It was all I could think to say right at that moment."

Aykroyd said it more to convince himself than to communicate information, then sighed deeply in frustration. After he dropped Ali and Evan off at their hotel, he drove back to Pretoria, to his office at the Bureau of State Security. He told the story to his two direct subordinates, Neil Logan and Pieter Kloff, though he did not tell them why this assignment was so important.

Neil Logan was the man who had tried to pick Ali up two nights ago in her hotel bar. Even in that setting, without trying, his personality was as dazzling as Ali had first believed.

Kloff was another story; he had never in his life dazzled anyone and he never would. He was a hard-working man, almost forty years old, but he had no more than an average intelligence and a limited imagination. His hair was sandy-colored, neither quite blond nor brown, and while his features were pleasant enough, they were in no way distinctive. He was the only person who remembered that he was Logan's senior in the organization by more than ten years. In everyone else's mind they were equals, and he knew that was only temporary; eventually Logan's career would soar past his. He could not hope to compete with him. He knew he would always stand in the shadows of Logan's talented glow. He wished that weren't the case, but he didn't resent it. He knew he would never be a leader, but he compensated for that by being the most loyal of followers once he was sure the leader he followed deserved that dedication.

"You told her you were with BOSS?" Logan asked.

"I didn't have any choice. If I hadn't, she was just going to keep probing."

"I suppose so," Logan said. "I did warn you about her."

"Not enough. You didn't tell me it was like dancing with a tiger."

Logan chuckled. "Oh, by the way, Rune, what exactly is it that you think this bird is going to do? Or has done," he added hastily.

"Why did you state it like that, Neil?" Aykroyd snapped. "Why did you think we suspected her of planning something rather than something that was already done?"

"Oh, for God's sake, do we have to think about every bloody thing we say around here now? Isn't it insulting enough that we aren't let in on anything? How long do you have to be here before they tell you the secrets?"

"You've had your share of secrets," Aykroyd said tightly.

"Not the really big ones, that's obvious. What do you have to do to get into this ruddy club?"

He didn't say it, but they all understood his implication. He meant that he was being left out of this investigation because he was not an Afrikaner, but of English ancestry. Afrikaners frequently felt a decided prejudice against the descendants of their once colonial masters. Aykroyd, however, knew he had given Logan every opportunity. He had nothing to feel guilty about.

"I don't know anything about it either, Neil," Kloff said. "Sometimes we're on a need-to-know basis around here. You know that."

"Yes, I know," Logan sighed. "And I suppose I'd consider it sensible if it weren't being directed against me.... Sorry and all that. My temper gets away from me at times."

Aykroyd nodded his acceptance of the apology and then Logan left.

"I'd better be going too, Rune," Kloff said.

"Close the door when you leave, will you, Pieter?"

Kloff closed Aykroyd's door behind him, then hurried up the corridor to catch up with Logan.

"Why did you do that, Neil?" he asked. "Can't you see this case is really important? He would tell you if he could, but he has his orders. You can see that. Why can't you accept it?"

You're so...average, Logan thought as he looked at Kloff. That was the worst thing he could say about anyone.

"You always do what you are told, don't you, Pieter?"

"I follow orders, if that's what you mean."

"Don't you realize that when they always know where you are it is so easy for them to overlook you?"

With that Logan turned and walked away. Kloff looked after him, watching his arrogant strut, as cocky and self-assured as ever, half-wishing he could be like Logan, half-relieved that he wasn't.

Rune Aykroyd sat alone in his office with his face buried in his hands. He wished Logan weren't adding to the pressure on him. At one time, pressure of any amount wouldn't have affected him. That's why he was so good at his job. He had never allowed personal feelings to interfere with his work either. Most people would have sworn he had no personal feelings. Now they were surfacing against his will, and he did not know how to stop them.

How could he tell Logan the Hayden woman was suspected of being a...? No, he couldn't even allow himself to think it. If he permitted the word to form in his mind too many times, it might just slip out, and to...the wrong person. At times in the past he'd taken chances on breaking security when he was certain it was the right thing to do in the circumstances. This time, however, there could be no breach; the stakes were just too high.

Why, then, was he allowing this to happen to him? Why was he letting Ali Hayden get to him? He knew what she was. His superiors were sure about her and so was he. At least, he used to be sure. The evidence against her, while circumstantial, was quite damning. Why, then, was he doubting it now? What was that woman doing to him?

There was no denying she was having an effect on him, and it went beyond the attraction he experienced the first day. She was causing him to have thoughts that he believed he buried, feelings he was sure he'd killed. He wished he could hate her, but could not. He had never wanted a woman so much. He wished he could take her away somewhere where the past and the future would cease to exist, where their separate worlds would not be able to pull them apart.

But there would be no little hideaway, he knew. Though right at that moment he personally didn't care at all about what she was, he would do his job with respect to her, as tenaciously as ever. He would find the truth about her and bring her to justice, as his duty to his job and his country required.

Then, alone, he would learn to live, yet again, with what that duty cost him.

Ali did buy Aykroyd's explanation. She attributed all of her doubts to the enigmatic man himself, not the situation. She felt a little down now, the way she always did when what seemed to be a great lead disintegrated into dust. But, as always, she was giving extra diligence to a routine task to make up for her lagging interest.

The routine task presently at hand was the update on the site of the gold mine that she had been sent there to do. As she paced around her hotel room she held her small tape recorder in her hand, listening to his speeches about mining. She always fast-forwarded over her own voice, particularly her irrelevant needling, which had seemed so clever at the time but which was now embarrassing.

Her mind was so glued to her work that she paid no attention to where she walked and she did not notice the little piece of carpeting that had pulled up at the seam. When her heel caught in it, she tripped across the room and fell into the wall. When the tape recorder hit the wall, however, it emitted a high-pitched whine.

Involuntarily, to stop the sound, her arm snapped the recorder away from the wall. Then slowly, deliberately, she placed it down again. Once again, it whined. She checked all four walls, in several spots, and two of them elicited that sound.

Now she was mad! She knew of only one thing that would cause the recorder to make that sound, and there was no reason why it should be in her room.

She rushed out of the room, leaving the door wide open, and ran down the hall to Evan's room. She rapped heavily on the door.

"It's me, Ali. Let me in."

Evan took his time about answering.

"What a time to be undressed," she muttered to herself, when there was really no reason why he should have been dressed.

When he finally opened the door, she pushed past him without explanation and started pressing the tape recorder to the walls of his room.

"What are you doing?" he asked.

"My room's bugged," she answered. "But yours appears to be clean."

If Evan was disturbed by her discovery, he managed to hide it beneath his excitement. He seemed to be particularly taken by her method of discovery.

"That's really neat!" he said. "How'd you ever learn that?"

"I've worked in Moscow. Everyone there learns.... Wait a minute. You've worked there too, haven't you? I've seen your pictures."

"Sure I have," he said defensively. "But no one ever showed me that."

She shook her head at him, wondering how someone of such incredible naiveté could have survived that long.

She cut his jabbering as short as possible and returned to her own room. She was outraged. At Aykroyd, of course, but also at herself for believing his glib explanations. Why didn't she stay with her suspicions? But she knew she had no time to waste on post-mortems. It was time for action.

She looked at her watch. Six o'clock. Perhaps he was home. She dug the number he had given her that morning out of her purse and dialed it. A maid answered on the second ring and told her he had just gotten in.

"I know it's late...Rune," she said when he got on the line, using his first name for the first time, "but I find I'm going to be free tonight after all. If you aren't busy, perhaps we could have that dinner together after all."

He accepted the offer with just the right touch of eagerness, damn him, and said he would pick her up in an hour and a half. She waited for him to hang up first, then slammed her own receiver down.

"Come into my parlor...." she started to say, then stopped.

She was not sure anymore who was the spider in this strange scenario and who was the fly.

CHAPTER FIVE

"*Dr.* Mantizima!"

Deborah Mantizima beamed proudly as she said that to her son. Though he had secured his Ph.D. many years ago, the triumph of it was still so fresh to her she could not view it indifferently.

Mantizima flushed with pleasure. "Yes, well I don't use that title very often, Mother. I think it's more applicable to the academic world than to business."

"That doesn't matter. All that matters is that you have it. Oh, I'm so proud of you, Terry. I only wish your father were here to see what you have made of yourself."

"So do I."

"Things are going well in your business, aren't they?" she asked, suddenly concerned.

"Very well. Why do you ask?"

"I don't know, I just thought.... Well, I was very surprised when I got your letter saying you were coming. You knew I'd secured a visa so I could visit you in Boston for Christmas, and that's only a few months away. I couldn't imagine why you would come here—you've never been back here—unless there was something wrong."

He looked at his mother with great affection. She was almost sixty years old now and, while she was strong and still retained a trace of the delicate prettiness she must have had as a girl, she looked every day of those sixty years. She'd had such a hard life, how could he make it any harder? How could he hurt her the way he was sure to do? He took the easy way out; he told half the story.

64

"I learned quite by accident that one of my employees, a Canadian woman named Nora Brand, had done something that promised to cause quite a messy situation if she wasn't stopped. I also learned she came here, so I came too, to try to stop her."

"You came in the hopes of keeping her out of trouble?" Deborah asked.

"No, it's too late for that. Besides, she deserves whatever happens to her. No, I just thought I could help the innocent people who might have gotten in her way. You see, Mother, Nora designed and built something whose only practical application is terrorism."

"I can understand your fears, but you aren't responsible for her actions just because she worked for you. Why didn't you hand the matter over to the police or—what is that organization in America?—the F.B.I.? They could have handled it. It's their job."

"She built this device on my time, using my equipment. I think that makes it my concern," he said a shade too defensively.

"That still doesn't explain—Oh, no!" she said, alarmed. "You're not in love with this woman, are you, Terry?"

"In love with her!" he snorted. "I can barely tolerate being in the same room with her. She's an abusive person and no more than a marginally-competent engineer. I was actually on the verge of firing her when I happened to chance upon her little moonlighting activities."

Deborah shook her head. She still didn't understand why the matter required his personal involvement. He must be changing, she thought sadly. At one time he was so single-minded he would not have allowed anything to tear him away from his own pursuits. Unless.... She looked at him with a sudden thought.

"This isn't...it isn't the whole story, is it? Tell me the rest."

He sighed and told her. He told her about the nagging doubts he had suppressed for years, which Nora's activities had catalytically resurrected, the fears that the battle he had left behind in South Africa was one that was his to fight, to share.

"And maybe it doesn't make any sense," he concluded, "connecting two things that are totally unrelated, but Nora Brand's project brought it to the surface. When I learned she was coming here, to South Africa, I was forced to think of it, the way I hadn't in years. And I think, I hope, that when I find Nora—and I intend to, though I haven't a clue on how to start looking—well perhaps, just perhaps, I'll find myself too."

"You've been reading Entato's newsletters, haven't you, Terry?"

"No, I haven't. Entato sends them to me somehow. I don't know how he smuggles them out, but they arrive promptly every month, and every month I put them away without reading them. I've been avoiding the question all these years. Don't you see that?"

Didn't she see it? What she saw—only too well—was that one of her children, the one she believed was safe, was willingly walking back into a hungry lion's den.

"Just tell me this," Deborah asked. "Who is it you think you owe your life to? To your people? Because if you do, believe me, the best thing you can do for us is to show us that another world exists out there where people can be free, dignified human beings. If you want to do something for us, go back to doing what you've done for yourself. I'm just glad your father isn't here to see this."

She could have killed herself after she said it. She would have done anything to take it back. She never liked to pile burdens like that on her children; guilt of that sort was contrary to everything she'd taught them. But it was her honest thought.

"I'm sorry this has to hurt you, Mother, but I have to do it. And it isn't a question of owing my life to anyone. I don't. I just have to know...."

"Whether you alone could have changed everything, could reverse the thinking of this society? Isn't that absurd?"

66

"When you state it like that, yes, it is. But that isn't what I mean. I just have to know.... Look, when I left here, I was very young. I believed everything you and Dad told me. I believed that I had to leave if I wanted to make something of my life, but now I'm an adult. I have to think for myself. And I don't really know that. I don't really know anything about South Africa as an adult. Now, I have to find out.... Well, let's just say this is an open chapter in my life and I have to finish it, one way or the other."

This time she succeeded in holding back everything she wanted to say. She even held back the tears, though they flowed inside.

"Well, then, if you have to, finish it. And be done with it."

"You're not going to fight me on this, Mother?"

"It's your life. You have to live it as you see fit."

She did it. She said the hardest thing she ever had to say. But just because she knew it was the right thing to say, that didn't make her feel any better. She knew he was happy with her attitude, however. He kissed her quickly on the cheek, then rushed upstairs to change his clothes, leaving her alone with her pain. She grieved for him and she desperately hoped he would be able to stay free of the chains that bound her. But there was nothing she could do to help him.

The Mantizimas ate a quick dinner, then Deborah went to work. She was a nurse in a clinic in Soweto. Since most of their patients worked during the day and would never be excused for something as frivolous as a doctor's appointment, nights were the busiest time for the clinic.

While he would have liked to have been able to spend more time with his mother, he was not sorry that she had to leave. He had plans of his own for this evening. He had a pressing need to see someone he hadn't seen in years and didn't want any excuse to put that off. Besides, it was nice to have a chance to be alone so he could get acquainted with her house.

That was not the house he had been raised in; it was a much bigger and better house than that one had been. They had acquired this house only five years ago, just before his father died. Actually, he thought, it was too big for his mother, even though Elizabeth and Entato occupied one room on their day off. But he knew that house represented the crowning achievement of a lifetime, not to mention a last link to a much-loved husband; nothing would prompt her to sell it. He smiled, remembering the pride she displayed when she showed it to him. It was hers, she had said, all hers.

At any rate, as much hers as was permitted.

Yes, it was worthy of that pride, he thought, as he took a last look at the outside of it from the sidewalk. They all were, all of the houses in that neighborhood. This was something the proponents of apartheid loved to point out, that not all non-Whites were poor and lived in the cinderblock shanties the government built for them; many, they said, made very comfortable incomes and lived in fine houses, a few in what were nearly palacial mansions. And that was true. This particular neighborhood could be part of a tract of higher-priced homes almost anywhere in the world, and there was a section only a half-mile away that rivaled the best homes in any city.

But this wasn't a city anywhere else in the world—it was a specially created township, a reservation, designated for workers who were not permitted to live anywhere else. However good that neighborhood might be, there was an element of enforcement about the habitation that could never be avoided. Those people could not go into some nice Johannesburg suburb and buy the same house, even if they had the money. And even here they lived by permission, not by right. They were able to own the structures, but not the land; that was retained by the government. They were lucky to get lifetime leases, and even then, they always knew, those leases weren't really secure. At any time, if they failed to comply with any one of the stringent rules of residence there, they could be severed from their possessions and shipped off to a place they had never seen and forced to start over.

Mantizima shivered a little as he thought about the conditions of their lives and wished, for a moment, he were snug in his own house in Hingham, Massachusetts, thousands of miles away from that nightmare. But he hadn't come there to be secure. He walked on.

There weren't many trains heading out of Soweto at that hour, so Mantizima and the few other intended passengers had to wait for quite a while. He noticed the anxious looks on the faces of the people standing on the platform with him. Probably servants having a day out, he surmised, worried that they would not arrive back at their employers' homes in time. Blacks, apart from live-in servants, were not permitted to be in White sectors after dark, and servants had to be indoors. In fact, many chose to disregard the law and were never apprehended. However, enforcement did occur at times, albeit erratically and arbitrarily, and arrest for even that minor a transgression was not pleasant.

Why are you all so afraid? Mantizima wanted to say to them. But he did not. In truth, he was a little apprehensive himself. He had his U.S. passport in his pocket, but he was not sure how much good that was going to do for him. His position was an odd one. He was not sure whether his citizenship would place him in a separate category or whether the color of his skin would supersede political divisions. He had tried to have his travel agent confirm his position before he left Boston, but the answers she received from official sources were always contradictory and vague. He finally came to the realization that the official position of the government of South Africa with regards to him was going to be decided by the first policeman he met. He hoped the decision wouldn't be reached in some jail tonight.

He had to change trains and buses several times, but he finally arrived in Kempton Park, an affluent White suburb of Pretoria, at a stately, old, hilltop Victorian home. While the area and architecture weren't that similar, he was reminded of San Francisco. That made him think of Ali Hayden, the woman he'd met on the plane, and he wondered if he would ever see her again. He'd been a fool to agree to be interviewed by her; he'd known that at the time. He had little enough control over his life as it was without having a reporter picking through the ruins. But she was a very unusual woman, he thought, and he wanted to see her again.

He knocked at the back door of that house and a small black woman answered.

"Hello, Elizabeth," he said to his sister.

"Terry? Is that you? Oh, I'm so glad to see you."

She threw her arms around his neck and he lifted her off the ground in a bone-crushing hug. Then he placed her down and looked at her. He had seen his father once since leaving South Africa and his mother a couple of times, but always in Boston. He hadn't seen his sister since he left and she had only been sixteen then. The years apart had served her well. She had been a fairly pretty girl, but had grown into a very attractive woman, a small, delicate one, who took more after their mother than he did. She still looked very young. Her overall appearance had not yet caught up with her chronological age, but her eyes, he noticed, had aged beyond it. They were old and tired and very frightened.

She brought him into an impeccably maintained kitchen and sat him at the table.

"Have you eaten?" she asked.

"Yes," he said, smiling, remembering that even as a girl she was much more domestic than their mother.

"Well, at least you can have some tea. It won't take me long to make it."

She busied herself silently at the stove, then said of the man who owned that house, "He's not here, you know. I mean if you came to see him. I don't know when he'll be back."

"I did want to see him, but I wanted to see you more. I'll wait for him."

"Good. That will give us time to catch up."

They spent some time reminiscing and filling each other in on the little things that happened in the years they'd been apart. She did not ask why he had come back to South Africa and he did not tell her. He did plan to, he was sure she would approve, but the subject never came up.

70

Then he asked her, casually, in the same light vein, about her husband. Her face clouded over.

"We're thinking about leaving South Africa," she said softly. "Like you did."

"Where would you go?" he asked, surprised.

"What does it matter as long as it's away."

"Why?"

"For a lot of reasons," she answered evasively, then sighed and continued more honestly. "Oh, you should be able to figure it out. There's nothing for us here, and...and...my time is running out."

"I don't understand." Was she dying? he thought with alarm.

"I believe they call it a biological clock. I'm thirty-two years old, Terry. I don't have that much more time left."

Tears came to her eyes and she hastily rushed to the counter to hide them. "I think that tea must be ready," she said in a choking voice.

He cursed himself for his insensitivity. He had always assumed they hadn't had children because they didn't want them, because they might have interfered with Entato's work. He should have known better. Even as a young girl, she was like a pied piper to the children of their neighborhood. He should have realized she would want some of her own. It was tragic, he thought, but also very telling; she and her husband had always talked about the hope they held for the future, but they weren't genuinely confident enough in that future to subject another generation to it.

"I'd like to help you if I can," he said. "I've met a number of influential people in the course of my work in several countries. I'm sure at least one of them would be willing to sponsor your immigration."

He hoped that she did not notice he didn't offer to sponsor them himself.

"I don't know if Entato could accept that from you after the things he's said about you. You know he never approved of your leaving, and he's...he's a proud man," she said, her head bowed over the counter.

71

"He should be, for the things he's done."

"What has he done?" she said angrily, suddenly whirling around to face him. "Nothing! He's accomplished nothing at all. One day a week of stating his mind on paper does not begin to balance out the six days he bows and scrapes and does what he's told. And now he doesn't even have that avenue of expression. He's been ordered to shut down the newsletter under penalty of being banned!"

Banning! The Sword of Damocles that hangs over the heard of every South African who holds anything remotely independent within that head. The victims are usually writers or public figures, but they can be any citizen who has dared to speak his mind. They are declared to be enemies of the State and, as such, are denied the right to appeal or due process of law, which is limited at best in South Africa. They are then forbidden to speak or write their ideas and are never permitted to be in the company of more than one person, usually for a period of five years, though that can be, and often is, extended for the person's lifetime.

"Banned!" Mantizima said, shocked. "Now I understand why you want to leave. But this changes the whole picture. You have to let me help you. You can't be too proud to accept it. Not now."

"What can you do? Our only hope is to stop making waves and hope they forget about us. Then we'll escape. Entato knows people who can help us with that."

"Escape? Why should you risk that?" he asked; then, remembering the way he secured his own exit visa, added, "Look, Elizabeth, I know a woman, an American reporter. I met her on the plane. She wanted to interview me, but Entato would be a much better subject. I'm sure she would be willing to stir up public support in your—"

"Oh, please, Terry, don't tell her about us. Talking to her might be all it would take to get him banned. Then we'd never get away," Elizabeth said with sudden alarm.

"But if they don't like the things he writes, you'd think they'd be glad to have an excuse to get rid of him."

72

"Are you really that innocent? Or have you just been away so long that you don't understand anymore? They don't want to get rid of him—they want to break him!"

She suddenly broke down in tears and rushed out of the kitchen in the direction of her room, leaving him alone at the table. She was right, he thought, he didn't understand any of it anymore. But he would learn.

Elizabeth returned several minutes later, composed, but embarrassed, and eager to let the subject drop. "Well," she said, too brightly, "you still haven't told me why you are here. Mother was quite surprised when she got your letter."

He couldn't tell her. Not now, when she wasn't strong enough to handle it. She would learn eventually, he wouldn't be able to keep it from her, but it would be easier later on.

"Just thought it was time to renew old acquaintances," he said.

"Is he one of them?" she asked again of the owner of that house.

"There are some things I have to discuss with him, yes."

"You won't know him, Terry. He's changed a lot."

"Who hasn't?"

"You haven't. You should see yourself. You're just like you always were, only more so, while he seems...oh, I don't know...less. You know, he asks about you. He has all these years. He tries to make it sound casual, as if he's just making polite conversation with me, but I know he's interested."

"I never think about him," Mantizima said, a little sadly. "Or hardly ever."

"I wouldn't feel guilty," she said bitterly. "He's probably only stayed interested in you because you're the one who got away."

She was right; he was the only one who got away. Their family had worked for his family for generations. Their grandparents had; their mother had worked as a nurse for their business's black workers until her husband died and she decided to work closer to her home, and their father had spent his entire adult life in their shipping department doing

73

manual labor; Elizabeth had worked as a maid for someone in that family from the time she left school.

Only Terry had managed to avoid the Mantizima family serfdom. What would that man say, he wondered, what would any of the people like him say, what would they do if they knew the one that got away had come back?

CHAPTER SIX

Neil Logan took a hefty gulp from his glass of neat whiskey and settled himself in his favorite chair for a rare evening at home with his television. Publicly, he often praised South Africa for being the last advanced nation in the world to admit T.V. and questioned the wisdom of allowing it at all. "It gives the people the wrong ideas," he was frequently heard to say, "and makes it harder to keep them in line." Secretly, however, he was glad of its existence. His personal favorites were the shows other people said were of the lowest quality; they made him feel so superior.

He laughed heartily at some clumsy attempt at classic slapstick by the characters in a popular American show and drained the last of his whiskey. He immediately rose to refill the glass. That would be his fourth in a little less than an hour, but it did not show. That was something people always said about him—Neil Logan could hold his liquor. As well he should. Practice does make perfect.

There were two things that were important to Neil Logan: to be in charge and to be wanted. That was the way he expressed it to himself. Someone a little more objective might have said he wanted both power and acceptance and would probably have considered those two elements to be contradictory. A ruler can never really be one of the people. But Logan didn't see it that way. He thought that with enough strength you could force people to accept you, even if they did not want to, and he saw nothing contradictory in that.

Neil must have made those key decisions early in his life because he started putting his philosophy into effect before most children even form one. Even in his infancy he flew into uncontrollable rages which far exceeded normal tantrums, and at the slightest provocation. By the time he was a toddler he ruled the household with his personal reign of terror.

He had been born to a successful banker, well into middle-age, and his young second wife. The elder Logan had been through child-rearing before and was not inclined to put up with his son's behavior, but he desperately wanted to hold onto the child-woman he'd married. Since she wanted to put no restrictions on her adored son, he put none on her.

Neil's temper grew worse in that unstructured environment, however. After a while even his uncritical mother couldn't deny that he had become a monster. At one point she took him to a prominent neurologist for confirmation that his problem was physical. The doctor could find nothing wrong with him, however, and suggested psychological counseling. His mother stormed out of the office, vowing to find a "real doctor" who "knew his business." She never did, however. She was afraid to see another doctor for fear that he would say the same thing. She knew that if enough people said her cherished baby was "crazy," eventually she would have to believe it.

When he was five years old he grabbed a kitchen knife and viciously slashed the arm of the chauffeur who had dared to speak crossly to him. When he was eight he savagely beat another boy who had scored too many points off his rugby team, putting the boy in a hospital for a week.

That was too much for Neil's father. He thought that the only way to turn his son around, if it was not already too late, was to make him pay for what he did. But he knew Neil would not be the only one to pay the consequences, it would cost his wife much more in public humiliation. She was such a lonely, frightened creature, painfully aware that she was no match, in either age, sophistication or social standing, for the wives of her husband's peers. She had worked so hard for her meager acceptance that he couldn't bring himself to rob her of it. The injured boy's family was bought off, the scandal hushed-up, and Neil was transferred to another school.

Before he left, however, the headmaster gave Neil a few words of parting advice. He was a kindly but weak old man who preferred to look for the best in people, and, if he couldn't find it, to simply look the other way. He suggested to the boy that one could catch more flies with honey than with vinegar. It was such a feeble old adage that it should have made no impression on him, but the sentiment had never occurred to him before and it affected him profoundly. He was smart enough to realize coercion was not always as successful as he would have liked; perhaps, he thought, manipulation would work better.

He gave it a try in his new school, ineptly at first, but with rapidly-improving ease, and was amazed at how effective the technique was. Of course, not everyone fell for it; the brighter, more independent students recognized that his honey was still liberally laced with vinegar, or cyanide, as one teacher liked to describe it. He hated the people who saw through him, but he was learning to handle his temper, to channel it into sly, long-range revenge schemes against those who still rejected him. After he had been there for two years, he ran a slick campaign for class leader, with an expertise that any professional politician would have envied, and won by a wide margin. The next year he was voted the most popular boy in the school.

He was accepted, he had arrived. It was a heady thrill. He had succeeded in transforming his early brutality into a dynamic presence that few could resist.

Around that time, however, he became aware of the political realities of his country. He had no innate prejudices—his contempt was universal—but he saw that people fell into different categories and would have to be handled accordingly. He knew that Bantus and Coloreds had no political standing, and he secretly admired the way the government controlled them. Yet he knew the "better" people treated them with courtesy and were liberal with respect to them, in words, if not in action, and he mimicked that behavior. He also learned that there were differences between white people, and those weren't as easy to deal with.

He had been so insulated as a child, his associates and schools so well-chosen, that everyone he knew was of English ancestry. He hadn't even realized that most of his countrymen shared a different heritage. He was shocked when he discovered that and shocked by how much that heritage meant to them.

When he was in his teens his father enrolled him in a school that was mixed. "They're bloody ignorant Boers, the lot of them," his father had said, "but you'll have to learn to get on with them." He quickly assessed the situation. The English, he saw, dominated the upper class, they held the lion's share of the nation's wealth, and they were frequently more polished—but it was the Afrikaners' country, and they didn't like sharing it with the descendants of their former colonial rulers. It was frustrating for him, but his old techniques did not work as well in this new setting. His classmates, he knew, did not dislike him for himself, but they were so infused with the beliefs of their forefathers, they couldn't see him for himself.

"If I'm English," he said, when it was time for college, "then I should be in England." His parents strongly objected to his decision; his mother didn't want to lose him, and his father, for all his British ways, was a South African to the last part of his soul. But they could never change his mind when it was made up.

He realized, sadly, however, after only his first week, that coming to England was a mistake. He felt even more out-of-place there than he had at home. He felt hopelessly tied up in political binds that were not of his making. The South Africans considered him English, the English considered him South African. Where did he belong? He finally decided the only chance he had was in the country of his birth.

He came home and finished his education in South Africa. But he never regained the level of popularity and control he had once known. He attributed all of his problems

78

to the English-Afrikaner prejudice. In truth, while it did exist, it wasn't the whole story. The fact of the matter was that he was dealing now with a wider, more diverse and experienced group of people than the innocent schoolboys he had duped. He wouldn't have believed that, however, if anyone had told him. The bigotry was a convenient strawman. He'd always need a solid enemy to fight in the pursuit of his ever-present goals of control and belonging.

For lack of anything else to do, he went to work at his father's bank when he completed his education. But he really didn't belong there. He found banking a little too tame for his taste and the bankers found him to be, though he tried to mask it, too ruthless for theirs. He had pretty much decided to leave the bank and was trying to decide what else to do when chance entered and changed his life.

He had been walking down a street in downtown Jo'burg when he came upon a Bantu riot. Though he was just an innocent bystander, he jumped in and helped the police. He defended it later as the action of a good citizen, but in truth he still liked smashing heads and hadn't gotten to do it in years. Nothing would have come of it if the Bureau of State Security hadn't sent a man named Rune Aykroyd to investigate the riot. Aykroyd saw Logan in action and recruited him on the spot.

Finally, and by accident, he had found his place. He was accepted in BOSS, not for what he pretended to be, but for the man he was beneath the pretentions. He was actually expected to do what he loved best: exercise control over his fellow citizens. Oh, he kept up the facade, as did they all, mostly because they needed to maintain illusions about themselves. Logan needed no illusions, but understood that it usually was not advisable to shatter anyone else's.

He started at the bottom in BOSS, but he rose quickly. The organization's wunderkind. Within a few years he was second-in-command to one of its senior officers. He did have to share his rank with Pieter Kloff, but that didn't worry him, Privately, he considered Kloff to be a fool. He was not like most of the sonofabitches in BOSS, he was a good, honest man trying to do the best job possible, albeit with limited equipment. Because of what he thought of those traits, Logan discounted him to the point of nonexistence. Of course, he would have to get rid of Kloff eventually, but didn't consider that either advisable or necessary at the present time.

Rune Aykroyd presented a far greater stumbling block, and one that genuinely worried Logan. Like Kloff, Aykroyd was also an honest man, but he couldn't be discounted as easily as Kloff. He was far more astute, and that made him a real threat. Bright honest men scared Logan. You never knew where you stood with them. They were always judging you, and you could never be sure of winning their confidence and keeping it.

Of course, he didn't have many gripes about Aykroyd. He knew he would not have his present position but for Aykroyd's personal recommendation. And his treatment of Logan was unusually fair. Logan knew that Aykroyd and Kloff communicated in Afrikaans before he came aboard, but switched to English out of deference to him. He was grateful for the gesture, but considered them both to be fools for doing it, particularly Kloff. If he had that edge with a superior, he would have maintained it.

He had tried to establish his own edge. He and Aykroyd were of the same class and, as such, had more in common than a shared ancestry. He tried to develop that commonality, tried to socialize with Aykroyd on the level to which they were both accustomed. But Aykroyd did not socialize with his co-workers. He did not have a single friend as far as Logan could tell, either in the Bureau or out. He was the complete loner, whose shell could not be penetrated. He could not be owned.

Logan eventually came to the conclusion that, despite Aykroyd's treatment of him, Aykroyd considered him to be nothing more than a useful tool that would always have to be harnessed. Which meant keeping him in a second-line position, and that was not in accord with the future Logan planned for himself.

A sudden loud sound from the T.V. brought Logan out of a daze he had slipped into. He'd been thinking about that future he desperately wanted; he was growing tired of waiting for it.

Frustrated, he rose and angrily snapped off the set. He walked to the counter where he kept his liquor bottle and poured himself another drink. He was feeling a little fuzzy around the edges now, but that didn't bother him. He did some of his best thinking drunk.

The fact that Aykroyd had decided to keep him out of this present case was proof that he really didn't trust him. Of course, Aykroyd hadn't told Kloff any more about it, but Logan never gave that a thought. His only interest was with himself. Somehow, he decided, Aykroyd would have to be removed from his path. Perhaps there was something in this present case that Logan could use to do it. If he could only think of something....

He continued to plot, to scheme, to plan a strategy that would destroy the man who had given him his greatest chance.

The telephone rang in the busy, pre-party home of Wade Petri.

"I'll get it, Rina," he said to his wife. "I'll take it in the den."

I'll have to get it, he thought; by the time she could walk to a phone, even the most patient caller would have hung up. Rina Petri stepped—the word that came to her husband's mind was "waddled"—into the living room and smiled gratefully. She was in her last month of pregnancy and was quite big. He looked at her shapeless body beneath the silk tent that had probably cost three hundred rand and the old, black, flat-heeled shoes that had once belonged to their maid and were now the only things she could fit into and shook his head. He could never understand the men who considered their pregnant wives' bodies to be beautiful, who wanted to be part of the "miracle" of birth. He never saw anything

81

miraculous about it; all it meant to him was pain and mess and blood and no damn sex for months.

He realized his thoughts must be showing on his face and remembered to smile reassuringly. He didn't want to upset her any more than she was. She had wanted to cancel this party until after the baby was born. She hadn't been sleeping very well lately and was feeling tired. He was eager to show off their big new house, however, and wanted to solidify his relationships with some of the influential people who had accepted their invitations. She had no right, he had told her, to put her personal considerations above his career and their future. She gave in reluctantly, but he really feared she might be spiteful enough to have the baby that night.

He was not looking forward to having the baby in their home. Who in his right mind would want someone around who had to be fed and cleaned and changed at all hours of the night? he thought. But what could you do? You had to have a family. Of course, it wouldn't be so bad this time. He had managed to convince her to put the nursery on the other side of the house, far away from their room, and to hire a wetnurse to attend to it. That hadn't been easy; she had put up quite a fight. But he told her a wife's first duty is to her husband. She had no business leaving his bed in the middle of the night to take care of someone else. Eventually he had managed to win her over, but he still didn't understand the problem. Why would a woman want to feed her child herself, and with her own body no less, he wondered, when she could pay someone else to do it?

He always won their conflicts, but it irritated him that she made problems where they didn't have to be at all. It wasn't that he didn't love her, he thought as he crossed to the ringing telephone in the den. He did. She'd been a good choice for him. She'd brought a lot of money and a prominent social standing to their marriage and did not mind using that position to further his. And she had never even once reminded him that she had married beneath herself. She was a good wife. In exchange, he was determined to live up to the faith she had in him.

A perfect marriage based on true love.

While he never permitted Rina to change his opinions, he did allow her father to influence him, as his own father had before that.

His grandfather had run a small neighborhood grocery store, which his father had parlayed into a small chain of gourmet shops. But there never had been any question of Wade's going into the family business. He was destined for better things.

His father made a comfortable living from his business, but they were never wealthy. In fact, he was always painfully aware that he served the wealthy, something his son would never have to do. He sent Wade to a better school than he could properly afford so that he might begin making good connections right from the start. Wade always made good grades there, though he had to work very hard to achieve them. He didn't understand why they were so important to his parents, however; after all, other students were content with average marks. But his father had said, "Grades are very important to a boy, the way money is to a man. It's what people judge you by."

Without having anything else said to him, Wade learned the first of the many lessons he was to learn in the course of his life, the lessons that were to become the foundation of his existence. He learned that the essential thing in life, more important than anything else, was what other people thought of you.

Of course, he did rebel at times. Once a poor but brilliant boy had come to their school on a scholarship. Some of the other children, filled with their parents' snobbishness, had made fun of him. Wade liked the boy and always took his side. One day he defended him in a fight and received a black eye for his efforts. His parents punished him severely when they learned the whole story. "It's not your affair," his mother had said. "Never get involved in other people's problems." "You've probably alienated all your other friends," his father had warned, "and you'll have to win them back. Nothing can do as much for a man as having the right friends."

From his second lesson Wade learned that friends are people who can do things for you.

He fought them on the choice of his career. He had wanted to be a doctor and believed his parents would approve of his choice. A man in that profession, he reasoned, always made a good living and was well-respected because of the nobility of the job. His father argued that the real wealth and, hence, the power in South Africa came from the resources within the earth; it was the earth that produced the true leaders in their society. He couldn't provide his son with a gold or diamond mine, he said sorrowfully, but he could give him the means to one day acquire his own. It was decided that Wade would study geology and, later, with an eye to the methods of the future, that was refined to geophysics.

That lesson taught him that while money is important, status and power are more so.

He got off the beaten trail again in his teens when he became involved with a girl who lived in his neighborhood. Her father was as successful as his, but no more so, and that was not what the Petris wanted for their son. Wade really cared for the girl, however, and continued to disobey his parents about seeing her until the girl confessed to him that she believed herself to be pregnant. He shared his fear with his parents and together they sweated out the days until her test returned. This time they punished him with a heavy load of guilt. They had done so much for him, they said, that he had no right to think only of himself. He had no right to throw away everything they had given him just when he was on the brink of building the life they had always planned for him. Fortunately, the girl's pregnancy was only a false alarm. She was promptly dropped.

This time the lesson he learned was that the selection of a wife is the most important career decision a successful man could make.

Anyone who witnessed it would have sworn his first meeting with Rina van Niekirk was spontaneous, a testimony to his mother's brilliant engineering. A spoiled girl, in one of her rare bouts of willfulness, Rina fell in love with Wade almost from the first. Probably because her parents didn't approve of him. They had nothing against him personally, but they, like the Petris, wanted their child to move up in marriage, not down. But Rina held out, in an unprecedented burst of insistency, and they were married.

Her father decided to make the best of the situation, seeing that Wade, despite his humble origins, did have the potential of being the right kind of son-in-law. He accepted the fact that he would have to give Wade the kind of position his daughter deserved, but did not want to hand it over immediately; he expected the young man to earn it.

He was the one who suggested that Wade enter government service for a while. "It will give you some good credentials," van Niekirk had said. "Shows you're willing to do your share. A successful man always recognizes his responsibility to return some of what he takes." He secured a key research position in the government's atomic facility at Pelindaba, he suspected with his father-in-law's help. He didn't like the work and the hush-hush atmosphere that was so heavily burdened with bureaucratic red tape made him uncomfortable. And there were strange things that happened there that would have made him nervous if he allowed himself to think about them, which he did not.

Still, he stayed there until van Niekirk told him it was time to make the move into private industry and offered to call Karel Aykroyd, a member of his country club, about finding a place for him. And only last week he said that he was pleased with Wade's progress and promised to finance a venture for him when he was ready for it. "I think I know a few people who would like to be part of the syndicate. Just put in a couple of more years soaking up information around Aykroyd's place before you try to put him out of business," he had joked.

He was on his way. He had learned his lessons well and now they were going to pay off.

He thought, as he picked up the receiver of the telephone in the den, that his in-laws were going to be at the party and he would have to remember to be particularly solicitious to Rina tonight.

"Yes?" he said into the phone.

"You won't ever say anything about Pelindaba if you know what's good for you," an unidentified male voice with an indeterminable accent said without preliminaries. "They probably won't get onto you, but if they do, remember, say nothing. Unless you want something to happen to that pregnant wife of yours...or even yourself."

"Wie is jy?" Petri said, unconsciously slipping into Afrikaans. "Who are you?" he hastily repeated in English.

"A friend. Just remember, you don't know anything."

"But I don't know anything," Petri protested.

"Stay that way."

With that warning, the caller abruptly hung up. Petri held the silent phone next to his ear until the dial tone returned to remind him the conversation was over.

"But I don't know anything," he protested aloud to the empty room. "I don't. I never do."

CHAPTER SEVEN

Ali gave her reflection in the mirror one final inspection. Though she was a naturally beautiful woman, she rarely took pains with her appearance. When she did, the result was spectacular. She wore the best dress she owned, a rust-colored silk dress that beautifully accented her hair, which she would probably not have even had with her had she not come directly from San Francisco. She considered herself quite impersonally and decided it would work very well.

She waited for Aykroyd in the hotel lobby, pacing a little anxiously for a while. But she did not have to wait long. As she expected, he was early.

His brisk steps stopped suddenly when he caught sight of her. His breath caught in his throat. Ali was quite pleased with the way she was obviously affecting him. The time she had taken preparing herself had paid off. He was thrown off-center enough to give her what she had wanted most in this encounter: the upperhand.

Aykroyd recovered enough to approach her and took her hand in his. "You look...beautiful, just beautiful," he said breathlessly. "Are you ready to go?"

"Not quite," Ali answered seductively. "I need...well, I wonder if I could persuade you to do a couple of little favors for me first."

"Anything. What do you need?"

"Well, first, I want you to ask the hotel to change my room. They'll do it for you, I'm sure" she continued sweetly. "and then I'd like you to explain why you had me bugged."

The alluring tone, in contrast to the nature of her request, and the fact that she had happened onto the discovery at all was all too much for him to take in. He stared at her in amazement.

"Now!" she ordered in an abrupt shift of tone.

"Will you lower your voice?" he said, recovering his.

"Not until I get some answers!"

"Well, you are not going to get them here!" Aykroyd said, joining in the shouting.

"Really? I'm not leaving here until I do."

By that point they were both oblivious to the curious glances they were attracting from the other people in the lobby.

"We shall see about that," Aykroyd said.

He roughly grabbed hold of her arm and pulled her towards the front door. Ali knew that Aykroyd believed he had taken charge of this conflagration, but, in fact, everything was going according to her plan. She was sure that if she had pushed him really hard she could make him angry enough to be careless, to reveal things he obviously did not want her to know.

On the sidewalk he curtly ordered the valet to bring his car around. When it arrived it was not the large American car he had used in his guise of a Haagen-Aykroyd executive, but a small Italian sports car.

"Nice," Ali said. "If I don't fit in, you can always stuff me in the trunk."

"Don't tempt me," Aykroyd said as he pushed her into the passenger side.

They drove in silence in the direction, if her geography was correct, of Pretoria. She assumed he was taking her to BOSS headquarters. She could feel the angry tension in him and even thought she sensed a touch of fear, but figured she had to be wrong about that because why would he be afraid of her? Still, she allowed herself to sink comfortably into the seat and smiled to herself. Unless she missed her guess, she was definitely onto something—something big—and she was the only reporter who had it.

He surprised her by taking her not to his office, but his home in a Pretoria suburb. She allowed herself to be led into the house and, once inside, roamed around the living room as if she were actually a guest there by choice.

The house did not surprise her. Had she thought about it, that was precisely the way she would have envisioned his home. The house itself was an old, well-preserved Victorian. Most of the furnishings seemed to fit the house. They were solid, traditional pieces, obviously expensive, but tastefully understated. Good, safe choices, all of them. But there were other pieces scattered about that were strangely at odds with the dominant theme of the decor. Bold, starkly modern pieces in dramatic colors that were like a defiant blast of cold wind in that stuffy, airless room. It was not a delicate and intentional blending of the products of different ages, the eclectic mix with which decorators are so enamored. It was a house at war with itself, the mirror of a man locked in an ugly struggle between the past and the future for which he obviously believed there was no resolution.

Aykroyd stood silently and watched Ali as she walked around. He studied the movement of her body beneath the delicate fabric, the body he could reach out and take with no effort at all. The effort, he knew from the aching in his loins, was in not taking.

"Interesting," Ali said at last. "Suits you. But do your taxpayers know about this?"

"By now you know enough about me to realize the taxpayers need not concern themselves about my expenditures."

"That's interesting, too," she said, "that you went to work for the government, I mean, instead of the business that obviously provides all of this."

"That shouldn't be too hard for you to understand. Your father must own half of San Francisco. Why aren't you working for him?"

"I don't think my father can possibly own more than a third of San Francisco," she said sarcastically. She said nothing else, but she noted that he knew more about her background than he had any legitimate reason to. "Aren't you going to offer me a drink?"

"I'm a simple man," he said. "A direct man. I have no ability to play the sophisticated sort of games you are used to, and no desire to learn. All I'm going to offer you is a chance to save your wretched skin."

The scenario was taking a strange turn, Ali thought. And for a simple, direct man, she considered him to be incredibly obtuse.

"Tell me what you know," he continued. "Now, before anything happens, and I promise you you'll get off easily, though God knows you don't deserve it. But if you wait, if you think you can go ahead with this, I'll see you hang. I swear I will!"

So he thinks I know something, she thought. Well, that wasn't too hard to figure. Why else would he have built up that elaborate charade, not to mention having her bugged.

"I mean it," he continued. "I want answers."

"Generally, the best way to get answers is to provide questions."

"Flippancy is not going to help you. And neither is being a woman. Don't believe that makes you safe. You wouldn't be the first woman I beat the truth out of. Nor the last, I trust."

"So you are going to maul me," Ali said calmly. "Wonderful. It'll make great press."

"It will never see print."

"Like hell it won't!"

They glared at each other angrily.

"Tell me what you know!" Aykroyd demanded again. "If you expect to walk out of here in one piece!"

It's a bluff, Ali assured herself. He wouldn't dare lay a hand on me, not when I could put it on the front page of every paper in the world. But she could not imagine what could have incensed him so. Nothing, she thought, was that serious.

"If you want me to talk," she said in the manner of a shrewd negotiator, "I need a drink."

90

He became silently livid, causing her to rethink her earlier assessment. At that moment, as preposterous as it sounded, she was sure he really wanted to hit her.

"A drink," she said again, and was confident her tone did not reveal the fear she was starting to feel.

He did not, however, hit her. With the utmost control, he walked to a liquor cabinet and started to prepare two drinks. She did not really want the drink, she just needed to gain a little time. This was definitely not going according to plan. Somehow, she had to figure out some of what he wanted to know if she was going to get all of it out of him.

He returned to her a few moments later holding two drinks, a tall whiskey and soda for himself and a short scotch and water for her.

He even knows what I drink, she thought. Panic started to rise within her. He seemed to know everything about her. And he didn't even take the trouble to hide it. Maybe he really wasn't intending for her to leave that room alive.

He was about to hand her one glass when, suddenly, he changed his mind and slammed both drinks down on the table next to her. He grabbed her by both arms and pulled her body close to his.

"Why, Ali?" he whispered desperately. "Why you? Why do you have to be—"

She realized he was not really talking to her, he was asking agonizing, unanswerable questions of himself. She also realized how deeply this man desired her and what that desire had to be costing him.

He's a fool, she thought, if he thinks I could care about him. And all I have to do to show him what a fool he is is to break away.

Yet she did not break away; instead, she leaned into him, pressing the length of her legs against his. She had thought all of that ended in his office, but apparently not. She despised everything the man stood for, pitied him for his personal agonies, but she could not stop her body from responding to his. She could not deny that the strength, the power, the promise still alive within him was an answer to her own.

"Does it really matter?" she whispered.

"God help us both, no."

I'll stop this in a minute, she thought. I can't let it continue. Just one more minute and I'll stop it once and for all.

But rather than stop it, she lifted her face to his. His arms went around her. His mouth moved down. She could feel his quick, warm breath on her face. In another moment....

She could not do it. She wasn't a perfect person, she knew, just a good one, trying to do the best she could and sometimes not making it. But one flaw she didn't have was dishonesty, particularly with respect to herself. She did not live with lies. She genuinely liked the vibrant, although sometimes harsh, colors of reality; she had no taste for the evasive pastels with which most people paint their lives. She knew that she was not responding to the man he was, but to the man he could have been, but chose not to be. And because he had made that choice, he was not a man for her. She knew that denying him now, when she'd given him every reason to believe that she felt as he did, was not right, but she couldn't help it. Why start something in joy, she thought, that can only end in pain?

She lowered her face.

But Aykroyd would not accept that wordless message. He had gone too far to turn back. He had cut the reins of his precious control, releasing years of emotions that had been harnessed too long. He jerked her face up and pressed his lips to hers in something that was not a kiss, but an act of violence. Ali tried to push him away, but that only made him hold her tighter; he locked her into a grip she could not hope to break out of. She was genuinely frightened. She knew what was going to happen in the next few minutes. She also knew it wouldn't be an act of love, but of abuse, a release of all the anger he had bottled up in himself. She shuddered to think of what would be left of her when he was finished.

Then someone, whom neither Ali nor Aykroyd had ever heard enter the room, suddenly cleared this throat, in a manner that feigned but was definitely not embarrassment.

"Am I interrupting anything important?" an amused voice asked.

Aykroyd, still holding Ali in his arms, looked across the room and saw a black man who had dared to enter his home and interrupt at a time like that. He was about to throw him out physically—Ali feared he might even kill him—when recognition dawned on his face.

"Terry?" he asked, his voice still heavy with desire.

"Hello, Rune," Terry Mantizima said wistfully. "As they always say in the movies, it's been a long time."

Seventeen years. A very long time.

They had met when they were seven years old. It had been a school holiday and Karel Aykroyd had brought his son to work with him so the boy could become acquainted with a business that would one day be his. Terry's father, who worked in the Haagen-Aaykroyd shipping department, knew that his superiors would both be off that day, so he took the chance of bringing his son, too, so the boy could see his father work. Two boys with loving, concerned, but busy fathers, so busy that for all but the start of the working day the children were left to their own devices.

Rune had wandered into the shipping department and saw Terry sitting off in the corner reading something. In the shy, stiff way that children have, the boys became acquainted.

"What are you reading?" Rune had asked.

"It's a catalog of electrical parts," Terry answered. "When I have enough money to buy them, I'm going to build my own radio."

"You can't build a radio. You're a Kaffir."

He had said it simply, without malice. An obvious, undisputable fact. He did know that some children did build crystal radio sets, usually older boys, but he had never known anyone who had done it. He was sure he couldn't have built one himself, so there was no way this black boy could.

93

"If I had the parts," Terry had answered, "I could do it."

On a dare, Rune purchased those parts in a local store, defying Terry to put them together. He watched in silence one afternoon after school a few days later as Terry fitted the pieces together. By the time he was half-way through, Rune no longer wanted to win that bet. When they picked up their first staticy transmission, their friendship was sealed.

That same day they pricked the tips of their fingers with a pin and mingled the scant drops of blood they drew, the way they had once read about boys doing.

"Friends," Terry had said, "Brothers."

"For life."

The friendship endured, despite the problems attached to it. They never discussed it, but both understood that it had to be kept a secret. Society, family, other friends would never understand.

But is is hard to keep a secret in childhood, the time in life when one is most closely watched. Deborah Mantizima learned of the relationship after a couple of months and told her husband that they would have to put a stop to it.

"That boy will drop him in time. As soon as his parents realize what he is doing," she had said. "And Terry will be hurt."

"Then he'll learn about these things, the way he will have to anyway," her husband answered. "This isn't something we can teach him. He'll have to figure it out on his own."

Karel Aykroyd discovered it too, and also decided to let the friendship run its natural course. He didn't talk about it to his wife, whom he knew would be very upset, or even to his son. He just trusted that the beliefs of many generations, which he had instilled in his son, would prove stronger than any temporary attachments he might form.

With everything going against it, the friendship should not have survived, but it did. There were other friends found along the way, but none that gave them what they were able to provide for each other. Their strengths and weaknesses, their varying attributes and talents balanced each other and filled needs that no one else could. They were equals in each other's eyes. Each knew the other was different from him, that they came from separate worlds, but they left the trappings of those lives outside of the shell they had built around themselves and believed the demands of those worlds would never be able to penetrate.

By some unspoken, mutual decision, there were things they did choose not to discuss, things that were part of that outside world that had no place in theirs. But there was nothing they couldn't have talked about if they wanted to. When they were eleven, Terry raised a thought that shocked Rune.

"Do you believe in God?" he had asked.

"Of course!" Rune said, looking over his shoulder, though he knew they were alone.

"I'm not sure that I do."

"I know what you're thinking, Terry. You're thinking that if there really were a merciful God, he wouldn't let...some people suffer," Rune had said, coming as close as they ever did to forbidden territory.

"Would you think that, Rune, if you were me?" Terry answered, bringing it out into the open. "But that's not what bothers me, anyway. It just doesn't make any sense. They tell us in Sunday school that God created the whole universe. But he's part of that, so who created him?"

They continued discussing, in simple, youthful terms, the ideas that would be echoed years later in college classrooms. Rune really feared for Terry, yet did not attempt to silence him the way outsiders probably would have. He would not let anything, not even his most fundamental beliefs violate the environment of open trust they had created between them. But he secretly prayed for Terry and asked God to forgive him.

Terry also worried about Rune. In that discussion he sensed for the first time that there was an essential difference between them. Not because Rune didn't accept his ideas—he would always defend Rune's right to think whatever he chose—but because he did not feel free enough to consider them. Terry feared that the binds of the outside world were starting to pull at Rune, but he vowed to fight for his friend's life with everything he had, never doubting he would win.

There had never been any question about what Terry was going to do with his life; he was going to be some kind of scientist or engineer. He didn't know which kind at that time, but he knew he was going to spend his life conquering the unknown.

Rune, however, never talked about his plans. He never gave any indication that he even had any. It was as if he didn't even realize the future existed, at least when he was with Terry. Once Terry asked him about what he wanted to do with his life.

"I don't know," Rune answered. "I suppose I'll go into the gold business. My father says I have a duty to maintain the order of our society."

"Then why don't you become a policeman?" Terry asked angrily. "No one can maintain order better than a cop."

Rune looked up, surprised. It was an idea that had never occurred to him.

"Look, Rune," Terry continued desperately, "what do *you* want to do? Don't you have a duty to yourself? Isn't it your life?"

"I don't think it is. Not completely. I wouldn't be here if my mother and father hadn't had me. Doesn't that make my life at least partially theirs? Don't I owe them for that?"

Terry began to realize that pulling Rune out of his parents' clutches might not be as easy as he had believed.

They saw each other less as their teenage years progressed. Mrs. Aykroyd imposed a very structured social life on her son. But the time apart made the time they had together even more precious. When they were together Rune always acted as if nothing had changed between them, but Terry knew it had. Rune was as warm and close as ever, but there was a desperation about him now. He was clinging to Terry as if he feared he could not make it alone. Terry understood that there were two Rune Aykroyds: the one he was with him and the one he was with other people, the boy

96

he wanted to be and the boy he thought he was supposed to be. He also knew they weren't equals any longer, they were a drowning man and a healthy swimmer. But Terry did not mind the burden. He was strong enough to handle it, and he would have done anything to help Rune become a whole, healthy person.

When they were seventeen, Karel Aykroyd told his son to join a particular club in school. Rune knew the members of that club were all Fascists and knew their "schoolboy pranks" were always vicious attacks against Bantus and Coloreds. He didn't want any part of anything that might hurt Terry, but he also knew he couldn't defy his father.

"I'll have to join, you know? I really don't have any choice," Rune had said.

"You always have a choice, Rune, you just have to take it."

"I can't do that to my father. I'll have to join, but I'll try to change the way they think. I really will, Terry."

"You're straddling a fence, Rune, and someday you're going to have to get off. On one side or the other. You're going to have to make a choice."

"I'd never choose against you, Terry. I'd never do anything to hurt you. Believe that," Rune cried desperately.

"I want to."

"Oh, why does it have to be so hard?" Rune asked. "I owe you both so much."

"Me? You don't owe me anything," Terry said in amazement.

"Don't I? Don't I lean on you? Now don't deny it. Haven't you given me what little strength I have...? Sometimes I feel as if I'm always struggling to reach you and you just keep moving farther above me. I just wish I could repay you somehow so we could go back to being what we were when we were kids. I really wish I could clear the slate."

A year later, Rune Aykroyd got that chance. When Terry's exit visa was turned down, he asked for Rune's help in reversing the decision.

"Rune, you know I have to leave. There is no future for me here. But they won't let me go."

"What can I do?" Rune had asked.

"You can't do anything, but your father can. He's an influential man. If you asked him, I know he'd do it. He'd probably be glad to get me out of your life."

But he doesn't know about you! Rune shouted in his own mind. And how could he tell him?

"Don't ask me, Terry."

"I have to. You're my only chance. You said you wanted to clear the slate, well, this will do it. I've never asked you for anything else, Rune."

Rune turned away. He couldn't bear to look at Terry. He knew what the opportunity to leave South Africa meant to him; he could almost feel his friend's pain. But how could he ask his father a thing like that? How could he tell him that he had been betraying their beliefs all those years? That throughout his whole childhood he had been living a lie?

"Terry...I can't."

Rune stood with his back to Terry for a long time. When he finally summoned the courage to turn around and face him, Terry was gone.

Rune did keep abreast of Terry's struggle to secure permission to leave South Africa, which was eventually gained through the efforts of a liberal white newspaper editor who made the denial a public issue. He never allowed himself to avoid the issue; he had to know what his cowardice had cost the only person he had ever really cared about. But he never saw Terry again.

Until now.

"Yes, it has been a long time. What has it been? Fourteen, fifteen years?" Aykroyd asked while he struggled to regain his composure.

Coward! Aykroyd said to himself. Why can't you admit that you know precisely how long it has been. Why can't you tell him that after seventeen long years you're still raw inside from thinking about what you did to him?

It's been seventeen years, Mantizima thought, and after all this time it still hurts a little bit. But he couldn't bring himself to say that.

"Yes," he said instead, "something like that."

Mantizima turned his attention to Ali. She looked so good to him that the sight of her almost took his breath away. But he did not forget that when he entered the room she had been kissing Aykroyd. He did not realize that it was so one-sided. He wants her badly, the thought, stealing a glance at Aykroyd, but they're wrong for each other. In a very short time she would tear him apart, if he didn't stab her in the back first.

He smiled at Ali. "Hello, Ali," he said. "I imagine you are surprised to see me again so soon."

"Not really. I knew we would run into each other before long."

"If I'd known you were going to look this beautiful the next time I saw you, I would have made it a lot sooner."

"Do you two know each other?" Aykroyd asked unnecessarily.

"Oh, yes, we're old friends," Ali said.

"We just met on the plane," Mantizima explained. "I would say that makes us new friends."

They just met, Aykroyd thought, and yet there was no strain between them. They acted as if they'd known each other for years. He noted bitterly that whatever desire Ali might have felt for him disappeared when Mantizima entered the picture. Coincidence? Not likely, he thought. He wondered whether she realized it herself. But he wants her, Aykroyd thought when he saw the look his old friend was giving Ali, very much, and he was well aware of it. But they're wrong for each other. He asked himself whether that opinion came from some unconscious prejudice, whether the thing that bothered him was that Ali was a white woman, but he was sure that was not it. They were wrong for each other because they would bring out the worst in each other; they would incite each other's most dangerous, most reckless instincts, and would lose whatever self-control they had.

"As a matter of fact," Aykroyd said, "Miss Hayden and I are new friends, too."

"So I saw."

The two men faced each other and all of their thoughts were communicated just as if they were spoken. Both knew where they stood. Ali was not privy to that communication, however; she merely sensed that something awkward had settled over the room, but she didn't know what it was.

"Maybe someone should warn her about the way you treat your friends," Mantizima said.

"I don't know what you mean," Aykroyd said tightly.

"No, you wouldn't.... Well, I had something to tell you— not something personal—but I obviously picked a poor time. Rune," Mantizima said, with a nod of his head, then turned to Ali and said, a touch sarcastically, "Bye, Ali. You can go back to getting...the third degree."

Both Aykroyd and Ali watched him walk towards the kitchen. Each thought—I have to stop him!—but neither moved a muscle. Then, when he was almost out of the room, Ali shouted to him.

"Terry, despite how things appeared," she said anxiously, "I was getting the third degree."

Mantizima snorted and turned to her, but the sarcasm quickly drained from his face when he saw how frightened she looked.

"Seriously," she continued. "He thinks I know something— God knows what—but he told me he would beat it out of me."

"Rune, is that true?"

"This is business, Terry," Aykroyd said. "My business, it doesn't concern you."

"Right, *Baas*," Mantizima said bitterly.

He had wanted to wound Aykroyd with that remark and, though Aykroyd's shock told him it obviously met its mark, he wondered why he didn't enjoy it more. He turned and once again marched towards the kitchen.

"Terry, wait!" Aykroyd shouted.

He ran after Mantizima and grabbed hold of his arm, twirling him around to face him. Mantizima stared at Aykroyd with black, angry eyes, but he did not pull his arm away.

"Terry, listen to me, I'm saying this for your own good. This has nothing to do with...with what happened between us. Believe me, you don't want to get involved with her. You don't belong here."

"Ali?" Mantizima asked, never taking his eyes off Aykroyd.

"I can handle it on my own if you really don't want to get involved," Ali said. "But I wouldn't mind a little help."

"Then it's decided," Mantizima said. "I'm staying."

"Don't be a fool, Terry. I know what I'm talking about."

"I'm staying, Rune. *I* don't let my friends down."

"Will you forget about us for one minute and use your brain? She is not your friend. She's no one's but her own. You don't want to be caught on her side. You really don't belong in this business."

"Rune—"

"Dammit, Terry, don't you understand what I'm trying to tell you? This woman is a terrorist!"

Ali's jaw dropped in shock. Had anyone seen her, they could not have doubted the honesty of her reaction, but no one looked at her. The two men still saw only each other, though most of their intensity was now spent.

"If that is true," Mantizima said conversationally, "then you're wrong. I definitely do belong here."

CHAPTER EIGHT

Trudi Schmidt sat perfectly still listening to the sounds made by the man outside her door.

"Are you there, Trudi? It's...me," he said, unwilling to identify himself even in a place where no one knew him. "It's our time, Trudi. Are you in there, my dear?"

His dear, she thought bitterly. That was a joke. She had never been and never would be anyone's dear.

He gave a single, loud, impatient rap on the door. "Trudi, are you there?" he demanded one last time.

She remained quiet through his angry mutterings outside the door and the petulant stomping that receded down the hall. When it was silent once again, she sighed deeply and lit a cigarette. He was gone, thank God, and with a little luck he would never return. Of course, with that kind of luck she could starve to death. At that moment, however, she didn't really care.

She angrily crushed out her cigarette, but lit a replacement a moment later. She just had to do something. The floor around her chair was covered with the pages of a newspaper, thrown down in disgust. She had been reading the "Help Wanted" ads. Of course, it was an academic exercise; her visa did not entitle her to work in South Africa. She reasoned, however, that if she found a job for which she might be qualified there, the same or similar job would exist somewhere where she was permitted to work. Unfortunately, the converse was also true.

Wearily, without ever forming the words that commanded the action, she slowly rose and walked in the

102

direction of the bathroom. The room was dark when she entered it, but she didn't even bother to turn on the light. Even in the dark she could find it, that bottle of pills that she'd been needing to sleep more and more often. The bottle hadn't even been opened yet; it was the extra she had brought from West Berlin. There wasn't any question that she would succeed. Finally, she would be good at something.

She reached out for it, her hand extending closer and closer. But then, suddenly, her arm stopped in mid-air and she couldn't make it move any closer.

Do it! she ordered herself. You'll never feel a thing! You'll never hurt again!

She couldn't.

Oh, for several moments she continued to hold her arm rigidly before her, but she knew it was over. In the moment of crisis she had learned she really did not want to take that out, though she didn't know why. A few moments later she collapsed faintly against the bathroom wall.

But the tension that prompted that action still raged within her. She had to get out! she thought. She didn't know where; the where did not matter. She ran out of the bathroom and, grabbing a jacket on the run, she raced through the living room, out of the apartment and down the hall.

She didn't stop running till she hit the street.

Bugged! Evan Michael Todd thought. Why would anyone have bugged Ali?

He glanced nervously at the walls of his own hotel room. He knew they were okay. As soon as Ali left, he rushed down to a shop in the hotel lobby and purchased a tape recorder with which he checked every inch of that room. There was definitely nothing there, but he felt uncomfortable nonetheless.

He returned to his earlier question for which he could find no answer. Why Ali? What could anyone possibly have on her that they would go to those lengths to watch her? She was clean, he was sure of that. She was just an ordinary, politically naive person whose life was an open book.

103

Ordinarily, he might have thought that she had angered the South African Government by the articles she had written the year before, but if they were really disturbed by her, they would never have granted her a second visa. Besides, he had looked up those articles; most of them were simply factual pieces about the diamond strike, far easier on the South African Government than many of her colleagues were. There was nothing there. There was nothing anywhere. There was no answer. Unless....

Aykroyd! he thought, taking a sudden mental leap and landing on what he was sure was the right answer. There was something fishy about Aykroyd. He hadn't sensed it, but Ali did. She must have or she wouldn't have asked those questions about him after their first meeting. Evan resolved to be more sensitive to her instincts in the future.

Aykroyd was probably some kind of cop, he decided. And probably not a flunky either or he wouldn't have been able to call up the resources he obviously had at his disposal. That was it all right, he thought bitterly. He had certainly underestimated that cold fish. But that still didn't answer his question: why were the police interested in Ali?

He sighed in frustration and glanced uneasily at the walls that didn't but could well have had ears. He shivered. The room gave him the creeps. In the morning he would ask the hotel to change it, if he could think of a subtle way to do it.

In the meantime, he had to get out of that place. He didn't care where. Just out.

Trudi wandered into a Hillbrow bookshop. Bookstores were terrific places, she'd always thought. You could browse around them for hours and never be bothered by anyone, thoroughly involve yourself in books that didn't interest you in the least, blessedly kill some of an overabundance of time and, best yet, convince yourself that you'd actually improved your mind in the process. Yes, she was grateful for bookstores.

While wandering through the "Self-Help" section, her attention was caught by a book from an American publisher on something called "displaced homemakers." A quick glance through the introduction told her that displaced homemakers were women who, through divorce or widowhood, were suddenly thrown out of the job they had done all of their lives. The book went on to say that housewives develop many useful skills in the course of their lives, which they just need to learn how to market out in the business world.

I could use something like this, she thought. Just then a clerk passed, giving her a pleasant smile. Trudi sadistically thought of asking him if anyone had written a book on displaced hookers, but managed to restrain herself.

Then a surprising thought occurred to her. In the course of her work she had also picked up a number of useful skills. Morality aside, she had run a business, and she had run it very well. Was it really so different from, say, running a store? Could she possibly do something like that? She had good clothes sense and had learned a lot about hair and make-up. Maybe other women would be willing to pay for her knowledge. Maybe she could succeed at something like that, she mused.

But she could also fail.

She glanced up from the book and saw an old man looking at her. He actually was only looking at her, with the indifference that people give to strangers who happen to catch their eye. Trude was convinced, however, that he was leering. Who are you kidding? she demanded of herself. Of course, you'd fail. Everyone, even strangers, could see what she was, nothing but a stupid tramp.

She slammed the book back on the shelf, embarrassed that she had ever picked it up, hating it for what it had caused her to think. She glanced around quickly, desperate to get away from there.

Travel, she thought. Where is the travel section?

Evan walked aimlessly through the Hillbrow streets, glancing into the windows of the shops and restaurants, most of which were open at night. He was glad he had heard about this place. Jo'burg was such a stuffy, up-tight town, but at least it had a section like this. A little too avant-garde for his taste, perhaps, but there was a slightly wild, unruly feeling about the area. It was a place where you could really cut loose and raise hell, he thought.

Of course, he wasn't doing any cutting or raising. He was just wandering around, without direction or purpose, hoping that he would stumble across something that would occupy his mind for a while.

He meandered around for a while, completely lost in his own thoughts, but every now and then he got the strange feeling that he was being watched. The first time, he glanced tentatively over his shoulder; after that, he just boldly turned around and looked. There were always people around, but no one had any interest in him.

Paranoid, in addition to everything else, he thought in self-mockery. The feeling continued to occur from time to time during his wandering, but thereafter he always ignored it.

He happened upon a bookstore and paused before it, deciding whether or not to enter. He didn't read much; no one ever wrote anything that interested him. But there might just be some adequate photography books that would help pass the time, maybe even teach him something.

He hadn't yet found the photography section when he noticed the profile of the girl with whom he had shared a few drinks on the plane.

"Trudi? Hi, remember me?"

She turned to face him. What in hell has happened to her? he thought, noticing a dramatic change. She looks like she was hit by an emotional truck.

Damn! she thought. The last thing she needed tonight was to meet someone she knew, and a potential John at that.

"Yes, I remember you," she said dully, not bothering to hide her reluctance to speak to him. "How are you, Evan?"

"Just great," he bubbled. "How are you?"

"I'm...fine."

He continued on for several minutes, trying to draw her into conversation, but all he elicited were sharp one-word answers.

Why won't he leave? she thought. He had to realize she didn't want to talk?

"Look, Trudi," he said after a while. "I don't have anything to do tonight, and it doesn't look like you do either, so why don't we do it together? We could get something to eat, maybe have a few drinks. It might be fun. What do you say?"

She snorted bitterly. "I warn you, you won't get—what is it you Americans call it? Lucky?—tonight."

"I don't really care about that. I'd just like a little company."

Why not? she thought. Wouldn't it be easier to lose herself with another person? Particularly a person as undemanding as he was?

"If I agree," she said cautiously, "you have to promise me one thing. No questions. I mean it."

"That suits me too."

"No questions," she continued, "no past and no future. You have to accept that. Just one evening of a little...company."

"Sure. If that's what you want. No problem."

She let out a quick breath, releasing more tension than she knew she had felt. It occurred to her in passing that this was probably a date. She had never had a real date at any time in her life.

"Where would you like to eat?" Evan asked. "You name it."

The only restaurants she knew were the expensive kind of places where rich men took the young girls whose company they had bought just to be seen. This man didn't look like he could afford that kind of restaurant. Besides, she wasn't sure she could stand a meal in a place with associations like that.

"I saw a little place around the corner," she suggested. "It looked like it might have good soup and sandwiches. Would that be all right?"

"Sounds good."

He unconsciously took her hand in his as they walked towards the door, but she abruptly stopped and pulled it away.

"Sorry," Evan said. "I didn't mean...."

Perhaps it would be all right, she thought. Bearable. It wasn't sex, after all, just a connection to another person. Something to remind her she was still a human being.

"No, I'm sorry," Trudi said, placing her hand back into his.

They walked out of the store together, with Evan making fragile, empty conversation to hold up his end of the bargain and Trudi trying hard to listen with all of her mind.

Neither noticed that a small, dark man with blond hair followed them out.

CHAPTER NINE

"I'm a what?" Ali shrieked.

He couldn't have said that, she thought, he couldn't have. Or if he did, he couldn't have meant it. It had to be a joke. Only he did not appear to be joking. She was suddenly cold with fear. In the course of her work she'd often gone to great lengths to report on violence, sometimes bending countless laws along the way, but never had she been in this position. Never had she been suspected of being the instigator of that violence, the kind of person any policeman in the world might feel justified shooting on sight. As a reporter she had always enjoyed a special sort of insulation. Policemen tended to place journalists in a unique category when it came to law-breaking, and they usually viewed themselves in that manner. But terrorism fell outside the boundaries of that insulation. Suddenly, she was stripped of all the protection she had come to expect. She felt naked, alone and very vulnerable. Then a thought occurred to her: this might just be something she could turn to her advantage. She stopped feeling like a suspect and started thinking like a reporter. A shrewd, calculating look spread over her face. She was in control once again.

"What did you call me?" she asked Aykroyd, this time in a calmer, almost conversational tone.

"You heard me. I said you were a terrorist," Aykroyd said.

Aykroyd sighed wearily. Mantizima's presence was forcing him to alter the way he planned to spring this on her. Now there was no choice but to take things as they were and to make the best of them. She still couldn't leave that house as a free woman without his permission and, at the moment, he had no intention of giving it.

"I can't believe that, Rune," Mantizima said. "There has to be some mistake."

"Terry, I wish it weren't true," Aykroyd said, looking sadly at Ali, "but it is."

"Just how did you happen to come upon this?" Ali asked.

Ali never looked at Mantizima. She did not want to encourage him to speak. She hoped he wouldn't feel the need to come to her aid, even though she had asked him to. At least, not just yet. And he seemed to sense her thoughts. He became quiet and thoughtfully appraised her.

"A friend of yours in Cairo stepped in front of an automobile and was killed, but not before he told the police everything," Aykroyd answered.

"Everything? He really told them everything?"

Aykroyd paused, then continued honestly, "He told them enough."

"Really?" Ali said, casually strolling around the room. "And just who was this friend? Does he have a name?"

"His name was Saeed Moheb. Does that mean anything to you?" Aykroyd asked sarcastically.

Ali smiled like a person who has just scored a point and committed that name to memory.

"Ali, you're really quite good," Mantizima suddenly said appreciatively, then turned to Aykroyd. "Can't you see what she's doing, Rune? She's pumping you."

"Of course she is. She's trying to find out what I know," Aykroyd answered.

"She's trying to find out what she doesn't know," Mantizima said with exasperation. "She's investigating a story. One that you threw in her lap."

Aykroyd studied Ali for the first time with just a shade of doubt in his mind.

"I'm not a terrorist," Ali said quietly. "I know that's exactly what I'd say if I were guilty, but I really haven't done anything wrong. I can't imagine why you think I have."

There was simple honesty in her manner—unless she was a truly great actress. Aykroyd found himself feeling torn and fought to hold onto his theory.

"Why do you suspect her, Rune?" Mantizima asked thoughtfully.

Aykroyd did not question his interest. "She was named by the dead man," he answered.

"He named me? I don't know the man! I never even heard of him," Ali shouted in sheer frustration.

Aykroyd sighed, then for the record gave them the complete history. "In July of this year a man named Saeed Moheb was hit by an automobile. Before he died he told the Cairo police that his terrorist organization was planning some monumental assault against Israel that would be carried out in South Africa. He warned them about an American reporter and he mentioned your name."

"He said Alison Hayden?" Ali asked in disbelief.

"He said...Ali," Aykroyd admitted, pronouncing it as the male name, as the dead man had.

Mantizima snorted in disbelief. Ali raged in sarcastic anger.

"Oh, well, I can see why you happened to settle on me. I'm the only person in the entire Middle East whose name is spelled A-l-i, not to mention the only American reporter in South Africa."

Aykroyd rushed to her and took her wrists in his hands. "Ali, do you think I want to believe this of you? Don't you know by now how I...." He let his voice trail off, then continued more impersonally. "Naturally, we have investigated every American reporter assigned here, and none of them have any obvious terrorist ties. And none of them have the name connection. You, on the other hand, are the only reporter to come here since July and, pronounciation differences aside, that is your name."

Ali angrily pulled her hands free of his hold and turned away.

"What about Evan?" she asked. "His name's not Ali, but he is an American journalist. Have you been badgering him like this?"

"Strictly speaking, Evan Todd is a photographer, not a reporter, although that might not be a significant difference. But, yes, we have investigated him thoroughly. Evan Todd is a simple, quiet man whose background is positively pure, while you have been known to associate with all sorts of questionable people."

"Of course I do. That's my job. I cover an area where terrorism is an accepted practice. Unquestionable people are not news."

"But your name—"

"Will you stop already with my name?" Ali screamed.

"It's a coincidence, Rune," Mantizima said. "It has to be."

"Irony," Ali muttered to herself.

"Whatever you call it, such things do happen, Rune, and sometimes honest people are railroaded by circumstantial evidence," Mantizima said. "Please tell us again, exactly, what this man said."

Aykroyd repeated the transcript that was now committed to memory. When he was finished, Mantizima and Ali looked at each other in disbelief.

"Stupid, incompetent police!" Ali said. "You take a thought, just a theory, and grind it into a rut until it gives you tunnel vision and you can't see anything beyond it."

"She might be right, you know?" Mantizima said absently. "Oh, not about you being stupid, of course, but she might be right about the tunnel vision. It's happened to me sometimes in my own work. And it could be happening to you. Now let's think about this.... The man in Cairo said to 'ask Ali.' That doesn't sound to me like the American reporter and Ali are the same person. More likely, Ali was a friend of his who also knew about the plan. Perhaps the individual in charge.... You also have no guarantee that the

American reporter is going to enter this country in that capacity. You won't necessarily know that he is a reporter."

"We do a very thorough check on backgrounds, Terry. Surely you remember that," Aykroyd said.

"And I imagine this individual could be just as thorough in covering his. It isn't hard if you really want to do it."

"This is absurd!" Ali suddenly exploded. "I am not a terrorist. I have never given anyone reason to believe I am. I don't even know what you think I'm planning. Do you think I'm going to blow up Tel Aviv or something?" She saw the startled look on Aykroyd's face. "You do. You think I'm intending to plant a bomb! Now that's the dumbest thing I ever heard. If I were planning to blow up Israel, what in hell would I be doing here?"

"Maybe there is something here that you need to complete your mission," Aykroyd said cautiously.

"Oh, yeah? Well, let me tell you something Mr. know-it-all Aykroyd, if I wanted to obtain a bomb I could go out any day in Cairo, anywhere, and for less than ten American dollars get as fancy a bomb as I needed. So, I repeat, why am I here? And what is all this fuss about one little bomb, anyway? Do you have any idea how many bombs have gone off in Israel since its inception?"

"The fuss, Ali," Mantizima said slowly, thoughtfully, "is that, unless I've missed my guess, this is not an ordinary bomb we're talking about. This bomb is nuclear."

Suddenly the room became still. Deadly still. Not even the sound of breathing could be heard. In the silence Aykroyd reluctantly found himself wondering about his old friend and what could not possibly be just a lucky guess. But Mantizima met his eyes openly. He seemed aware of the doubts that would enter Aykroyd's mind, which he expected and was prepared to meet.

"Now, I'm sure my sister has gone to sleep," Mantizima continued, calmly taking charge, "so I suggest one of us make coffee. I think this is going to be quite a long night."

A while later, with tempers under control, reason entered the conversation. Mantizima paced restlessly, speaking in a manner that was more like thinking aloud, while the others watched him.

"It was definitely a control panel for some sort of explosive device. There was no question at all about that. But, no, there was nothing about Nora's plan that indicated it was for a nuclear bomb," Mantizima said in answer to Aykroyd's question. "Truthfully, that didn't occur to me for quite some time, but some things about it kept puzzling me until I figured them out.... Now I don't know that much about terrorists and their weapons—certainly not as much as you must—but even I know that the kinds of bombs they make don't need controls that sophisticated. They don't need controls at all. They put a timer on them that allows the bomber to run away before the device goes off. But the device that Nora designed should have had a very long range. Maybe as much as a thousand miles. I kept wondering why this bomber felt he had to be that far away. It wasn't to avoid detection—the police rarely catch them. I also didn't understand why he would have gone to the expense and taken the risk to hire someone to make this control panel for then when it wasn't necessary for most bombs...unless it was necessary for his."

"So you decided it had to be a nuclear device?" Aykroyd asked.

"No, not really decided. I thought about it, but I really didn't accept the possibility until tonight when I saw how disturbed you were about it and when you mentioned to Ali the possibility that this terrorist needed something readily available here in South Africa," Mantizima said.

"Uranium!" Ali said with sudden inspiration. "Right? From *Schmokkeling Reef*. From the diamond stream. You said that uranium was in the ore people carted off there."

"I was suspicious of those damn diamonds ever since they turned up. Where did they come from? Why weren't there any others?" Aykroyd demanded.

114

"You think someone seeded the stream? But why?" Ali asked.

"Perhaps to create a smokescreen. No one thought the people at that site to be anything but ordinary prospectors. People looking for diamonds and maybe settling for a little gold. The fact that there was uranium ore connected to that gold never entered the picture," Aykroyd said.

Ali said that she thought it was an over-complicated scheme. She looked at Aykroyd as she said it. While he seemed perfectly content to allow her to participate in the conversation as an equal, it was clear his distrust of her was only partially assuaged. He had opened his mind to other possibilities, but the original theory had not yet been replaced. She felt as if she would go through life with a scarlet letter on her clothes if she couldn't find some way to clear herself, and that letter wouldn't signify anything as tame as adultery.

"The very complexity of it eliminates all risk. You saw that area then. It was completely chaotic. There is no way to single out anyone who was there as our bomber or even as someone working for him...or her.... It is true that it is ridiculously expensive. Someone threw away eighty thousand rand on those diamonds. But I think you'd both agree that whoever is behind this has a very large budget," Aykroyd said, looking at Ali very pointedly to remind her that theirs was only a temporary truce.

"You're still just guessing," Ali said. "You don't know that any of this actually happened."

"It is more than a guess. What we have learned, rather belatedly, is that there were two Palestinian terrorists among the prospectors. We know they were there, though we do not know how they entered South Africa or when they left. We have no record of them in our files. There was also another man, a physicist, an American, who was here on some legitimate business, but who now appears to have disappeared from the face of the earth."

"Did he have a name, this physicist?" Ali asked.

"Alan Warrick. Does that mean anything to you?"

"No," Ali snapped.

"Ali, Rune, please stop this bickering," Mantizima said, then waited until they did before continuing. "Now, assuming your theory is correct, Rune, I don't believe you have anything to be concerned about. Understand, I agree it's being tried, but it can't be done. A private individual or even a number of them cannot build a nuclear bomb."

"It hasn't ever been done, Terry," Aykroyd corrected, "except in student exercises, but there is always a first time."

Mantizima shook his head and said, "No, it can't be done. I roomed with one of those physics grad students at M.I.T. who wrote his dissertation on it. I'm not a physicist and I don't keep up on the field, but I'm sure there isn't any way to do it."

He went on to explain about the different grades of uranium. Weapon-grade uranium is required, he told them, meaning it has to be an enriched uranium isotope.

"Now, in books, people just steal weapon-grade from government installations," Mantizima continued. "But I think that's easier said then done. Governments are a lot more careful with that material than their critics claim. The only other alternative is to enrich the ore yourself, but that requires a gaseous-diffusion plant, which would cost a couple of billion dollars to build, not to mention the power plant you would need to run it. No one has the ability or the money to put one of those things in their backyard. And how could you hide it? I repeat: it cannot be done."

Aykroyd looked like he was about to say something to contradict Mantizima, but hesitated and finally decided to clamp his mouth shut. Ali glanced at him cautiously, trying to decide whether to say what she was sure he was thinking, or whether it was safer to just let the whole thing slide. Definitely safer, she thought, but safety be damned.

"You're wrong, Terry," she said, "there is a much easier way to enrich uranium. The—well, that is, it is believed—that the scientists here in South Africa, at the government research facility at Pelindaba, have developed a much cheaper, easier way to do it."

116

Aykroyd glared at her angrily, all of his suspicion quickly returning. But he also appeared to feel a little respect for the woman who kept surprising him.

"An open secret! Everyone knows it!" Ali protested to Aykroyd, then turned back to Mantizima. "They haven't even confirmed that they have such a formula, but it is believed that they do. Some people think it might be done with lasers." Returning her attention to Aykroyd, she said, "The Science Editor from *The Toronto Sun* told me about it once when we shared an airport layover. I swear that's how I know."

Ali said it sarcastically, in mockery of his suspicions of her. She allowed herself a triumphant little smile. Oh, she was still up to her neck in it, she knew, but she had one-upped him again. She was starting to believe that he was no match for her, no matter how much governmental power he had on his side.

She didn't know it, but Aykroyd almost shared her belief. Was there nothing she didn't know? he demanded irritably. He debated momentarily whether to continue, then, while not quite admitting the accuracy of her statement, said that the security at the Pelindaba facility was the tightest in the country.

"No one could possibly get to such a formula," he assured them. "Assuming it even exists."

"Oh, it exists, and no security is worth a damn," Ali said.

"Really? I supervised the designing of that system myself," Aykroyd said stiffly.

"Then you should know I'm right," she said. "Look, Rune, if we were sure we had a couple of weeks to spare I'd break into the plant and steal the formula myself, just to prove it could be done. But we don't have a couple of extra weeks. We don't know how much time we have."

"We?" Aykroyd demanded eloquently.

Ali chuckled softly. She hadn't even realized that she had used that word. But somehow her mind had unconsciously provided the avenue she had sought.

117

"Yes," she said, "we."

"Oh, no," Aykroyd said. "You don't have a chance. I don't know yet what I'm going to do with you, but including you in this isn't even a possibility. You're not a citizen of this country— you couldn't get clearance. You probably couldn't get it in your own country."

"And why not?" Ali asked indignantly.

"Because you are a reporter, a person with a notorious urge to tell everything you know."

She reminded him that throughout history reporters have been known to sit on some pretty important stories when there was some greater good at stake. She also said that working with him was the only way she could clear herself with certainty.

"You owe me that!" she told Aykroyd.

"I owe you nothing."

"Yes, you do. You built this case against me. You have to let Terry and me help you with this."

Mantizima was surprised by her inclusion of him, but not disturbed.

"Terry, tell her this is insane," Aykroyd said.

"I don't think it is," Mantizima answered. "Rune, I came here because one of my employees used my money and materials to build something I don't believe in. I could have handed this over to the F.B.I., but I came myself because I don't like being used. Now I intend to stop Nora from handing those controls over to whoever commissioned them, or at least stop him from using them. I intend to do that with or without your help."

Aykroyd couldn't believe what he was hearing. They really are alike, he thought, and they do bring out the worst in each other...but they're both so alive.

"You're both insane!" he said. "You're amateurs. You don't know what you're getting into. You'll both be killed."

"So you're just going to handle it all on your own," Ali said in response to a sudden thought. "Isn't it too much for one man to do alone?"

Aykroyd protested that he wouldn't be alone, that BOSS was a huge organization with immense resources.

"Big organizations are sometimes full of holes," Ali said, and was pleased to see that she drew a guarded reaction from Aykroyd. "You know, Terry, he was going to bring me to his office—I'm sure of that—but instead he brought me here. I don't think he felt safe talking about this in his office. I think he knows he has a leak."

"Really? Is that true, Rune?" Mantizima asked.

Aykroyd reluctantly admitted that he did suspect that there was a leak in his office. He didn't know how high up it went, he hoped not too high. He didn't know which of them he could trust, and this problem was too big to take chances with. At present he was working alone on it under the direction of the Director of BOSS and the Minister of Defense, using subordinates purely on a need-to-know basis.

"But I still can't allow either of you to get involved in this," he summarized. "It's absurd. It's totally...unconventional."

"So's building a nuclear device in your kitchen," Ali noted.

"What it comes down to, Rune," Mantizima said, "is that we're all going to be working on the same thing. It makes more sense to combine forces than to fight each other."

It was unconventional and, above all else, Rune Aykroyd was a very conventional man. But the desire to repair his relationship with Terry Mantizima was very strong. He wasn't sure he could say the same thing about working with Ali. Though she had not alluded to it, even in expression, he knew what had happened earlier that evening. Had he not been interrupted, he would have raped her. He still could not believe that he had allowed such a thing to happen, that he had lost control that way. It was an unforgivable outrage against her, but also against himself, against the professionalism that had always been the cornerstone of his existence. What had he been thinking of? How could he have hoped to build a case against her if that had happened? And how could he even consider working closely with her now?

Then he looked into her eyes, eyes that were waiting for his decision, and saw that no sign of the feelings she would have been justified in having. For her, it might not have even occurred. He did not understand that it had simply waned in importance when compared to the chance to clear her name and the opportunity that investigation held for her.

Perhaps it would work, he thought. This was his chance to prove to himself that he was the man he should be and, maybe, if she were actually innocent, to her. If she were guilty, however, he was taking a terrible risk, but he took those with the members of his staff, too, even if he did not give them the whole story. Was the risk of betrayal any greater, he wondered, with someone he trusted than with someone he was free to openly distrust? He just didn't know.

Aykroyd was not the only one in that room with doubts, nor the only one thinking about betrayal. Mantizima realized that at some time during that evening, he had let his guard down. He let go of the anger he felt towards Aykroyd and let their relationship slide back to the way it was before Aykroyd let him down. He knew that was dangerous. By letting time roll back, he was giving Aykroyd the chance to re-create the incident that had hurt him so much. But it felt so good being back together again, just like old times. He couldn't help himself.

"What about your story?" Aykroyd asked Ali in an accusing tone. "Even if you are innocent in this matter, how can I be sure you won't jeopardize my investigation by writing about it too soon?"

"I want that story, of course. And I expect you to protect my exclusivity in exchange for my work. But I'll hold off on breaking it until it's over. Until you give the word. That's a promise."

He heaved a heavy sigh of surrender and said, "You realize that when I find this person I'm going to do whatever I have to do. You could both get caught in the middle."

Mantizima looked at Ali for the confirmation of her commitment; she nodded decisively.

"We know that," Mantizima said. "Where do we start?"

CHAPTER TEN

SEPTEMBER 10, 1979

The investigation began.

Alone and together, Aykroyd, Mantizima and Ali Hayden poured through reams of computer printout in search of something they feared they might not even be able to recognize if they found it.

They bypassed the records of American journalists, since a search of those had already proved fruitless, and looked for another route to the same destination. The start they settled on was a check of the financial records of every person who had worked at the Pelindaba facility for the last two years. No small task. Since security checks were run on each of those people at the time of employment, with those of dubious ideology being eliminated, money seemed to be the most likely motive. Other motives were not overlooked, however. The personnel reports were also carefully scanned. Someone with an ignored gripe against a superior just might have considered sabotage a fitting retribution.

And because the security of his own organization might have been penetrated, Aykroyd asked Interpol to run a check on all of the employees of BOSS. He did not pin much hope on that investigation, however, even though Interpol's terrorist files were extensive. But anyone within BOSS with access to sensitive data and the knowledge of how to alter it would also know how to cover his tracks.

The investigation wore on, hour after weary hour. They all experienced a sense of urgency because they did not know how much time they had that was oddly coupled with a like portion of disbelief, because none of them really accepted that the thing they feared was actually being done.

Deborah Mantizima came home for work late one night to find her son in the exact spot where she left him that morning, at the small desk in the guest room in her home which he occupied.

"Terry, you're not still working?" she said. "Have you had anything to eat?"

"What?" he asked, looking up absently. "Oh, yes, I think I grabbed something a few hours ago."

"Grabbing something isn't going to sustain you when you're working like this. Now come down and I'll make you some dinner."

He followed her downstairs only because it was easier to give in than to argue, but while his body went to the kitchen, his mind remained upstairs with those papers. Sorting, sifting, he continued to try to integrate those unrelated facts into some kind of order, even though the letters of all those words had long since become indistinguishable to him.

"What exactly are you looking for?" Deborah asked.

"I wish I knew. Something...something that just doesn't sit right, I suppose. Some coincidence that's just a little too good to believe."

"You realize, Terry, that you are looking for a needle in a haystack. It can't be done."

"I don't know about that, Mother. It doesn't seem so impossible to me. After all, a needle looks nothing like a piece of hay. If you look carefully enough, it has to stand out."

"I admire your optimism. But you do know that if you're not watching it all the time, a needle is very likely to stick you. You will remember that, won't you?"

"I'll remember it," Mantizima said to reassure his mother, even though he knew he had scarcely given the idea of danger a thought.

At the same time, alone in his office, Aykroyd looked up from his reports and was shocked to see how late it was. He had been working so hard that he hadn't even thought about the passing time. Now that he did, he realized he must be very hungry—it had been many hours since he had last eaten—but he was almost too tired for the sensation to register. He thought briefly about going straight home, but knew if he did he would not eat. It was too late to wake up Elizabeth, and he was too weary to fix anything for himself. Finally he decided he had better get to the employees' cafeteria before it closed.

Despite the late hour, the cafeteria had a good many last-minute diners. Most of them were people assigned to the night shift, mainly from the data processing department which did the bulk of its record-keeping work at night. But there were also a number of operatives and supervisors, like him, who had been kept at their desks long after normal hours by some pressing assignment. He saw Neil Logan across the room amusing a table full of female clerks with his silly chatter. Aykroyd was surprised to see him there. He should have finished his assignments hours ago. But he knew that Logan considered the night shift girls, most of whom complained about the difficulty they had meeting men due to their irregular hours, to be easy pickings.

Well, he thought, suddenly remembering Ali, each to his own.

There wasn't much choice left on the food line and what was there, scant amounts of indistinguishable entrees covered in grease that had congealed when the steamer trays cooled, had long since lost any appeal. But Aykroyd did not notice. He accepted what was offered to him and carried his tray off to a remote corner table where he hoped no one he knew would notice him.

He ate most of his meals during working hours in the cafeteria, and he usually ate them alone. Fortunately, most of his co-workers respected his desire for privacy, but they did not understand his need for it. In fact, it wasn't that he simply didn't want to be with anyone, it was that he needed that little bit of quiet time, the chance to clear his mind and throw off the pressures of the job.

Tonight, however, he couldn't stand the sight of any of them. Someone who worked in that building, perhaps someone in that room at that very moment, had probably sold out his country, had prostituted it for a few pieces of a terrorist's gold.

He tried not to be too critical of that person. He had always had more than enough money to meet his needs. He knew he had no sense of what it was like to feel deprived, to want something so very badly and have no way to get it. He could really understand that someone might want the money that he took for granted as a motive, perhaps even to the point of entertaining an illicit proposition, but he couldn't understand that person actually accepting it. And he couldn't forgive him.

Treason! Someone with whom he worked side-by-side had probably committed treason, to Aykroyd, the worst offense possible. Far worse, he thought, than a murderer who had left a score of bloody bodies in his wake. Murder was just a crime against an individual, but treason was a crime against the State, which, in his mind, was larger and more important than any or all of the citizens who comprised it.

He reminded himself that if a nuclear bomb really was in production, then a far greater crime was being perpetrated against Israel, against mankind as a whole, and that should outrage him even more. But it did not. An action taken against some country across the globe could never hurt him like a betrayal against the land to which he owed his life.

He knew that if he tried to explain the way he felt to Ali or Terry they wouldn't understand it. He supposed they loved their country and would be just as angry at someone who had betrayed it, but it wasn't the same. They were both so individualistic, so complete in themselves that they wouldn't understand what it was to simply be a part of something, just as he couldn't really understand their self-sufficiency.

Well, he thought with a sigh, you are what you are. You can't fight it. God knows he'd tried that long enough. He was the son of South Africa, of the mother who was the land and the father, the State, and his duty was to protect them from the enemy within or without who threatened to weaken them. To kill or be killed, if it came to that.

The only question was, who was that enemy?

Alone in her hotel room the next day, Ali felt just as fatigued and just as perplexed. She sat on her bed, covered in sheets of papers, trying to make some connection that, in her exhaustion, had passed through her mind without conscious detection.

It's here...somewhere, she told herself, as she looked out on the materials that had seemed to consume her legs. But where?

She started sifting through the papers again, in search of something that was just beyond her reach. After a while, however, she realized she was no longer capable of making progress.

"Jello!" she shouted. "That's what my brain's become."

She threw the papers off her lap and rose and stretched. Of the three of them, it was she who found Aykroyd's bomb theory the most believable. It wasn't that she knew anything they didn't, it was just that her life had trained her to expect the unusual. The very essence of her work was recording the unusual, the violations of the norm. The things that were not to be believed, had they not happened. By this time in her life she had seen so many of those violations that she now knew anything to be possible.

There was another thing that set her apart from the two men. Aykroyd was only doing his job, protecting his country's international reputation. Terry, she suspected, was going through some kind of personal baptism by fire. But she was a suspect. She was suspected of committing a most heinous crime against humanity. Of course, she was doing her job, too, and she tried to keep her focus on that. While she was a widely-respected reporter, breaking the story of the world's first—she hoped only—attempt at a privately constructed nuclear weapon would elevate her to a new level.

It would be the making of her career. She had to remember, however, that unless she cleared her name, she would not have much of a career. A shadow of guilt would be cast over the rest of her life. She had to get rid of that. She had fought too hard for the position she now held to lose it to whispered suspicions and innuendo.

She walked to the window and watched the passing rush-hour traffic down the street. So many people, she thought, and any one of them could be the bomber. What did he look like?

Were it only that simple. She remembered when she worked the City Desk on *The Star* and was assigned to interview the neighbors of a convicted mass murderer. "He was such a nice man," they all said. "I never would have believed it of him. He just didn't look like a murderer." Well, what did a murderer, or a bomber for that matter, look like? If you could tell from looking at someone, things would never happen, people would be prepared; but it was impossible to be sure just by looking at someone and, even if it were possible, did anyone want to live in a place where that was the basis of justice?

She thought about the bomber a great deal, beyond the scope of the investigation. At odd times of the day, when she was alone and when she was with Evan, she found herself wondering where he was or what he was doing. And even more, she thought about his motives. Why, she wondered, was he doing this? For money? Of course. Power, too. But it had to go beyond that. What kind of person would do such a thing?

Her thoughts were interrupted by a rap on the door.

"Ali, it's Evan. Are you almost ready for dinner?" said Evan's voice through the door.

"Almost," she shouted, as she hurried to gather up her papers.

She took all of the reports and stuffed them into a dresser drawer where they would be out of sight when she opened the door. She had told him that she was pursuing a lead that she had to follow alone, to explain the time she was

127

spending away from their assignment. She couldn't let him know what she was really doing.

She stepped out into the hall and smiled at Evan. His face, as always, was undeniably attractive, but so bland and simple. Even the well-known tragedies of his youth appeared to have left no mark on it. If only everyone had this expression, Ali thought wistfully, it would be so easy to pick out the bad ones.

Several evenings later the three of them met at Aykroyd's house to discuss their findings.

"We've had some success," Aykroyd told them. "Both a janitor and a secretary at Pelindaba have known ties to Palestinian terrorists, and each has a small, but not insignificant, bank account in Switzerland."

"And that didn't show up when they were hired?" Mantizima asked.

"No, nor on the periodic security checks we run."

"Any idea who suppressed that information?"

"None," Aykroyd said disgustedly. "I don't think that individual's going to be as easy to detect. However, that still doesn't tell us anything other than the fact that terrorists were interested in what was being done at Pelindaba. That doesn't mean they learned anything. Neither of those people had any access to top-secret material."

"There's always a way," Mantizima said. "There's always someone you can get to."

"And I know who!" Ali said.

Both men looked at her.

"Wade Petri!" she announced triumphantly.

Aykroyd burst her bubble by laughing.

"Seriously!" she said, trying to hold down her anger. "As I understand it, the head of each sector is in charge of seeing that security measures are followed in his area. Right?"

Aykroyd nodded.

"It follows then that the supervisors have the easiest job of breaching security. Now Petri was the head of the most sensitive sector of that research project. And he spends too much money for what I'm sure your father probably pays him now. Where did he get all that money?"

"Wade Petri has a rich wife and no courage. Granted, he would give his soul and ten rand to see his name in a society column, but he wouldn't have the nerve to take a chance like that, and he doesn't need the money," Aykroyd told Ali.

"There are reasons other than money that might prompt a person to sell out, Rune," Mantizima said thoughtfully. "Such as political beliefs."

"He has no political beliefs. As Ali so correctly pointed out, he is the kind of person who will always 'buy the party line.' He believes whatever it is prudent to believe. No, based on everything I know, he's the last person to be involved."

Ali said nothing, but was obviously not convinced.

The next morning the three of them drove up into the northern Transvaal to Pelindaba, the "Meeting Place," as it was called in Afrikaans. Ali didn't know quite what she had anticipated, but what she saw was not it. She supposed that she expected the main experimental facility of the South African Atomic Energy Board to be frightening and sinister in its appearance, but it was not. With stunning modern buildings surrounded by lush lawns that were dotted with beautiful desert rock gardens, it was an uncommonly lovely environment.

"Who would have thought that with what they do here they would surround themselves with so much beauty?" Ali muttered to Mantizima as they approached the entrance.

"Maybe they have to," he answered.

They met first with the Director of Security for Pelindaba, who nervously assured Aykroyd that no breach of security could possibly have occurred while he was in charge. "Inconceivable!" he had said, without a shadow of doubt. But if it had, he added, covering all bets, he would be the one to find the perpetrator. He told Aykroyd he was running the most exhaustive checks on all of the people assigned here, knowing full well that he was also being subjected to just as thorough a scrutiny.

129

Next, they were given a demonstration of South Africa's unadmitted process for enriching uranium. That was an unprecedented event; outsiders were never even given a hint that the process existed. But Aykroyd's clearance came directly from the Minister of Defense, and his orders had to be obeyed. The engineer supervising the demonstration didn't bother to hide what he personally felt about those orders, however. Ali wondered whose presence he resented more, hers or Terry's, and finally concluded that she was the more offending party.

Without a technical background, the demonstration meant little to her, and that was very apparent. Just a few minutes into it she was sorry she had come. She wasn't learning anything there and was wasting time that would be better spent reviewing those reports.

To Mantizima, however, it was a fascinating experience. He wasn't a physicist, but had enough knowledge of the subject to realize what a breakthrough the process was. He was sorry that its primary purpose was to facilitate the production of destructive weapons, but that did not alter the awe he felt for the mind that had overcome what every other physicist in the world found to be an insurmountable problem. His questions were so intelligent, his interest so genuine that he even succeeded in warming up their hostile guide, who managed to forget that he was speaking to a Bantu and just thought of him as someone who spoke his language.

"Why did you come?" Mantizima asked Ali as they were leaving, in response to her grumbling. "You must have realized you wouldn't understand any of it."

"I just thought that being there, seeing it, might trigger something in my mind...but it didn't."

"Don't punish her, Terry," Aykroyd snapped. "Sometimes that works for me, too. It was a good thought."

The two men glanced at each other over Ali's head. They were as close as they ever had been, as they were as boys, but there was one difference in the relationship now. There was a woman between them. They didn't think about it often, but they always knew it was there. May the best man win, each thought, both knowing full well he only meant it if he were that man.

"Is there any place else you would like to go?" Aykroyd asked.

"How 'bout a uranium mine?" Ali asked a little timidly.

"It's worth a try."

They drove to a mine whose owner Aykroyd knew through his father and were given a tour. Ali was very disappointed. Again, it did not measure up to her vague expectations. In most ways it was exactly like the gold mine. There were the same sort of installations there, the same multi-languaged signs, everything was similar, except the ore, which she did not see. Nothing about the place suggested anything to her. She felt very foolish for ever asking to come.

Apparently the men shared her feelings because they walked through the compound towards the exit in silence. They passed a miner sneaking a cigarette in a crevice near the entrance of the mine and Aykroyd instinctively ordered him to put it out.

"Why did you do that?" Ali suddenly demanded.

"It was a conditioned reflex. It comes from being around the mining business all my life," Aykroyd answered, then, noting her intent expression, continued, "I know what you are thinking, that I was unduly harsh or that it was none of my business, but— "

"Stop telling me what I think!" Ali ordered. "Tell me why you did it. What was the reason?"

"Well, you can see the signs. Smoking is strictly forbidden. And that isn't arbitrary. It's a matter of safety. There are gases in the mine that— "

"So there's a real reason for it?" Ali continued. "Would anyone associated with the mining business know it? Even someone who didn't actually work at the mine? Is it as important to everyone else as it is to you?"

"Yes, everyone knows it's a cardinal rule. Something as simple as one cigarette could cause an explosion, a cave-in that might claim hundreds of lives. But why— "

"When we were at *Schokkeling Reef,* Wade Petri— " she stopped suddenly, seeing the look on their faces, then continued with great determination. "Now hear me out, dammit! Wade Petri saw a man smoking just like this man was and he approached him but then turned away and pretended he did not see him. At the time I thought he was simply avoiding me, but he didn't look as if he even saw me. Now that I think about it, I believe he just didn't want to get involved. And you said that about him. That he wouldn't get involved."

"But this man, at least as you two describe him, is a very proper individual," Mantizima argued. "Would he stand by and look the other way while someone walked off with his country's most prized secret?"

"That's the question, isn't it?" Aykroyd said, stunned by a thought that hadn't occurred to him. "I think it is time that Mr. Petri provided some answers."

CHAPTER ELEVEN

SEPTEMBER 15, 1979

"They are nearly ready in the interrogation room, Mr. Aykroyd."

Aykroyd looked up from the paperwork on his desk and saw his secretary standing in the doorway. Thank God for the Afrikaner secretary, he thought, what would we do without them? His secretary was a fairly plain girl who might be pretty if she chose to do anything with herself, but she did not. Girl! he snorted to himself. She must be as old as he was, or nearly, though he did not know that for a fact. He didn't know anything personal about her. She was true to a type frequently found in South Africa; humorless, devoid of emotions, at least while on the job, and the model of brilliant efficiency. He knew that visiting American businessmen frequently found Afrikaner secretaries to be too coldly impersonal compared to the secretaries they had at home with whom they shared warmer, more casual relationships, but Aykroyd was grateful for their existence, and this woman's in particular. Her dispassionate attachment to her job suited his personal working style very well.

"And I have put your guests in the observation room as you requested," she continued.

There it was again, he thought, the perfect efficiency. Not an inkling of what she thought about those guests, and she must have thoughts about those particular guests—an American woman and a Bantu who were being permitted to invade BOSS's most secret sanctum. But nothing showed.

"Thank you, Petra," he said "I'll be along in a few moments."

He watched her exit, thinking about the times when he had felt a little guilty for his part in their very detached relationship. Once Logan had told him that the day before had been her birthday, and another time he'd heard from another secretary that Petra and her husband had just celebrated their tenth wedding anniversary, when he hadn't even realized she was married. At times like those he'd often thought about loosening up a little, at least to the extent of congratulating her, if for no other reason than to let her know how much he appreciated her. But he was loathe to do anything that might alter the order of their working existence.

Now he was glad that he hadn't given in to the impulse. He was well aware that she might be the traitor. Within that sphere of reflected power that secretaries enjoy, while she lacked his authority, she shared his access to classified documents. Every door and file within the Bureau was as open to her as it was to him. Of course, knowing her, he did not consider her a very likely candidate for selling-out, but did he know her? How could he know how much rage or anger or lust for danger might exist beneath that prim facade.

Yes, he thought, it might be Petra; she was a viable candidate. But it just as easily might be anyone else. He thought about an incident that occurred the other day between Kloff and Logan.

After Ali Hayden's brainstorm about how Wade Petri might be involved, he knew that Petri had to be interrogated. He did not want to do the interrogation himself, however; he wanted to be free to observe Petri's reactions. That meant that someone else had to ask the questions, but the person could not be given the real reason for it. Aykroyd brought the subject up during a meeting with his two subordinates.

"I need a favor from one of you," he said. "You know I routinely oversee the security at Pelidaba. Well, we might have have had a breach in security about a year or so ago. A minor incident, nothing serious, but we can't just let these things go by. The man who might be responsible for it is a geologist named Wade Petri. Unfortunately, he now works for my father, and I know him quite well. If he is innocent, as he probably is, it could be quite sticky if I talk to him. So I think I'd like one of you to interview him instead."

There was nothing unusual in the request; it had happened before on a few other occasions. From the way that Aykroyd described it, it shaped up to be a "soft" interview, and Kloff was BOSS's specialist at those. He did not have what it took to be really ruthless, but he was quite effective at gently prying information out of unwilling subjects. Because of that, Kloff naturally expected to be chosen, and unconsciously prepared his mind to accept his orders.

"Perhaps you could do it, Neil," Aykroyd said suddenly, surprising them both.

Logan was just as shocked as Kloff at Aykroyd's choice but was always quick to recognize an opportunity.

"Of course, Rune, I'd be glad to," he said, much too eagerly.

"Good. I'll get back to you about the approach I want you to take."

Kloff was angry and hurt by the slight, and for once, decided not to be good-natured about it. He summoned up his courage.

"Rune, I've had more experience with this type of thing than Neil, and—" he stated.

"I know, Pieter," Aykroyd interrupted. "But I want Neil to handle this one."

There was nothing else Kloff could say to that. He nodded acquiescence, shrugged and dismissed the matter. But he knew he would not forget it. Then the meeting was concluded, and both Logan and Kloff left the office. Aykroyd forgot about them until he happened to overhear a conversation of theirs later in the day.

"Have you noticed the old man seems kind of strange lately?" Logan had asked.

"He isn't old. He's younger than I am," Kloff answered absently. "But now that you mention it, he hasn't been acting like himself lately. He seems...troubled by something."

135

"It's you, old man. He's fine around me, but he doesn't seem too fond of you anymore. Have you done something wrong?"

"Not that I know of," Kloff said thoughtfully.

"Not been telling tales, have you?"

"No, I wouldn't do that," Kloff said hesitantly.

"You don't have to convince me, Pieter. I know you wouldn't. It would take a bit o' the bottle for you to do something like that. But just because I believe you doesn't mean he does."

Kloff did not respond.

"I mean it, Pieter. Keep your nose clean, as the Yanks say. In this business, a chap's career can go up just like—that," he said, snapping his fingers right in front of Kloff's nose.

With that, Logan ambled off with a cocky stride, leaving Kloff alone with his worries.

The conversation left Aykroyd quite shaken. In truth, he hadn't suspected Kloff; he hadn't suspected either of them. Logan had more money than he could even spend, and Kloff, he had always believed, to be an exceptionally good man. The only reason why he had chosen Logan to do the interrogation was that it wasn't going to be nearly as "soft" as he had given them to believe, and Logan was a much better candidate for the job. Now, Aykroyd was genuinely concerned. He didn't like the sound of Kloff's less-than-convincing denials of guilt. He did realize that an honest, if not too intelligent, man might respond the same way if he were really thrown by the implication, but he also remembered that Kloff was a poor man with a large family. It didn't look good for Kloff.

It couldn't be Kloff, Aykroyd thought, but if it wasn't Kloff, who was it?

He remembered the time and returned his attention to the work before him. He was updating his report on this investigation. Since he was the only operative working on it, he tried to keep his records complete, since Kroonhof, the Director of BOSS, and the Minister of Defense would need those if anything happened to him. Not that he expected anything to. Usually he scratched them off very quickly, often before going home for the day, but today, he agonized over possible inclusions.

He, himself, had built up the case against Ali and had written nothing to soften it during the whole time of their unofficial joint participation. That was a scrupulous effort to keep his personal feelings for her out of his work, but now he wondered whether it wasn't just as wrong to punish her because of those feelings. He really believed her to be innocent; no one could lie that well. Finally deciding, he wrote, "Hayden appears to be the victim of nothing more than flimsy circumstantial evidence. I do not believe her to be involved."

Then he came to the problem of Terry Mantizima, and found including him to be far more difficult. He had foolishly evaded the issue of Mantizima by putting off any mention of him in his reports, but he knew that practice could not continue. The information about Nora Brand's design was too important to be ignored, and so was the surprising return of Mantizima after all these years.

After all, he thought in a professionally detached manner, he believed Terry to be telling the truth, but he could not prove it. Looking at it as someone more objective would, he knew Mantizima's story of his employee's contribution might be nothing but a ruse for his own involvement. It was conceivable that the whole operation was nothing more than Mantizima's plan to embarrass South Africa. He had to include Mantizima in the report.

But what if something did happen to him? Aykroyd thought. What if he were no longer there to protect Mantizima and defend his innocence? What chance would he, a black man, have against all of White South Africa? He wouldn't have a prayer. He would be made a scapegoat, taking all the blame. He would be tossed into prison and left to rot.

He couldn't write Mantizima's name in that report, Aykroyd thought. It would be like throwing him to the wolves.

But he had to. Duty demanded it, and he had always vowed never to put anyone before that. He had to do it. He had to.

He could not.

Hastily, before he could change his mind, he wrote something about receiving an anonymous tip about an American engineer's design for a remote detonation device, then quickly sealed the report in an "Eyes Only" envelope addressed to Lukas Kroonhof. He knew that item wouldn't stand up to much scrutiny but trusted himself to handle it, were he ever questioned.

Defending his lie was not his problem, living with it was. He felt simultaneously ashamed and proud of himself and honestly did not know which was the moral response. How long, he wondered, could he go on being pulled apart like that?

None of this would have happened if Terry hadn't returned, he thought bitterly, while hoping he would never again leave.

Ali and Mantizima sat alone in the observation half of one of the Bureau's many interrogation rooms. They glanced occasionally at the one-way glass on one wall, but the "subject" had not been brought into the other room yet, so there was nothing to see in the Spartan room next door.

The door opened just then, and Neil Logan popped his head into the room.

"Oh, sorry," he said, backing out. "I was looking for Rune Aykroyd. I thought he would be here."

"Hello, again," Ali said, stopping him.

"...Oh, it's you," he said, recognizing her. He approached and extended his hand. "I told you we might meet again, but I didn't expect it to be like this."

"I'm full of surprises."

"I told Rune I thought you would be."

Aykroyd entered in time to hear that remark. "You should have made sure I believed you," he said to Logan and gave a quick disarming shrug to Ali.

Logan gave Ali a warm smile of leave-taking and took a step towards the door. He never so much as noticed Mantizima.

"Neil, wait," Aykroyd said. "There's someone else here I'd like you to meet. A very old and great friend of mine, Terry Mantizima. Dr. Terry Mantizima."

Logan gave a sharp surprised look at Aykroyd. A Bantu friend for Mr. Official South Africa! he thought. Who would have believed it? He quickly recovered, however, and extended his hand to Mantizima.

"Dr. Mantizima, it's good to meet you," Logan said smoothly. "We don't get to know enough of Rune's friends."

Just then, the door in the interrogation room opened, and Wade Petri entered. They all silently watched as he ambled over to the small stool that was the only chair in the room.

"Well, I'd better—" Logan started to say.

"Not yet," Aykroyd interrupted. "Let's give him a few minutes to think about it."

The minutes passed.

Wade Petri sat quietly and patiently on the little stool, expecting the door to open at any moment, but it did not. As the time passed, he glanced at his watch once or twice.

"I'm a busy man," he muttered to himself. "They've no right to keep me here like this."

He thought briefly about going out and saying that very thing to the secretary who had shown him in, but he did not move. It was just a thought.

Sitting there, with his back erect, his body so well-dressed and faultlessly groomed, the little beads of perspiration that were forming on his upper lip were hardly noticeable. He took a deep breath and glanced impatiently at the ceiling. He wrung his hands slightly, then, noticing the palms were damp, rubbed them dry on his impeccably-pressed trousers, something he would not have done had he known anyone was watching him, but the thought that anyone might have been just did not occur to him.

He did notice the mirrored wall. In fact, he rose at that point and took some pride in his reflection. He looked like a successful man. He walked closer to it and adjusted the knot of the expensive silk tie he had bought on a trip to Rome just a few months before. Then, slowly, it dawned on him. There were people on the other side of that glass, unknown faces, watching him, studying him, trying to read his mind, his soul. He quickly retreated to the stool, trying to keep his eyes off that mirror that now seemed to be taunting him. He never again regained the faultless bearing and composure with which he had entered.

He hadn't intended to, but he jumped up when Logan entered the room.

"Good morning, Mr. Petri," Logan said, as he sorted through the file of papers he brought in with him. "Please sit down and be comfortable."

"It's a little hard to be comfortable on that," Petri said indignantly about the stool.

"Yes, well, one must adjust, musn't one?"

Logan told Petri that there was a possible security breakdown had occurred at Pelindaba.

"Why are you telling this to me?" Petri asked. "I haven't worked there for quite a while."

"This happened while you were there. In your sector, for that matter. And you were responsible for its security."

"I always followed security procedures to the letter. I admit that I found them to be a bit difficult. So many regulations, you know. But I always did exactly what I was told to do. Exactly."

"I'm sure you did, Mr. Petri. My question is, did you ever do anything beyond what you were required to do?"

"I don't think I understand what you are saying."

"Yes, well, let's move on."

"I didn't see anything, if that's what you mean," Petri suddenly protested.

Logan looked shocked, as if that idea had never occurred to him. "I don't believe I said anything about seeing something, did I, Mr. Petri? Did I?"

"Well, I didn't see anything. I didn't."

Logan just looked at Petri, his face expressionless. But he thought, you poor fool, you poor, gutless fool. You should have just kept your mouth shut. But I've got you by your ruddy balls now.

In the other room, beyond the glass, three faces watched the proceedings with varied interest. There was a professional detachment about Aykroyd. Though the outcome of this interview was more important than some he'd witnessed, he had seen so many in his career, too many to feel any intensity about it. It was a first for Ali, however, and she couldn't hope to maintain the same level of indifference. She stood at the glass, watching every inflection, her body taut and rigid with tension. She felt responsible for this interview, responsible for its outcome. She felt that somehow Petri had to get her off the hook. Mantizima took yet another position. He sat comfortably in one of the observers' chairs, thoughtfully studying the subject beyond the glass. It was more important to him to get to know the man beyond the glass, to read the statements his body made. There, he was sure, if nowhere else, they would find their answers.

"Moving along," Logan continued, referring occasionally to his notes, "Your file shows that when you were at Pelindaba, you were quite friendly with a woman named Sylvia Turner, were you not?"

"There was nothing between us. I'm a married man."

"Have I suggested that there was anything between you? But you were friends, weren't you? She was your secretary, I believe."

"I didn't have a private secretary, but she did some of my work, the unclassified things, mainly."

"But you took her out to lunch quite often, didn't you?"

"Why shouldn't I have? She worked better when I gave her some reward. She did my work first.... Oh, just a moment, if this is something to do with Sylvia, I know nothing about it. I'm not involved in it."

"I haven't said that Miss Turner did anything wrong. But supposing she had, would you have done anything about it? If you had seen her involving herself in matters that were beyond her security classification, would you have done anything?"

"Of course."

"What would you have done?"

"I didn't see her do it—if she did anything, that is. I didn't see anything."

"But if you had, what would you have done?"

"Reported her, I guess. Of course, that's what I would have done."

"At the risk of alienating a secretary whose favor you were currying? At the risk of finding yourself, perhaps, in the middle of a full-scale investigation? Would you have done that?" Logan pressed.

"Yes, yes, of course."

"You would have gotten involved?"

"Yes!"

"Would you? Have you ever gotten involved in anything that you weren't required to? Would you ever risk messing up your perfect life like that?"

"No, you wouldn't," Ali whispered intently beyond the glass.

"Yes, yes I would. I swear it."

"Tell me," Logan said softly, "about Katje Retief."

The sweat began flowing freely from Petri's pores. "I don't think I remember—I don't know her, I mean."

"You were right the first time, Petri. The word is remember. But I think you do remember her, and I'm sure that she still remembers you."

Petri pulled out a stiff white handkerchief and pressed it to his dripping forehead.

When he was in college, Petri was believed to be the only witness to an attack on a young girl. The girl, Katje, cried for help to a passing male student, but the boy ignored

142

her pleas. The police believed that boy to be Petri and asked him to testify at the trial, but Petri continued to deny he was the witness. Without his testimony, the rapist could not be convicted.

In fact, Petri was the witness, and the guilt of letting it go unpunished gnawed away at him for years, sometimes, even to this day. But his parents had always taught him not to get involved in other people's problems, to put nothing in the way of his pursuit of position, status and prestige. That had been one of his earliest lessons. "Who is she?" his father had asked. "A nobody. No one worth getting involved in something as controversial as a trial for." The trial would undoubtedly be controversial, Wade knew. Not because of the rape, but because of the highly unpopular views Katje was known to hold. It was anyone's guess how many people he would alienate coming to her defense. "She's just a little tramp," his mother had said before closing the subject. "Probably asked for, brought it on herself."

But she wasn't a tramp, and he knew that. She was an innocent victim of an unjust outrage. Sometimes, when he lay awake late at night, he could still hear her cries for help in his mind. But what could he do? It wasn't that he simply lacked the courage to disobey his parents. It wasn't the fear of their anger that prompted him to remain silent, it was the fear that if he had questioned even that one tenet of the value system they had given him, the whole thing would unravel, leaving him with nothing. That still frightened him, and he still clung to it as tenaciously. He understood that he would be nothing without it.

"You heard that poor girl cry for help, and you did nothing to stop it. You wouldn't even help punish the animal who did it," Logan said viciously.

Throughout the interrogation, Logan was like two men. He was able to put just the right touch of horror in his accusation, when, were he in the same position, he would have remained just as uninvolved as Petri, unless there was something in it for him. He didn't experience any guilt, however; nothing that lessoned the genuine sound of his

143

outrage. He felt contempt for Petri, for anyone not as skilled as he in maintaining a phony dichotomy in his life.

"I wasn't there!" Petri protested. "I didn't see anything."

"You did see it, and you looked the other way. Just as you have all of your life. Just as you did when Sylvia Turner violated security."

"I didn't see Sylvia do anything, I didn't."

"You did, but you won't admit it."

"I didn't! I swear it! I never saw her copy that file."

Logan turned away from Petri and exhaled deeply. He looked into the mirror and raised an eyebrow in what he believed to be Aykroyd's direction. It was all over now, except for the mopping up. They had the admission they wanted.

No one had ever told Petri that the secretary, Sylvia Turner, copied a file.

In the observation room, beyond the one-way glass, there was complete silence. But it wasn't a tense silence any longer—all of the tension had drained away with Petri's last statement—it was the silence of catching up.

After a few moments, Mantizima broke the silence. "She copied the file," he said ironically. "It's so simple, it's anticlimatic."

"Yes, well," Aykroyd said, "I think we have to assume that since they had access to the formula that they put it to use. Somewhere out there, a nuclear bomb factory is in full production—if it isn't already finished."

On his return to his office, Aykroyd ordered a trace put on Nora Brand, even though no one with that name had entered South Africa or even applied for a visa, but they had her description, and he initiated an investigation of every scientist in both private and educational facilities, who might have, in some way, contributed to the building of the bomb. He also ordered a watch on Wade Petri. Still, none of those measures seemed like enough. Suddenly, and for the first time, he really believed in the existence of the weapon that had been only hypothetical, and the thought of it frightened him more than he ever remembered being.

"You had better leave by the back exit," Aykroyd said to his guests.

"Why?" Ali demanded. "We were good enough for the front door when we came."

"I shouldn't have let you come in that way," he said absently, missing her point. "It was too dangerous. Someone might have seen you. My only defense is that I really didn't believe in it until just now."

"Who do you expect to see us?" Mantizima asked.

"You never know, Terry. We don't know what they know. They always have the advantage over us."

"Mightn't they see us if we go out the back way?" Ali asked.

"It's unlikely," Aykroyd assured her, assuming her to be frightened. "A tunnel goes under the basement of two neighboring buildings and lets out in an alley a block away. No one knows about it. We use it all the time."

He escorted them through the long tunnel. Ali noted that it got quite a bit of traffic for a secret tunnel, but then BOSS was a large organization with many operatives who had reason to hide their association. Eventually, Aykroyd opened the door to the alley for them and stepped outside to say good-by.

"I don't know exactly where we go from here," Aykroyd said. "But I'll keep you both informed, of course."

"I have a few ideas of my own to pursue," Ali told him. "The foreign journalists assigned to a country usually form into a tight, little community. If anyone's been acting suspicious, someone will have noticed. They'll tell me before they'd tell you."

"And I think I'll do some checking around in the scientific community," Mantizima said. "I know the right questions to ask."

Secretly, Aykroyd was convinced that nothing would turn up from either pursuit. They were duplicate efforts his organization could perform more effectively. Were that his only reservation, he would have said nothing, but it was not his only concern. They were both intelligent and determined, but so naive—too new at that game to know how rough it could be played.

"I'm not sure that's a wise idea," Aykroyd said cautiously.

"What are you so afraid of?" Ali demanded angrily.

"Only that you'll both be killed."

Suddenly, shots rang out from a neighboring rooftop. Seeing that there was no cover, they all reacted instinctively. Ali, having found herself on impromtu battlefields before in the Middle-East, immediately threw herself on the ground. The men, however, found themselves responding to some probably unacknowledged values within them. Mantizima's first reaction was to protect Ali, and he threw his body on hers, while Aykroyd's first thought was to shield Terry, and he crouched down in front of him.

Several shots were fired, and one met its mark. Or at least, a mark. It buried itself in Rune Aykroyd's back. In a few moments the shooting was over, but it was too late for Aykroyd.

Mantizima rolled him over onto his back, and he and Ali knelt beside him. They all knew it was useless to call an ambulance; it wouldn't arrive in time.

"I swear to you, Rune," Mantizima said in a hoarse whisper, "I'll get whoever did this to you. I won't let him get away with it."

"No...Terry...authorities...let the...authorities...do it...proper channels...," Aykroyd said slowly, with blood trickling out of his mouth.

The authorities, the proper channels, Aykroyd had lived with them all of his life. They had been the backbone of his existence, the girders of the society he served. He had always been nothing more than a part of that society, only one piece of a giant collective. But men don't die collectively, they die alone. They learn in death what some of them fail to realize in life, that in the final analysis each man must be complete in himself. For the first time in his life, Aykroyd learned what it was like to be whole and wished he had discovered it sooner.

"No...you do...it.... Find him...carry on...all up to you."

Mantizima swallowed hard as he tightened his grip on his friend's hand.

"Friends," he said gruffly. "Brothers."

"For life."

"Forever."

A slight trace of what must have been a smile softened the lines of pain on Aykroyd's face.

"Terry...the slate?"

"It's clean. It's clean."

"I'm...glad."

With that, the hand in Mantizima's went limp. From that moment on, Rune Aykroyd never again had to struggle, as the man said, alone and afraid in a world he never made.

Mantizima closed his eyes for a moment, then quickly tried to recover his composure.

"Come on, Ali," he said, his voice choking. "We have to get away from here."

"Terry, he's dead. We can't leave him."

"We can't do anything more for him, except leave."

"Uh...no...I—"

"Will you just be quiet, and for once in your life listen to someone else? I know what I'm talking about. We can't be found here. They'll hold us until they investigate, and we have things to do. Now come on!"

She did not appear to agree, but neither did she resist when he took her hand and pulled her away. They ran down the alley, but he stopped at the end and turned back to the body.

"I'll finish this for you, Rune," he said simply. "That's a promise."

CHAPTER TWELVE

Mantizima took Ali to a *sheeban,* a black bar, in Soweto. It was a shabby, old wooden shack, run-down well past the point of redemption, filled even in the middle of the day with men hollowed out by fear and anger, whose hostile eyes told Ali she was not wanted there. With that sort of welcome she should have found the place uninviting, but, instead, she considered it surprisingly comforting. No one would think to look for me here, she thought. She just felt like being lost for a while.

They took a corner table in an unoccupied back room. At Mantizima's request, the proprietor produced a surprisingly good bottle of a local Cabernet Savingnon, one that Ali would have considered a fair rival for those produced by her native California if she had even noticed what she was drinking.

Then, without even realizing he was doing it, Mantizima started talking. He told her about the boyhood friendship he shared with Rune Aykroyd and the things that happened along the way to pull Rune away from him and shape him into the man he had become. Ali did not say much, she just listened with an understanding that he needed to talk. After a while, with the subject spent, his voice just trailed off into silence.

"He loved you, you know?" Ali said. "No matter what happened in the past."

"I know. I felt the same way about him. I always have. I tried to fight it for years, to deny it because of what happened. Now I don't have to anymore.... He was a good man. He tried to be, at any rate. He just wasn't sure what that required."

"Why do you think he was killed? Do you think it was related to this case?" Ali asked. "Or some other case? I suppose a man in his position makes a lot of enemies."

"I'm sure he does, but I don't think one of them...killed him," Mantizima said and paused, before continuing gently, but quite deliberately. "I don't think Rune was the target. I think the sniper was gunning for you."

"For me?" Ali said. "Impossible. What enemies do I have?"

"Probably none, personally," Mantizima said.

"Then how can you say...?"

"I think our friend, the American reporter, wanted to give the appearance of eliminating the weakest link. The way organized crime does."

"Ridiculous! How did they know I was even a suspect?"

"It wouldn't be that difficult to ascertain, Ali. If Rune and his superiors were able to build a case against you, these terrorists could do the same. They probably saw you with Rune, maybe they even saw us go into the Bureau. They probably saw Petri, too. They know how they used him and know he couldn't be trusted to lie effectively. So they tried to eliminate what appeared to be the one link the authorities had to the operation."

"No! I won't believe it!" Ali snapped.

She lapsed into an angry silence of denial. Mantizima said nothing until she continued.

"Did you mean what you said back there?" she asked. "That you intend to go on with this?"

"Yes, I did. And it's not just because of Rune's death. That only makes it more important. You see...."

He told her about the personal quest that brought him back to South Africa.

"So you see, I have to do it. Of course, it doesn't necessarily follow that I'll find my answers through this mission, but I have to do something, and it was Nora's design that brought me to the point of making the decision. It seems right to me that I follow it. And now I have an added incentive.... But I'm not sure you should be involved in it. Perhaps you should leave South Africa."

"I have a vested interest in this, too, Terry."

"Why don't you just let me handle it for you? I'll prove your innocence and I'll gather the material for your story. You don't have to be here."

"I do my own work, thanks."

"Ali, if someone tried to get you and missed, he won't stop at one attempt."

"No one is trying to kill me!" she shouted. "Is that clear? No one!"

She angrily lowered her head, refusing to even consider the suggestion. Mantizima felt frustrated. He was not sure whether he tried too hard or not hard enough, only that South Africa was no place for her. It was ironic, he thought; he did not care at all about the danger he might be facing, but he didn't want anything to happen to her. He looked at her left hand, pressed to the table in front of her, and changed the subject.

"You've never married," he said, as a statement rather than a question, in the manner of a peace offering.

"Is it that obvious?" she asked, a little stiffly, but accepting the truce.

"As a matter of fact, it is. Is marriage just incompatible with your work?"

"I've said that long enough, I really ought to believe it," she laughed. "But I guess I don't. My mother says that I've avoided commitment because I'm afraid of failing in the relationship, afraid that I'll be disappointed in the man I've picked. Given it a lot of thought since she said it, and I think there might be a grain...or maybe, if I'm honest, a bushel of truth to it. But I don't think that's the whole story."

"What is?"

She shrugged. "Disappointed idealism, I guess. I just think that when people come together they should add to each other. They should give each other so much that they are each more together than they would have been alone. Only, somehow, it doesn't seem to work that way. Not often, at least. The people I see always seem to subtract from each other. They're drawn together and stay together out of their weaknesses rather than their strengths." She laughed, a little embarrassed at revealing so much of herself. "Guess maybe I expect too much. What about you?"

"Oh, there's no great mystery in my life. More of a chiché, actually. I suppose you would have to say I just never met the right woman. Although I haven't been looking either."

"My mother also says that when you are ready, you don't have to look. Seems it just happens to you."

Mantizima looked quite pointedly at her for a long moment. "Maybe she's right," he said.

When she left Mantizima, Ali returned to her hotel room. She had felt uncomfortable with him and was eager to get away for reasons she did not choose to explore, but now that she faced the prospect of an evening alone, she felt restless and uncharacteristically lonely. Perhaps she could have dinner with Evan, she thought. Even that would be better than being by herself. But Evan was not in. He had shoved a note under her door saying he would be out all evening and reminding her of the appointment they had the next morning with a Native Studies professor at a local college.

She closed the door and stared at the walls of the empty room, feeling terribly lost. It's the death, she told herself. It wasn't every day that she lost...well, not a friend, but a comrade. But she knew all of that emotion wasn't being spent on Rune Aykroyd.

No one was trying to kill her, she thought at last. They didn't have any reason to. But even facing the issue openly did nothing to dispell the shroud that had filled her mind.

She ordered dinner sent to her room, but when it arrived, found she wasn't very hungry. She pushed the food around on her plate for a while, then decided that what she needed was to get out.

151

She left the hotel and walked to a nearby shopping area, closed for the night, and passed the time looking through darkened store windows. Then she came upon a neighborhood bar. From the outside it looked like a quiet, homey little place. Just what she needed, she thought.

From the moment she entered, she knew she did not belong there. Apart from a few closed glances, no one even looked at her. She wouldn't find any companionship there. But she had no place else to go. She took a seat at the bar and ordered a drink. For a while, no one paid any attention to her, except for a young man—really just a boy, Ali thought, scarcely old enough to drink—who came in after her. After a few moments, with a hostile look on his face, he approached her.

"You're an American, aren't you?" he asked in a surly tone.

She nodded.

"Then why don't you go back where you belong?"

"Because, at the moment, this is where I happen to belong. I'm a reporter. Been sent here to do a job."

"A reporter!" the boy said, as disgusted as he would have been had she admitted to being a carrier of fatal diseases. "I might have known. We don't want you here. You must be able to see that. Why didn't you leave while you still can?"

Ali looked around the bar for some support. It was obvious everyone had heard what the boy said; they were all watching her. But it was also clear from their faces that he had expressed their sentiments. No one was going to raise his voice in her behalf.

"Why don't you mind your own business?" she said to him.

She finished her drink, then got off the stool and walked to the door.

"It was nice," she said sarcastically to the room in general. "We'll have to do this again."

She walked out of the door. The boy watched after her for a moment, then followed her out.

Ali retraced her steps back in the direction of the hotel. She chided herself for ever going into the place to begin with and accepted the fact that she would probably feel lousy all night. She did not notice she was being followed.

As she approached the entrance to an alley that ran perpendicular to the street where was walking on, however, the boy caught up with her and pulled her into it. He pinned her up against the wall of a building. Perhaps it was because he was so young that, despite his obvious strength, she really did not take him very seriously.

"I told you to leave," he said, "but you just wouldn't listen. Now I'll give you a little inducement."

Without warning, the boy suddenly belted her in the stomach. She doubled over in pain. He hit her in the face, throwing her back against the wall. And slammed her again in the stomach.

Just then a couple of young English tourists out for an evening walk happened past the alley and saw what was happening.

"You there," the man shouted. "What do you think you're doing?"

The boy looked up and swiftly ran away. The Englishman took after him, while his wife helped Ali to her feet. A few moments later the man came back, alone.

"Sorry," he said. "He was too fast for me."

"What happened?" his wife asked.

"He was a mugger," Ali said. "Wanted my money and I wouldn't give it to him."

She wasn't sure why she lied; her conscious mind had not caught up with her unconscious. She just knew that something had happened that she had to stay on top of.

"Not smart, love," the man said.

"I know that now."

"Well, that's enough talk for now, dear," the woman said. "We'll have to get you to a hospital."

"That's really not necessary," Ali said. "I'll be all right. If you could just get me a cab.... Really. You've both done enough."

The English couple did not really agree that that should be the extent of their ministrations, but Ali was so insistent they let it go with finding a cab for her.

"I suppose you want to go to Johannesburg General," the driver said kindly when she climbed into the back seat of the cab.

She closed her eyes for a moment. She knew she should have medical care, but she did not know how to handle it. No matter what she said, she knew they would call the police. She felt things slipping away from her, when she suddenly had an idea.

"No, here's where I want to go," she said, as she rummaged through her purse.

She produced the business card Terry Mantizima had given her, with his mother's working address and telephone number on the back, and handed it to him.

"This is in Soweto," the driver said. "I can't take you there. Whites aren't allowed to go there. Besides, I couldn't pick up another passenger there."

She knew what he meant—he couldn't pick up a white passenger there, and that cab was reserved exclusively for them. She reached into her wallet, pulled out a twenty rand note, and extended it without saying a word. The driver gave it a sour look. For a moment she thought he was going to throw her out of his cab, but then he snatched the bill out of her hand and turned the meter on.

Ali was physically in shock by the time she reached the Soweto clinic, so she was not prepared for or up to handling what awaited her there.

When she opened the door, she was confronted by a waiting room filled with people, all of whom were openly shocked by the presence of what was possibly the first white person to ever enter that place. There was a short line of people waiting to check in at the now-vacant nurse's desk, who moved aside to allow her to get in front of them as she approached. She hated that automatic show of deference that is required of Blacks in South Africa and thought it particularly wrong there where she was the intruder, but she did not know what to do about it. She couldn't jump ahead of the line and yet she felt too weary to explain her position. Instead, she just stood in the middle of the room, feeling dumb-struck and very helpless.

Just then, a competent-looking black woman in a nurse's uniform entered the waiting room. She, too, was startled by the presence of a white woman in that room.

"Excuse me," Ali said, finding her voice. "Could you tell me if Mrs. Mantizima is here?"

"I'm Mrs. Mantizima," Deborah answered.

"I'm Ali Hayden, a friend of Terry's."

"I know who you are, Miss Hayden."

Deborah then looked Ali over, taking in the battered face and torn clothing, and the surprise melted away.

"Sorry," Ali said, "but I didn't know where else to go."

"Yes, well, we'll have the doctor take a look at you, then decide what to do. Come with me," Deborah said with professional courtesy.

"These people were ahead of me."

"We always take emergencies first. Come along."

Ali followed her into an examining room, suddenly feeling worse upon learning how she appeared to someone else. In the examining room, Deborah helped her undress, then spread a sheet over her once she was on the examining table.

"I'm going to call Terry," Deborah said.

Ali nodded, but later never remembered hearing that exchange.

A few moments later, the doctor, an elderly man, entered, obviously having already been briefed about the patient in that room.

"You know, you really should be at Johannesburg General," the doctor said.

Ali very decisively shook her head. "They'd call the police."

"Would that be such a bad idea? You were attacked."

"I don't want to have to answer questions. Can't you take care of me?"

"I'm not supposed to, but I'll make a deal with you. If I find anything seriously wrong, anything that requires extended treatment, I'm going to call for an ambulance to take you to a White hospital. But if you aren't seriously hurt, we'll just keep it between ourselves. That's the best I can offer you. Is it a deal?"

Ali nodded; she was too spent to argue.

The doctor pushed the sheet aside and pressed his fingers into her abdomen. "Does that hurt?" he asked.

She made a face. Doctors! she thought. They were all alike. They manhandled you and asked if it hurt.

The doctor must have read her expression. "I mean unduly," he said.

"No, it's tender, but there's no real pain."

"Good."

He continued with her body for a while, then had her sit up and examined her swollen eye, whose violet hue was just beginning to bloom.

"You're a lucky girl," the doctor said when he finished.

Ali snorted.

"I mean it. This could have been very bad, but you don't appear to have any internal injuries and your eye looks all right to me. You'll look awful for a while, probably feel awful, too, but then your pretty face will return and you'll be none the worse for wear."

"Thank you, doctor."

The doctor hesitated for a moment, then said, "Miss Hayden, I don't know what you're involved in, but humor an old man and listen to a bit of advice. You only have this one body—it can't be replaced. Don't let anyone do this to you again. Don't put yourself in that position. You might not be as fortunate next time."

Ali nodded contritely.

156

"Enough said. Now get dressed. A friend of yours is waiting to see you in my office. Mrs. Mantizima will show you the way."

She couldn't imagine who the friend was, but when she saw Mantizima in the doctor's office, she realized she should have expected him. He angrily glared at her for a moment, then wordlessly walked over and took hold of her chin, positioning it so he could get a better look at the eye.

"Lovely," he said. "In another hour it will be a perfect match for your blue suit."

"I'm the victim, Terry. Remember? You act like I did this to myself."

"You might as well have. I warned you that you were in danger, and in spite of that you went out alone, and at night. Now tell me what happened."

She sighed wearily, but carefully related the entire incident to him in the manner of a skilled reporter, with a scrupulous adherence to facts, without interpretation.

"He followed you into the bar," Mantizima said when she finished. "I told you—"

"I said: he came in after me."

"But he definitely followed you out."

Ali nodded; she couldn't deny it.

"Well then, I don't think there's any choice now. You have to leave South Africa. You are not safe here."

"Aren't you letting your imagination run away with you, Terry? We don't know that this is related to...this afternoon."

"Ali, how many other people have ordered you out of South Africa? How many men go around beating up strange women?"

"Not everyone is as chivalrous as you are. Besides, he wasn't a man, just an angry boy with an anti-American prejudice. Believe me, he wasn't alone. Everyone else in that bar felt the same way. They aren't shedding any tears for me tonight."

"Maybe not, but how many of them would have done the same thing?"

Ali shrugged noncommitally. Deborah Mantizima entered the room then and stood quietly with her back to the door. Neither Ali nor her son appeared to notice her, allowing her to silently watch them. Before tonight, Alison Hayden was just a name. Now she was more than that. Deborah wanted to learn more about this woman's relationship with her son.

"You have to leave," Mantizima continued. "Now. Before it is too late."

"Forgetting something, aren't you, Terry? Assuming the South African Government would even let me leave, which is highly doubtful, I don't want to go. I have a shot at the greatest story of my career. That's what's at stake here. Not to mention my personal reputation. Besides, what guarantee do you have that the people whom you think are after me won't come looking for you?"

"I can take care of myself."

"So can I!" Ali protested.

"So you can. You did a fine job of taking care of yourself tonight."

They glared angrily at each other, while Deborah stared glumly at her son. She feared the worst, but she had to know.

"Ali, if anything happened to you...." Mantizima said softly.

Deborah closed her eyes in grief. She learned what she had wanted to know when she entered that room, but she didn't feel very good about it. She should be happy, she told herself, she had succeeded as a mother. In spite of all the injustices perpetrated against their people in South Africa, she had taught her children to be color-blind. To judge people as individuals, not according to someone else's divisions. And the lesson took with Terry. That really was the way he dealt with people. But just because he chose to ignore the divisions didn't mean other people did. She could see that her son already cared for this woman, probably more than he realized himself, certainly more than Ali did. What would she do to him? she wondered. Would she be another Rune Aykroyd? Deborah never learned what really happened between Rune and her son, but she knew it was something that wounded Terry deeply. At that moment she desperately feared for Terry and she thought that she probably hated Ali, not for anything she was personally, but because she held Terry so firmly in her power.

"Terry, I appreciate your concern for me. Really. And I wish I could tell you I'm not scared—only I am. But I have to stay in spite of that.... I've walked away from a lot of battles in my life. I'm not proud of that, but not ashamed either. I just never knew those fights had my name on them. This time, however, I can't evade that."

She paused momentarily and rubbed her hand over her eyes, wincing slightly when she unconsciously touched the bruised eye. Mantizima waited for her to continue.

"I don't usually go in for such long-winded explanations, but.... I lied when I said that it was simply my story and the suspicions against me that were holding me here. True, they are important, but not everything. There's something much larger at stake here, and it's gotten under my skin. I'm a reporter—I'm supposed to concern myself with facts and leave the judgments to others. But I'm still a human being. I live in this world. I don't have to tell you that if that bomb reaches its intended target, there won't be any State of Israel, at least not as we know it. But it would be just as wrong if it detonates anywhere else along the route. I don't know if I can stop it, but maybe I can. At least I have to try. I don't know why life chose to give this burden to me, or to you, but it has, and I can't walk away from it. If I did, I'd have to admit to being a coward, and I'm not brave enough to live with that.... Terry, you, of all people, have to understand. This is my fight."

Mantizima smiled at her. He walked closer and took her hand in his. "It's ours," he said softly. "We'll fight it together."

Deborah Mantizima had to look away.

Ali went home with the Mantizimas.

Terry had said, "It's too late for Ali to go back to her hotel tonight, Mother. She'll have to come home with us."

"Of course."

"Oh, no," Ali protested. "I can't impose anymore. You've done enough for me."

"It won't be any imposition," Deborah said. "We have plenty of room. You're a little taller than my daughter and I, but between us I'm sure we can find something for you to wear."

Deborah spoke courteously to Ali, but there was no warmth in her voice. She was not trying to convey her feelings for Ali through her speech—actually, she would rather have hidden them, but she could not. That was really the way she felt. Yet, as a nurse, she came to Ali's defense when, as they were driving home in the car, Mantizima wanted to brainstorm some of his ideas about this investigation off of her.

"Don't badger her, Terry," Deborah had said. "Can't you see she's had enough for one night? Whatever you have to say will keep till morning."

But the hard edge returned to her voice once they arrived at the house, despite her best efforts to keep it out.

"The only extra room I have," Deborah explained as they walked upstairs, "is my daughter's and son-in-law's, but they aren't here tonight."

Deborah pointed the bathroom out for Ali and apologized for the presence of a large piece of furniture that blocked off half the hall just outside the bedroom Ali was to use. The offending piece was a large dining room breakfront. A beautiful piece, obviously well cared for, but being kept in a strange place, Ali thought.

"I meant to ask you, Mother," Mantizima said, "Where did you get this?"

Deborah paused, then continued sadly, "It belonged to one of my neighbors. She never worked. Her husband had a good job and they could afford for her to just keep house. But he died suddenly last year and she couldn't get permission to stay in Soweto. They sent her to live in

Transkei, the Xhosa homeland near Port Elisabeth on the Indian Ocean."

"That's hundreds of miles from here," Ali said.

"I know," Deborah answered with a long-standing resignation. "She couldn't afford to take everything with her and she needed money to start over alone, so most of the neighbors tried to buy what she wanted to sell. I don't have any place for this, but I've always loved it. I hope to be able to give it to my daughter someday. I keep thinking that eventually she will have a home of her own."

Ali looked sadly at the breakfront. The years of care that had been lavished over it were as obvious as the many coats of polish. It was so lovely, she thought, so valuable, but it had been discarded like a piece of junk, the way her government had discarded its owner.

Ali bade the Mantizimas good night and quickly slipped into the room assigned her. She dropped all of her clothes in a pile on the bedroom floor, found a robe that almost fit her, and, after a quick shower to get rid of the alley's dirt, climbed into bed. She could not sleep, however. There was too much to think about, too many demons running loose in her mind.

She was not the only wide-awake person in that house. Downstairs in the kitchen Deborah sat alone, very ashamed of her behavior towards Ali. After a while she decided to bring her a peace offering. She entered Ali's room a short time later carrying a cup of hot cocoa.

"I thought you might have difficulty sleeping tonight," Deborah said, a little stiffly. "I can give you a sleeping pill if you would like, but I think this might be all you need."

Ali nodded gravely and accepted the cup, but she didn't say anything until Deborah was about to leave.

"Mrs. Mantizima," she said.

"Deborah, please."

Ali nodded, but did not repeat the name. "I sense that you don't like me very much. Would you rather I not stay here tonight? It's not that late. I could still leave."

Deborah was shocked by Ali's direct frankness, but not displeased.

"You're very much like Terry," Deborah said, without answering the question.

She was very much like Terry, Deborah thought. She did not know that Rune Aykroyd had thought them to be wrong for each other because they would bring out the worst in each other, but had she known, she would have disagreed. In just the little time she had seen them together, she had to admit they were good for each other. They spurned each other on, gave each other strength. And what was wrong with having a friend who was good for you? Couldn't she make herself take the chance? Deborah thought. Couldn't she risk extending a little trust to this girl for Terry's sake?

Deborah smiled and said, "Before I met you...Ali, you were just a name to me. A name associated with something I didn't want to see my son involved in. I think I was inadvertently blaming you for bringing the problem about. But you're not the cause, I know that now. You're the victim."

Ali smiled sleepily, happy to be relieved of that worry. Deborah sat on the edge of the bed and they talked for a little while. They talked easily about little, unimportant things in the manner of two old friends, or like a mother and daughter.

CHAPTER THIRTEEN

SEPTEMBER 16, 1979

"A nuclear bomb!" Neil Logan said when he finished reading the pages of the late Rune Aykroyd's reports. "That's the last thing I would have suspected. He never even hinted—that is...I mean...."

Lukas Kroonhof, the Director of the Bureau of State Security watched Logan's reaction without expression for a moment; then, apparently deciding it was the expected one, passed on to other things. Kroonhof was a fat, gross-looking man with an overstuffed stomach, thick jowls and heavy eyelids that all combined to make him appear much older than his forty-eight years. But while he had surrendered to his personal battle of the bulge many years ago, that did not mean he accepted his condition. He knew the cliché that inside every fat person is a thin person fighting to get out was true in his case. Inside he was a lean and hungry man, at least as dangerous as Cassius was said to have been. But his shape did have decided advantages. To most people's minds, a fat man is jolly, he isn't cunning and ruthless, he isn't the sort who would slit someone's throat without giving it a second thought. In his business it paid to be underestimated, sometimes even by those who worked for you.

He wondered briefly whether Logan was doing it right now.

"You do understand now, Neil, why Rune—may he rest in peace—had to play this so close to the vest? If this had leaked out...well, I'm sure you see what I mean."

163

"Oh, quite, sir, quite."

Kroonhof continued to study Logan without saying anything, watching, evaluating, deciding. He had called Logan to his office with the idea of offering him Aykroyd's job, but with so much at stake he couldn't afford to make a mistake. Logan was a young man, perhaps too young for the job, and he was English-speaking; that would not sit well with some of the powers that be. But he was bright and ambitious. Too ambitious, Kroonhof knew some people would say, but he had also been "too ambitious" at that age—if he hadn't been, he would never have achieved his present position. Besides, ambition was such a transparent motive; it was always obvious, he thought, when it went out of control.

From the other side of the desk, that bright, young, ambitious man took advantage of Kroonhof's silence to assess the situation he found himself in. He was genuinely stunned by the things he had read in Aykroyd's report, and the shock had enervated him, but not enough to let opportunity slip away from him. He had not been summoned to that office to engage in small talk, he knew; Kroonhof was, at that moment, deciding his future. Logan summoned every last ounce of his strength and threw it into a facade of youthful vigor, and he wracked his brain to come up with something to say—anything—that would push Kroonhof into making that decision the way he wanted it made.

"Excuse me, sir," Logan interrupted. "If I may offer a suggestion. I'm sure you have your own ideas of how to proceed now that poor Rune is...gone. But I have some contacts in the scientific community that might be useful to us. Just some chaps I went to school with, but many of them are in very high positions. Talking to them really might be quite useful."

You're a clever little liar, aren't you? Kroonhof thought of Logan; you're grasping at straws. But that did not bother him. He liked it when his men lied their way into corners—that meant they had to work their way out. That lie, however, provided all the assurance Kroonhof seemed to need.

"That's really up to you Neil. It's your investigation now, if you want it."

If he wanted it? He'd have killed for it.

Logan accepted the promotion with enthusiasm tempered by just the right touch of thoughtfulness. He threw a few more of his ideas before Kroonhof, all just as much hot air as the first, but his manner made them sound intelligent, some, almost inspired. His purpose in pursuing the discussion was to find out, without asking, what the boundaries were on his authority.

Cutting through the rhetoric, Kroonhof suddenly said, "As the Americans say, it's your ballgame. If you succeed, this will only be the beginning for you. If you fail, well, I don't think I have to tell you what that will mean for you, for all of us."

"No, sir," Logan gulped.

Logan made all the proper sounds about not letting the team down and quickly made his escape from Kroonhof's office. Once in the hall, however, his confidence deflated like a broken balloon. The responsibility, the problems, the whole thing scared the hell out of him.

He made his way back to his own office like a somnambulist, barely noticing Kloff when they met in the hall.

"So he found out about you?" Kloff said.

"What?" shrieked Logan.

"The old man. Kroonhof. He noticed your existence and offered you a chance at the brass ring, as they say. Am I right?"

"Oh, yes. How did you know?"

"You know what the rumor situation is like around here whenever someone gets summoned to the tenth floor. You might like to know the heavy money was on you," Kloff joked. "Congratulations," he added with just a tinge of regret in his voice.

Logan accepted Kloff's wishes with more grace than most people believed he possessed and wandered off down the corridor in the direction of his office. Somewhere enroute, however, it occurred to him that little cubbyhole he'd been occupying for the last couple of years wasn't his office any longer. He was the boss now!

With some of his arrogance returning, he walked back in the direction of what had been Aykroyd's office. He slipped in quietly, a little grateful that Petra, the secretary, was not at her desk—he didn't feel like making explanations yet—and closed the door behind him. When he sat in Aykroyd's chair, he was himself again.

It was worth it, he thought. Everything...was worth it. He allowed himself to drink in that heady thrill and resolved to worry about the problem, as he termed the investigation, later.

Later, however, the problem was still there. He read through Aykroyd's notes again and again, but he still didn't know what to do. He wished there were someone he could ask, but that, he thought bitterly, was the negative part of authority. That was what it meant to be in charge. He thought he would just discuss it with a friend, just to get his impressions, but then had to admit he did not have any friends. Oh, he knew people, of course, the chaps he drank with, but they weren't the sort with whom one could discuss something like that. When he realized there was no one else he could turn to, he ordered his secretary to call Kloff.

Logan handed Aykroyd's notes to Kloff without a word and watched as he read in silence. To Logan's annoyance, Kloff accepted the matter much calmer and with much more practicality.

"So someone's finally tried it?" Kloff said. "I always thought it was just a matter of time until some terrorist group tried to build something nuclear. Right up their alley, so to speak. I never thought it could be done, but it seems Rune did, so I guess I was wrong."

That's the average mind for you, thought Logan nastily; always willing to accept the obvious.

166

"What do we do?" Kloff continued. "It appears that Rune set some things in motion. Do we—"

"All of those things will take time. Too much of it. Interrogating scientists, hunting for some bird who may or may not have entered South Africa, following some bloody fool who already told us everything he knew—all of those things will take forever. I'm going to cancel them all."

"Is that wise, Neil? I mean, if Rune thought—"

"Rune is dead, Pieter. I'm in charge now. Is that clear?"

"Perfectly."

"Good. Now, as I was saying, what's needed is a shortcut. Somehow, we have to find—"

Suddenly, he got an idea of how to proceed. It was an idea that came, not in words, but as an image in his mind, and as a sharp rush of fear in his gut.

"I have it!" he said. "There were two people with Rune the other day. They were with him when he watched me interrogate Petri. One of them was that Hayden woman he had me meet when she first arrived—she's mentioned in the report. Exonerated, apparently. The other was some Bantu."

"A Bantu? Here? Watching an interrogation?"

"Yes," Logan answered. "Interesting, wouldn't you say? And judging by the timing, they were probably with him when he died."

"Out there in the alley, you mean?"

"Right," Logan answered absently.

"And they left him?" Kloff asked, appalled.

"What would you expect them to do? Hang around until some fool of a policeman accused them of murder? What would you do?"

"I don't know, but leaving a body doesn't seem decent, somehow. Who is this Bantu?"

"If you would stop talking for a moment, I'd think of it.... What the hell was his name...? Mantizima! That was it. Never forget a name. Terry Mantizima. *Dr*. Terry Mantizima," he added sarcastically. "Those two people are involved in this in some way. I know they are. I want them watched round-the-clock. Use as many men as you need."

"If you're sure they know something," Kloff suggested, "why don't we just bring them in for questioning? We can make them talk."

"No. Let's just give them some rope," Logan insisted.

Kloff considered that and said, "Good idea, Neil. We'll give them enough rope to hang themselves.... There's just one thing that bothers me. What if they don't know anything? What if they hang themselves, so to speak, on circumstantial evidence?"

"Better them than me," Logan muttered to himself, then added to Kloff, "After all, I have a career to think about."

Ali gingerly eased her aching body out of the cab that brought her to the campus where she was to meet Evan for their interview and slowly walked to their prearranged meeting place.

She had awoken that morning to the sound of a groan, unaware until her mind was more conscious that she had made the sound herself. She was then confronted by the unique sensation of being, by the pain emanating from them, vividly aware of each and every one of her muscles. At first, she couldn't recall why she happened to feel that badly.

Then she remembered.

With a sigh, she swung her legs out of the bed and planted them on the floor. Not a smart move, she realized, as her stomach, outraged by the events of the night before, made its presence known by violent heaving that she was some time in quieting down. Once that truce was signed, she staggered over to the dresser mirror to inspect the damage.

"Redheads," she said, with profound disgust, after a long, expressionless glance, "should never wear purple."

Requiring more effort than she would have believed, she slowly dragged herself to the bathroom.

Physically, she felt much better after her shower, but in contrast to that, she experienced a strange sense of emptiness which she could not define, but concluded was probably just a little depression as a result of the attack. Then, as she dried herself, she happened to catch a glance of herself in the full-length mirror on the inside of the bathroom door. Perhaps it was because of what had happened to her the night before, perhaps it was because she had been alone for a while—for whatever reason, she found herself feeling more aware of her own body than she had in a long time. She dropped the towel to her feet and stood before her reflection. Even now, with the swelling and the bruises, it was a beautiful sight. In an unconscious way, she'd always been proud of her body, of her long, slim lines and full breasts, but only consciously allowed herself to enjoy that pride on rare occasions.

Her body tingled as she wrapped a rough terrycloth robe over her skin. She felt excited by what she had just experienced, a pleasurable sensation of her own heightened sensuality, but also, by contrast, more vividly aware of that feeling of emptiness that still lay beneath it.

She opened the bathroom door and stepped out into the hall. Just then, the door to Terry's room opened and he stepped into the hall, too, wearing, as she was, only a robe. It wasn't an unusual situation; house guests wearing night apparel have been meeting outside of bathrooms ever since plumbing came indoors. But the way it affected those two people would not be found in the house guest's Book of Rules.

"Morning," Ali said awkwardly.

Mantizima just nodded stiffly.

With only an instantaneous break in their strides, together they entered that part of the hall made narrow by the piece of bulky furniture, pausing only a moment when their eyes met and their bodies brushed against each other, before moving on to their own destinations. The encounter only lasted a second, but it wasn't until Ali was safe in her own room that she was able to breathe again.

Even now, as she remembered it, her breath quickened and a warm aching spread through her body. But the memory had to be shoved aside because Evan looked up from the newspaper he was reading and saw her approaching.

"What the hell happened to you?" he demanded.

169

"I had a fight with a truck," she said sourly, a little angry at learning the ravages of the attack were as obvious as she had feared they would be, even though she had applied her make-up with a putty knife. "The truck won."

"Honestly? Oh, no, you're kidding. Right? What really happened?"

She sighed. What could she tell him? "Nothing unusual. I was mugged."

"I didn't think they had much of that here."

"Evan, it only takes one."

After what seemed to Ali a considerable amount of time and innumerable assurances from her that, no, she was not seriously hurt, and, yes, she had seen a doctor, Evan moved onto other things as they walked across the campus to the professor's office.

"Did you read about your boyfriend?" he asked.

Ali looked up sharply.

"Aykroyd, I mean. He was killed."

"Yes. I...read it."

"Did you get a load o' this?" he asked, handing her a section of paper while he juggled his camera equipment. "It says he worked in some government accounting department. Not for Haagen-Aykroyd, although we knew that was a crock."

"Did we?" Ali asked.

"Well, I did, at least. I thought you saw through him, too. And I don't buy this accounting department crap either."

"It might be true, you know. Why would they lie about it?" Ali asked cautiously.

"Are you kidding? Why would an accountant bug your room?"

Ali laughed softly. She'd had an answer ready for him for days but never had occasion to use it. "Oh, that. Aykroyd said, and I believe him, that they just do that routinely to foreign reporters. At random. Happens all the time."

"No kidding?"

"No," Ali lied. "And they say this isn't a police state."

"At random, huh? Well, better you than me."

"Who knows? Maybe now they are listening to you."

Evan tripped. He fell flat on the sidewalk, with his camera gear stuffed under him and his perfectly coiffed hair tossed every which way. Ali bent over to help him up.

"Evan, are you—"

As she leaned closer to him, she saw something. Something miniscule, something insignificant, which struck her speechless. She was glad that in that position he couldn't see her face.

CHAPTER FOURTEEN

"You've hardly touched your drink."

Ali looked at the glass, which, due to melting ice, now had more liquid in it than when the waiter placed it before her. She looked up at the man across the table, the man who called himself Evan Michael Todd.

"Been so busy, I forgot about it," she said brightly.

She had just managed to convince herself that her voice had sounded real, convincing, when what started out as a normal swallow developed into a gulp in her throat. She hoped he didn't hear it, or, if he did, it didn't mean anything to him, then chided herself for making such a big deal out of a small deception.

What do I have to be worried about? I'm the one with a clear conscience, she thought, momentarily buoyed by the confidence the remembered remnant of some childhood maxim gave her, until she recalled that the maxim only promised death without guilt to those with a clear conscience; it said nothing about pain.

She quickly lowered her eye to the photographer's loop pressed against the proof sheets she held, which were definitely not the work of the great Evan Michael Todd.

The revelation that this man was not really Evan Todd came to her that morning when he tripped on the University sidewalk. The discovery she had made then was really rather insignificant in itself, but it triggered an avalanche of thoughts that brought days of unacknowledged doubts into sharp focus. She had had to struggle to maintain her composure through the interview, then rushed to Mantizima's house with the news.

"Evan," she said, triumphantly, "dyes his hair!"

Mantizima said nothing, but his eyes gave a shrug.

"Didn't you understand what I said, Terry? Evan dyes his hair."

"So what? I didn't know you were that provincial. Lots of men color their hair. Maybe he's prematurely gray."

"His roots are blond, not gray! Now maybe he just likes brown hair, but there's just as good a chance that he darkened it because—"

"Because you were expecting to meet a man with dark hair!"

"Right!"

They both knew what that discovery probably meant, but they did not allow themselves to jump to conclusions until they were sure their landing would be safe.

"Let's not be hasty," Mantizima warned. "You told me Evan Michael Todd is a famous photographer. Would he be that easy to get rid of? Where is the real Evan Todd?"

Ali quickly shook her head, unaware that it was not clear what she was disputing, and, without a word of explanation, picked up the phone. She placed a call to the London number she had been given for Evan Todd. A recording told her the phone had been disconnected. Questionable, she thought, but not conclusive.

Then she dialed the number of a Fleet Street acquaintance named Tim O'Hara and was lucky enough to find him in. She briefly outlined the favor she wanted of the London reporter and promised to wait for his return call. That call came much sooner than she expected.

"You're pullin' me leg, aren't you, darlin'?" O'Hara asked. "Not that I care, mind you. It's just that I like to know."

Ali solemnly assured him that she was doing no such thing and asked what he'd learned.

"Well, I knew I'd heard something about Evan Michael Todd recently, but I couldn't remember what until I checked with my editor. It seems a little barmaid named Lucy—what was her last name?" he said, as he flipped through some papers on his desk. "Danner. That's it. Lucy Danner. Anyway, little Lucy told the police that something must have happened to Todd because he didn't come to meet her after work the way he said he would. She wanted them to drag the river. She said there was something troubling him the last time she saw him, something about some man he'd met who kept asking him questions about his personal life, but Lucy didn't know the whole story. When the police didn't pay any attention to her, she brought the story to us. We checked it out, but we couldn't do anything for the girl, either. There's no story here; the poor thing just got jilted. The police say Evan Todd is alive and well and on an assignment in South Africa. But here's the interesting part. He's working for *The San Francisco Star* with a reporter named—are you listening, Ali, me love?—with a reporter named Alison Hayden.... Now what would be going on down there?"

Ali did not answer his question directly. "Tim, you might suggest to the police or Scotland Yard, whoever is handling it, that they compare Evan's prints to any John Does they happen to have in the morgue."

"Seriously, love?"

"Very. And I would appreciate it if you didn't tell them where you heard it. Not yet."

"All right," O'Hara sighed. "I'll do it, and I won't ask any questions because I know you won't be giving any answers to them. But when you can, you will remember your old friends, won't you, darlin'?"

"Never forget 'em, Tim."

She hung up and turned to Mantizima. She didn't have to tell him what she learned, her face did that.

"Who would have thought it? We all overlooked him."

"Only because he acts so incredibly stupid. But that's bothered me all along, I just didn't do anything about it. He is not the man my editor described to me. He's too tall, too thin, not nearly shy enough. He obviously hasn't led Evan Todd's life. But more importantly, Elliott would never have hired someone so obnoxiously dumb. This man must have really underestimated Evan Todd's gentleness."

"He's pretending to be a man he didn't understand."

"Do you think...?" Ali mused. "Now I know Rune Aykroyd believed the American reporter carrying this out and the physicist who planned the whole thing to be two different people, but do you think that—"

"That they are one-and-the-same? It's very possible. I always thought Rune might be wrong about that. I'm sure the man who could think of all of this wouldn't leave it to someone else to carry out."

"Terrific," Ali muttered. "What in hell have we gotten into? We can't afford to make his mistake. We can't underestimate him, Terry. He's a whole lot smarter than we've believed. Much smarter, much craftier, much more ruthless or he wouldn't have gotten even this far."

Mantizima nodded thoughtfully. They were both frightened by the prospect of tangling with this man, perhaps more frightened than they could admit to themselves. But they were also exhilarated by the prospect of finding a window in a room believed to be without doors.

They plotted out the rudiments of a working plan, now that they had some idea of where they were going. Mantizima called his brother-in-law, who put him in touch with a man who worked as a cleaner at Ali's hotel. It was that man's day off and he agreed to loan Mantizima both his passkey and uniform so he could search "Evan's" room. Ali called "Evan" and arranged to meet in their hotel bar on the pretext of reviewing the proofs of the pictures he'd shot so far. Were he really a competent photo-journalist, he might have taken offense at her assumption of authority, but he seemed eager to show off his work.

When they parted at the employees' entrance of the hotel, Mantizima reminded Ali that she had to give him the time he needed.

"Forty minutes," he said. "Thirty at the very least. I'll call you later from my mother's."

Ali tried hard to give Mantizima that time, but she wasn't able to.

"What do you think?" "Evan" had asked of the proofs moments before.

"Great," Ali had said with enthusiasm, while thinking, average, with none.

But her deliberate stalling was making him restless, and flattery only partly assuaged it.

"Look, Ali," he said after a while. "Why don't you drink up? I have some other things to do tonight."

Ali didn't dare look at her watch, but she was sure that they had spent less than twenty minutes in that bar.

"I'm not finished," she said, panic rising in her throat. "They're so good. I don't want to miss any."

"Evan" seemed to glow with the praise, but for the first time, she noticed there was a hint of mockery in his smile. How stupid he must think I am! she thought angrily.

And still he wouldn't allow himself to be kept there.

"Well, there's a simple solution," he said, rising. "You stay here and finish them. Have another drink on me. You can shove them under my door later."

"No!" she shouted, then forced herself to calm down. "No, I'll go with you. I'll finish them in my room."

Twenty minutes. Terry wouldn't be finished yet, she thought. Her whole body trembled as they crossed the lobby. Her legs barely carried her. At one point, she dropped the proofsheets on the floor in a clumsy, desperate attempt to gain time, but "Evan" scooped them up quickly with his ever-attractive agility.

Her heart beat so loudly in the elevator that she was sure he must have heard it, even though he made no sign of it. Once they reached their floor, she tried to hook him into every feeble form of conversation she could devise, stopping every couple of feet, as if she couldn't walk and talk at the same time. She only ceased that ploy when she saw he was becoming irritated with her; she didn't want to inflate that irritation into suspicion.

176

Despite her best efforts, they reached the door of "Evan's" room only a few minutes after they left the bar. He said good night, unlocked his door and closed it behind him, leaving her alone in the hall.

She waited there for what seemed like an eternity. Her heart wasn't pounding now—it seemed to have stopped. She couldn't even hear herself breathing. This, she thought, must be what it feels like to be dead. She continued to stand there, as still as it is possible for any living body to be, waiting, listening for any sound of a struggle beyond the door. As soon as she heard it, she vowed, she was going to scream that hotel down!

It never came. She heard nothing, not even the sounds of "Evan's" movements. After a while, she wearily wandered down the hall towards her own room, exhausted enough to have lived ten years in those three minutes.

With her mind still taken up by what might have happened in the room across the hall, she unconsciously opened the door to her own room. But for the hall light spilling in through the open doorway, it was pitch black. Absently, she groped at the wall for the light switch, when suddenly the darkness seemed to strike her as a solid mass, a frightening substance, terrifying because it was not supposed to be there. Knowing she would return after dark, she had put a light on before leaving the room earlier in the day. Her breath caught in a final gasp, and in the stillness that followed she could feel the presence of another person in the room. She was frozen in terror. In that instant she debated whether to take the brave course and throw on the light or to back out of the door and run like hell.

She never got to make that choice.

A man's hand suddenly clasped over her mouth, trapping a stillborn scream in her throat. His arm coiled around her waist, his fingers pressed into the spaces between her ribs. Suddenly stripped of all personal power, her energy for action was channeled into her mind and emotions, producing thoughts and feelings of rapid and unparalleled clarity. She was intensely aware of the strength in this man's body, of the

177

tautness of the muscles pressed into her spine, of his personal power and the deliberate control his hands seemed to need to exercise to remain where they were. She had never been so frightened in her life, never so sure she was about to die, but neither had she ever felt so vividly alive. And she hungered for some final affirmation of that life from a living force as great as her own, as great, perhaps, as that of the stranger who held her.

Using their two bodies as one, he leaned against the still open door until it clicked shut. Then, taking his hand from her mouth, he flipped on the light. Inexplicably, she shut her eyes in the same instant, choosing to stay in the place the darkness gave her.

But she had to know. She opened her eyes and turned within the circle of his arms until she saw the face of her attacker.

It was Terry Mantizima.

She buried her face in his chest and sighed softly, in relief for the safety the light brought...and regret for the things it took away.

After a moment he lifted her chin and brushed the surface of her face with his fingertips. As his hand brushed over her mouth, her lips trembled under his touch.

"I apologize for frightening you, Ali," he said softly, "but I couldn't let you scream. If they ever found me here...."

She nodded her understanding and let her head fall back against his chest, where it seemed to belong. But even as she did it, she allowed a form of self-destruction that is peculiar to humans, the kind that mascarades as self-preservation, to come between them. Her conscious thought—the excuse, the lie—was of the penalty and the indignities she would face if he were found there; the thought she hid from herself was: this is a man I couldn't walk away from.

His hands awkwardly fell to his sides as she eased herself out of his arms, and he angrily thrust them into his pockets to keep them still. He watched her back as she walked away, studying the posture that seemed both confident and unsure at the same time. She came to stand before the dresser mirror, and he positioned himself so that he could catch her eyes in it if she ever looked up.

"Did you find anything?" she asked, as she might have a stranger.

"Enough. I took a glass he'd used. I'll give it to a policeman I know to check his fingerprints so we can find out who he really is. But what's interesting is that he had reports on a lot of people, including you and the real Evan Todd, from both private detectives and his personal observation. There isn't any legitimate reason why he should have had those."

"So there isn't any doubt," she said, as she looked up and was startled to find his eyes meeting hers in the mirror. "About 'Evan,'or whoever he is, I mean."

He paused for a moment, then said with great deliberation, "For me, there isn't any doubt...about anything."

She held his eyes in the mirror, not hiding what she felt, but not acting on it, either. What's wrong with me? she asked herself. Why was she hesitating? She had never shied away from risks in the course of her work. She'd taken more chances than she could count over the years, many in life-threatening situations. But personal risks were different. They scared her too much. She'd always run away from them. And none had ever frightened her as much as this one because she'd never wanted anything so much.

His eyes remained fixed on hers. He did not mask his desire, but neither did he attempt to influence her with it. He had made his decision; the choice now rested with her.

Suddenly, she turned away from the mirror and walked past him towards the door. He was sure she was

179

going to walk out of this room and out of his life. But she stopped at the door.

Sometimes, in this life, she decided in that moment, you have to take what you want and let the consequences be damned.

She reached up and slid the deadbolt closed.

Slowly, he approached her from behind. He wrapped his arm around her, as he had when she entered the room. He held it there for a moment, allowing them both to recapture what they had felt in that first encounter, then, taking a right that was not his then but was now, moved his hand over her breast. He felt it grow hard under his hand, and in the same instant heard her moan softly.

She turned in his arms, grasping desperately, and pulled his mouth down to hers, taking his hungry kiss. Their tongues entered each other's body, meeting, exploring, as a prelude to the joining that was to follow.

He lifted her up, but did not carry her to the bed; instead, he lowered her onto the floor. They couldn't wait as long as it would take to cross the room. They swiftly undressed each other. There was an urgent neediness in their actions, as if they believed that intensity that great could not be prolonged much longer, it had to break.

He explored every crevice of her body with his hands and with his mouth, discovering, with the exciting newness of the first time, a much greater intimacy than first-time lovers are supposed to achieve. It was as if they had known each other all their lives, but just now met; as if they had consciously wanted each other all those years, but just learned how vast that acknowledged desire was.

With each touch, every nerve in her body cried out in a pleasurable agony. They screamed for mercy. No greater ecstacy could be endured, she knew. But instead of begging him to stop, she hoped it would go on forever.

His excitement was just as great, but he couldn't allow himself to finish it. Not yet. His need for her was so enormous, so seemingly insatiable, that he lingered over each movement, savored each sensation, until there was only one thing left for them to experience.

Then he parted her legs and entered her body.

She trembled at that first touch and thought that no greater feeling could possibly exist. He had filled her, physically and emotionally, took everything she had, and demanded more. Driving harder and harder, reaching and reaching, they soared together to unchartered heights.

This was the celebration of existence they had both unknowingly yearned for all of their lives, the affirmation she had sought from what she believed to be the stranger at the door, the answer to all of the tumultuous mysteries life had thrown in their paths. This was what she had wanted to experience just once before she died, but now that she had, dying was the last thing on her mind.

Life was all there was. Life, in its most vital and ultimate sense. They continued to clutch at that level of living, grasping for everything in their reach until they arrived together in climax at the state when everything that is, was theirs.

Then they languished together as one in that unsurpassed feeling of invincibility, in the quiet sense of forever that has to be the closest man will ever come to immortality.

CHAPTER FIFTEEN
SEPTEMBER 17, 1979

The early morning sunlight streamed in through the thin white drapes at the window, waking Ali with its gentle touch. She stirred, then threw the sheet covering her body aside, allowing the warmth to fuse into her body until she felt one with its pure, eternal energy. She moved in a lazy, languid stretch and rolled over onto her side, allowing her hand to fall on the sheet where Mantizima had been. He was gone from her bed now, but his presence was still with her, still a part of her.

She noticed a note written on hotel stationery propped up on his pillow. It was written in his unmistakably bold, clear print, but the lines were uneven, as if he had written it in the dark. It read:

Ali— Thought it would be better for both of us if I left before the hotel awoke. I've gone back to my mother's house. Call me as soon as you are free.

Terry

The note was so like him. To-the-point, business-like, almost impersonal. But there was a postscript on it that made her flush with satisfaction. It said:

P.S. You smile in your sleep.

She was smiling now, she knew. She could do nothing but smile. She was sure she was going to break out in inexplicable grins at odd times throughout the day every time her mind drifted back to last night. She walked to the window and threw the drapes aside, allowing her body to drink in the early morning sunlight and silence. She had never felt so happy, so free, never so proud of an accomplishment.

Then, like a heavy cloud covering her sunshine, there was a knock on the door.

She suddenly felt cold and very frightened and she did not move to answer it. She couldn't. The police, she thought. It had to be. Who else would knock on her door at that hour? She did not react at all until she heard the second knock. Then she picked up her robe and wrapped it around herself, but slowly, as if she were prolonging the inevitable. But she considered everything while she did it, and by the time she fastened the sash with a sharp, decisive tug, she was much stronger again. She was not afraid anymore because she was armed with the knowledge that she had something no one could take away from her.

It was worth it, she decided. Whatever they did to her, whatever indignity they imposed on her, it was worth it. She pulled the door open.

But it wasn't the police. It was worse than that. It was "Evan."

"Hi," he said, bouncing into the room. "Hope I didn't wake you. Had some things I forgot to tell you last night."

He noticed her bed had been used by two people the night before and, like a little boy sneaking a look at a dirty magazine, he stifled a smutty smile. He threw a quick glance at the open bathroom door to see if he might learn who the man was, but no such luck.

"What is it?" she asked evenly.

She stood at the door, her hand tightly grasping the knob, until she realized that she was afraid to be alone with him with the door closed. She chided herself with being foolish. She'd been alone with him many times. It was not

her he was planning to destroy. But her mind drifted back to that night in the alley and the boy he might have paid to beat her up. She shut the door, but she walked across the room and stood leaning against the wall, keeping several yards and a little bit of running time between them.

"Oh, yeah, I just wanted to tell you that I'm almost finished here in Jo'burg, so I'm flying to Cape Town in a few days. Thought I'd spend a day in Durban, then a day or two in Kruger National Park before heading back to London."

"Why?" she asked, hoping her voice wasn't trembling too much.

"Why not? You said on the plane coming down here that there was no reason why we had to work together all the time. Besides, I have to get to those places eventually, and I'm almost finished here. Should have been done days ago, but you work slowly. Your paper must have some budget."

"Yes, well, this has been somewhat of a working vacation for me," Ali said absently, as she tried to decide the best course of action to take.

"Well, it wasn't supposed to be for me, and I have other assignments to think about...."

He continued on, telling her about his plans after he finished in South Africa. She had to admit, it would have sounded very convincing if she didn't know better. Exactly what the real Evan Michael Todd would probably be doing. Perhaps, she thought, this man stole a glance at Evan Todd's itinerary before he.... She had a sudden image of the body drawers in London's morgue, one of which was almost certain to have contained the remains of the real Evan Todd. What a price he had paid to be part of this man's destiny.

She studied him as he spoke, wondering how she could have been such a fool. She had been so quick to accept him as a simpleton, and only when the truth became apparent could she see which one of them was actually simple. Of course, she had noticed the difference between him and what she had known of Evan Michael Todd; she noticed his perceptiveness and his occasional bursts of incisive reasoning and never saw his reputed moodiness and temperment, but

183

she never pursued those observations. Looking at him now, however, she could see quite clearly where the lines of the mask ended and the real man began. She saw his cunning and the pride he took in fooling everyone and the contempt he felt for fools, and she was sick because she knew those things had been there all along.

Suddenly, while she still felt a good dose of healthy caution, she wasn't afraid of him any longer. She was angry and quite determined to make him pay, somehow, not just for the things he planned to do, but for the person he was.

I may not be as quick as you are, she thought, but you'd better keep looking over your shoulder, my friend, because I'm going to be right behind you.

"Well, I know you're going to be busy in the next few days, and you probably won't get to Cape Town till after I'm gone, so I guess I'll just say good-by right now," "Evan" said, extending his hand. "It was nice working with you. Perhaps we can do it again sometime."

"Yes," Ali said cryptically, taking his hand, even though she couldn't stand the touch of it. "Let's make sure we get together again."

"So they spent the night together," Logan said in response to Kloff's stiff-lipped report. "And in the hotel. That Terry sure has balls. I guess our little Alison could tell us exactly what they look like.... You really have to wonder."

"How could she do it?" Kloff asked.

"How could she do it with him when she could have had me?" Logan said indignantly, then added, "But she was too old for me anyway."

Kloff attributed that statement to sour grapes since, from what he'd observed of Logan, his grandmother wouldn't be too old for him if she were the best he could do on a given night.

"I tried to reach you last night, but you weren't in," Kloff continued. "So I just had your orders followed to the letter. In the future, perhaps you should leave a number where— "

"What did you need me for?"

"Neil, haven't you been listening to me? I told you, they slept together. If you want to arrest them, we have to get there before the evidence is destroyed."

"You mean before they change the sheets."

"Uh, yes," Kloff said uncomfortably, thinking it was easier to enforce the law if you didn't allow the details to become too graphic in your mind.

Logan giggled. Had it been later in the day, Kloff would have wondered whether Logan had had a few too many at lunch, but since it was only an hour after breakfast, he ignored the irritating sound.

"What do you want me to do about it, should it happen in the future?" Kloff asked.

"Do? I don't want you to do anything. I certainly don't want them arrested. Why should you care that they're screwing each other?"

"The man is a Bantu!"

"So what? Haven't you ever had your maid? Or, better yet, your maid's teenage daughter?"

"Certainly not."

"Then you're the only white man in South Africa that hasn't. I bet your wife's been laid by your gardener a dozen times."

Kloff reached out and lifted Logan out of his chair by his tie.

"You stupid *saltprie!* I could kill you for that! My wife does not—"

"All right, Pieter!" Logan shouted, while suspended from his tie. "I'm sorry. I didn't mean it."

Slightly assuaged, Kloff lowered Logan back to his chair, but whatever working rapport they might have had was shattered.

"I'm sorry," Logan repeated. "I was only making a point. But you invite it. You really are so pure. You believe it all, don't you?"

"I don't know what you mean. What do I believe?"

185

"All of the official shit they shove down our throats from the time we can walk. White supremacy. Separate but equal. Apartheid ordained by God. All of it. You swallow it all."

Kloff was shocked by so bold an attack from Logan on principles he'd never considered challenging. Part of him wanted to terminate that conversation immediately, but in a small part of his mind, he grasped that he was being given a rare glimpse into the essence of a man he'd worked beside for years but never really knew.

"Yes, of course, I believe it. That's the law I've sworn to uphold. I could not have made that commitment to something I didn't believe."

"I always knew you were a twit, but I never realized how much of one. Don't you know that the things we say are just to justify the things we do? We do all right by them, remember. We have an enormous, cheap labor force, which, incidently, I don't see you refusing. How many people in your position without inherited wealth, in other parts of the world do you think have as many servants as you do? Or any, for that matter? But more importantly, we hold power over them. We have them by the throat! And we love it. But you don't believe that. Oh, no, you have principles."

"And you don't?" Kloff asked tensely.

"Only one—might makes right."

"And what will you do, Neil, if that might is ever on the other foot?"

"You mean if the Bantu, that great sleeping giant, awakes?"

Kloff nodded.

"Don't make any mistake about that, old chap. It isn't a question of "if," but "when." It's going to happen someday, and when it does, I'll do what every other South African does. Beg those bleeding hearts in the U.N. for help, for leniency, for time to adjust, when in my heart I'll know it was a damn good show while it lasted."

"I couldn't do this job if I thought like you," Kloff said.

"Well, then, the joke's on you, mate. Because when we hang, you're going to swing right along with us in spite of your bloody principles."

Kloff nodded sadly. Suddenly he felt old and very tired.

"Cape Town?" Mantizima asked.

"So he said," Ali answered. "Supposedly flying down in a few days. Haven't had a chance to check on his plans yet."

"He's making his move. This is what I have been waiting for."

"I'm glad you're so thrilled."

"Aren't you?" Mantizima asked.

She shrugged. "It was inevitable, I suppose. That he'd want to lose me, I mean. Too much to hope that he'd be stupid enough to just lead us to the bomb. But it's gonna be damn hard to catch him at this."

Mantizima studied her for a moment. "You sound discouraged."

"Just realistic. I've chased people to the ends of the earth before. I know how hard it can be. Too many places to hide. And this bastard, whoever he is, is as slippery as an eel."

"As to the "whoever he is," I'm working on that. I gave his glass to my friend, Kenny—he's a policeman—to do whatever they do with fingerprints. It may take him a while. He'll have to give his superiors some story about why he wants those prints run without making them suspicious, but Kenny's creative. He'll think of something. Regarding the rest of it, don't worry, I have an idea."

Ali snorted. "An idea? Terry, this man is a dangerous terrorist. It's going to take more than ideas to trap him. How, for instance, are we—"

Mantizima put his fingers over her mouth to stop her from speaking and smiled. Then he lifted his fingers and gave her a gentle kiss.

"Trust me," he said. "We'll discuss it later."

"But—"

"Later."

He took her hand and led her upstairs to his bedroom. For a short time the man calling himself Evan Michael Todd and all the problems he'd brought into their lives went away.

She awoke some time later alone in his bed. She felt rested and rejuvinated again, and once again she was smiling. This man does amazing things to me, she thought, and felt a slight shiver go through her whole body as she remembered just a few of those things.

A moment later, Mantizima entered the room, fully dressed, carrying a pad and pen, and apparently quite preoccupied.

"You're never here when I wake up," Ali chided.

"Yes, well, at the risk of being unromantic," he said while planting a light kiss on her forehead, "that's something you're just going to have to learn to live with. I never sleep much. Hate it, actually, particularly when I'm restless and have things to do."

"And have you been doing things?" Ali asked.

"A great many of them."

He lifted his eyebrows in a look of mock, almost comical intrigue. Ali knew he was joking, but grasped, from the nature of the joke, how much he was actually enjoying himself and how difficult relative inactivity must have been for him.

He sat on the bed and Ali curled up next to him.

"Now that your desires have been satisfied," she said, "are you prepared to answer some of my difficult questions?"

"Fire away."

"How are we going to pull this off?"

"I thought you said you were going to ask something difficult," Mantizima said. "That's easy. We're going to follow him."

Ali laughed and said, "Terry, you don't know what you are talking about. Have you ever tried to follow anyone?"

"I've never had the need to, but I have—"

"Let me tell you what it's like cause I've followed plenty. Many people have reason to avoid reporters. It's hard enough when you don't care if you are spotted. All kinds of things force the mission to be aborted," she said, matching his comic intrigue. "Red lights, sudden turns, getting cut off by slow drivers. If you have to stay hidden—well, if you're not a professional, it's probably impossible."

Mantizima was undaunted., "It may interest you to know, my darling, that I've learned a thing or two in my job, also."

"About following people?" Ali asked, unable to believe that.

"...In a manner of speaking. Now, if you have no more questions, I have a few things to discuss with you. I have a couple of little jobs for you to do, if you don't mind."

Ali smiled and shook her head. She still didn't understand anything, but his confidence was becoming infectious.

"First," Mantizima said, "I'd like you to rent a car. I'll pay for it, but it will be easier for you to get."

"The paper will pay for it."

"Better still. Next," he said, holding his pad between them, "I want you to buy a few things for me. Again," he sighed, "it will be easier for you to get these things without raising suspicions."

Ali looked the list over. The words meant nothing to her, but his enthusiasm had won her over.

"And then, finally, we have to find someone who can gain our mystery man's confidence and perhaps stay close to him."

"In the time we have?" Ali demanded. "Impossible. He doesn't know anyone here apart from the people we've interviewed and those we met on the plane coming—"

Suddenly, she remembered an image of "Evan" looking like a lovesick calf.

"On second thought," she said, "that just might be possible after all."

CHAPTER SIXTEEN

SEPTEMBER 18, 1979

Pieter Kloff entered Logan's office just as Logan was shoving a liquor bottle into a desk drawer. Maybe I'd drink, too, if they'd put the burden of this investigation on my shoulders, Kloff thought generously. But he still didn't like it. The stakes were just too high. If Logan couldn't keep his wits, who knew when they would all be blown to kingdom-come?

"Well?" Logan asked. "Did you have something to say or did you just come in here to gape?"

"Sorry," Kloff said. "My mind was wandering. I have some things to report."

It was strange, Kloff thought. He had always known, and reluctantly accepted, that Neil was destined for authority and had always assumed that Logan would handle it well, with too much arrogance, perhaps, but with competence. He wasn't, however. Oh, the arrogance was there, along with an equal measure of rudeness, but the competence that Rune Aykroyd had brought to the job was clearly missing in his successor. And the strain of trying to fill Aykroyd's shoes, as well as, perhaps, an overabundance of liquor, were starting to ravage Logan's handsome, young face.

"Still wandering?" Logan asked after a moment.

"Collecting my thoughts. It's...odd," Kloff said hesitantly. "Mantizima went to visit a man who teaches at a Black college. An engineering professor. And he came away a couple of hours later carrying an armload of books."

190

"So? Didn't you tell me he was an engineer in the States? Terry, I mean."

Kloff nodded.

"Then I don't understand why you're concerned."

"I haven't finished. The woman, Hayden, went to visit a girl first thing this morning. Named...." Kloff paused to consult his notes. "Named Trudi Schmidt. West German national on a visitors' visa. The local police say Schmidt is a call girl. And she came here on the same plane with Hayden and Mantizima. I took the precaution of having their calls monitored. She had quite a job tracking the girl down. It seemed very important to her."

"So? Hayden's a reporter. She wanted to interview the girl."

"Alison Hayden is a foreign correspondent. She doesn't write stories on hookers. And that's not all. She spent the remainder of the day on a strange sort of shopping spree."

"I don't see anything strange about that. All women love to shop."

Kloff didn't argue that point, he just continued. "What she bought were electronic parts."

Logan looked up, surprised. "Actually?" he laughed. "That's wonderful."

Kloff did not follow Logan's logic and he didn't understand what there was to laugh about. He felt as if he had just heard the punch line of a joke and, without knowing the rest of it, couldn't find it funny. But he sensed that this was a joke only Logan was privy to.

"Well, you see what that means, don't you?" Logan demanded. "They *are* involved in this. They're building something related to that bomb."

"That's what it could mean, Neil. But there are other possible explanations."

"Such as what?"

"I...don't know. But this is too simple, too easy. Neither of them are stupid enough to trap themselves like this. Mantizima owns an engineering firm. If he wanted the parts to build a nuclear bomb, he'd have ways to buy them so that they were untraceable. He wouldn't send his...girlfriend out to retail stores for them. There has to be another explanation.... I just wish I could understand...."

Logan studied Kloff for a moment, as if trying to decide what approach to take.

"You've done good work here, Pieter, and I intend to make sure Kroonhof knows it. But don't muck it up now by overestimating this Bantu. I know he's involved. Don't you see— he's our man. He's the one behind all this. I knew it, I always knew it! Rune must have known it, too. That's why he was being friendly with him. That's the only explanation, knowing Rune. He was giving Mantizima the opportunity to trap himself, just as I am. And I want it to continue."

"But—"

"No buts. That is an order. I want them watched constantly. By as many men as you need to get the job done. I want every policeman in this area, in the whole country, if need be, in every branch to know who they are. But I don't want them approached or molested in any way. If they are speeding, I don't want them stopped; if they kill someone, I don't want them apprehended. Not until I'm ready to reel them in. Now, if you have any problems with this, Pieter, I want to know now. You're not leaving here until I know I have your full cooperation."

"You've already ordered me to cooperate. What more do you want?"

"I want your understanding and agreement. Do I have it?"

Kloff nodded his understanding; his agreement, he thought, was not so easily given.

It was late afternoon when Ali wove her way through the crowded Johannesburg streets. It had been a long day and she was tired. The eyes behind her sunglasses were glassy with fatigue, but they were also bright with excitement. She was proud of her successes.

When she went to the first electronic store, she was not sure what approach she should take. She wasn't sure how

192

common it was to buy those things and whether she would arouse any suspicions by doing so. But, as luck would have it, she did not have to be too inventive. A private boys school had just given its students a building assignment for a science project. Given that they were all of the computer age, most of the students apparently chose to build electronic projects. In every store she found herself in the company of either those boys or their mothers. So she simply told the clerks that she was buying those things for her son and no one questioned her.

She was even more pleased by the time she spent with Trudi Schmidt. Mantizima had wanted to be the one to talk to Trudi, but Ali had insisted on doing it herself. "In her line of work," Ali had argued, "she can't really like men. You'd be going in with a disadvantage. I think a woman will have a much better chance with her."

She was not as confident when she arrived at Trudi's apartment. The girl seemed to take an instant dislike to Ali, and, while she agreed to listen to what Ali had to say, her attitude made it clear that the stone walls were firmly in place.

Ali had already decided that she had to be fairly honest with Trudi, but as she spoke she found herself telling a more complete story than she had planned. She told her everything, leaving nothing out. Trudi listened to Ali as she had promised, but she never waivered from her defiant posture. She only interrupted once.

"Evan?" she said, shaking her head. "I should have known he was too good to be true."

Ali brought the story up to the present and made her appeal for Trudi's help.

"We want...that is, Terry and I hoped that somehow you could get yourself invited to go along with him wherever he's going. We need to have someone who can get close to him."

"And you just happened to choose me!" Trudi spat out angrily. "I wonder why."

Ali did not respond.

"Why don't you go?" Trudi demanded.

"Because he wouldn't ask me."

"Then you came to the right place, but you came for the wrong reason. You don't need me to get invited on his trip, you need me to teach you how to. And I can do it. I know every trick, if you'll excuse the expression, in the book when it comes to men. And I'll be glad to share that knowledge with one of my 'sisters.' Of course, you are getting a little old for this profession, but some men do have a strange interest in their mothers, don't they?"

"Am I right in assuming you're refusing?"

"Of course I am. Do I strike you as insane? I could get killed doing that."

The telephone rang. Both women looked at it, startled by the intrusive sound, then Ali turned back to Trudi.

"And you obviously have so much to live for, don't you?"

Trudi steamed in angry silence until the ringing stopped.

"Get out!" she said then.

"Look, I'm sorry. I didn't mean to offend you. I didn't come here to judge you, I came to ask for your help."

"There's nothing in it for me," Trudi said.

"There certainly is. I'm not asking you to do this for me or any of the people that might be affected by it. I'm asking you to do it for yourself because it's also in your interest."

Trudi obviously did not believe that.

"These people are terrorists," Ali continued. "And very shortly, they will have a horrible weapon at their disposal. There won't be any stopping them. Do you want to live in a world that they run?"

"Politics mean nothing to me. I can get by anywhere. Every society needs hookers," she said, then added as an after thought, "few, however, need reporters."

Ali lowered her head in defeat. She wished now that she had let Mantizima come instead. He probably would have done better than she was doing; he certainly couldn't have done worse.

"You're so smug, so superior," Trudi said, while pacing in angry frustration in front of Ali's chair, "so sure I've picked the easy life."

Ali looked up in surprise, but not in anger. Even though Trudi was doing her best to insult her, Ali did not take offense from her remarks. She suddenly felt as if she had stepped back, out of the picture, and was able to view both Trudi and herself in a detached, observant manner. She was struck, not so much by the girl's anger, but by her need to express it. For the first time since she had arrived there, she was able to pierce through both her preconceived image of a call girl and the facade Trudi projected on the plane, to reach the real person behind them, and the real pain she felt.

"Easy? No, I don't think your life is easy at all," Ali said, then, playing a hunch, added, "I just think that, for you, the alternative is so much harder.... Why did you come here? To South Africa, I mean."

"Why not?" Trudi said, a little uncomfortably. "I'd never been here."

Ali shook her head. "Nope. I don't think so," she said on a hunch.

"Look, Miss Hayden," Trudi said nervously, "I've listened to everything you had to say, and I don't really want to hear any more. I'm sorry if I was rude to you, but I really think you'd better leave now."

Ali ignored that request as if she had never heard it. "What did you want to be? When you were younger, I mean. What did you want to do with your life? You couldn't have intended to do this."

"Please, Miss Hayden. I've had enough men ask me 'What's a nice girl like you....'Believe me, there isn't an answer."

"Sure there is," Ali pursued. "What is a nice girl like you doing in a life like this? You must have wanted something else. No little girl dreams of growing up to be a hooker."

"Someone should tell little girls not to dream at all," Trudi said absently, then caught herself and added, "I've been very patient with you, Miss Hayden, but I really think—"

Ali did not realize it, but she had taken on the same aggressive manner that she normally displayed in interviews. And she was just as ruthless in her determination to force Trudi to talk to her.

"I'll leave when you answer me," she bargained. "What did you want—"

"All right.... I wanted to be an actress."

"Then why don't you?" Ali exclaimed, moved by the rush of her own success. "You're young, pretty. I don't know if you're talented, but—"

"Oh, I'm talented, all right," Trudi said bitterly. "Just ask any of my satisfied customers whether I'm a good actress or not. But I couldn't do it. You see, I've been doing it too long. Acting, lying—it's the same thing to me now."

"There must be something else you'd like to do. Something that wouldn't tear you apart like this."

Trudi had a sudden image of that night in the bookstore, the evening she met Evan. She remembered the dream she had allowed to grow in her mind that night, and she remembered the way that dream had hurt her.

"Nothing," she said, slamming the door on her recollection. "There's nothing at all."

Emotionally spent, both women sat in silence, not speaking, not even looking at each other. Finally, Ali broke the spell.

"You know—I hate to say it—but you and I are a lot alike."

"Really?" Trudi asked. "I would have said you were very discriminating."

She had meant it as yet another insult, but something had happened between them that made that impossible. It came out as a joke to be shared by confidantes. That was the way Ali took it.

"Seriously. The particulars of our lives are very different, but in one way we're both alike. To varying degrees, we're both afraid."

Trudi looked at Ali, wanting to deny it, but unable to do anything but nod in understanding.

"Vulnerable, that's what we are," Ali continued. "Even though we don't let anyone see that. Afraid of being hurt. Of failing."

"You can't fail if you don't try," Trudi said softly, to someone who would understand.

"Can't succeed, either. At least, that's what people tell me. Lately, I've been wondering whether they're right. It seems as if they have something we don't, that they derive something from finding out what they are made of."

"What happens to them, I wonder, if they find they are not made of anything, that there's nothing there?"

"Maybe the trying makes that impossible, proves there is something."

Ali waited for a moment, but Trudi did not respond. She rose reluctantly.

"I'll leave now...Trudi. Sorry.... Well, good-by."

Ali felt sadly inadequate. The words just didn't say anything, but maybe, she thought, too much had been said already. She walked to the door, but Trudi's voice stopped her before she reached it.

"What would I have to do? About Evan, I mean. What would you want me to do?"

Yes, she did okay, Ali thought as she drove back to Mantizima's house with the electronic parts. She'd had a profitable day. She was so lost in thought as she drove, she never noticed that a car had been following her for hours, nor the driver, Rahmire Jones.

The telephone on Wade Petri's desk rang just as he was leaving his office for the day.

"Damn!" he muttered. "What is it now?"

He really couldn't complain. It was early, well within the official Haagen-Aykroyd business day, but he had reasons for wanting to slip out now. The baby was due any day and Rina was becoming a whining bitch. That should be reason for avoiding home, but he had found that if he paid her extra attention by coming home early and listening to her complaints first thing, he could spend the rest of the evening in relative peace; whereas, if he did not, he had to spend hours listening to a graphic description of every ache and pain she felt. As if it were his fault.

"Yes?" he demanded into the phone.

His secretary informed him that a Mr. White was on the line who wouldn't state his business except to say that it was very important.

Petri hesitated for a moment. Important to whom? he thought, then finally agreed to get it over with. White would probably just keep calling if he didn't. As it turned out, however, the call was of great importance to Petri. Jason White was a businessman, he said, whose time was money; he would get right to the point.

His voice was young, Petri thought as he listened to that introduction, too young for the position he implied he held. But it also had the note of authority and the sort of brusque confidence that Petri always admired in natural leaders, which he wished he could emulate himself. That alone won his attention.

"I've bought a mine," White said with succinct caution, seemingly wary of anyone who might be listening. "A small mine. Cheap. The owners believed it to be played out, but my geologist thinks differently."

Petri's pulse quickened. He'd always wanted to get in on the ground floor of a dramatic find. Like many South Africans, gold fever was an infection he had never become immune to.

White went on to explain that he didn't have much of a mining background himself, and he had too many other interests to allow him to get involved in the daily workings of a mine. So he was looking for a partner—an equal partner—who could manage the company in exchange for his share.

"I've been watching you, Petri," White said. "For a long time. I think you might just be the man I need. Could we get together today to talk it over?"

Talk it over? Petri would have agreed right then, without knowing another thing. It was an answer to his prayers. But he didn't want to destroy the chance by being too eager. Yes, he told White, after some manufactured consideration time, he would be glad to get together to talk it over.

Petri had expected to go to White's office, but White insisted on meeting at the site in an hour. As he drove out to it, Petri did consider that a strange meeting place. He would have to see it, of course, before they concluded their agreement, but he considered it unusual to view it at their first meeting and at five o'clock in the afternoon. He dismissed that as miners' paranoia, however. Everyone worried about word getting out before announcing a strike. Besides, with a deal like this, he couldn't allow trivialities to get in the way. It was perfect, everything he'd always wanted. He couldn't wait to tell Rina's father that he was half-owner of a mining company and that he'd accomplished it on his own.

He noticed a 'For Sale' sign on the perimeter of the property as he approached it and thought that White must have just acquired it and not had time to remove the sign. Or perhaps he didn't want anyone to know the mine had been bought. Of course, he thought, that was it. White was a sharp operator, all right; he was going to be proud to be in partnership with him.

Petri parked his car and pulled a slip of paper out of his pocket that contained White's directions to their meeting place. He was obviously not there yet, at least there wasn't another car in sight, but that would give Petri a chance to look around a little. He thought again about the strangeness of the meeting place, but only because he was not dressed for climbing over rocks.

He found the meeting place all right, a little valley near the entrance to the shaft, and waited. For all his thoughts about looking around, he just stood there; he really was not prepared for any serious investigation. He waited and waited, not impatiently, because his mind was filled by a dream come true.

He heard the sounds of someone approaching on the rocks behind him. He thought briefly that he had never heard the sound of a car approaching, but he didn't hold onto that thought. He started to turn around to greet his future partner, but he didn't turn quickly enough.

From the time the rock smashed into the back of his skull, he never felt a thing.

After dinner, Terry Mantizima spread the electronic equipment Ali had purchased out on the kitchen table. The books he had borrowed from the professor were stacked to one side, ready if he needed them, but he was reasonably sure he could accomplish his task without their help. When he had everything assembled, he paused. Only then, with his concentration momentarily broken, did he notice that his mother and Ali were standing quietly behind him.

"This is going to take some time, ladies," he said. "But it should go quicker without an audience."

"Enough said," Ali remarked sheepishly.

"Come on, Ali," Deborah said. "Why don't we take a walk while the genius is at work?"

The women walked in silence for a while, meandering through dusk-toned streets, neither seeing nor caring where they went. Ali felt certain Deborah's purpose in suggesting that walk was something other than simply killing time. She was sure Deborah had something to say to her, but waited until the other woman was ready.

"Ali, are you frightened?" Deborah finally asked.

"Not really," Ali said, lying a little. "Anxious, perhaps, but that's only because of having to wait for 'Evan' to make his move. Never have liked working on someone else's schedule."

Deborah nodded thoughtfully, digesting that statement without comment.

"But you don't have to worry, Deborah. We're not fools. We won't take any ridiculous chances."

"You're already taking a ridiculous chance. Have you forgotten those bruises you received just because they are almost healed?"

"No, but I'm really not convinced that incident was related. Particularly since I know it's 'Evan' who's behind this. He knows me, he's with me all the time, he has to know I can't hurt him."

"But you are in a position to hurt him. Why shouldn't he realize that? Because you think you've been careful? You're working in the dark, how do you even know what careful is?"

Ali did not say anything. It was true; there was no answer to it.

"If you're worrying about Terry, don't," Ali continued. "'Evan' doesn't even know him, he doesn't know anything about him. He's not in any danger."

"I am worried about him, and I'm worried about you, too. You're both in danger, and I'm not talking about just the obvious ones. There are all kinds of risks out there that you aren't even thinking about."

Deborah stopped suddenly and turned to Ali. "Ali, promise me you won't try to be a martyr. Don't think you can change this system all by yourself just by not complying with it."

"I don't think I can change it," Ali said, not really understanding. "I'm not that powerful. But I can't comply with it, either. I'm not part of it."

"You are! You must understand that. As long as you're here, the color of your skin makes you a part of it. And if you don't respect that, you'll be endangering Terry, as well as yourself.... Don't you think people can see what you are to each other?"

Ali looked shocked; she was sure they had hidden it.

"You may think you're being very private and discreet, but I can see it, and if I can, other people will. What do you think some of these stupid Boers will do to a black man who has dared to touch a white woman? What will they do to the woman who has allowed it? If you don't believe me, look around you right now. Look at the stares we're attracting, and we're two women."

Ali noticed their surroundings for the first time. Deborah was right. The people out in front of their houses were giving them a variety of looks that ranged from suspicion to amazement.

"You're so caught up with each other, you don't even notice other people, but, believe me, they will notice you. They won't respect your rights. They don't know what that means. You're two civilized people trying to live in a jungle. Promise me you'll act accordingly."

Ali nodded sadly. She had thought of her relationship with Terry as an island, removed, remote, untouchable. Partially, she didn't want to view in connection with anything else because she did not want to have to think about where it was going, but also because she wanted it to be theirs alone, out of the reach of everyone else. Now she realized that such a reality was impossible as long as one lived in a society of men, and particularly in a society such as that one. She mourned for the loss of something precious that she knew was gone forever because it never really existed, except in her mind.

With her purpose accomplished, Deborah suggested that they go back to the house. They walked in silence again, until Ali broke it.

"Deborah," she said softly, "my parents live in San Francisco. If anything happens...."

"I'll tell them," Deborah said tightly.

Ali nodded thankfully. They said nothing more about it; there was nothing more to say. Deborah simply slipped her arm around Ali, and they walked back to the house together in silent understanding.

Kloff sat alone in his office. It was late at night; everyone else had gone home for the day. But he couldn't leave until he made some sense of the problem before him. He was not a quick-witted man. He was probably, he thought, dull and plodding, but he was thorough. He didn't

202

let a thing go until it had a solution with which he could be satisfied. He picked up the pile of reports on his desk and went through them yet again, as he had for hours.

It didn't make any sense, he thought, as he ran a mental tape of the things Logan had said that afternoon. Logan had said that they shouldn't overestimate the Bantu, Mantizima. The time-honored bigotry he had been reared with accepted that for Kloff. In the next breath, however, Logan had accepted Terry Mantizima as the bomb-builder, the man they were seeking. How could he be both? How could a man that had to be discounted, by his very nature, be a man every rational person had to fear?

No, it didn't make sense.

Kloff went through the reports he'd had ordered on both Mantizima and Hayden, detailed dossiers on their entire lives. They weren't really people to him—he'd never even seen either of them—they were just names on sheets of paper. But he had learned in the course of his professional life that those names he read about generally acted in an orderly fashion. He couldn't believe that two people who had lived their lives in such an open, honest way could change that dramatically. People did change, of course, but even then, their changes were for what they considered to be logical reasons, and in logical ways. He couldn't find anything in either of those reports to support the idea that Mantizima and Hayden had altered their ways of thinking that radically.

No, he didn't believe they were guilty.

But Logan had believed it, and Logan, he thought, was much brighter, much better at these things than he was. Why had he been so willing to accept Mantizima's guilt?

Of course! Kloff grasped after a while. Neil needed a scapegoat; he was protecting his job. His future demanded that he apprehend a bomber.... But no, that wasn't right—he needed both the builder and the bomb. If he apprehended the wrong man, his job would still be in jeopardy when the right man ultimately detonated the bomb.... Perhaps he really had been overestimating Logan all these years. Maybe Logan was stupid enough to think he could scrape through this by just stalling for time.

Kloff rolled that idea over in his mind for a while. While he hadn't expected that, he had to admit the solution was a better fit than any other he could come up with. It wasn't the whole answer, he knew, but it was a good working hypothesis.

That didn't settle the problem of Mantizima, however. Even if he were an innocent man being framed by circumstance, that didn't explain his need for those electronic parts. Of course, Kloff knew, he was an engineer; he might just be building something for his own use. But the timing was just too pat to be a coincidence. And Mantizima was just a Bantu, he reminded himself, something that needed no further elaboration in his mind.

He reread the background section on Mantizima's educational accomplishments with some awe, which his own background forced him to discount. Even with that bias, he had to admit it was impressive. He was definitely an unusual Bantu, Kloff had to admit, an unusual...man. Could he possibly be a man mentally capable of the task of which he was suspected. It seemed unlikely to Kloff. But even if he were, was he morally capable of it?

Kloff sighed and shook his head. He had no answer. He hadn't solved that problem, but he was too tired to pursue it. He walked to the door and turned out his light, but he still couldn't let it go. He turned to the darkness and, prompted by centuries of deep-seated beliefs he did not dare to challenge, asked a question similar to the one the same beliefs had raised in Rune Aykroyd years ago.

"What could he be building? He's a Kaffir."

He waited, but the darkness did not respond.

CHAPTER SEVENTEEN

SEPTEMBER 19, 1979

Trudi Schmidt waited on the sidewalk outside the main entrance of Ali Hayden's hotel, just beyond the line of vision of anyone exiting. She'd been standing there, patiently prepared, for quite a while, but when the man who called himself Evan Michael Todd came out, her heart skipped a beat on the way to her throat.

That she could be so wrong.

She had always considered herself to be a good judge of people, particularly men. It was not much of an accomplishment, as achievements went, but it was something. She was so needy for them, she grasped at anything. Finding out now that she had so misjudged this man gave her an unhealthy dose of humility that adversely affected her confidence.

"Evan" started walking in her direction. In hindsight, she could see that he wasn't the man for which she had taken him. He was stronger, more capable, much more ruthless. Those things must have always been there, she thought, but were more obvious now because, believing himself to be unobserved, he was not wearing his act. He also appeared to be deep in thought at the moment and very tense. From what Ali told her, he had good reason to be.

Probably because of his own distractions, he still had not noticed her, however. There was still time to get away, she thought suddenly, to walk in the other direction and forget the whole crazy, suicidal thing. But she didn't have much self-respect, certainly none to spare, and Ali had made all too clear what walking away would mean in terms of Trudi's personal courage. The risk of living with herself afterwards almost seemed greater than the physical risks involved.

She had to do it.

Maybe she would fail, she thought, grasping still for an out. Maybe he had no more than a casual interest in her, maybe, even if he were interested, he would be smart enough to realize he should not have an audience in what he was doing.

No, she decided, she couldn't even think about failing if she was to get out of this what she needed. She had to be committed. She had to give it everything she had. Slowly, she took a step in his direction.

"Trudi?" he said, suddenly noticing her. "What are you—"

"Evan, *mein Freund!*," she said brightly. "Just the man I wanted to see. I was coming to visit you."

"Me? You were coming to see me?"

He spoke absently, with just a trace of irritability. She sensed that he wanted to get rid of her, and she feared it was not going to work.

"I wanted to thank you for that night we spent together. It was so wonderful. Just what I needed."

"Great. I'm glad you enjoyed it. I did, too. Now, I really—"

"And I wanted to apologize for the way I acted. I can't imagine what you must have thought of me. You see, I was feeling so low that night we spent together, and—"

"Don't you think I understood that? We all get like that sometimes. I was a little troubled myself that night," he said, then added with subtle calculation, "Although, you know, strictly speaking, we didn't spend the *night* together."

She blushed on cue the way she had always been able to when she thought that would work with a particular man. She looked up at him in a way that emphasized her tiny stature in relation to his greater height. She smiled, a little sweetly, a

206

little seductively. She looked so young, so innocent, and yet so ready for whatever he wanted to do to her. That look, that illusion had worked on hundreds of men, had made hundreds of men feel ten feet tall, had made hundreds of men forget they were paying for it.

"We could always correct that omission tonight," she said softly, "if you like."

It didn't show on her face, but her stomach was tied in knots. She had given it her best shot, but what if she were wrong in her calculations? What if another approach would have been better with him. Would it work? she worried.

Without even realizing he was doing it, he ran his tongue over his lips. He couldn't wait. It had worked!

"You won't have to talk me into that," he said, then remembering something, added, "But I have some things to attend to right now. Maybe—"

"Oh, I'm sorry, I didn't even think. Perhaps we should see each other tomorrow instead of today."

"No, that won't do. I'm leaving Jo'burg tomorrow."

She looked crushed. "Oh, that's too bad. I thought—that is, I'd hoped, we could see more of each other. I'd really like to. I think so much of you."

She'd laid it on too thick, she feared, much too thick. He'd never fall for it. But he did.

"Well, maybe we can work it out. If you don't have anything else to do, why don't you come with me on my errands. But you'll have to wait outside," he cautioned, then added quickly, "I've got to interview some people for my article, and they won't talk in front of a witness. How 'bout it?"

If she'd ever had any doubts about the things Ali told her, she wouldn't have any now. A photographer does not interview people. How stupid he must think I am, she thought angrily. She successfully hid that private emotion, however, as she had been doing for years.

"I'd love to!" she exclaimed. "I think your work must be so exciting. I'd like to hear more about it, although I guess we don't have much time," she added wistfully.

"If you're a good girl, we just might have more time than you think," Evan said. "Come on, we'd better get a move on. I'm running late."

A good girl! In a pig's eye, you ass! she thought contemptuously, as she shyly slipped her hand into his.

As they walked away, she felt a curious tingle throughout her whole body. It wasn't from his touch, she was sure; he made her sick. It was strange, she thought, it felt like pride. But how could she be proud of doing the things she'd been ashamed of for years? She shrugged and ceased probing it. It did not matter what the feeling was or what caused it. What mattered was that it felt so good.

Ali pressed her face to the window of her room, trying to get an angle that would allow her to watch Trudi and "Evan" in the street below. When she checked in, she had complained about having to take a front room—the traffic noise would be awful, she had said—but the hotel was full, so there was no choice. Now she was grateful for it.

She heard the sound of her door being unlocked and jerked around, but it was only Mantizima slipping in with his copy of the passkey. She turned back to the window.

"Are we on schedule?" Mantizima asked.

Had Ali been less engrossed in what was happening outside of her window, she would have noticed that even though Mantizima's choice of words was casual, his voice was tense.

"Ahead of it. They're holding hands."

"She's a fast worker," he said, sitting on the bed for a moment, then rising restlessly a moment later.

"Isn't that what we wanted?" Ali demanded. She pressed her face closer to the window, then moved it around, but they were out of her view. "They're gone," she said, turning away from the window. "I hope she'll be all right."

"I hope she doesn't destroy everything."

"Something wrong, Terry?" Ali asked.

"Nothing we haven't already discussed. I know we didn't have any choice, but at least permit me to have a few concerns, will you, Ali? After all, she is a hooker."

"And that makes her completely different from everyone else, right? She's not so different from me. And she has her reasons for doing this. At least as important as ours. As yours."

"I know. You've told me. Several times. And from what you said, she also has reasons to run away. She always has. I hope her courage holds out this time."

"It will!"

"We'll see."

They glared at each other angrily for a moment, but were unable to hold the anger.

"Is this a fight?" Ali asked.

Mantizima nodded. "A little one, I think."

"I'm worried," she said to explain her tension.

"So am I. But you, Miss Hayden, have a temper and a strong will."

"Look who's talking," she laughed. "You didn't risk sneaking into my room just to pick a fight with me, did you?" she asked, noticing how tense he was.

He shook his head and sat on the bed once again. "I have some things to tell you that I'd rather not say on the phone. I happened to catch a little bit of the news before I left the house. There's no easy way to tell you—Wade Petri is dead."

She sat down heavily on the bed next to him. "Poor slob," she said. "I didn't like him, but his only crime was being a fool.... How...?"

"He was killed at an abandoned mine site. The property's up for sale. What we in the States would call a real estate agent came to show it this morning and found him. I don't think 'Evan' thought he would be discovered this soon. He did his homework well, he just had a little bad luck. This was the first time they'd shown the property in months."

Ali just shook her head.

"He's leaving tomorrow, remember. He has to tie up loose ends," Mantizima continued.

"Is the bastard going to kill everyone who worked for him?"

"Just the ones he can't trust, and I'd say there aren't many of those. Greed makes a much more binding alliance than non-involvement. It's ironic though, Rune had a man following Petri. His successor obviously pulled him off. If he'd kept that watch on Petri, they'd have the man they are looking for. At the very least, they could charge him with murder."

"Murder. Sometimes it's still hard to take in. Looking at him down there," she said, indicating the window with a toss of her head, "I still have trouble thinking of him as anyone but Evan Todd."

"He's not."

"Don't I know? I talked to Tim O'Hara in London again. Evan Todd was in the morgue. Fished out of the Thames a couple of weeks ago. The body's in bad shape. They would never have identified him without the tip I gave Tim."

"Will the police try to make your friend tell them who gave him that tip?" Mantizima asked.

"I suppose so, but Tim will hold out."

"Give thanks for small favors," he said thoughtfully. "Oh, there was something else. My friend Kenny got the results back on those prints he ran for me."

"Who is he, Terry?" Ali asked. "Was your friend able to learn that?"

"Uh-huh. It took a while for him to find it. The man is not a criminal, believe it or not. He's only been fingerprinted because of a security clearance he needed on some job."

"Don't keep me in suspense."

"The name won't mean anything to you. It's Alan Warrick. He's an American physicist—actually a graduate student—from Southern California who dropped out of sight—"

"About a year-and-a-half ago. I know. Don't you remember, Terry? That name. That was the name of the physicist Rune said was prospecting at the diamond site."

"So it was."

"Stupid move, entering South Africa under his own name," Ali said. "Our Mr. Warrick makes mistakes. Wouldn't you agree, Terry?"

Mantizima did not respond; he did not appear to have heard her. He stood up and walked across the room, absently tapping his fist into his other palm as he did. Ali watched him as he walked away, noticing that his back was stiff with tension and that the sound of the pounding fist was growing louder. She knew that something was seriously wrong, something was agonizing him.

"Terry," she said softly, "what is it?"

He turned to face her, his expression not bothering to hide what she had already recognized. He started to speak, then shrugged helplessly, then started again.

"I didn't tell Kenny the real reason why I wanted this man's name. I said you needed it for a story you were writing. Fortunately, I never mentioned that the owner of those prints was calling himself Evan Michael Todd. You know the British are going to make an inquiry of the South African police eventually, if they haven't already. They know he came here. I don't think that inquiry will filter down to Kenny's level. At least, he hadn't made any connection as of today."

"So what's the problem?"

"I...I feel a trifle guilty about it. Not telling him, or at least someone, I mean."

"Is that what you want to do, Terry?" Ali asked cautiously. "If it is, I could call Logan, Rune's subordinate. He'd know who's in charge now."

"I don't know. I just don't know what to do.... I'm trying to be honest about it. I want to solve this myself. Very badly. I don't know why, I don't have anything to prove to anyone certainly...but I feel as if this is a path that keeps opening to me that I have to follow. It may not make any sense, but I can't help thinking that the answer I want, I need, will be at the end of it. If we hand over what we know to Rune's successor, we won't be involved."

Ali nodded. As frightened and lost as she felt at times, even though she had thought of it herself on occasion, it was really not something she wanted to do. She didn't want to give their investigation, their quest to someone else. It was against all of her instincts. She was a reporter and there was a story here. Her natural inclination was to guard that. But there was more than a story at stake here. For some unknown reason, she, too, felt that she had to follow that path, that life and circumstance had given it to them. She couldn't just hand that over to someone else.

"But I'm not just thinking about my own desire," Mantizima continued. "At least, I don't think I am. Whoever has replaced Rune on this investigation is really doing a poor job. Not only did he let Petri go, a lead that would have nabbed the bomber for him, but he's obviously stopped following up on routine leg-work, too. He isn't integrating leads the way Rune would have. By now, he should have received that information about Evan Todd. He should know that someone entered this country on a dead man's passport. But he apparently doesn't know, or they would have questioned Warrick by now."

"He's probably pursuing another lead. Investigating someone else," Ali said.

"I can't imagine who. I'm trying to be honest. In good conscience, I can't hand this over. But on the other hand, I don't want to be responsible for any more innocent people dying."

Ali listened, letting it all sink in, but there really wasn't any question in her mind. "Then we can't let any more innocent people die," she said simply. "We'll just have to stop it. Too many have died already. What right had he—"

"He doesn't have any right, not to do what he's done, what he plans to do."

"Well, then, let's stop him."

Her decision confirmed his, removing the last of his doubts.

"Let's."

Rahmire Jones sat alone on the bed in his shabby motel room, his dinner on his lap. He was tied in knots. His father—damn him!—a big, beefy man, ashamed of the puny, restless son he'd produced, once said, "That boy's nothing but skin and nerve endings." If he could see Rahmire now, he'd notice that nothing had changed, only now, those nerve endings were aroused to an intense pitch.

It was almost time! he thought anxiously. Almost time. He couldn't wait.

Impatiently, he pushed his meager dinner off onto his unmade bed. Some of it fell over onto the dirty spread, but he did not notice. In that room, no one would have.

The motel was a dump, the cheapest place he could find. The place did not bother him, however; he literally did not notice his surroundings. He was actually proud of finding it. It was centrally located, close to the people he needed to watch, yet not nearly as expensive as the accommodations they had chosen for themselves. He wasn't opposed to spending money. He would spend it when it was needed—to fulfill his mission—but would squander no more than necessary on himself.

He noticed the food on the spread and reluctantly carried the dishes out to the unit's little kitchenette, more to have something to do than for any hygienic reasons. As he rinsed off the dishes, he thought, yet again, about the future. With a fervor that never lessened, he thought about his cause, his mission, his homeland, the only things that mattered in his life.

Rahmire was more like an animal than a man. Like a dog, he loved the hand that fed him, that patted him on the head and told him he was a good boy, and he hated those he was taught to attack. Unlike some of the more vocal people within his organization who paid lip-service to rights and justifications, Rahmire never thought about morality. The concept had no meaning to him. He was taught to want certain things, and he did; he was taught to fight for them, by whatever means necessary, and he did; he was taught to follow orders, and he did. The people whose lives were spent in the process meant nothing to him.

Even now, when he was out on his own, he was still a follower. He followed the vision they had given him of their rightful homeland, fighting for it along the lines he had copied from others. Were he less of a dog and more of a man, he would have realized that, even in success, he would be no closer to that ideal. When the bomb he was working to protect was finally detonated, the land they struggled to claim would be uninhabitable, perhaps for generations. His leaders, who actually cared less about claiming that land than destroying the people who occupied it, knew that.

Rahmire, poor fool, did not.

"Just one more stop," Alan Warrick told Trudi as they pulled into a service station, "and then we'll go back to the hotel."

His voice was a little shaky as he spoke and his breath was coming in short, shallow gulps. He wants it badly, Trudi thought. She tried to give the illusion that she felt the same way, when in fact what she felt was a cross between dread and boredom.

He had wanted her all day, of that she was certain, but she had managed to stay free of his grasp. Initially, his "errands" kept them apart. She had accompanied him, in a manner of speaking, but she always had to wait outside or in cabs or nearby coffee shops. She had

214

memorized those addresses, however, and repeated them frequently to herself when she appeared to be listening to him.

The last of his stops was to rent a car for the "working vacation" he planned to start the next day. With that accomplished, he wanted to drive back to his hotel immediately, but Trudi insisted on having dinner first.

Over dinner, she was her most charming and seemingly unconsciously seductive. During coffee, he finally asked her to join him on the trip. She stalled over dinner as long as she could, knowing that prolonging it would intensify his desire, and, hopefully, solidify her position with him.

He suggested that they stop by her apartment so that she could pack some things and mentioned, quite casually, that he might just come up with her. That would never do, she thought; she had to have some time alone there. She quickly agreed to it, however, hoping that at that hour he would have difficulty finding a parking place. As she had expected, he did not find one and was forced to circle the block while she packed.

She packed quickly, just in case he happened to find a parking space, but she did take the time to write down the addresses of the people he visited today and hide the list under the phone. When it was all over, someone would come and find it...if she did not return.

Then, finally, they had to stop at a service station and fill the car's tank so they could get an early start in the morning.

"Just one last thing," Warrick repeated as he cut the engine. "Then it will be time for us."

He stepped out of the car and gave his order to the station attendant. Trudi stepped out, too, in an idle manner of simply stretching her legs.

"I'll be right back," he told her. "I want to get a map."

"Don't be too long, *Liebchen*."

As Warrick disappeared into the service station's office, Trudi casually strolled to the back of the car. Idly watching for him, she quickly slipped something out of her pocket which she secured under the bumper of his car. She was leaning on the car, patiently waiting for him by the time he came out of the office.

"Did you miss me?" he asked cheerfully.

"Never thought of anything else," she answered truthfully.

PART TWO:

THE DETONATION

CHAPTER EIGHTEEN

SEPTEMBER 20, 1979

Amidst the normal traffic heading out of Johannesburg that morning was a strange little caravan, a collection of allies and adversaries whose lives were now inexorably bound together.

In the lead car, the man who called himself Evan Michael Todd took a perverse sort of pleasure in not driving faster than the legal speed limit, the way law-abiding people were supposed to. He glanced into the rearview mirror on occasion, but only out of his normal driving habit. He did not expect to be followed, so he did not watch for it.

Mantizima and Ali, in their rental car, followed at some distance. Mantizima drove and Ali, in the passenger seat, sat with a box on her lap, the result of her electronic shopping and Mantizima's efforts. He had built a direction receiver that responded to the transmitter Trudi had placed under the bumper of Warrick's car.

There was also a third part to the puzzle, of which neither of the other parts were aware. Rahmire Jones held the middle position. Not possessing Mantizima's directional equipment, he was forced to maintain a close visual connection with Warrick. He knew that to be risky, but because he believed that travelers were only aware of the cars around them, not the people in them, he planned to exchange his rental cars at every possible opportunity.

And there was a fourth element, unbeknownst to any of the other three—four cars of policemen and women, disguised as tourists, backed up by an even larger contingent of replacements, but unaware themselves of the total picture of which they were only one part.

Held in the grip of growing apprehension, experiencing the gamet of all human emotions, that unusual collection of friends, lovers and enemies, the final lines of which were not yet drawn, drove on, bound for a destination unknown to most of them, and the triumph or disaster that awaited them there.

The countdown had begun.

Alan Warrick, you're a smart son-of-a-bitch! Warrick told himself.

Alan Warrick. It seemed funny to think that name again. For the last month he'd been Evan Michael Todd, and there had been so many different names and identities in the months prior to it that he'd almost forgotten his own. He reminded himself that he had tried to forget it. More than a year ago he had come to the conclusion that severing all connection with his name and his past was a necessary ingredient in his survival and success. But now, he had both survived and succeeded. He could afford himself the luxury of thinking that name one more time before forgetting it forever.

He wouldn't be sorry to shed Evan Todd, he thought. Being that jerk had been a real drag. Evan, the loner, the shy, stammering photographer who'd had a legitimate reason for going to South Africa, had been too good a cover to turn down, but Warrick was really getting tired of him. He had worried a little about the set-up. He hadn't looked forward to working closely with Ali Hayden. He had her background checked and found her to be a bright, tenacious reporter. But people, even the smart ones, were so stupid. They took their own circumstances as given and never questioned them. He trusted that she would do the same, and she did. It was funny, though. When that guy Aykroyd got onto things—Warrick's contact hadn't known how when he asked—he latched onto Ali as a suspect, and she took all the heat. And he was even lucky there; he'd had to get rid of the guy, of course, but he was able to disguise it as a favor for his contact.

Life was ironic, wasn't it? he thought. When you were on the bottom, you just couldn't get up. But when you were riding the big one there was no way you could wipeout.

He caught a glimpse of his own face as he adjusted the rearview mirror and he flashed his reflection a smile. The action brought back the memory of a similar action on that day in Los Angeles two years ago when it all began, when he first met Ali Sabas, the Palestinian terrorist who had commissioned the building of the bomb. Then, the purpose of that smile had been to boost his sagging confidence and to allay the fear he felt at the prospect of meeting a man whose hands he knew regularly bathed in human blood; now, it was one of celebration.

It was strange, but Warrick still didn't understand how Sabas happened to choose him for the assignment or why he had been so sure Warrick would succeed. He knew how Sabas had learned about him—a Los Angeles paper had run an article about a Cal Tech Ph.D. candidate whose dissertation outlined the construction of a nuclear bomb—but that could not have been the deciding factor. True, it was an uncommon subject for a dissertation— uncommon enough for some of his professors to threaten to block his degree, which he never did stick around long enough to claim—but not unheard of. Other students had written similar papers; how did Sabas know that his would be the one that would work?

He remembered the strange response he got from Sabas when he raised that question: "I lack your technical background, Mr. Warrick, so I'm unable to judge the plan on its own merits, but I know men. If I didn't, I wouldn't be alive today. I could go out into the street, any street in the world, and pick out the few men destined for sainthood, just as I can see the destiny you've chosen for

221

yourself. Your politics, if you have any, may be different from mine, Mr. Warrick, but inside you are one of us."

Warrick never really understood what Sabas meant by that. Who the hell chooses a destiny? Alan Warrick possessed an exceptional mind—even his critics acknowledged that—but he took pains not to exercise it outside of his area of interest. He was particularly uncomfortable examining that murky area, which for want of a better word might be called the human soul. He didn't really want to know why he had accepted the commission; he didn't want to run into any remnant of a conscience he might still possess. He did have two stock answers to the question of motivation that arose occasionally in his own mind: he was a scientist, a man whose job it was to find solutions to problems; what happened to those solutions after they left him was not his concern—and he wanted money, enough to live in comfort for the rest of his life, enough to erradicate the impoverished roots that still embarrassed him, and why should he care how he got it since no one else did? He repeated either or both of those justifications to himself whenever any doubts arose, but he hadn't had to think of either of them for a long time. By now, he had come too far to allow any doubts to get in his way.

He did feel a little uneasy about working for Sabas, knowing, or rather guessing, what he did about the man, but he need not have worried. He hadn't seen Ali Sabas or any of the other members of his group many times since that first day when it was decided, and had little contact of any sort with them in the last year. They had kept their part of the bargain. They did not interfere with his work, while providing an unlimited source of funds for him to carry it out. They apparently never worried about his cheating them. They knew, he surmised, that he was smart enough to know how they would deal with someone who did. They also never seemed to worry about his failing. They understood that success mattered just as much to him as it did to them. He had just as much to prove.

Now he had proven it, and he was intoxicated by the thrill of it. Here he was, he thought, at only twenty-seven years old, a man with the power to pluck an out-of-control world up by the scruff of its neck and to hold it, dangling, until it cried for mercy and promised to obey. A man with the capacity to shock a world believed to be beyond it. The man of the future, here to claim it. His only regret was that no one knew it.

How he wished he could tell someone what he had done. It seemed to petty, he thought, but damn it! he wanted to brag. He wished he could see the faces on those professors at Cal Tech when the bomb went off. The ones who said it couldn't be done, and especially the ones who said it shouldn't be. They would talk about if, of course. Every scientific establishment, every person in the world would talk of nothing else for weeks, perhaps even months to come. Would they think of him when it happened? Would they remember his plan and be awestruck by the coincidence? No, he decided sadly, they'd already forgotten him. He was just part of a sea of faces that swept through that institution, pausing on the crest of a wave for a brief time before being washed out the door.

Yes, he wished he could tell them. Gloating would feel so good. But it didn't really matter; he was going to feel great anyway when it was over.

Or was he?

He was still riding high on exhilaration, but he felt a slight foreshadowing of the letdown he would probably experience when it was over. It was funny, but he never in that whole time gave a thought, beyond the money he would possess, to his future. He thought about it now. What would he do? He was still so young and would be so rich that the possibilities were endless. One thing he was not going to do, he decided, was continue as he was. He was not going to go on building bombs for terrorists.

That was a once-in-a-lifetime thing; no one could live at that pace forever. Besides, he had good reason for not wanting a proliferation of nuclear bombs in the hands of terrorists—he might just get caught in the detonation of one!

Maybe, he thought, when he collected the big bundle promised to him at the end, he would settle down and get respectable again. That would be a good joke on everyone. Sure, that was the thing to do. He would settle down somewhere—not LA, where too many people knew him—but somewhere else. He would buy a business that he could go to at least a few hours a day and buy a big house and put a pretty, young wife in it. One of those snooty, rich girls of the sort who were always willing to go out with him, but would never have considered him as a prospective husband. He would father a couple of beautiful children, hopefully a boy and a girl. He took great relish in the idea of raising a couple of little snobs that would look down on the kind of person he had once been.

His fantasy grew in his mind, fleshing out in every detail, but there was an unreal quality about it. He did not realize that he had turned a corner that day, two years ago, and he could never go back, even in sham.

His thought of a wife made him think of the woman sitting next to him. He threw an uncomfortable glance at Trudi, feeling a tinge of regret. She was not the sort of wife he envisioned for himself, but how he would love to keep that little hooker around permanently. He'd had the hots for her from the time he'd laid eyes on her. He'd had to fumble his approach, however, the way Evan Todd would, but it all worked out in the end. She was great in bed and she really looked up to him. Admiration and great sex were two things he would never get from a spoiled, nagging wife who always had a headache.

Of course, Trudi did put on airs. How could she think she could hide what she really was? He'd been buying women, professional and otherwise, for as long as he'd

224

had money. He did not want or trust anyone who could not be bought. Besides, in a way, he was a member of that same ignoble profession himself, and every dog knows his own. And she was so stupid, she believed everything he told her.

Still, she was great to have around; he would miss her when she was gone. But dead men tell no tales, and Alan Warrick was the last man who would deny equality to a woman.

He leaned over and gave her knee an affectionate squeeze.

"Honey," he asked, "are you getting hungry?"

Time was the enemy. There was not enough of it, Ali thought. Not enough to do everything that should be done, to take every precaution, to cut off every possible avenue of escape. And there was too much. The waiting for something to happen was unendurable.

Tension bore down ruthlessly. She supposed that she felt its effect all over her body, but the only part she was aware of was her jaw. It ached from hours of unconsciously gritting her teeth together. She looked over at Mantizima, intent on his driving, and saw that the muscles of his neck and shoulders were taut. She slipped her hand behind his neck and began massaging that rigidity away.

He smiled gratefully and his eyes lingered on her for a moment before returning to the road. It was hard to remember, he thought, that she had only entered his life a matter of days ago. She seemed an integral part of it. But they were living on an island, he knew, an island of time. What would happen when they crossed the strait separating them from the mainland that was the real world? What would the future hold for them? If it held anything.

"Their position's holding," Ali said suddenly, looking up from the box on her lap.

"It's lunch time," said Mantizima, glancing at the dashboard clock. "Let's drive on ahead to see where they are before taking care of ourselves."

The found the place with Warrick's car in the parking lot, then faced the problem of what to do about their own lunch. They couldn't simply go into another restaurant; Mantizima would not be welcome.

"We passed a park a mile or so back," Ali said. "Why don't I get some take-out from that place up ahead and we can go back to the park."

A simple enough solution, or so she believed. When they arrived at the park, however, they found, as they should have expected, that it was divided into White and non-White sections.

"Got another brainstorm," Ali said over-cheerfully. She opened the trunk of the car and pulled out a blanket she had borrowed from her hotel room. "Thought we might need it. Who knows when we might have to sleep in the car?" she explained. "All we have to do now is spread it out on the dividing line. You stay on your side and I'll stay on mine."

Ali's false enthusiasm did not brighten Mantizima's mood, but the fact that she was trying so hard did. Against his better judgment, he agreed to her suggestion.

Ali asked whether she should take the directional receiver with her.

"Better leave it here. We don't want anything to happen to it," Mantizima decided. "But turn up the volume so we can hear it when they start moving again."

So they began their picnic, on opposite sides of the line that society drew between them. Almost immediately, however, Ali realized it was a foolish idea. There weren't a lot of people in the park, but those that were there looked at them with unvarnished hostility. Ali suddenly remembered her promise to Deborah and realized that she had already broken it.

"We aren't doing anything to them," Ali said resentfully.

226

"We're challenging their beliefs. To some people, that's the worst thing you can do."

They did notice that there were two couples in the White picnic section who paid absolutely no attention to them, who seemed not to have noticed them at all. That bothered Mantizima, although he did not say why.

"So they're liberals," Ali said.

"Perhaps."

After a short time, however, despite the tension around them, Ali relaxed into having a good time. For a while she was almost able to forget why they happened to be there, and was just able to enjoy their surroundings. The grass smelled so fresh, the breeze was warm, and the sky was clear. The wildflowers, which would be at their best in another month, were just coming into bloom. It was an inviting, picturesque spot.

"What are you thinking, Ali?" Mantizima asked after watching her face for some minutes.

"Something I'm only struck by on rare occasions when I'm here," she answered. "That this is such a beautiful country."

"Yes, it is," he said, with neither pride nor antagonism.

"There's so much here, the land, the people, the natural resources. So much, and yet...."

"It's a place where so much should be possible," Mantizima said with difficulty, though he'd thought about that subject a lot lately, "but nothing is. A place that should have a great future, but has none.... I know I should hate it here, but I don't. I don't hate the place, I don't even hate the people. I just feel sorry for them. I feel sorry that they've lost what they never knew they had, that they've never missed it."

Mantizima paused for a moment. His fingers absently played with a blade of grass until the anger spread to his extremities. He broke the blade with a swift, brutal snap.

"I care, you know, more than I like to admit. I care about the young people here. Maybe it's because this is where I spent my own youth, but more likely it's because, wherever you go, youth has always been the hope of the future. Tomorrow has always been theirs, their place of promise, of triumph, if they earn it, their place to conquer. But here, youth is trapped in a static past, their natural hope stillborn within them. I bleed for South Africa's young, both White and Black. I really do. Because they have no chance. Because South Africa is a land of yesterdays in a world of tomorrows."

When he finished speaking, Ali said nothing, but she wondered if he understood what those sentiments implied about his future.

Then they heard the beeper on the transmitter in their car grow louder.

"They're on the move," Mantizima said abruptly. "Let's get going."

They hastily bundled up their possessions and headed back to the car. In minutes they were on their way. They drove to the restaurant where Warrick and Trudi ate. At the entrance they nearly crashed into a red Volkswagen in a terrible hurry to leave, but Mantizima's quick reactions averted an accident. While he kept the car idling in the lot, Ali rushed into the restaurant's ladies room. There, on the mirror, written in bold, lipsticked letters, where everyone but any man could see, was the prearranged message they'd been waiting for.

Ali quickly scrubbed the lipstick off with a soapy paper towel, then rushed out to the car that was on its way before her door was closed.

"Vrede!" she said succinctly. "Van der Wyk Machine Works."

Mantizima stretched out on the rooftop of a small industrial building facing the van der Wyk Machine Works. Ali was off somewhere in the neighborhood

228

asking the sort of perfectly normal questions expected from reporters.

The scene Mantizima saw when he adjusted his binoculars was a deceptively harmless-looking one of workmen loading wooden crates onto a flatbed truck. The only thing unusual about it was that Warrick was giving the orders to the men, while someone, presumably van der Wyk, assuming there was such a person, stood nearby, as nervous as an expectant father. Trudi sat in Warrick's car, which was parked near the factory, filling her obvious boredom by filing her nails and chain smoking cigarettes.

Mantizima heard the sound of someone climbing the fire escape ladder on the other side of the building and turned quickly, but relaxed when he saw Ali climb over the ledge. She slid in place next to him and, refusing a turn at the binoculars with a sharp shake of her head, simply watched in tense silence.

"It's there, isn't it?" she asked after a while.

"Somewhere, certainly," Mantizima answered. "But I don't think we've seen it yet."

Though they had been aware of its probable existence for quite some time, being this close to the no longer hypothetical bomb, had a chilling effect on her. It was real to her now. She asked whether Mantizima thought it had been built there.

"No, definitely not. It wasn't built by one person, I'd say. My guess is that Warrick hired a number of different people to work on it, each contributing parts within their area of expertise. He probably assembled it himself—he wouldn't trust that to anyone else—and had it brought here for packing and delivery as part of an innocent shipment of machine parts."

"What do you suppose it looks like? I always thought it would be shaped like a missle."

Mantizima laughed softly and said, "It could be a sphere, but more likely, it's built in a pipe. At least, that's how I would do it, were I him."

"Those boxes are pretty small," Ali said. "It can't be very big. It's not as big as I expected."

Mantizima explained that it didn't have to be very large to do an immense job.

"The bombs they used in World War II were much larger, but considerably less efficient than the ones that are built today, but still they got the job done. Today, the technology has come lightyears ahead, and any man who could do this on his own has brought it even further. If we know anything about him, we know he's good."

Ali remembered to tell him the things she had learned by talking to some of the people in that business neighborhood. Van der Wyk, they said, had been on the verge of losing his shirt when he attracted a large sum from an outside investor. Mantizima snorted eloquently at that semantical choice. Since then, however, the company had been holding its own.

"You know, Warrick's been very lucky in finding people who need his help as much as he needs theirs," Ali said.

"It isn't luck; it's a law of nature. They—"

Mantizima stopped suddenly, his body instantly alert. "There it is!" he said.

"Where?" Ali asked impatiently.

"There," he said, pointing. "The one with the red spot painted on the corner. See how gingerly they're handling it.... So someone's really done it? I wouldn't have believed it."

Now it was real to him.

"Terry?" Ali asked in a low voice.

"Yes?"

"Do you think it's...safe?"

He turned to her and saw that she was really frightened by it. She had expected his immediate assurance. She counted on it. But it did not come.

"I...think so," he said honestly. "But I don't know it. I know I won't rest until 'the button' makes its appearance."

"The button?"

"The control panel. Nora Brand's contribution to this venture. The thing that brought me into it. I won't feel comfortable until that's in Warrick's hands."

She did not understand why she wanted Warrick, of all people, to have it, but things started happening below that diverted her attention before she could ask him. The packing of the truck was finished and, without any fanfare, considering its cargo, was soon on its way. They heard Warrick shout, "Two minutes, Trudi," to the girl in the car, then saw him enter the building with van der Wyk, presumably to make the final payment.

No one watching her would have doubted that Trudi had reached the tolerable limit of her boredom. She lit the last cigarette in the box and, after only a brief pause, flung the box out of the open window with spiteful irritation, just as Warrick was returning to the car.

He never gave a thought to the box lying on the ground, but Mantizima and Ali did. As soon as Warrick's car drove away, they rushed down the ladder to retrieve it.

"Harrismith," she read from the inside of the box. "Motel Kennedy."

She dropped it back on the ground as they hurried to their car. Only moments after they had gone, however, another car drove up to that spot. A woman, who to every appearance could be nothing more than an average housewife, jumped out of the car and purposefully picked up the discarded cigarette box.

Unlike Ali, she did not leave it where she found it.

CHAPTER NINETEEN

Kloff entered Logan's office to give him a report, but found Logan absent. He hesitated, not wanting to leave if Logan was going to be back soon, but also not wanting to wait for too long. He decided to write a note asking Logan to stop by his office before going home. As he hunted for a piece of scratch paper, however, another sheet of paper happened to catch his eye. It was an official request from Scotland Yard to the South African Government to trace the whereabouts of a man traveling under the name of Evan Michael Todd. It went on to state that the real owner of that passport had been murdered.

Todd? he thought. Where had he heard that name? Of course! Evan Todd was the photographer working with Ali Hayden, the man they believed she and Mantizima to be following.

Kloff could hardly contain his excitement. Clutching the request, he ran from the office, colliding with Logan in the doorway.

"Neil, did you see this?"

"What do you think you're doing reading my private mail?" Logan demanded.

"Neil, this could be our turning point. Todd is the man Hayden and Mantizima are following. He could be—"

"Naturally, I'm keeping all that in mind, Pieter. I'm not so stupid as to miss the significance of it. But just as you pointed out that circumstance might be hanging Mantizima, it might be doing the same to this man. For all we know, this man might be Todd and the dead man someone else. We only have their word for it being the reverse. And even if it's true, I'm not going to upset the equilibrium of this investigation just to make the British Government happy."

"But, Neil—"

"No buts, Pieter. Now in the future, I suggest we adhere to a strict division of labor. You do your job and I'll do mine, and mine, if you recall, is being in charge. Is that understood?"

Kloff nodded reluctantly. He didn't have any choice. He slowly seated himself in a chair in front of Logan's desk. He tried to use the time to regain his composure, to pretend to Logan that nothing significant had happened. But he did not lie to himself. Something had happened. He had just watched Logan throw away the best lead they had. He wished there were some logical explanation for Logan's ridiculously poor judgment, but he couldn't think of one.

He tried to relax in the chair, but it just wouldn't come to his stiff, unnaturally erect body. It was odd, he thought, with Rune Aykroyd, God bless his soul, with whom he had a very formal relationship, he was always at ease; whereas, around Logan, who, till very recently, was his equal in position and for whom he had not a shred of respect, he could never feel like himself. On some unconscious level, he always felt as if he had to be on his guard, but he didn't know why.

The bottle and glass were out on the desk now. No more hiding or half-hiding them in desk drawers. And Logan's eyes were beginning to look blurry and unfocused, the way they always do in the early to middle stages of inebriation. Maybe he always drank like this, Kloff thought. He'd heard enough rumors to that effect, but in truth, if Logan always had been a heavy drinker, it had never before affected his performance of his job. That was no longer the case.

"Well?" Logan said rudely. "What do you want?"

"You told me to report whenever I had anything new," Kloff said, controlling his temper and keeping his voice as impersonal as possible. "They stopped for the night in a motel in Harrismith."

"All of them? Both parties?"

"Yes."

"How the hell does Mantizima get to say under the same roof as those white people?"

"It's an 'International' hotel," Kloff said curtly.

"Oh."

Less than five percent of South Africa's hotels and restaurants had switched to an "International" designation, meaning they did not discriminate on the basis of color. Needless to say, few white South Africans patronized them, not even the white liberals who wrote stirring letters-to-the-editor on the subject of discrimination while underpaying their many black house servants. Most South Africans claimed the owners of the "International" establishments only chose that designation to appeal to foreign visitors, whose numbers seemed to shrink every year. Cynics maintained the South African Government only permitted that easing of apartheid laws to gain respect in the eyes of the rest of the world. The general thinking was that the government would continue to allow the "International" status unless the trend grew, which it was not expected to do.

Logan chuckled lecherously. "I bet Mantizima and the Hayden woman aren't sharing the same room. Those places aren't that liberal," he said.

"They are registered in adjoining rooms, but the only activity seems to be in the woman's."

"Activity, eh? That's interesting. Do you still want to arrest them?"

"That no longer seems advisable," he said tightly.

"No, of course not," said Logan smugly. "Was there anything else?"

"When Mantizima and Hayden stopped in a public park for lunch, a local policeman checked their car. It had tracking equipment in it. That's what he built with those electronic parts. Apparently, it's very sophisticated. They think it will work from a number of miles away."

"He's a *slim* Kaffir, our Terry-boy is. You have to grant him that."

Kloff felt his face becoming hot and tight. He didn't know what was happening to Logan. He never used to talk like that. He had always enforced the law as his job required, but privately he was often critical of it, though not as much as many English-speaking South Africans. What had happened? Kloff wondered. Had his promotion gone to his head and solidified him with the official government position? Or was the liquor simply loosening his tongue and revealing what he actually always believed?

He also wondered about himself. What was happening to him? He had never reacted like this before. It almost seemed as if he and Logan had changed sides.

"What's the matter?" Logan asked. "You don't like that expression anymore. You used to use it often enough."

"I don't know what you are talking about," Kloff said stiffly.

Logan shrugged in a "have it your own way, but we both know what you're really thinking" manner.

With his report over, Kloff started to leave, without even waiting for dismissal. But he paused at the door and turned back to Logan.

"Maybe you ought to eat some food," Kloff said.

"Why should I?"

"Because most people find it keeps the body going better than alcohol."

"Sod you! You lousy son-of-a-bitch. Who the hell do you think you're talking to? Have you bloody well forgotten I'm your boss now?"

"How could I when you tell me so often?"

Kloff was angry with himself as he walked back to his own office. Why the hell had he let Logan get to him like that? Logan was right, he had used the word, Kaffir, many times. Oh, not to their faces; that was against the law. Of course, his position would have allowed him to do it anyway, but he never abused that position. He always gave them all the respect the law required, no more, but no less either.

Until now.

He had never questioned apartheid. It was ordained by God and enforced by the State he was sworn to serve. Why had it suddenly changed? Why was this one Bantu, this...man, whom he didn't even know, causing him to challenge the very foundations of his existence? But the more he read about Terry Mantizima, the less able he was to go back to that.

He slumped into his desk chair and let his hand fall on a sheet of paper on the desk. That paper was the report of Mantizima's tracking equipment. No, he couldn't deny it anymore. Mantizima was not simply a Bantu, a legally designated inferior creature. He was a man, and an unusually talented one at that. Kloff had to admit that he couldn't have designed that equipment, not if his life depended on it. He probably couldn't do many things that Mantizima could do. He was genuinely surprised that that realization did not threaten him.

He was beginning to feel a strange sort of kinship with Terry Mantizima, a man he had never even met, a man who didn't even know he existed. What he didn't yet realize was that his loyalties were in the process of being divided, nor the choice he had already made.

Ali anxiously sat at her darkened motel room window with her eyes glued on the open courtyard separating the two buildings of rooms. They were taking a great risk by staying in the same motel as Warrick and Trudi, and an even greater one by leaving the room. But it had been a warm, dry day and they both desperately needed the cold drinks that Mantizima had gone to buy.

She had been the one to decide they would stay there. She made the choice as soon as she saw the word "International" on the motel sign. She told Mantizima that if they were careful, it was worth the risk to be able to keep a closer watch on Warrick. Actually, that had little to do with her decision. She just couldn't bear the thought of his being put through the indignity of having to stay somewhere else or, even worse, sleep in the car.

She pressed her face to the glass and looked for Mantizima. He had been gone a long time. She was very worried about him. He had invested so much of himself in this thing, too much, she thought, and it was wearing him out. For once, his well-paced energy seemed to be waning. She hoped he lasted until the end, whenever that might be, but more importantly, she hoped he was finding whatever he was looking for.

In truth, they were both feeling the strain, they were wrung dry with fatigue, but not so much that they lacked the energy for the act that would fill their night. She closed her eyes and felt her body melt into a warm liquid at the thought of what the next few hours would bring, when as both the conquered and the conqueror, she would grasp his body inside of hers, and they would renew each other, give each other the strength to go on.

The passion that was part of their nights was not only a part of the night, however; it was there in the day, too, present at all times, to be felt in every casual touch, every glance. Occasionally she would look up and find him watching her, a proud look of ownership on his face. At one time she would have rebelled against any man who assumed that right, but she didn't resent him; she shared his pride. For the first time she understood what that shopworn cliché, succeeding as a woman, meant. She felt triumphantly successful in her sexuality because she belonged to that man.

The tie between them was not based solely on physical attraction, however. In a short time he had become an important part of her life. On some implicit level, she couldn't even imagine giving that up and going on without him, but because she was not ready to deal with what that implied, she forced herself not to look beyond the present.

Her thoughts were interrupted when she caught sight of a man walking through the courtyard towards the parking lot. He was a strange-looking man, with distinctly Middle-Eastern features and strawberry blond hair. Definitely bleached, she thought about the hair, though she couldn't imagine why he had done it. It looked so silly. But the man hadn't simply caught her eye because he was different-looking. There was something familiar about him, though she could not place where she had seen him.

Cairo? she thought. No, if she had come across him in the course of her regular life, she would have remembered. It had to be in South Africa. Of course, she thought after a moment, snapping her fingers. He was the driver of the red Volkswagen that almost hit them when they pulled into the restaurant to retrieve Trudi's message. How odd that he would have chosen to stay in the same motel. But when the man reached the parking lot he didn't go to a red Volkswagen—there wasn't even a red Volkswagen there—he went instead to a blue Ford.

He had to be a different man, she decided. Still, she had an uncomfortable feeling about him. It was at least a curious coincidence, one she really ought to share with Mantizima as soon as he returned. Then she saw him approaching the room. His walk was brisk, but that did not hide his body's exhaustion. How could she burden him with anything else, and particularly something that was probably nothing more than her tired mind playing tricks? It was nothing, she finally decided, as she jumped up and ran to the door. Nothing.

She opened the door as soon as he reached it and greeted him with a smile that seemed to ease some of his fatigue. She went to the bed and, without ceremony, flopped onto it, while Mantizima took her place at the window. For a long time they didn't speak, they simply allowed the cool liquid to rehydrate their parched throats. It was an untroubled silence, the kind that only those people who can communicate without words can achieve. Neither questioned its presence between them; it seemed so natural.

After a while Mantizima asked, "Ali, do you like it? Reporting, I mean."

"What a strange question!" she said.

"I don't think it's so strange. You don't talk about your job that much. Does it...well, does it give you everything you need from it?"

Had she been less tired and more observant, she would have noticed there was a leading quality to the question, but she did not notice.

"It's been a good life for me. Given me a chance to travel, to meet people. And I love writing."

"What about books? Do you ever think about writing those?"

"Not books...novels. I used to think about writing those...sometimes. Haven't in a long time," she said. "Someday...perhaps."

"When are you going to do it?" he pressed.

"I suppose when I've found a story where the whys are more important than the whats, the way they are in newspaper pieces," she said in dismissal of the subject.

Mantizima weighed the things she said and the things she did not say for a moment. "Afraid of it, aren't you?" he asked. "Afraid of exposure of yourself, by yourself, to yourself. Right?"

"...Something like that."

"That isn't what you told that girl, Trudi, when she said something similar." He shook his head.

"No, but I did tell her that she and I are a lot alike. You wouldn't understand, Terry, you've never been afraid of anything."

"Don't you believe it. I've been afraid lots of times. And never so much as the night I decided to come back here."

She heard in his voice just how much that memory hurt him.

"But you didn't let it´ stop you," Ali said a trace wistfully.

He shrugged at the obvious. "It's your choice, Ali, but speaking for myself, I don't want to live with what might have been."

Ali suddenly had an image of herself as an old woman still talking about the novel she was going to write...someday.

"If you ever decide to," Mantizima said in a voice that tried to sound casual, but didn't quite make it, "I know a great place to write it, Ali. It's right on the ocean, the real ocean, not that meek, little pond you people have out in California. And it comes equipped with a den, not to mention one terrific lover." He stopped, then quickly continued, "Who knows? You might like it so much you'll want to stay there permanently."

He could not see her face across the darkened room, but he heard her sharp intake of breath. When she spoke, however, her voice was fully controlled.

"Terry, we haven't known each other very long."

"Time isn't going to change anything. We both know that. At least I do."

"We're in the middle of a crisis. People don't make decisions of that magnitude at times like this."

"They do, you know. All of the time. And they're usually right. A crisis has a way of clearing away the fluff and showing you what's really important. But, since we are in a crisis, I suppose you know what's important to you."

"Do you know what's really important to you yet?" she asked. "I mean, have you decided where you are going to live your life? Can you really offer that house?"

He was silent for a long time, then said, sadly, helplessly, "No, I can't."

We're so ironic, she thought. They were both trembling on the brink of taking that step towards an essential commitment, but neither could take it. She was unable to make a commitment to another person and, while he could do that, he couldn't make the most important one to himself. We're like two lemmings, she thought, tied together, but trying to swim in opposite directions. Then she wondered why she had thought of them in terms of that animal.

"But we could work something out," he grasped desperately. "No, I'm not asking you to sacrifice yourself here...."

Sacrifice? he thought. Why had he chosen that word? If living in South Africa would be a sacrifice for her, what would it be for him?

"I don't know what or how," he continued hastily, "but I know we could work something out if we really wanted to."

"Why don't you keep a light in the window?" Ali asked, surprising herself by making even that much of a concession.

"It's already there. But don't wait too long. Lights need fuel, you know?"

Before she could say anything else, something in the parking lot caught Mantizima's eye and his head turned in that direction.

"Ali, come here," he whispered, even though no one could hear them. "Come over here. No, don't turn on the light. I want you to see something."

She rushed to his side and looked out the window.

"Do you see that woman in the parking lot? The one just getting out of the car?"

He pointed to a short, plump woman in her early twenties, who wore obviously expensive, but badly-fitting, clothes and carried a canvas bag in lieu of a purse. When she passed under a parking lot light, it was clear she hadn't washed her hair lately, but she also carried a good leather attaché case. With all of her conflicting parts, the woman made a strange picture.

"What about her?" Ali asked.

"That's Nora Brand."

"Nora...? You mean the girl from your office. The one who— "

"The one who built the controls, yes, that's her."

They watched her walk through the courtyard in the direction of Warrick's room.

"I wonder what she's doing here tonight," Ali said. "Do you think she's carrying some papers in that case that she had to show to Evan, I mean Warrick?"

Mantizima laughed and shook his head. "Darling, you must be very tired. Your mind has gotten rather slow tonight. That case is the controls."

"The button?"

"That's right. 'The button' has arrived."

Ali trembled inside, but she didn't know that she also shook outside until Mantizima put his arm around her and held her close.

"Don't worry," he said. "I've been expecting this. It doesn't really change anything. Warrick wants that bomb to stay intact until it's delivered as much as we do. For the moment, that case is as safe with him as it would be with us."

Ali wished she could believe that.

Alan Warrick sang in the shower of his motel room, loudly and defiantly off-key.

Trudi hated the sound of his voice almost as much as she hated him. At least while he was in the shower he couldn't be in the room pawing her, so even listening to that voice had its compensations. She dreaded the idea of another session of having sex with him. It was not an active, virulent emotion, however, just a pervasive gloom that kept seeping out of a container on some back burner within her where it perpetually simmered. Fortunately, his tastes were average enough, nothing bizarre, and he was mercifully quick.

That woman had come and gone. He hadn't hid the presence of Nora Brand from her, nor had he hid the case. Of course, he hadn't explained them either, but she could make a good guess about its contents because of the things Ali told her.

Her mind paused a moment on the subject of Ali, and she wondered how she and Mantizima were doing. Had they found her messages? she wondered, but quickly assured herself that they had. She had to believe that they were close at hand, ready to give her help when she needed it. She wasn't only worried about herself, however, she was worried about them, too, especially Ali, with whom she felt particularly close. It was an unusual experience for her to have a relationship with another woman. If you could call two brief meetings a relationship. She would not have at one time, but coming to South Africa seemed to change everything. Everything. Now, she was enjoying the sensation of being genuinely involved with another human being.

Her thoughts returned to the case when she caught sight of it across the room. There it was on the dresser, locked, but in plain sight. No, Warrick hadn't bothered to explain its presence to her. He never explained anything. He thought she was just a dumb hooker, she thought, who didn't even warrant a lie. But she knew that wasn't the only reason. He was not a stupid man; if he let her see things he wouldn't want her to talk about, she knew he must not intend to leave her around where she could do any talking.

That thought frightened her, but not as much as it might have. She had lived with so much fear that day, actually since she made the decision to come with him, that she figured she was becoming immune to it.

That was partially true, but she did not realize that there was another side to her lack of fear. She did not realize it, she couldn't see it in herself, but in the course of one day she had become a dramatically stronger person.

Warrick cracked a particularly high note which grated against Trudi's nerves.

God, how she hated him! She hadn't when he was pretending to be Evan Todd; then he had seemed to be a harmless sort of person, a person in whose presence you could lose yourself because he offered no judgments. Now, she knew him for what he really was. A whore, like her, who would sell himself to the highest bidder.

In the past few days she had come to despise that trait in him and in herself. Maybe, she thought, she had always hated it, she just didn't know it. But, for the first time, she was able to draw a distinction between the deed and the person who performed it. She grasped that she could hate the things she had done without hating herself for doing them. She was learning that she could give herself the love and approval she had always wanted from her parents. That, in the final analysis, a person always has to give them to himself.

She had finally forgiven the past and she was healing.

But she couldn't let Warrick off as lightly. His whoring was not as innocent as hers. She, at least, had never hurt anyone but herself, while he did not care how many people he destroyed. Sometimes she believed he actually enjoyed the hurting.

Her reverie was interrupted when Warrick leaned out of the shower and called to her.

"Hey, Trudi, honey. I forgot my shampoo. Can you get it for me? It's in my suitcase."

She told him she would, taking particular care to keep the venom she felt out of her voice. That wasn't difficult for her; she'd been doing it so long it was second-nature.

The suitcase was lying on the bed, closed, but unlocked. Without really giving it much thought, she walked over to it, flipped up the top, and searched for the shampoo. When she found the bottle, she was about to close it when she caught sight of a small ring with a couple of keys. She knew what they unlocked. Bypassing a thought process, her eyes immediately flashed to the case.

Should she? No, it was an unnecessary risk, and there was nothing to be gained by it. She could not resist.

She brought Warrick his shampoo and waited for the singing to resume again. Then she quietly rushed to the case. She knew she had only a few moments, and she wasted some of that time by repeatedly looking over her shoulder. She was a fool to be doing it, she knew. If he caught her, it would be all over immediately. She slipped one of the keys in the lock. As she was turning it, it occurred to her that it might be rigged. Maybe it would blow up in her face. But the key turned easily. Quickly, with remarkably steady hands, she parted the two sides of the case.

And there it was—the first of its kind.

She didn't know what she was expecting, but this certainly wasn't it. What she saw was an unassuming solid state panel with a pressure sensitive timer and a few simple controls. From appearances, it could have been a part of almost anything. An appliance, maybe, or a toy. Why did it have to be part of a nuclear bomb?

The experience was a very revealing one to her. She had always looked with disdain at the need for power in other people. Personally, she had always believed herself to be immune to the desire. Now, when she held the fate of a good part of the world in her hands, she found she was not indifferent to pull of power, as she had believed—she was repulsed by it. She was disgusted to think that anyone would want to put his finger to that red button.

Yet she knew that for Alan Warrick the very idea of it was a thrill.

CHAPTER TWENTY

SEPTEMBER 21, 1979

When he pulled into a roadside restaurant just outside of Ladysmith, Alan Warrick was feeling very pleased with himself. Everything was going according to plan. The "thing," as he thought of the bomb in his own mind was on its way, and he did not anticipate any problems with it. Customs officials had never troubled themselves over van der Wyk's shipments, which was partially why Warrick had chosen him for the venture. He had the "case," as he described the controls, and would deliver it in good time. It was all over now but the shouting. And what a shout it was going to be!

Yes, he was feeling all right.

He hadn't abandoned the details. He still intended to follow the shipment to Durban, where it would be loaded on a ship bound for Cairo, when it would be met by someone designated by Ali Sabas. He wouldn't be able to supervise the ship's loading as he had the truck's, but he would be close at hand nonetheless. Then he would personally carry the control panel to his meeting place with Sabas, at the same time collecting the number of that very large Swiss bank account. No, he hadn't abandoned the details, he just didn't focus on them. They had been a part of his life for the last two years; he had worked them and reworked them, memorized them, lived with them for so long, they were now a part of him.

He also had to deal with Trudi, he remembered uncomfortably. He would keep her as long as possible, he had already decided; as long as she cooperated and didn't ask questions. With a little luck, he could keep her all the way to Durban, but then.... He didn't like to think about it, but he knew he would probably strangle her and leave her on the docks. If he could time it right, he would have sex with her first so the police would think she'd been raped. In these violent times, he thought sarcastically, every major city has at least a few rapists at large; that MO was bound to coincide with one of Durban's.

When he cut the engine in the restaurant parking lot, he was so confident, so sure that he had avoided detection, that he didn't even notice that the driver of the blue Ford that had been behind them all day, had also pulled into that parking lot and preceded them into the restaurant. It wouldn't have bothered him if he had.

"Get a table, will you, Trudi?" Warrick said when they entered the restaurant. "And get me some coffee."

As he ambled off in search of the restroom, there was a cocky air about him. He was a man without a care in the world.

Then, suddenly, everything changed.

It happened when he was washing his hands. He saw it all unfolding in the mirror, but it happened too fast to do anything to stop it.

A man suddenly appeared behind him. Warrick did not know where he came from—he was just suddenly there. An absurd-looking man, with dark skin and thick, strawberry blond hair. A small man, who shouldn't have been much of a physical threat were it not for the surprising degree of tone showing in his tightly flexed muscles. Before Warrick could so much as think about the threat, the little man had slipped a knife across his throat and dragged him into one of the stalls.

This can't be happening to me! Warrick thought. Not now! Not to me! He struggled a little, then stopped fighting until he could assess the situation. The man was surprisingly strong, but so was Warrick. They were probably evenly matched. He could probably get free with a little effort, but would he be fast enough to avoid that knife? No sense getting himself killed if all the guy wanted was a little money. He decided to play it cool until he had some idea of why this was happening.

"What the hell do you think you're doing?" Warrick demanded.

"My name is Rahmire," the young man said in a hard, hoarse whisper, in a manner that implied the name should mean something to Warrick. "Rahmire Jones."

Holy shit! Warrick thought. Was he the brother of some girl he'd laid? Quickly, he tried to remember the names of the bodies that had passed through his bed over the years, but they just hadn't been important enough to stay with him.

"I work for Ali Sabas!"

That opened up an entirely different can of worms. But why the hell would Sabas pull something like that? He did know one thing, however, he knew he would have to play this one carefully. Rahmire was scared, he sensed. Terrified. That might work to his advantage, but after more consideration, he realized that only made the situation worse. A frightened man did not think—he might do anything, he'd never consider the consequences. Yes, he was going to have to be very careful.

"Think you got the wrong man, buddy. If you let me go, I'll forget all about this. I don't know anyone named Ali. I used to work with a woman named Alison. Called herself Ali. But I don't know any guy—"

"Enough, Warrick. I know all about you. I know why you are here. I know all about your project. But you've bungled it, you fool. I'm here to take it over. I'm here to save it!"

Christ! Warrick thought. How the hell could this have happened?

"Does Ali know what you're doing?" Warrick demanded.

"That is not your concern."

248

No, Sabas did not know, Warrick concluded, but what good did that do him? In the present situation there was no way he could get Sabas to call off his dog.

"Where is the case?" Rahmire demanded. "I want it."

"What case?"

The knife pressed tighter. It was very sharp. It cut the surface of the skin. Warrick felt a trickle of blood run down his neck.

"It's in the trunk of the car," he whispered.

"You left it there, where anyone could steal it? You idiot! You—"

"It's less conspicuous there than carrying it around and as safe as anywhere else. Now if you want it, let's get it. Then you can be on your way."

Rahmire's smile was ugly. "It's not that simple, Warrick."

Rahmire gave Warrick his instructions. They would walk through the restaurant casually so as not to attract attention. But they would be close together. Any false moves and the knife would go into Warrick's side.

Warrick's mind raced as they left the men's room. There had to be some way to overpower this clown! he thought. Some safe way that would guarantee he wouldn't be slashed to ribbons. Strangely enough, with all the chances he'd taken in the last two years, this was one he didn't want to risk. But he couldn't let him have that case.

He noticed Trudi sitting at a table reading a menu as they walked through the restaurant and realized Rahmire either did not know about her or had forgotten. Warrick quickly looked away, hoping she would not see him. Rahmire would be easier to handle without her around.

Trudi did see him, however. She looked up and saw him walking away with a strange man, leaving her.

"Evan," she shouted, "where are you going?"

Warrick shot her a sharp look, ordering her to keep quiet. She understood his implicit message, but it was too late. Rahmire had forgotten about her, but she was forgotten no longer.

"That's your woman," Rahmire sneered.

"I don't know—"

"Don't lie! She's coming with us. Get her over here."

Warrick motioned Trudi over with his head. "Trudi, we're leaving here now. We—"

"Leaving? We haven't eaten yet."

"Don't argue with me, damn it. This guy...." He looked around to make sure no one was close enough to hear them. "This guy'll kill me if you don't come."

Trudi looked justifiably terrified. Not for Warrick—she did not care what happened to him—but for herself. She also worried about the job she had come to do. She had no way to warn Ali and Mantizima.

"Now!" Warrick insisted as he and Rahmire moved to the door.

Mantizima and Ali ate in their car, which was parked in a rest stop off the side of the road a couple of miles south of the restaurant. By all of their calculations, and if yesterday was any judge, Warrick's car would be passing the rest stop in thirty or forty minutes. They had plenty of time, they thought, for a leisurely break themselves.

Their calculations were wrong, however.

"They're starting," Ali said and quickly tossed her own half-eaten lunch in a bag.

"That's strange," Mantizima said, though he didn't consider it cause for alarm. "All right. I'll move the car where we know they won't be able to see us, and we'll give them enough time for a head start."

As Mantizima moved the car, Ali picked up the receiver, but as she studied it a question grew on her face.

"Terry, this thing's going crazy," she said. "It shows them as heading in the wrong direction."

"Maybe they've gotten off onto surface streets for some reason. Perhaps they need gas. It's probably nothing to worry about."

"They're going north. Back in the direction they came from!" Ali insisted.

"Let me see that."

Mantizima studied it for a moment and checked to see that the receiver had not malfunctioned, then quickly handed it back to Ali.

"Something happened in that restaurant, Ali. It must have. And we'd better find out what it was."

They arrived at the restaurant as quickly as possible, owing to the fact that their car was pointed in the wrong direction. Ali jumped out.

"I'll try to find—"

"I'm coming with you."

She questioned the wisdom of that decision, but said nothing.

They found the waitress who had served Trudi, a lazy, indifferent woman who was too busy to talk to them until they hinted at an offer of money. The waitress was still a young woman, probably not much more than thirty, but of the type who seems to rush towards middle-age with open arms. She had a fat body, a loose, doughy face and dry, ineptly bleached hair.

"The man is probably in his late twenties. American. Tall, slender, with dark brown hair. The girl's young, small and blond. And she has a German accent," Mantizima said.

"Did you see them?" Ali demanded anxiously.

The woman ignored Ali, but she studied Mantizima with open speculation and gave him a seductive little smile of the sort that had been known to cause strong men to vomit.

"Why do you want them?" she asked.

"They're...friends," Mantizima explained. "We were supposed to meet them, but we got our directions crossed."

251

A black man with white friends. With a white woman who was a lot more than a friend, if she read them right. Now that was interesting, the waitress thought. She'd always wondered what it would be like with a black man. She'd heard things, of course; who hadn't? And she really wondered whether they were true. What would it be like?

Fantasize about him later, Ali thought, reading the woman's obvious idea, on your own time!

"Were they here?" she demanded impatiently.

What would it be like with this man? she wondered. Pretty good, she figured. Not that she'd ever find out. She was a married woman, totally faithful to her husband...except, of course, for those times with Harry, her boss, but that was just to keep her job. Although, lately, that was all she'd got. All that fat slob of a husband she had did was drink and watch television. She wondered whether black men burn out. She hoped not. A tongue slithered out onto the woman's thick lower lip and she melted inside, visualizing Mantizima naked, at least from the waist down.

"Oh sure, they were here," she said at last, answering Ali's question to Mantizima. "They didn't leave me any money."

"They didn't pay you?" Ali asked.

With great annoyance and obvious envy of Ali's looks and nerve, the woman finally turned to her. "Isn't that what I said? She ordered coffee and they never paid for it. They didn't drink it either, but that doesn't matter. It has to be paid for."

"Why did they leave so suddenly? Did you see anything that might have made them go?"

Just then a fat man in cook's whites came out of the kitchen. He was just looking around idly until he spotted Mantizima.

"Hey, you, boy," he shouted. "You can't come in here."

"They're just asking for directions, Harry," the waitress said. "He's her driver. They'll be gone in a minute."

"Well, make sure they are," Harry muttered on his return to the kitchen.

The woman's smile to Mantizima bragged of her quickness and demanded all the gratitude required when one is pulled out of a burning building. She revolted Mantizima, but he struggled to hide it.

"No, there was nothing," the waitress said. "Nothing made them leave. They just came in, ordered coffee and left. I think he just wanted to use the men's room. I don't know why she sat down. But there was nothing that made them leave."

"Think!" Ali demanded.

"I am thinking!" the woman said angrily. "And nothing happened. Nothing!"

Ali shrugged at Mantizima as they turned towards the door, but the waitress' continued speech held them.

"...Nothing, that is, but meeting their friend. Hey, maybe he's a friend of yours, too."

They looked at her in silent amazement.

"Small, little guy, dark skin. Colored, probably. He shouldn't have been in here. I thought he might just be one of those A-rabs you hear about, you know, with all the oil, only he had hair the color of mine. So I guess he's got to be colored."

Ali's eyes widened in sudden shock. She had a vivid recollection in her mind of a small, blond Arab walking through their motel parking lot the night before. She felt sick.

Mantizima stuffed a twenty rand note into the woman's hand. "For their coffee," he explained. "Thank you. You've been a big help."

He took Ali's arm and guided her towards the door.

"Funny thing, though," the woman shouted after them. "They were really chummy when they walked out, but they didn't seem to know him when he came in."

Mantizima and Ali looked glumly at each other.

Trudi gripped the steering wheel of Warrick's car with white, stretched knuckles. She glanced occasionally at Warrick, sitting beside her in the passenger seat, sending a silent appeal for help, but Warrick had more on his mind than her safety. They did share the same fear, however: the man in the back seat with the very sharp knife.

"You're a fool, Jones," Warrick said bitterly.

"Time will show us who is the fool. Now turn around so I can watch you."

"The...package will sail tomorrow, and I would have delivered the case in person in a few days, as arranged. Everything—"

"I told you, my comrade in Cairo—"

"I don't care what he told them. Everything is under control. No one, no one breathing, that is, knows anything."

Warrick's confidence drained Rahmire's. He seemed so sure. Perhaps he had been too hasty...but no, he had to be right. He'd come too far not to be. There was no turning back now.

"What about her?" Rahmire asked of Trudi, in a sudden burst of defiance.

"What about her? She didn't know anything till you pulled this stupid stunt. Now she knows too much, and that's your doing."

Trudi gripped the wheel even tighter. She didn't need elaboration to know what that meant. Where was Ali? she thought. Where was she?

"It's not too late to change your mind, Jones," Warrick continued. "We can still follow my plan. We can do it together."

"I have my own plan, Warrick. The shipment will go as scheduled. It doesn't need me. But I'll take that case out of South Africa in my own time, my own way. I don't need you any longer."

Jesus! Warrick thought. He's crazy! He made himself calm down and tried to address the problem coolly and rationally. There was no doubt that Rahmire intended to kill them both. It was just a matter of time. Even if he managed to scrape through somehow, however, he was still a dead man. He'd let this maniac get hold of the case; those terrorists would not take that failure lightly, they'd have their revenge. And even if he succeeded in eluding them, where was he? He'd never collect his payment. He'd be back where he was two years ago. It would all have been for nothing. He might as well be dead.

He stole a quick glance at Rahmire over his shoulder. Out of his depth, Warrick thought. He's crazy and scared and in way over his head. The longer it took, the more frightened and dangerous Rahmire would be. He'd been right in not resisting in the restroom; they'd been too close. But conditions were different in the car. They had the seat between them. Now the odds were better in his favor.

He had to try, he concluded, and soon. Now. Now or never. It was his only chance. Everything he had was riding on it.

Without warning, Warrick suddenly reached over and grabbed the wheel from Trudi's hands. Trudi screamed. The car went into a frightening spin. Rahmire leaned over the seat, slashing his knife wildly. Warrick ducked.

But not enough.

CHAPTER TWENTY-ONE

"I wish I had told you about him," Ali said regretfully.

As Mantizima hurried to catch up with Warrick's car, Ali had told him about the young Palestinian with blond hair whom she had seen in the parking lot the night before.

"If you had, I wouldn't have done anything about it, other than write it off to coincidence."

"I'm a reporter, trained to distrust coincidence. I should have pursued it."

"You were tired, Ali. Under a lot of strain. Now stop beating yourself. It's done. All we can do now is try to correct it."

"Who do you think he is?"

"Someone from the terrorist group that commissioned Warrick to build the bomb, I'd say."

"But the waitress said Warrick did not appear to know him."

"I doubt he knows many of them by sight," Mantizima said.

"No, I suppose he doesn't. They wouldn't be careless enough to leave a path that traceable.... But somehow, this doesn't strike me as being a part of the well-ordered plan. Feels more like a curve from left field."

Mantizima nodded his agreement. They drove in silence for a while, trying to recapture lost time.

"I just keep thinking about Trudi," Ali said softly after a while. "She's in the hands of, not one, but two

nuts in what has got to be a terrifying situation. I just
hope she has the stuff I think she has. Hope she comes
out of it okay."

"Whatever happens is not your fault."

"Isn't it? Remember, I got her into this."

"She got herself into it. For whatever reason."

Just then, a slow-driving car, desiring for some
whimsical reason to be in Mantizima's lane, leisurely
pulled in front of their car.

"Get out of my way, you stupid bastard," he muttered
tightly as he skillfully changed lanes.

Ali studied him quietly. It wasn't like him to be that
irritated by anything. He was losing control, he was
nearing his limit, she thought. They both were. And they
had no idea how much more would be demanded of them.

"What did you mean when you said 'for whatever
reason?'" she asked.

"Just a thought. You won't like it."

"I'm listening," she said.

"All right, consider this. Maybe you just played right
into her hands. Maybe you gave her the chance she
wanted."

"Terry, I had to talk her into it. I know. I was there."

"Perhaps. But then again, maybe she just read you
correctly. Maybe she understood that the best thing she
could do would be to push you until you begged her to
take this little jaunt. Then all she had to do was to find
an accomplice and wait. It doesn't take much intelligence
to realize how valuable that case would be to the Israeli
Government. They'd pay anything for it."

Instead of flaring up as Mantizima expected, Ali
played with the idea for a moment. "You're saying that
my little heroine is really after the big score."

"It has been known to happen."

"I don't think so, Terry. Granted it's an idea that
occurred to me. Oh, not in connection with Trudi. But I've
been concerned about the obvious marketability of that
case from the time you told me it might have existed. But

257

I just don't buy your scenario about Trudi. I can't. I know her. Not very long, but very well. She wouldn't do what you're suggesting. I'd stake my life on that."

"You probably have."

With no answer to that, she lapsed back into silence. They remained like that for quite a while, until Ali, gazing absently out of the window, happened to notice something in the bush at the side of the road. Something that definitely should not be there.

"Terry!" she shouted. "I saw a hand at the side of the road."

"A what?"

"A hand!" she shouted impatiently. "A human hand."

Without a word, he cut across three busy lanes of traffic to catch the exit just ahead of them. But even with such quick action, at the speed they were traveling, they'd covered a lot of ground. He backtracked a little, then parked the car and set out on foot to find it. They searched for quite some time without any success. Mantizima was nearly ready to call it quits.

"Where did you see it, Ali?"

"I don't know. Around here somewhere...I think. Oh, it all looks the same. I don't—" She stopped in her tracks and pointed. "Look! There it is!"

They ran to the body, fearful that it might be Trudi. They were relieved that it was not, but not really surprised by who it was. They knew they should have expected it.

"It's Warrick," Ali said.

For the second time in what he considered to be too short a period of time, Mantizima knelt beside a dying man. Only this time the man was not a friend. Ali looked over his shoulder. In a moment Warrick opened his eyes and recognized her, but in his disorientation he did not find her presence there incongruous.

"Ali," he said weakly, offering a feeble version of that illuminating smile. "Case...stolen...stolen," he muttered.

"By whom?" Mantizima demanded.

"Stolen.... All...over."

Mantizima grabbed him up off the ground by the shoulders. "Now listen to me, Warrick, you don't have much time," he said cruelly. "Tell me who took the case."

"No money," Warrick muttered bitterly. "No...nothing."

"Who was the man, damn you, who took the case? Where was he headed?"

"All gone...all...gone."

"Where?" Mantizima shouted. "Do you hear me? Where was he going? Who was—"

Ali gently touched Mantizima on the shoulder. "Terry, he's dead."

Mantizima closed his eyes, helpless before a part of nature stronger than any man. He pulled his hands away from Warrick's shoulders and let the body fall to the ground. Then he and Ali stood before it, not in some form of respectful mourning, but simply to allow the fact of his death to register.

"He who lives by the sword...." Mantizima said bitterly, believing it to be a fitting eulogy for the man before him and, in fact, the only one he was going to get.

Why does any one man happen to die? Ali wondered, viewing the inexplicable mystery of death like a child confronted by it for the first time.

Was it simply chance? If that man in Cairo hadn't died, the arm of the law would never have reached out for Warrick. So much had happened beyond his control that, in retrospect, it was almost amazing that he'd held things together that long. Or was Mantizima right? Was there a form of justice in the universe that condemned to destruction those who worked in the cause of the destruction of others?

She did not know; she hoped it was the latter. In Alan Warrick's case, it certainly seemed to be.

"Let's get going," Mantizima told her. "Let's take care of the living."

"That man Evan Todd—or the man calling himself Evan Todd, whichever it is—is dead," Kloff told Logan.

Logan hadn't been paying a lot of attention to Kloff, but when those words filtered in, his face jerked up. "Dead? How?"

"He was knifed. Bled to death."

"Did Mantizima—"

"No," Kloff said as if that were unthinkable. "But he found the body. He and Ali Hayden. The police team saw them, but waited until they left to investigate about what they discovered."

"You mean they left the body? They seem to do that a great deal. You're right, it's not quite 'decent' of them."

For the first time in quite a while, Logan seemed his jovial old self, but he was joking, Kloff thought, about a dead man.

"I don't think they had any choice under the circumstances."

"No, no, of course not. No one wants to be caught with a stiff.... Did they take anything away with them, did the police notice?"

"Did they rob the body, do you mean?" Kloff asked disgusted by the implication. "I hardly think so. The police found his wallet on him. That's how they made the identification."

The seed of a budding idea, small, young, fragile, sprouted in Kloff's mind, but it was too elusive for him to grasp fully. His mind, however, gave him a shadowy, unexplained hint of what it would be when it was allowed to grow.

"Why did you ask if they took something?" he asked suspiciously.

"No reason." Logan insisted.

Kloff sat down heavily in a chair. How he wished he were a brighter man, someone who could pull those loose ends together in a snap. But he wasn't. He'd just have to go about it as he always had, with long hours and hard

260

work. At least, he thought, he was a man who wouldn't let it go until he had it.

"Neil, have you...thought about this? What this means?"

"Of course, I've thought about it. I've thought about nothing else since Kroonhof gave the bloody job to me."

"No, I mean Todd, or whoever he was. Neil, he traveled here on a phony passport. He's suspected of killing an innocent man. Yet you're treating him as if he were a model citizen. There's a very good chance that he was our bomb-builder. Everything points to it. The cover he must have taken was perfect for him."

Logan appeared to roll that over in his mind. "You might be right about that, Pieter. But if you are, then our job is done, isn't it?"

"Done? Neil, there's still a nuclear bomb loose out there somewhere! And Todd, for lack of another name to call him, is dead. Someone killed him. Someone, perhaps, who now has that bomb."

"Mantizima," Logan said instantly. "I always told you he was involved in it, didn't I? A little falling-out between fellow travelers, perhaps. Or maybe Mantizima always intended to get rid of him. Excess baggage, as it were."

Kloff looked at Logan in disbelief. He was grasping at straws. He'd believe anything now, no matter how illogical. How did he get through to this man? Or did he? He told himself he should let it go. It was not his responsibility. His job was to help Logan, not to fight him or work around him. But he couldn't turn his back on it, he knew that. Not if he intended to continue living with himself. He'd just have to keep it...somehow.

"You're doing an excellent job, Pieter. Truly excellent. Don't know what I'd have done without you. Keep it up," Logan said in dismissal.

The flattery meant nothing to Kloff; it came from a person whose opinion he did not value. He nodded feebly, for lack of anything else to do, and slowly walked out of the office, his burden weighing heavily on his shoulders.

He was halfway down the hall when he was suddenly given another, this time greater, glimpse of that embryo idea. It was a startling thought to say the least, too much so to be believed. He was pierced by a momentary stab of disloyalty. Still, he looked back in the direction of Logan's office in stunned disbelief. He ought to forget the idea, he knew. It was preposterous, unthinkable.

But he couldn't let it go. It made too much sense. Much too much.

He was going to kill her, Trudi knew. After what happened to Warrick, damn him, there wasn't any doubt of that. He was going to kill her when she ceased to serve a purpose for him, when he no longer needed a hostage. And what, she thought desperately, could she do to stop it?

She had lived like that for hours, in hopeless terror, but it was as if the fear operated only on one level of her mind. On the other, she carefully, deliberately, monitored their position, constantly keeping track of where they were. The sign at the side of the road which they had just passed said "Welkom to Amersfoot." That name did not mean much to her—it was just a small town—but it told her they were traveling northwest. She kept a firm grasp on her sense of direction at all times. She had no idea what she could do with the information she was collecting, but she gathered it with strict diligence nonetheless. It was all she had to hold onto.

They had gotten off the National Road at Volksrust, but continued to travel in the same general direction on surface streets. She hoped—desperately hoped—that Mantizima and Ali were able to make sense of it. She knew that following had to be much harder over those city streets.

Rahmire ordered her to turn right at the corner, and she did, without comment, but she was starting to get the idea that he had no idea where he was going. He was running scared. That, she thought glumly, made the situation even worse, even more desperate for her. If that were possible.

She had tried to inch the speed up several times, in the hopes of being stopped by a policeman, but Rahmire caught on to what she was doing and ordered her to keep it level. She did not dare to try it again, and she had no other ideas.

Just then, she saw a disabled car parked at the side of the road up ahead. A family stood next to the car, waiting for help. If only she could attract their attention. She got an idea. If speeding did not work, she'd try something in the opposite direction.

Without warning, she suddenly slammed on the brakes. The sudden stop threw Rahmire into the dash as she had hoped, but it also caused another car to slam into her bumper. She felt a surge of hope as she threw her door open. Rahmire was quicker than she thought, however, and stronger. She should have remembered how quickly he reacted when Warrick tried something similar. He grabbed her wrist and yanked her towards him. He pressed the knife into her side. Out of the corner of his eye Rahmire saw the other driver, the one who had hit them, approaching on foot. He ordered her to drive away. Immediately.

As she drove off, she noticed that the family members at the side of the road, who had looked up at the sound of the collision as she had hoped, had already returned their attention to their own problem. They had no way of knowing how badly she needed them.

The other driver still stood in the street, shouting at her for leaving the scene of an accident, but his voice was drowned out by the sound of the engine.

No one out of all those people noticed or cared about the injured little transmitter dangling precariously from the smashed bumper.

"It stopped!" Ali shouted. "The signal stopped."

They looked at each other in horrified dismay. That was the only link they had to Trudi and the controls. They couldn't lose it, but they didn't know how to hold it.

Then slowly, undramatically except by implication, like a human heart of someone who had died and been brought back to life, it beat once more. Then again and again. The signal remained weak and erratic, but it gave them enough of a direction to follow.

Ali took an audible gulp of air in relief. Mantizima pressed down even harder on the overworked accelerator.

Their desperation held them in a tight silence for a long time. Each was completely lost in his own thoughts. Ali's thoughts were totally devoted to Trudi, but Mantizima's it appeared, went in an entirely different direction.

"Ali, I think there's something else at work here, there's something involved that we're missing completely," he said at last, speaking more in the manner of thinking aloud than holding a conversation.

"This blond Palestinian. He's an unknown factor."

"Not now. We don't know his name, but we know he exists. That rules him out as an unknown now. No, there's something, someone else here."

"Who?"

But Mantizima did not answer. He drifted away from the auditory to the mental without even realizing he had done it. Ali did not press him.

"Rune's death," he said after a time, as if that explained everything or even anything.

"What about it? You said the sniper was gunning for me."

"What if I were wrong?" he asked.

Ali told him she had never really bought his theory.

"Because he never tried again after what we've been calling the second attempt, right?"

Ali nodded.

"What if that boy in the bar was just what you said—a redneck on a personal vendetta? What does that say about the shooting?"

"That the killer was after you, which seems unlikely, or Rune, which is very probable."

But she added that Rune's death did not have to be related to their current mission. A man in his position made a lot of enemies, she reminded him. Any one of them might have come out of his past to take revenge.

"You're the one who told me to distrust coincidence," he told her. "No, it has to be related."

"So Warrick killed him," Ali said.

"Probably, but why?"

"Because he knew Rune was getting closer to him, or at least that he knew something of Warrick's plan. He had to get rid of Rune. I'm sure someone else took over, but the interim confusion in BOSS bought him a little time."

Mantizima questioned that confusion. Intelligence agents get killed all the time, he told her, and yet their organizations recover quickly. They have to. They're prepared for it.

"And besides, how did Warrick know Rune was a threat to him?" Mantizima asked.

"Maybe someone told him what that man in Cairo said before he died.... No, that won't work. He would have called it off or laid low for a while if he knew all that. Maybe he was just being cautious, in case the authorities knew something.... Nope. Still won't work. There are a lot of people in BOSS. It doesn't explain how he happened to settle on Rune."

Suddenly, the solution hit her like a lightning bolt.

"The leak!" she shouted. "There was a leak in Rune's organization. He admitted as much to us.... My God! We completely forgot about him. That's your other factor."

"That's it," Mantizima said.

"We don't know him," Ali said glumly.

"But he knows about us, Ali. I'm sure of it. He wouldn't let our involvement get past him. And make no

265

mistake about it. If we don't find him, he is certainly going to find us."

"Good God, man! Are you still here?" Logan asked Kloff with mock surprise.

Kloff looked up but did not respond. The answer, he thought, should have been obvious, even to Logan.

"I thought you were such a good family man," Logan said. "Your family probably doesn't even remember what you look like."

"It's not yet quitting time? Why should I leave?"

"Because with the hours you have been putting in, you have it coming. It's due, Pieter. Why don't you take your wife out to dinner? Surprise her."

Kloff couldn't believe he was being asked to leave in the middle of this assignment. Or was he being told to leave?

"You're so conscientious," Logan laughed. "You'll probably be here long after quitting time, as usual, won't you?"

"I might be. Why does that bother you?"

"Bother, did you say? Of course, it doesn't bother me. Why should it? Well, maybe it does make me feel a bit guilty because I'm not staying. I'm on my way out now. Or I will be soon. I have a date tonight that I'm not going to miss for anything. Why don't you leave too?"

Kloff looked at Logan with disgust that he was sure was not disguised. How could a date be more important than what they were working on? How could he put anything above that? Why should he have to explain how important it was?

"The reports keep coming in, Neil."

"That's what the night men are for. Let them handle it. They have your telephone number if they need it."

Why was Logan pushing so hard for him to go? Kloff questioned. Was it just what he said? Was he afraid of being shown up by a subordinate? He was so ambitious,

266

that might be possible. But it might also be something else.

"I'll stay a while more to see what turns up."

"You bloody twit!" Logan exploded. "Do you think this show of devotion to duty is going to do you any good? Do you think anyone notices? Have they so far? How old are you? You haven't gotten anywhere with it by now, and if I have anything to say about it, you never will."

With that warning, Logan stormed off to his own office. Kloff looked after him in disbelief.

It was almost beyond his comprehension to believe it, but Kloff was sure Logan desperately wanted to get rid of him. Why? He had two possible explanations in mind. One was that Logan knew he was failing miserably at this investigation, but had a plan of his own to pull it off somehow; that he intended to present some rigged solution, such as the farfetched one starring Mantizima that Logan liked so well, and push it through without having Kloff around to steal his thunder.

The other solution, the one too monstrous to allow himself to put into words, Kloff feared was the correct one.

He wouldn't think about it, Kloff decided. Yet even as he made that decision he opened a desk drawer and reached to the back of it. He took out something that he had not needed for a long time, since he stopped working in the field, an old friend that had saved his life more than once.

His gun.

He took out the stained, but laundered, old cloth that he had always used and went to work on it. He oiled it, caressing it as gently as a bride on her wedding night, easing it out of retirement until it was fit and ready once again.

But ready for what?

267

CHAPTER TWENTY-TWO

Rahmire pricked the skin of Trudi's arm with the point of his knife, drawing a small drop of blood. It was not his intention to hurt her, although he did not care if he did. He simply wanted to get her attention and disliked speaking to her any more than necessary. Now that he had learned what a "working girl" was, he had even more contempt for her than when he considered her to be merely a useless woman.

The knife prick had hurt her, however, causing her to momentarily lose control of the car.

"Watch where you are driving!" he ordered.

Trudi struggled to bring the car back into its lane.

"You should have told me you needed petrol," Rahmire continued. "Get off the road at the next station."

The fuel indicator was now below empty. Damn! Trudi thought. She had been hoping he wouldn't notice that. She'd planned to let the car run dry. Now there was no hope of that, she thought, but perhaps when they got to the station....

Her hopes were dashed there, too. When she cut the engine in front of the gas pumps, she started to open the door.

"Where do you think you're going?" Rahmire asked.

"Please. I have to use the ladies room," Trudi begged.

"No. You stay here. Keep the windows rolled up and the doors locked. And don't try anything or it will be the last thing you ever do," Rahmire said as he started to get out of the car.

For an instant, it appeared that Rahmire had forgotten about the car keys. But Trudi hadn't. She thought she would be able to drive off as soon as he was out of the car. She forced herself not to look at the keys, not to even think about them, lest the thought show on her face. Her efforts were for nothing. Rahmire had the same thought a moment later. With a wry smirk on his face, he leaned back into the car and jerked the key out of the ignition.

"You won't be needing this for the moment, will you?" he asked sarcastically.

Hope died in Trudi's eyes. She sagged against the steering wheel, burying her face in her arms for a moment, then forced herself to sit up and survey the possibilities. Since Rahmire had anticipated most of them, there weren't many left. The station had been stuck on a remote piece of land on the outskirts of the town of Breton. There wasn't so much as a house in sight. If she tried to run, where would she go? And how far could she get on legs that were stiff with fatigue and tension? How long would it be before Rahmire and his knife caught up with her?

Her only hope was catching the eye of the attendant. She lit a cigarette and posed herself seductively. At the very least, she thought, the attendant would have to tell her to extinguish the cigarette since she was parked in front of the pumps. But the attendant, when he finally appeared, was a slow, stupid boy, indifferent to both his job and his customers. His only interest, if it could be called that, was in Rahmire, a person of obviously mixed heritage and indeterminable race, whom he resented having to wait on. Trudi knew it was hopeless as soon as she saw the boy. She tried not to give in to despair but, despite her best efforts, her eyes traveled to the large reddish-brown stain on the back seat.

So much blood, she mused, shaking a little at the thought. Who would have thought there would be so much blood?

Rahmire stretched when he got out of the car to loosen the kinks and to ease some of the tension. He tried to act casually. He didn't want either Trudi or the attendant to know how scared he was. There was nothing to be afraid of, he assured himself. It was true that he had had to kill Warrick, and at a time when he hadn't planned to. But he would have to have done it eventually in any case, and one hostage was easier to control than two.

There really was nothing to worry about, he told himself again. Everything was going according to plan. He had arranged to meet a man in the morning who was going to smuggle both him and the case out of South Africa. From there he would be home-free. "As long as you're not too hot," was the man's only reservation. But there was no problem with that, Rahmire thought; the authorities might have been onto Warrick, but they had no suspicions about him.

He smiled to himself. The future was beginning to look very bright. In his mind he saw glowing images of himself moving up into a position of authority. Finally, he would be respected, admired, instead of snickered at. He would be an important man. Whenever he became afraid, he thought of that, and the fantasy kept him going.

He glanced at the attendant filling the car. He could sense the boy's resentment, but instead of making him feel inferior as it usually would, it made him cocky. Still giddy from his dream, he thought, you wouldn't treat me like this if you knew what I was doing. You wouldn't dare to!

He walked around the back of the car, floating on his internal euphoria. Then he stopped.

He saw it—the transmitter dangling from the damaged bumper.

All at once, everything changed. His fragile dreams shattered into a million pieces within him. They knew. They knew all along. *She* knew, he thought, looking at Trudi through the back window of the car. He wouldn't have believed it possible to hate anyone as much as he hated her in that moment.

He had to think. What was he going to do? He couldn't meet with that man now, not with the authorities onto him. He would have to find his own way out of South Africa. The fact that the man would probably not know he was being watched simply did not occur to him. But what should he do? he thought feverishly. Call Ali Sabas? No, he wasn't even sure where he was. Besides, Sabas would kill him if he ever learned how Rahmire had bungled this operation.

He waited until the attendant's back was turned, then ripped the beeper off the bumper. Acting as nonchalant as the blood pulsing in his veins would allow, he ambled over to the side of the station's lot and gazed into the field of sunscorched bush next to it. Then, glancing once over his shoulder to be sure no one was looking, he flung the beeper as far as it would go.

He had to act normally, he thought, as he stuffed some money into the boy's hand and climbed into the car. He had to act as if nothing had changed. And, though he was sure he was pulling it off, he wasn't even close.

He ordered Trudi to drive into the city of Breton, of which they were on the outskirts. He pulled a road map out of the glove compartment, which, since it was starting to get dark, he studied with the help of a penlight flashlight.

Something had happened out there, Trudi thought, immediately sensing the change Rahmire was sure he had hidden. She knew that the fear she had felt all day was just a prelude for what she was to feel now. Instead of destroying her, however, it forced her to gather the little strength she had left. This, she knew, was what she had been keeping it for. This was it. She also felt a small surge of hope because she had an advantage Rahmire knew nothing about.

It had always been her habit to study the maps and brochures of the places she planned to visit. She liked to

271

really know a place before she moved there. It gave her a feeling of belonging even before she arrived. She had studied that map before she came to South Africa, and probably knew it nearly as well as the man who had drawn it. She knew it well enough to read it, quite literally, backwards. She waited, watching, studying, until the small beam of light came to a stop. Then she stealthily scratched the name of that place into the steering wheel padding with her fingernail.

"Here it is," Ali said, holding the transmitter on her palm for Mantizima to see.

They had been searching in the field next to the service station for the last ten minutes, trying to determine whether their equipment had simply malfunctioned or whether it had done its job. Its last job.

"End of the road." Ali said.

"No, it isn't!" Mantizima shouted. "Think for a moment, Ali. What would you do if you were trying to run away and you knew someone had been watching your car?"

"Ditch it and get another one."

"Right!" Mantizima said. "Now let's find that car and see if Trudi left us a message in it."

"And if she wasn't able to?"

"Then that's the end of the road."

They found the car about an hour later, abandoned on the fringe of a grocery store parking lot. With the help of flashlights, they began searching it for some sort of a clue that would direct them further, first in the obvious places, then the less obvious, and now, in any place that would prolong the necessity of having to call it quits.

Finally, with a sigh, Ali stepped out of the car. Short of ripping the seats out and tearing up the rugs, she couldn't think of anyplace else to look, and she would gladly have done those things with her bare hands, if necessary, only she knew they wouldn't do any good. In frustration, she slammed her fist down onto the roof of the car and never even felt the pain.

She was about to speak to Mantizima when she glanced out onto the street and saw a police car approaching. Oh, my God! she thought. What would they think when they found a black man rummaging through a car? What would they do to him? Her voice froze. All she could manage to do was to tug at Mantizima's shirt and point.

"Yes," he said, unconcerned, as he stepped out of the car and turned off his flashlight. "They are probably reporting in right now. We'd better leave so they can come and pick this car as clean as we did."

Ali stared at him in amazement.

"For a 'professional observer,' you haven't been terribly observant. They've been watching us since we left Jo'burg. Probably before that," he said.

"Who has?"

"All of them. Local police, Security Branch. Probably reporting in to BOSS. I'm surprised you haven't seen them," Mantizima said.

"They can't have been that obvious," Ali answered, "or I would have."

"No, I'll grant you, they haven't been obvious, except by omission. I started getting suspicious yesterday. We were passed by several police cars, and not one of them showed the least bit of interest in us."

"Why should they have? We weren't doing anything wrong."

"You can tell you're white," he laughed bitterly. "You aren't used to being stopped by the police and questioned for no reason. As if a black man and a white woman alone together weren't reason enough in their minds. Believe me, these past two days have been highly unusual. Unless I've missed my guess, BOSS has set up a national police network to watch us, but not to stop us. We should be flattered. We seem to have entered into an unprecedented partnership with them. Only, if we succeed, they'll take the credit, and if we fail, we will."

"You've known all this and you haven't done anything about it?"

"What could I do? For all of your years in foreign countries, you know, you still think like an American. You don't fully understand a police state. The individual is powerless against them. If they want you, you can't get away from them. There is nowhere to go, no way to run. Besides, I'm an engineer, remember?"

"What the hell does that have to do with it?" Ali demanded angrily.

"I only try to change the nature of things when they are going against me. When they're working for me, I leave them alone."

"And how are things working now?"

"They're not."

Silently, they both stood in the parking lot, staring into the dark interior of the open car. They both knew they were finished, but neither could admit it. In an effort to have something to do, anything that would put off making that admission, Mantizima flipped the flashlight on and absently aimed it into the car.

The beam of light just happened to land on the top of the steering wheel. They both noticed the etching at the same time. They looked at each other briefly, unable to believe they had missed it, then, with renewed energy, climbed back into the car to read it.

"S...U...D...," Mantizima slowly read aloud.

Then, in a flash, he grasped the whole message and looked at Ali in horror.

The Sudwala Caves are a breathtaking natural phenomenon located about two hundred miles west of Pretoria. Particularly unique is the fact that the beautiful subterranean maize of caves and caverns are continually cooled by a fresh breeze, the origin of which, even after years of searching, is still unknown. Attracting thousands of visitors a year, they are one of South Africa's most popular tourist attractions.

Not to mention a great place to hide a body.

Mantizima shook the dozing, old black caretaker awake while Ali watched. It hadn't been hard to break into either the park or the caretaker's shack, but the time it took seemed like an eternity. They knew it was Trudi's time and might be all she had left. The old man awoke with a start and was frightened by the presence of a strange black man and, even more, by that of a white woman in his cabin. The caretaker got to his feet more swiftly than seemed physically possible and bowed his head in Ali's direction. She tensed at that action but did not consider it to be the ideal time to protest it.

Mantizima did not even notice. He wasted no time on preliminaries. "Where are your workers?" he shouted. "And your lamps?"

The old man either did not understand much English or was more frightened by Ali's presence than they realized. Mantizima took a deep breath to slow himself down and asked Ali to wait outside. Then he forced himself to be patient with the old man, speaking to him first in Xhosan, then a couple of other native languages until he found the one the man spoke. He explained the situation briefly and asked for the man's help.

Once he understood the problem, the old man told him that the caves were illuminated by permanently-placed electrical lights and that the park's maintenance men lived in a dormitory not far away. Within minutes, the lights were on and they had gathered a team of men to search the caves. But they all knew the Sudwala Caves were such an enormous labyrinth, it was physically impossible to cover them completely, even with that many people. Ali secretly believed that it was probably already too late and she cursed herself for ever getting Trudi involved.

There was no talk of giving up, but everyone involved was beginning to consider it hopeless, when they found her. Ali spotted her first and shouted for the others, her voice beating against the stone walls in

275

voluminous echoes. Rahmire had used both his fists and his knife on Trudi. Her face was badly battered and her dress was slashed to shreds and soaked with blood. Mantizima was the first to her side. He snatched up her wrist, holding it for an instant, then tossing it down in frustration. He pressed his fingers against the side of her neck, then looked at Ali in relief.

"She's alive!" he said. "Just barely, but alive."

Then he looked at the white skin under the bruises, which looked even paler than normal due to the loss of blood and the harsh artificial lights. How could he bring a white woman into a hospital? The police might be handling him with kid gloves, but the treatment wouldn't extend that far; the hospital wouldn't know about it. There would be questions asked, and that time might be all that Trudi had.

He didn't know how to get around the problem, but his conscience demanded he try. He felt responsible for her, all the more so because he had doubted her.

Swiftly, he made his decision. He spoke to the caretaker in his native language, causing the old man to rush out of the cave when he finished.

"What was that about?" Ali asked.

"I told him to call an ambulance. I'm taking her to a hospital."

"Not without me."

"You can't come, Ali. We're not going to a White hospital."

"What?"

"It's the only way, Ali."

"How will you—"

"I don't know how. Not yet. But I'll think of a way. It's the only chance she has."

"You can't take that risk. Let me take her," Ali said.

"It'd be harder for you. You'd get caught up in official inquiries. You wouldn't be able to avoid it. It will be much easier in our separate world where justice moves a whole lot slower."

Ali nodded reluctantly to indicate that she understood, even if she did not like it.

"Besides, I have another job for you," Mantizima said. "One you're better qualified for. There's a hotel in Montrose, not far from here, if I remember correctly. Hotel Meridith. Go there and register. That'll give you a chance to rest and a telephone to use. Get the home number of the Director of BOSS. You're a reporter. You'll know how to do that, won't you?"

"Won't be easy," Ali warned. "It's late, but, yes, I think I can do it."

"Good. Call that man. I think his name is Koonhof or Kroonhof or something. I can't remember what Rune called him. But anyway, find out from him who has taken over Rune's job. And then call him. I'll meet you back at the hotel later."

With that, Mantizima started to walk out of the cave.

"Terry, wait a minute. What do you want me to say to this Kroonhof when I reach him? How do I explain my interest?"

"He'll know who you are and why you are interested. Believe me, he'll know."

"And what about this other man?" she asked. "The one with Rune's job. What do you want me to tell him?"

"If I am wrong," Mantizima told her, "you're on your own. But if I'm right about things, you will not be the one doing the talking."

CHAPTER TWENTY-THREE

It hadn't been too hard to make the drivers of the Black ambulance take Trudi. They hadn't wanted to for fear of losing their jobs. Mantizima had had to cut them off before he learned the names of all the umpteen children they supported between them. But, fortunately, they were not strong men, so the force of his will and his swift assurance that he would accept all responsibility took the starch out of their resistance.

He knew that not everyone he would have to convince would cave in that easily, however.

When they reached the hospital, he took a deep breath and stiffened his spine. As the drivers wheeled the gurney towards the entrance, Mantizima took Trudi's hand, giving it a firm squeeze.

"Hold on, child," he said softly. "We're going to make it."

The young nurse at the front desk was startled when she saw the color of Trudi's skin. "Oh, dear, she's white," she said, half in her own native tongue and half in English. "You've come to the wrong place."

Then she noticed that, unlike Trudi, Mantizima was not white. The confusion reduced her to stammering. "Oh, that's not...it. I mean, you're...Oh, dear...."

Mantizima said nothing. That girl, he knew, would not be the one to make the decision. He would not waste his arguments on anything less than the heavy artillery she was sure to bring out.

As he expected, the young nurse turned to her superior for help. That woman, probably the night head nurse, was a short, stout woman with enormous breasts and a tightly-girdled body that was squeezed into a stiff, white cotton uniform. None of the soft pastel ones for her, Mantizima thought irrelevantly; nothing new would be as good as something old in her mind. She had a face that looked like it had collided with a train; he wondered how the train looked.

The battle-axe barreled over to stand next to the young nurse at the desk.

"Oh, no!" she shouted. "You'll have to get her out of here. There is a pay phone near the restrooms," she said, pointing vaguely down a corridor. "You can call a White ambulance from there."

"She's dying. She won't make it."

"Well, I'm very sorry about that," the head nurse said in a tone of complete indifference. "but we can't take her here. Rules are rules, you know? They're for everyone's good. Everyone benefits."

She loves this system, he thought. She thrives on it. She doesn't mind being on the bottom, as long as she's on the top of that bottom. In fact, she prefers it. The big fish in the very small pond. In oppression there was order, structure, a way of stepping on others, even if it meant she was stepped on herself; in freedom she would be lost. This, he thought, was the fallacy in the view of the white liberals, the people who classified all downtrodden souls as noble. What they often failed to see in their streamlined view of reality was that people of all ethnic groups were essentially the same in their differences. There were good people and those who were not good, and those, like this woman, who were their own worst enemy.

"I want to see a doctor, a surgeon," Mantizima said.

"Out of the question."

Without another word, he snatched a standing microphone attached to the hospital's paging system off the desk.

"Will a surgeon please report to the front desk in the emergency ward? At once."

"Look here! You can't do that," the battle-axe protested.

Mantizima couldn't decide whether she was more disturbed by his affront to her authority or by his flaunting of the rules. He figured it was a toss-up.

"I'm going to call a security guard to throw you and this girl out," she continued. "Mary," she said to the other nurse, "call—"

"Don't bother, Mary," Mantizima said. "It's done."

Mary, the young nurse, was not sure what to do, but, fortunately, the decision was made for her by the doctor who arrived just then. He, too, was a little surprised at seeing Trudi there, but he also took in the fresh blood seepage on the sheet covering her.

"He brought her in here, doctor," the head nurse said. "I told him that he couldn't. I said rules are rules, but he wouldn't listen. He...." Her voice trailed off when she saw the doctor wasn't listening.

Apparently unaware of anyone but Trudi, the doctor peeled the sheet back. He looked at the slashed dress with professional detachment. He pulled up her eyelids and took her pulse. Only then did he address Mantizima.

"Did you do this to her?"

"No, but I intend to find the man who did."

"Have her prepped for surgery," the doctor told the head nurse.

"But you can't do that. She's white. I'll report—"

The doctor shot her a threatening look that silenced the woman. The young nurse picked up the phone and gave the orders. The doctor waited silently until some orderlies came to wheel the gurney away, then walked away himself, with Mantizima following after him.

"Doctor, I'd like to wait, at least for a while, if I may," Mantizima said.

The doctor nodded and told him where the nearest waiting room was to the operating room.

"She's lost a lot of blood, you know," the doctor told him. "And there's a great deal of internal damage. I can't make any promises, Mr. ..."

"Mantizima."

"She might not make it, Mr. Mantizima."

"Just give her your best."

"I give that to all of them."

As the doctor went off to scrub, Mantizima marveled that the man never mentioned Trudi's race. Once his initial surprise was over, he probably never thought of it. He probably did not think of her as a person at all, but as a patient. Some people, he thought, might find that cold, but cold, deliberate dedication was exactly what he'd been hoping to find when he brought her there. Disinterested skill would do a lot more for her than tears.

Mantizima settled into an uncomfortable vinyl chair to wait. The other occupants of the waiting room were two women, a young woman and an older one who were so preoccupied with their own concerns they did not notice him. Within seconds he was lost in thought, so much so that he did not notice what was happening around him. After a while, however, it became so obvious that even he could not miss it.

Like a raging fire, word had spread around the hospital about the man who had brought in a white woman. Everyone who could possibly invent an excuse to be on that floor came to sneak a look at him. From the looks on the faces of the passing spectators, he could guess that they all took him to be Trudi's lover. Knowing that people tend to complicate their own feelings and simplify others', the assumption did not surprise him. What other than love would cause a man to risk all that he had for a woman? There were other motives, as he well knew, but they would not occur to other people.

Apart from that one common assumption, however, the thoughts reflected on those faces were not the same; they were many and varied. Some of the people who came to gawk at him were merely curious and eager to grasp at any sensation that happened to touch their unsensational lives. Others, however, were openly hostile. The Black separatists were easy to pick out; their anger allowed that people were either with them or were traitors, no other classifications were possible in their scheme of things. Their looks said that they would cheerfully slit his throat should the situation ever present itself. Men leered in his direction with undisguised congratulations on a point scored. Some of the women, to a one, plain and dull, resented his turning to a white woman before all black women had had a crack at him, even though some of them were his mother's age.

The experience had a sobering effect on him. While the girl on the operating table meant nothing more to him than a responsibility, their assumptions would have been correct were Ali in her place. In effect, their assumptions *were* correct, it was only the object that was wrong. With their private relationship suddenly made public, he was forced to reassess his own view of it.

He had thought about their racial differences, of course, but only in reference to his present situation. He had been attracted to her from the first, when she approached his table in the plane's cocktail lounge. More than any woman he had ever met. Naturally, he speculated about her, but since he was bound for South Africa, he backed off. Even after circumstance brought them together, however, and he decided she was worth the risk, the anti-miscegenation laws were his only concern. Had he met her in Boston, he was sure, he would never have given that difference a second thought.

Now, he was not so sure.

His skin prickled uncomfortably. He felt like a freak in a side show, an object of scorn by people he didn't even know. He'd been on the receiving end of bigotry before, but always dismissed it. He had never cared what people thought about him. He didn't care now, he told himself, but this was something different. Could he go through the rest of life facing this, as he had planned to, if Ali were willing? Could so private a man willingly become so public an object of curiosity? Would the judgments hold them together or would it drive them apart? He was sure Ali would say it did not matter, but how would she feel in time? Was it fair even to ask her to try?

Questions, new questions, kept arising from out of the blue, for which he had no answers. Maybe the solution was to proceed more slowly, he thought, to give it more time, and not to be surprised by the answers.

Then the doors to the operating room next to Trudi's opened and a reluctant doctor came out, dreading the task of having to tell the waiting women that he had not been able to save their husband and father.

Death. It was everywhere. It always was, he knew, as just another part of life, but now it seemed to be claiming a larger share. Its shroud weighed heavily on him, pressing in tighter with every passing day. Two men had died in his arms, a woman lay a few yards away fighting so as not to be claimed by it, and the death of thousands of people was no further away than the press of a "button." He felt it closing in on him; he felt as if he couldn't get away from it.

Then he thought of Ali. He had never felt so alive as when he was with her. Life was so short. It had taken him thirty-five years to find her. If he let her go, mightn't it take as long to find someone else of the "right" color? If he ever did. It would be a lonely life, more so now because he knew what it would be missing, but it would be a life without stares.

Let them stare, he decided. Their condemnation, their praise, those things did not matter. Crowds could never be a life-giving force in any case. Only one person could do that for him.

With that, life and death made peace within him. The questions were answered, those questions, at least. Maybe, he thought, they were all that simple if you let them be.

Logan hadn't gone home.

Kloff repeated that to himself over and over again, as proof of some charge he could not, or would not, name. Logan had said he was leaving early, he said he had a date, but quitting time had come and gone and Logan was still there.

Everyone else had left. Their entire section was dark, but for two small beams of light coming from offices occupied by men who had not uttered so much as a word in hours. It was as if they were unaware of each other's existence. Kloff was not sure whether Logan had forgotten about him, but knew he had forgotten nothing.

They waited together in, for the most part, uninterrupted silence. Waited for what? For the same thing? Kloff wondered. He did not know, but that was his only question. He had none about Logan anymore. He did not voice his thoughts, however, not even to himself. He just waited, patiently gathering data, like a policeman building a case.

Kloff occupied his time with thought and the chain-smoking of cigarettes. He did not allow his tension to build as the hours passed, but merely to maintain, to stay in a constant state of readiness for whatever happened.

Logan, he knew, filled his time with liquor.

Kloff remembered hearing when Logan reached what must have been the end of the bottle. "Shit!" he had shouted. "Too bloody little in these things." Then he had hurled it into his empty wastebasket, which toppled over from the force. Kloff had thought then that Logan would go out and get another, but something apparently more important held him there.

He thought back to the argument they had had that afternoon when Logan tried to get rid of him. The fight was not that unusual. Neil blew up easily—he had a terrible temper—but he usually cooled off just as quickly. Not because he cared what Kloff thought, but because he considered apologizing to Kloff more prudent than allowing him to hold a grudge. That night, however, the apology had not come. Though there had been nothing unusual in the words, something unprecedented had happened. Something had happened that might well affect his future. But even if Logan did succeed in getting him fired at some time in the future, that would not stop what he planned for that night.

The phone in Logan's office suddenly rang. He snatched it up before the end of the first ring.

"Yes, I understand. Perfectly," he said, after listening for a short time. "I'll be there. As soon as I can. Do nothing until you see me.... I don't care how you stop him. Just do it. Wait for me. See that he does, too."

"That's an order!" Kloff half-expected him to add, but he suspected the person on the other end was not someone who would care about Logan's orders. He did not know who Logan's caller was, but he could hear the effect that person was having on Logan. The call had nearly devastated him. Kloff noted and filed away for later the fact that Logan asked no questions.

Logan hung up and immediately placed an interoffice call. He ordered a small aircraft prepared for him and a driver to take him to the airport. Then he rushed out of his office, not even pausing to turn off the light. He had broken into a trot by the time he passed Kloff's office and was running, judging by the sound of the footsteps, by the end of the hall. Kloff heard a door slam; apparently unwilling to wait for the elevator, Logan took the stairs.

Kloff resisted the desire to follow him. He wanted to, but there were things he had to do first. He checked with the operator to find the identity of Logan's caller. It surprised him, but told him things were starting to come to a head. He had intended to follow Logan's lead, to have a driver and plane readied for him, too, but then he had a better idea. One that did not go through official channels.

He placed a call to the airport himself and asked to have a plane prepared for flight, but only after Logan's had taken off. He would drive himself to the airport, he decided, and would give the pilot his flight plan only after he arrived there. Secrecy and surprise, he thought, were his best weapons.

He forced himself to settle back, to wait. He would need one more report on Mantizima and Ali to learn their present location. Then it would be time for action.

Mantizima was still seated in the waiting room chair, only now he was bent forward with his hands cupped over his mouth. If hospital staff members were still coming to take a look at him, he did not notice. He had too much to do to dwell on personal problems that were not problems any longer.

Most people seeing him would have said he was doing nothing; some, perhaps, that he was thinking, but he was actually a man at work. He was sorting it all out, every single thing that had happened in the course of their venture, trying to put it all in its proper place. Like a whodunit reader, he was trying to solve the mystery before he got to the last page, sorting out the red herrings which life scattered more promiscuously than writers, knowing full well that this story was being acted out in all-too-vivid living color.

He glanced at his watch, then at the operating room doors. It was taking a long time in there. He hadn't wanted to leave until it was over, but he knew he could not wait too much longer. He had some time, however, not much, but some, and the quiet in the waiting room made it a better place than most for what he had to do.

He worked it through laboriously, bit-by-bit, trying to fit things together, moving or discarding what did not. And, finally, he was sure he knew all the answers. He wished he had a last page to consult for verification, but he really did not need it. He knew what had happened. He had figured out the only way things could have happened.

With that settled, he stood up and stretched. That was the first time he had moved and he was quite stiff. He looked at his watch again. Only two minutes had passed since the last time he had consulted it. With his work done, he knew that time would now pass more slowly. He thought about calling Ali at the hotel. She didn't have that much to do, and it had been a long time. He knew that she must be sick with worry. But he had waited so long to hear the outcome of the operation. If the doctor came out when he was off telephoning—no, he would wait a while longer.

It wasn't much longer, however; in only a few moments the operation was over. A bone-weary doctor emerged. He slipped off his hat and mask, but was too tired to care about the bloody hospital greens. Mantizima practically leaped at him, but he saw the tired reaction in the doctor's eyes. He had people jumping at him every time he walked out that door, Mantizima thought, but he still isn't used to it.

"Do you have time for some coffee, Mr. ... it's Mantizima, isn't it?" the doctor asked.

"Yes, it is, and yes, I have time."

"Good, I need it."

It killed him, but Mantizima did not press for an answer to his unasked question. He was not too discouraged, however; if it were the worst, the doctor would have wanted to get it over with.

When they had cups of coffee in front of them at a table in the employees' cafeteria, Mantizima decided he had waited long enough.

"How is Trudi?"

"Is that her name? I didn't know."

"It's Trudi Schmidt. She's a West German. She's...she was a rather pretty girl."

"Can't tell that now with the swelling, but I looked the face over. There doesn't seem to be any damage. She'll be pretty again when the swelling goes down...if she makes it."

287

Mantizima waited.

"I'm not going to lie to you," the doctor continued. "She has a chance, but just a chance. She'd lost so much blood and there was so much damage. I think I got all the cuts. I tried. But I can't be sure. The next twenty-four hours will tell. She may have to be opened up again, and in her condition.... But she's got a strong will, very strong. Seems strange to have so much in such a little body."

Mantizima was surprised by how much this man cared about the fate of a girl whose name he never even learned. This was the answer, he thought, to the people who would describe people like him as cold. This was the proper time and place for compassion.

"She must have a lot to live for," the doctor said speculatively.

"She does," Mantizima said, smiling, "but it's not me. It's herself."

The doctor nodded absently. He seemed to be wrestling with a problem. Mantizima gave him the time he needed without pushing him.

"She came close to consciousness when we were putting her under the anesthetic and she muttered some things. They do sometimes. I don't usually listen to it—kind of an unfair violation of their privacy I always think—and I never repeat it," he said with just a touch of defiance, as if he were warning Mantizima. "But this time.... Well, tell me something, if you will. This isn't simply a matter of some girl being beaten up, is it?"

"No, it's much more."

"I thought so. If you could have seen your face when you brought her in.... Well, she said a name...." The doctor was still not sure; he paused and sighed. "Jones," he said finally. "Rahmire Jones. A strange name. That's why it caught my attention, that and the fact that it seemed so important for her to tell someone. Is it important? Is that the man who hurt her?"

"Probably. I know who he is, but I don't know his name. But it is important."

The doctor was relieved, his conscience assuaged.

"Now, tell *me* something, if you will," Mantizima said. "What's going to happen to you? For operating on her, I mean."

"Oh, they could take away my license and put me in jail. I'm not supposed to touch her precious white skin, you know, although everything I touched was either red or black-and-blue. But they won't. By now our local White hospital has been informed of it. We have a nurse here whom I believe you met who takes care of that sort of thing for us," the doctor said with amused sarcasm.

Mantizima smiled, but he found it interesting that his impressions has been confirmed.

"The police will come here tomorrow or the next day and they will interview everyone who came into contact with her— Trudi. When they realize what kind of condition she was in, they'll let me go with a slap on the wrist. They're not monsters, you know, they're just foolish little people afraid of losing what is theirs. They would rather it be the reverse, a white doctor operating on a black woman, but they know emergencies don't always work out that way. In a life-and-death situation, the rules which are rules, to paraphrase someone, usually weaken a little."

"Will they move her?" Mantizima asked.

"Not until she's stable. But please don't worry, It was my decision. I knew what I was doing."

"It was my decision to bring her here," Mantizima said. "If I can, I'll be back by then, to take the heat for you. But if...I don't make it, I am sorry, but you are on your own."

The doctor did not miss the significance of his statement. "This is a dangerous business you're involved in, isn't it, Mr. Mantizima? You will try to see you don't end up in the same shape as Trudi, won't you?"

Mantizima assured the doctor he would try like hell.

289

CHAPTER TWENTY-FOUR

Mantizima walked into the lobby of the Hotel Meridith. He saw Ali immediately. She had jumped up with a start at the first sight of him and held her breath. Looking at her now, with the distance of space and the time they had spent apart, he saw that she was paying a very heavy price for her involvement in this mission. In one sense she had aged; the heavy responsibility had cut tight lines in her face. And, by that hour, there was none of her morning make-up left to hide it. In another way, however, it had rolled back the clock. The eyes that looked out of that tired face were those of a little girl which looked at life with a child's unforgiving view of good and evil. A child who was in pain because her friend had been hurt. A child who neither understood nor wanted any part of the perverted subtleties of the adult world.

A warm sense of caring swept over him. He wanted to take her in his arms and tell her everything would be all right. But he knew that wouldn't do. He knew the little girl was only a part of the adult woman who knew that things were definitely not all right and wouldn't be without making them so. This wound was not a scraped knee, and it would take more than a kiss to make it go away.

Ali waited while Mantizima approached her across the lobby, her breathing so shallow it did not even move her blouse. She waited for him to tell her.

"She's alive," he said without preamble. "She has a chance. We were fortunate. We lucked out with a good doctor. He'll do everything he can."

"That's something, I guess," she said bitterly; it was not what she had been hoping to hear.

"She'll make it, Ali."

"Did the doctor tell you that?" she asked, her hopes bouncing up again.

"No, you did."

Ali held onto her hope and her belief in a girl she barely knew.

Mantizima glanced around the lobby. It was empty, save for them and a lone desk clerk, who was keeping his eye on Mantizima. This was a White hotel. Non-whites did enter it, of course, but in cleaning uniforms, through the back door. They did not come in through the main entrance. But the clerk had obviously decided to do nothing as long as Mantizima did not make trouble, which Mantizima thought was just too bad for him because he definitely did intend to make trouble.

"What has been going on here?" Mantizima asked.

"Logan's here!" Ali said as if she were dropping a bomb.

"Really?" Mantizima said, with no surprise in his voice.

"That doesn't shock you?"

He shook his head. "I more or less expected him to put in some kind of appearance, though I wasn't sure it would actually be in person. This is even better than I'd hoped. Where is he?"

"Up in my room. I was shocked when he told me he'd come immediately. And he did mean immediately. Must have flown here. I wasn't sure whether I wanted to be in there with him initially. Thought it would be pick-up time again, like the first time I met him in the bar. But let me tell you, that boy has more on his mind tonight than girls. However, I still couldn't stay. He was so restless, he made me more nervous than I already was, so I came down here to wait for you. And he kept pestering me to tell him where you were."

"What did you tell him?"

"That I didn't know. I didn't think you wanted his company."

"Good thinking. What room is he in?"

"I don't remember. It's on the key. I'll call him down here."

"No, I'll go up, and I'd appreciate it if you'd wait down here. I don't think either of us is going to want a witness to this. I'll tell you about it later."

"Terry, you can't—'

"Ali, I'm going. I've had enough tonight of people telling me what I can't do. Now give me the key."

Reluctantly, she pulled the key out of her pocket. "Here," she said. "I don't think it's locked, but that's the number.... Terry, was it hard getting Trudi in at the hospital?"

"It was an experience, I'll say that," he said, smiling about it in retrospect. "I had some interesting thoughts there. I'll tell you about them...someday."

Wishing he could tell her then and wanting a substitute, he reached his hand behind her neck and pulled her to him and kissed her lightly on the tip of her shiny nose. The desk clerk's eyes bulged.

Seeing that Mantizima was headed for the elevator, the desk clerk ran to it and threw his body in front of it.

"See here, this has gone far enough!" the clerk said. "You can't really think you can go upstairs."

Mantizima had really had enough of that for one night, enough for a lifetime. "Get out of my way, little man, while you still can."

I think he actually means it! the desk clerk thought in amazement. A Bantu was actually threatening him. Unthinkable, but it was happening. Because he believed the threat, after only a moment's hesitation, the clerk meekly crept out of the way. Mantizima punched the elevator button, the doors opened, and in a moment he was gone. Only then did the clerk's nerve return.

"Cheeky Kaffir bastard," the clerk muttered to the empty lobby as much as Ali.

She looked at him and, though she really hadn't intended it that way, her expression frightened him.

"Oh, he's one of the educated ones," he hastily explained. "You can see that. They're not as bad as.... Oh, I could tell you some stories."

"Don't bother," Ali answered, turning away.

Mantizima entered room #427 without knocking. Logan, who was sitting on the bed, hadn't even noticed him until he was already in. Mantizima stood with his back to the door, his fingers reaching behind him to quietly slide the deadbolt closed.

The soundlessness of his entry, the few instants of catching Logan unaware, gave Mantizima the chance to assess the situation. The sight of the normally-dapper Logan rumpled and slumped over on the bed was a surprising one. That was not what Mantizima had expected to find himself facing, but he was not displeased by it. Far from it. He had been prepared to find a man totally strung out on tension. What he found instead was a man who had been in that state, but who had passed through it. Oh, Logan was still tight, but no longer at that level. The body can only sustain that degree of anxiety so long. Neil Logan's edge was not as sharp as it once was.

Logan looked up and saw Mantizima at the door. "So you finally decided to make your appearance." He tried to jump up then, but his rise did not happen that fast; his speed was gone. "Took your own sweet time doing it, too."

"I took just the right amount of time, judging by the way you look," Mantizima said softly.

"You arrogant black bastard. Who the hell do you think you are?"

"I know precisely who I am."

293

"You listen to me, boy. I don't know what your game is, but you are up to your neck in this thing. If you don't want to spend the rest of your life in a cell, I'd suggest you remember our respective positions."

"It has been many years since I was a boy," Mantizima said. "If you feel you have to call me anything, I'd advise you to use my name."

"I dare say you do, but why should that matter to me? I'll call you anything I want...boy."

"Call me that again and you won't walk out of this room alive."

He said it calmly, in a non-threatening manner, but his sincerity came through loud and clear. For the second time that night, someone thought of Mantizima: he really means it!

"Yes, I think that's the way we should settle it," Mantizima continued. "A fight to the finish with the better man walking out of here. You're younger than I am, but I'm in better condition. I think it'll be a fair fight."

"You're insane!"

"Perhaps."

"Someone will hear."

Mantizima tapped the wall with his fist. "Solid. This is an old hotel. They really built them well back then."

"They'll find you," Logan said in a panic, taking his own defeat for granted. "You'll hang, I swear you will."

"I'll take my chances."

Mantizima slowly removed his coat and tossed it on the bed. For the second time, Logan thought incredulously, he means it, he's really planning to beat the hell out of me. He noticed the body beneath Mantizima's rumpled fitted shirt. Slim, but strong. He saw that, while there were dried perspiration stains under Mantizima's arms, the shirt was dry now, whereas, he was drenched in sweat. In a contest he didn't have a chance, and he knew it.

"No, you don't have to," Logan said while easing back to the bed, believing that to be a more comfortable place on which to knuckle under. "Sorry. Sometimes I speak without thinking." He threw a sly glance at Mantizima to see whether the humble act was working; it usually did. "This has all been a bit much for me."

"It's been of your own making."

"If you mean that I accepted the job, you're right."

"That's not what I meant."

Panic fleeted across Logan's face. He quickly masked it, but not quickly enough. Mantizima walked across the room and leaned against the table there. He wanted to be comfortable; he was planning to enjoy this. But he still wanted the psychic advantage of towering over Logan.

"Rune knew there was a leak in BOSS. That's why he involved Ali and me. He couldn't use his own people without including a traitor."

"I know," Logan said evenly. "He suspected Kloff."

"Perhaps he did. I don't know Mr. Kloff, so I don't know whether he acted suspiciously. But that doesn't matter. Rune died without ever knowing who had betrayed him."

Logan's breath quickened, but he never took his eyes from Mantizima.

"I know, however, that it was you."

"You can't prove that!" Logan shouted.

Mantizima wanted to laugh; that was not the reaction of an innocent man.

"I don't need to prove it, but I know it," Mantizima continued. "Look, Logan, we're alone here. That's why I asked Ali to wait downstairs. There are no witnesses. Why don't we stop this cat-and-mouse game?"

Logan deliberated, then plunged in. He had never considered honesty to be anywhere near the best policy, but in his present situation it was worth a try.

"I didn't know he was building a nuclear bomb! It absolutely floored me when I learned it. I wouldn't have been stupid enough to get involved in something like that. I thought he was running guns to the natives or something. You would have approved of that."

295

"I've rarely thought that guns settled anything."

"Easily said now. At any rate, this chap, Warrick, came to me a year or so ago. Don't know how he happened to settle on me."

"I do. Go on."

"Well, at that time I happened to be pissed-off."

"At Rune?"

"Too bloody true. I happened to see a copy of his evaluation of me. He wrote that I needed harnessing. He was holding me down. He was going to keep me in a secondary position. When Warrick asked me for help with getting people into Pelindaba—he already knew we did the security checks, I don't know how—I agreed. I didn't take any money, you know. I did it for spite. Mr. God-almighty-perfect Aykroyd was ruining my career."

"Is that why you had him killed?"

"That was Warrick's doing, old man, not mine. I didn't know anything about it."

"But you told him that Rune was investigating his project?" Mantizima suggested.

"Of course I told him. What choice did I have with what he had on me? I didn't know it—not really—Rune didn't always let me in on things. All the signs pointed to it, however. But Warrick was the one who decided killing was necessary."

"That worked out awfully well for you, didn't it? How convenient that someone else removed the stumbling block from your path to the top."

"All right," Logan suddenly shouted. "I asked him to do it. Is that what you want to hear? Does it shock you? I wanted to get rid of him, and I did," he bragged.

"You're a fool, Logan. Warrick would have killed Rune anyway. He needed to. But you gave him the papers on yourself. He owns you now."

"Maybe, but despite what you're thinking, you don't."

Logan rose from the bed and idly walked around the room. He seemed stronger now, mentally, in spite of his

296

physical appearance. The division of authority in the room was shifting subtly in Logan's favor.

"You do realize, Mantizima, that I'm going to have to take you up on your offer to fight it out now, albeit with a little extra help on my side. Help that's no more than a phone call away. Witnesses or no witnesses, I can't let you walk out of here with what you know."

"You're forgetting, Logan, that I'm protected."

Logan laughed heartily. "You poor fool. What kind of protection could you have? You're no match for me. Who in this country is going to care if one bloody Bantu just disappears? And don't bring up your ties in the States. I talked with your secretary back there. She doesn't know where you've gone or when you'll be back. I think she misses you, incidentally. Too bad. You really slipped up this time."

"You're right about me," Mantizima said without worry. "but you are forgetting about that woman in the lobby. She does have ties. You can't keep her locked up forever. People will come looking for her, people with the power of a free press behind them. And when she gets out, you better run for cover. Because if you think I'm tough, you can't even imagine what she'll be like if she can't find me."

Logan considered that and knew it was true. He said that maybe it did have to come down to a fight to the death. After all, what did he have to lose now? Mantizima told him not to be too hasty.

"I'm not a policeman, Logan," Mantizima said. "I didn't come here to apprehend you. I came to make a deal."

A sly form of hope flashed in Logan's eyes and he asked what sort of a deal.

"First, I want to go over what I believe to be your intended scenario, just so you see which avenues are closed to you," Mantizima said. "You knew Warrick was dead?"

Logan nodded.

"And yet you didn't tell your superiors about him, I assume. You knew what he was."

Logan looked away evasively. His eyes traveled to the locked door. But Mantizima anticipated him. He crossed back to the door and leaned on it once again.

"A man with any shred of honesty—or sense—would have done just that, but not you. You had another idea in mind. You had Ali and me followed. Yes, I knew it. Your stooges weren't quite as unobtrusive as you might have liked. You decided to let us do all your work, to find the bomb. But a bomb isn't any good without a bomber. Perhaps Mr. Kloff would have worked, perhaps you considered him, but I suspect you finally cast me in that role. You were probably intending to have us killed. Dead men cannot contradict you. You would have brought in the ultimate prize. The world's first homemade nuclear bomb and the man who designed it. My background is not quite right, but only other scientists and engineers would realize that. Politicians would never know the difference. You would have been set."

"Yes, I would have been."

Mantizima told him he still could be. Logan protested that Mantizima would never let him get away with it, not after what he did to Rune Aykroyd. After all, he said, Aykroyd was Mantizima's friend. The hardest thing Mantizima ever did in his whole life was to tell Logan, very casually, that "friend" was a relative term.

"But don't worry. Do what I ask and you'll come out of this clean. I'll never repeat a thing." Mantizima paused to give Logan time to consider, then continued, "Now what I propose is a partnership, an official partnership. I don't know how you'll arrange that, but that will be your problem. I'll find the man with the case. His name is Rahmire Jones, incidentally, if that means anything to you. And you'll go after the bomb. You'll get to Durban as fast as the plane that brought you here can carry you. You'll find that bomb and you'll put it where it can't hurt anyone. Just in case Ali and I don't make it."

298

"What's in this for you?" Logan asked. "Why should you bother?"

"That does not concern you."

"How do I know I can trust you?"

Mantizima snorted. "Show a little intelligence, man. If I wanted to blow the whistle on you, I wouldn't be standing here now talking about it. Ali would have phoned in her story hours ago. Your demise would have already hit the streets."

Logan nodded; it made sense. He still wished he knew why Mantizima was doing this, however. He wished he understood Mantizima's motives. Important things, motives; they told you how best to betray a man.

"Stop wandering off, Logan," Mantizima ordered, recognizing, but not understanding the nature of his musing. "You can daydream when this is over. You need to keep your wits about you till then. Now, there are some other things we'll need for you and you'll have to arrange them. Now. Before you leave this room."

Mantizima told him what he wanted in great detail. Logan agreed and walked to the phone to get started.

"Fine," Mantizima said in closing. He picked up his jacket and put it back on. "Then we have a deal. Remember what I said about my part in it."

He unlocked the door and was about to exit when Logan stopped him. "Mantizima, wait!" Logan said, smiling sarcastically. "How do you know you can trust me?"

"I can't. Never imagined I could. But I'm reasonably sure you'll do what I ask. You'll at least go through the motions. You know I have too much on you to do otherwise. Even if I can't prove it, Ali can raise enough of an issue to bring you down like a house of cards. So, as I said, I know you'll make somewhat of a show of cooperation. But then at some time, when you're all alone with the bomb, you're going to realize that you'd better do what you've promised because you're the closest one to it."

Logan's sarcastic smile promptly sagged.

The elevator doors opened and Mantizima entered the lobby. Once again, a weary Ali waited for some word.

"Well?" she demanded.

"We're on the payroll now," he said cheerfully. "In a manner of speaking. We're not on the B-team anymore."

"What happened up there?"

Glancing over his shoulder, Mantizima muttered a safe, "Oh, things"

"Things? Now listen to me, Terry, I've done what you asked because you seemed to know what you were doing and because I was too tired to argue, but I'm not going to be left out anymore. This is a partnership, remember? And the waiting alone is killing me. Now I don't want any more of it."

"No more," he agreed. "I'll tell you everything later, when we're alone."

With a toss of his head to the area behind them, he told her to look around. Turning to follow his directions, she saw the much too curious desk clerk busying himself nearby them. She shot him a warning look—she now knew what that did to him—and he swiftly returned to his post.

"You can tell me now," she said. "At least generally. Where's Logan?"

"He'd better be upstairs telephoning. He was when I left him. And to tell you generally, we talked. We shared information, in a manner of speaking, exchanged truths and lies and made promises."

"Will they be kept, the promises?"

"His had better be. Mine won't."

Ali nodded, though she understood none of it. She watched as Mantizima spread a roadmap he had taken from his pocket out on a lobby table. She saw that the exhileration he'd come back with, the high he felt as a result of whatever happened upstairs, was fading fast now that it was over. She helped him open the last few folds of the map. He stared at the map for a while, then rubbed his tired eyes.

"If you were the man who dumped Trudi in the caves—imagine you are for now—where would you go from here? You have the case. You have to get it and yourself out of South Africa, but you have a back trail that you have to lose. Where would you go?"

Ali studied the map for a moment. "No question about it. The smartest place. If he knows anything, he has to know that."

"Where?"

"There's only one choice. Surprised you can't see it."

Her finger came down on the map. It landed in the middle of Kruger National Park.

CHAPTER TWENTY-FIVE

SEPTEMBER 22, 1979

5:00 a.m.—Kruger National Park

Kruger National Park. The largest and most famous of South Africa's game reserves. Eight thousand square miles of wild animals and twelve hundred miles of seemingly endless roads. One hell of a place to hide.

Mantizima and Ali approached the Malelane Gate of the Park just before daybreak. They had the look about them of people who had burned their bridges behind them, who did not yet regret it, but who knew they might in time. It was a terrible gamble and they knew it. They had staked the world against house odds. Eventually, maybe sooner than they'd like, that little, spinning ball was going to come down on a number, and it might not be theirs. But what choice did they have? Life, like roulette, is frequently an all-or-nothing game.

Going there was the logical choice for Rahmire to make. But could a man who had behaved as erratically as Rahmire had be expected to perform logically? Perhaps not. On the other hand, maybe he was smarter than the evidence left in his wake would indicate. For all they knew, he was curled up snug in a hotel bed right at that moment, the case tucked neatly away in some closet ready to be innocently mailed the next morning. That would be the smartest course, to get it out of his hands as soon as possible. But they were betting their lives on the theory that they were not seeking a very smart man.

The Park was dark as they approached, very dark. To two people who had lived their whole lives in the round-the-clock glow of city lights, it was a frightening, forbidding zone. A black hole into which one might fall and never come out of again. And it was quiet. Apart from the occasional rumbling of a distant nocturnal beast, the roar of their engine was the only sound to be heard. They felt, quite justifiably, that they were trespassing on a domain that was not theirs, a place where the two-legged were tolerated as long as they followed the rules, but where they really did not belong.

Kruger was only open during daylight hours. Visitors did spend the night, often several during the course of their stay in the Park, but they were confined to cabins called *Rondavels* in rest camps after dark. The nighttime gates were not well guarded, however; it was believed that only a madman would climb a fence and proceed on foot in a wilderness where wild animals roamed freely. But Rahmire was a man with very little to lose. They thought he would be willing to take the risk to make his way through a small part of the Park in the dark until he could find a sleeping rest camp, where it would be a simple matter to steal a car. They were banking on the idea that that was exactly what he had done.

They hadn't known what to expect when they reached the Park; they weren't sure whether Logan had kept his promise to Mantizima or, if he had, how well. He had, however, arranged all that they expected of him. The guard office at the gate was a beacon of light that guided their final approach. Their car idled outside the locked gate for only a moment before a black ranger ran out of the office to swing the gate open for them.

The man's khaki uniform was neat and crisp, which was more than could be said for him. He had clearly been pulled out of a deep sleep to be there. But he was cordial and cooperative, even if he did not attempt to hide his curiosity about an unprecedented situation. He had a right to be curious, he thought; he'd been robbed of several precious hours of sleep. He wished he'd had the same right to answers. How did this man, he wondered, a native, rate this treatment? And who was the woman? She was an American; he had guessed that long before she spoke. In his job of greeting tourists all day, you learned to pick out nationalities quickly. What were those two people doing there, he wondered, and how had they come to claim so much authority?

Not knowing what to expect when they arrived, Mantizima had been prepared to tell whomever greeted them as much as was required, but was glad to find that degree of detail to be unnecessary. He told the ranger simply that they sought a man whom they believed had entered the Park sometime within the last few hours and described what he supposed to be Rahmire's transportation plan. His skimming over details had been to save time and to lessen the degree of panic that might ensue if too many people learned of the terror threatening them all, but there was also an element of benevolence in his decision. The ranger was capable of facing danger, he did it every day, but his seemed so innocent compared to theirs. Let him go back to that sleep their arrival had taken him out of, Mantizima decided, and the dreams that awaited him there, without ever knowing the nature of the nightmare that kept them awake.

They told the ranger to instruct all of the other ranger stations to inform their men as they came on duty about their search and to be on the alert for a stolen car report. They exchanged their car for one of the Park's radio-equipped Land Rovers.

Then they set out, with only a map and a set of headlights to guide them through the wilderness in search of a man they knew virtually nothing about and a case, about which they knew too much.

6:00 a.m.— Durban

This just might work! Logan thought as the police car that had picked him up at the airport approached the Durban waterfront. I dare say I might pull it off yet!

Finding an out from the dead end in which he had cornered himself had given Logan renewed strength, not robust vigor exactly, but enough energy to carry out what he had ahead of him. He was still only a poor copy of his normal self, but enough of his personal style had returned to make him recognizable as the formidable opponent he usually was. It wasn't over yet, but he was breathing a lot easier now. He was confident that he would come out of it clean, maybe even a hero. And wouldn't that be a joke! He was certain Mantizima would stick to his end of the bargain. That was one of the advantages of dealing with honest people, he'd always believed, you could count on their being truthful; it was their Achilles Heel.

Yet Logan felt no gratitude for the man who had given him the chance to save himself. Mantizima had made him swallow too large a dose of humility. No one had ever done that before and got away with it. Logan did not have the time or energy to think about dealing with him at the present time, but revenge was never far from his mind.

The car turned a corner and the *Annabel Lee*, the ship carrying van der Wyk's machine shipment, came into view. She had been set to sail at five-thirty that morning, but Logan had ordered her held in port. He hadn't given any reasons to the local police, however. Let them sweat, he decided.

The *Annabel Lee* was of Liberian registry, but her captain was an Englishman. Their shared heritage ought to give them a common ground, Logan thought, but only in fairy tales. The two men met in the captain's office, glaring at each other like a pair of surly pit bulls.

305

The captain, one Henry Chambers, was a working-class Englishman and proud of it. A big, tough man, who looked like he belonged on the docks he'd probably worked his way up from, more than the bridge of a ship, a man who, though he now spent all of his time on that bridge, still had a thick layer of dirt under his nails. Henry Chambers had no love for these English-speaking South Africans with all their fancy ways and public school talk, when everyone knew they weren't real Englishmen. And Logan, on his part, felt just as little regard for the captain.

They were not off to a good start.

Logan gave the man a chance to cooperate. Were he not involved, he should have been eager to. He wouldn't want to incur the wrath of the local authorities, and his ship was rapidly losing the tide. The captain did not avail himself of that opportunity.

"Don't know what you want, mate," he said. "I keeps me records in good shape. No one can say nofink about the way I keeps 'em."

"Show me your cargo records," Logan demanded.

"'Oo wants 'em?"

When Logan presented his identification, the captain was forced to present his log. It was no help, however, It listed the cargo by the name of the shipper and its destination only. That was not what Logan wanted.

"This doesn't say anything about where in the hold these things are located," Logan said.

"No reason why it should. It's all goin' to the same place, mate."

That "mate," Logan thought irrelevantly, was getting on his nerves. He wished he had more time. He had no idea about the paperwork ships keep, whether this was the normal procedure or not. He suspected it was not. This log, he thought, was just something the captain prepared in case the police chose to investigate. But it would take too long to find out for sure. Time was of the essence. He had to put his hands on the bomb as soon as possible. Logan made his decision with little deliberation.

"Handcuff him to the chair," he told one of the policemen.

"'Ere! Wot's that?" Chambers protested. "'Oo do you think you are?"

Chambers shouted loudly, he cursed, he screamed for help, but no one listened to him. In moments, he was cuffed to the chair, with his hands bound behind him.

"Get everyone off the ship, but hold them out on the dock," Logan ordered. "And leave me alone with him."

In a moment they were alone in the office. Chambers' dark eyes threatened Logan's life and Logan answered that threat with his own malicious grin. Calmly, he took off his jacket and loosened his tie. He rolled up his sleeves. He took off his belt and held it in his hands. And he smiled. There was no question that he intended to enjoy himself.

"Now, 'mate,'" Logan said with undisguised enjoyment, "there are two ways we can do this. The hard way and the easy way. It's your choice."

The captain chose the hard way.

Logan had hoped he would, time pressures notwithstanding. It did take longer than he expected. Chambers was no push-over. Logan had to keep reminding himself that a man beaten senseless could tell him nothing. The temptation to go too far was great. There was so much hostility trapped inside of him that he'd had no release for until now. But Logan was an expert in "interrogation," one of BOSS' best, and his training held out till the end. Eventually, Chambers caved in, he told Logan what he wanted to know. They always did under Logan's hand.

Logan took a moment to catch his breath. He was soaked in sweat, but took comfort from knowing that the liquid Chambers was soaking in was blood. He wished he'd had time for a drink, time to search Chambers' office for something, but knew that would have to wait. He walked out of the office, leaving the battered man bound to the chair.

"Have them open the hold," Logan shouted to the police officer in charge of the men he'd commandeered. "I know where it is."

He had learned where in the hold the van der Wyk shipment had been stowed, but the bomb...? That was another story. He didn't know what he expected it to look like, but he was not prepared for the floating warehouse he found. A quick check he personally performed told him the crate with the red spot was not close at hand. He ordered that part of the hold emptied and stood off to one side while both the policemen and the ship's workers moved things out.

"They buried it well, didn't they, Neiman?" he asked the police lieutenant waiting with him.

"That's probably to be expected, sir."

"I suppose," Logan answered absently.

His mind drifted back to his session with Mantizima. He felt a fleeting sense of fear and hoped that black bastard had managed to put his hands on that case and would report in soon.

"If I may ask, Mr. Logan," the policeman said hesitantly, "What's in that crate? What are we looking for?"

"Lieutenant, you don't want to know."

7:00 a.m.—Kruger National Park

It's all right, Rahmire Jones assured himself. Everything was under control. He reached across the front seat of the car he had stolen and gently touched the cool leather of the case. From time to time he needed to reassure himself that it was there, that it was his. Yes, he repeated, everything was under control.

In fact, everything was far from being under control. Rahmire was completely frazzled by fear. He was a speeding car with an unconscious driver at the wheel; it was only a matter of time till he crashed. But he did not know that. His deluded view of himself saved him from facing the truth. Actually, that delusion was all that stood between him and complete insanity, a lucky thing for all concerned. As he was now, he still had something to lose.

He had made a few mistakes, he admitted. He should have checked Warrick's car over carefully. But if Warrick hadn't realized he was being followed, how was he to guess that? He also shouldn't have dumped Warrick's body so close to the road. Someone must have found it by now, he was sure of it. He'd listened to periodic news reports on the radio and had heard no mention of it, but that might only mean the police were suppressing it. He'd shown more sense, he thought, in getting rid of the whore. No one was going to find her for hours. By that time he'd be safe.

"Safe" was his word for the successful completion of his vague plan to sneak across South Africa's border. He was not worried about being able to pull it off. He'd illegally penetrated the borders of many countries and moved about them freely without papers and without being detected. But never, he forgot to add, without help. In the past there had always been people to help him, to tell him what to do, and now there was no one. That thought did not occur to him, however, nor did the idea that the manhunt might not be limited to South African soil.

It was almost all over now, he thought. He was safe where he was. He could even stay there for a while if he wanted to. He wasn't in any danger there, he reminded himself. That was a jungle, wasn't it? No one would think to look for him in a jungle. In fact, those dry plains did not even remotely resemble a jungle, but that was yet another delusion that protected Rahmire from a reality that would have destroyed him.

The day was beginning for both the inhabitants of the Park and its visitors. For many of the animals, that was the most active time of their day, and a number of tourists rose early enough to catch that activity. Most of the cars were not on the road yet, but some of them were. In that huge Park there should have been plenty of room for all of them, but a couple of cars had managed to get in Rahmire's way. Dawdling, gaping, acting as if they had all the time in the world, which, in fact, they did have. In a fit of anger, he'd forced one car off the narrow road. He didn't worry about getting into trouble because of that, however; whoever heard of policemen in a jungle?

He was not concerned about the presence of the animals either. When he felt a little warm, he rolled down the window, something, had he entered the Park in the normal manner, he would have been warned never to do. He wasn't afraid of them. He didn't notice them unless they happened to meander across the road in front of his car. They were part of the scenery, no different than the rocks and the trees, and to his mind, no more dangerous.

Rahmire was a man who had crossed the line into a dream-world. He looked into the rearview mirror, but did not see that his skin was as pale and pasty as dough. He felt the sweat running out off his scalp, but did not notice the air was cool. He did not react to the tremors that shook through him. He didn't know that at that moment his body had all the strength of gelatin. He could not see himself as he was, only as he imagined himself to be. As the victor, the hero, the winner, he was in his own mind.

I've made it, he thought. I'm almost there. He saw himself ultimately being met by the cheers of his comrades, by their congratulations, their gratitude, their acceptance. He saw himself effortlessly leading squadrons of men to victory. He saw himself where he always wanted to be.

He did not know that his thoughts almost exactly paralleled the ones Warrick, another man whose victory existed only in his own imagination, had when he was in the same position. And had he known, he wouldn't have cared. He knew he could not possibly meet the same end.

The roads were becoming progressively more crowded. People were cutting down on his speed, they were getting in his way. He made a sharp turn, driving past a sign that read, "Service Road—Authorized Personnel Only Beyond This Point."

He kept driving. It took more than a sign to stop a winner.

7:30 a.m.—Kruger National Park

Pieter Kloff arrived at Kruger.

He did not enter through the same gate as Mantizima and Ali. He employed a plane and, later, a helicopter to bring him closer to where he knew they were by now. He did not see the same gate guard that they did, but he was met by the same curiosity when he displayed his identification. By that time, every one of the Park's many employees knew that some sort of a manhunt was underway.

Kloff did not satisfy the man's curiosity. Like Mantizima, he simply took a Rover and a map, but also made arrangements to be kept in radio contact with his office.

"Do you want me to notify the others?" the ranger asked as Kloff prepared to leave. "To tell them that you are here?"

"Not...yet," Kloff answered. "I'll find them."

The ranger considered that to be highly optimistic, but said nothing.

Kloff drove off feeling hopelessly lost, yet moved by a desperate sense of urgency and a fear that he would not arrive on time, when he had no clear idea what he had to be on time for.

CHAPTER TWENTY-SIX

8:00 a.m.—Kruger National Park

Ali felt tired. Very tired. She was so weary that the fatigue almost felt like a physical pain. She'd gone without rest before, sometimes for long periods of time. She'd always prided herself on exceptional endurance, but she had never pressed that hard for that long on something that mattered that much.

And she was sick. She was hungover from an extended bout of guzzling her own adrenalin, and now she was paying the price of that overindulgence.

She felt awful, and yet she wished she thought Mantizima were doing as well. He showed less of the outward signs of abuse than she did, but his hope, his spirits, she sensed, were falling. As the hours wore on without any success, his natural optimism slid down a spiral of negativity. He said nothing about it, but she could feel it. She thought she had to stop that descent before it reached despair, but she didn't know how. Somehow, she had to help him to hold out, but for how long?

There was still no end in sight.

They drove on, as they had for hours, their red-rimmed eyes forced open, straining beyond their limit, searching for some sight, some sound, that would bring their quest to an end. Ali had to remind herself that it had only been last night when they found Trudi in that cave, less than twelve hours ago. Two days ago they were still in Johannesburg. Only two days. It seemed more like years. It felt like they had lived the lion's share of their lives in those two days, yet the experience still had a curiously unreal feeling about it. Like it couldn't really be happening.

The trek through Kruger might have been a bizarre, unprecedented event in their lives, but for the inhabitants of the Park life went on as it had since the beginning of time. Herds of wildebeast and their traveling companion, the zebra, flocked to Kruger's many watering holes, as they did in the cool of every morning. Sleek impalas ran past in the shadowy distance, so fast they appeared to be flying. Funny baboons gathered on the *koppie,* the strange and sometimes beautiful rock formations found throughout the South African veld. Giraffes loped alongside the car in their awkward but elegant way, pausing occasionally to nibble at tree tops.

Ali watched the animals without comment, but she felt uncomfortable. Not afraid, just out of place. This was another world, unlike any she had ever occupied. She tried to tell herself that it wasn't any different from a zoo, but it was different. Here, with the marked absence of humans, they weren't visitors, they were intruders.

Her feelings didn't only stem from the unusual inhabitants of that place, however, but from the place itself. She felt as if she were living in some bizarre science fiction movie, as if in her sleep she'd been transported to some strange, alien land. A harsh, cruel planet where only the strongest survived. Everywhere she looked, she saw the effects of an oppressive sun: the burnt bush, the bone-dry dust, the terrible, pervasive desolation. She watched the cracks in the dried mud road disappear under the car and felt not as if they were progressing, but as if something were slipping away from them.

Mantizima must have been reading her mind. "In another month," he said, "when the rains come, you wouldn't recognize this place. It will be as lush and green as a tropical garden. Very welcoming."

"I wish it were green now."

"I know how you feel, but you really wouldn't want that. With rain comes mud. Most of these roads would be a mess, some unpassable."

She still longed for some sign of that welcoming green, but also thought that it might be right that their search had brought them to that land just as it was. She thought that fierce, inhospitable place where life had been stripped to its cruelest essentials might be a fitting place for it to end.

If it ever did.

"We should have heard something by now," Mantizima said.

"Not necessarily. Some people sleep late. They are on vacation, remember? Maybe someone simply hasn't noticed yet that his car was stolen."

"If it actually was stolen. For all we know, we might just be wasting our time here, Ali."

Ali did not mention it, but she'd had the same thought an hour ago. They had a helicopter at their disposal, which was of no use to them in its hangar, but would be of no more use there unless they could tell the pilot what kind of car to look for. She had forced that thought out of her own mind then, however, as she intended to push it out of his now.

"Look, Terry," she said with more optimism than she actually felt, "I've pursued more false leads in my life than you have, and I've learned one thing. You give 'em your best shot. If you don't, there's no way to know they're false."

"And when you're sure, what do you do then?"

"You try something else. At least you know what doesn't work."

Both knew, but did not say, that that advice was all well and good when you weren't running a timed event with disaster.

They kept driving. They passed a cut-off to a service road with a sign telling visitors not to trespass. Ali merely glanced at it, but Mantizima took the time to read the sign.

They'd been lucky during the time they'd been driving through the Park. Animals had slowed them down at times, but few cars had gotten in their way, and those they had always been able to pass. September was the start of what was considered to be the best time of year to visit the Park, and many of the available cabins were occupied, but with so much roadway available, the cars were generally well scattered. Generally, but not always. Just ahead of them a car had stopped, blocking their way, in a narrow stretch of road where, due to heavy dried bush at the side, it was impossible to pass.

Mantizima stopped the Rover behind the other car and irritably threw it into neutral. The tourists were watching a pair of grazing giraffes. The young one was awkwardly attempting to emulate his mother's reach to a high branch. His efforts were in vain until the older giraffe grasped the branch with her mouth and bent it down until it touched her baby. Ali envied the animals and the timeless order of their existence and the tourists, the sense of peace they must have been deriving from watching it.

Then suddenly, seemingly from nowhere, a cheetah raced towards a watering hole in the distance. Instantly, the other animals scattered. Hords of them streamed around the two trapped cars until their colors almost blended into a muted blur. It was a terrible, magnificent sight, so commanding it robbed Ali of the frustration she had felt just before it happened. She watched the event with great interest, but without involvement. She was not a participant in it, despite its frightening closeness to her; she had her own fight. She was not able to share the animals' fear of the cheetah. Somehow, its savagery seemed so innocent, so clean, compared to the animal they chased. Still, it held her in fascination until she happened to notice that Mantizima was not watching it, that he was lost in thought.

"Terry," she said.

"There was a cut-off back there. The sign said it was a service road."

"Yes, I know. I read about them in the brochures I took from the office. They're off-limits to the public. They're only for rangers. Don't know where they lead. They're not on the map."

"That's where we should be, you know."

"Terry, didn't you hear me? They're not on the map."

"So we get lost," he shouted in frustration. "Aren't we now? And that's where he would go. It stands to reason."

It was risky, Ali thought. But it was the first sign of optimism she'd seen after hours of watching the strain wash his spirits away. They weren't getting anywhere as they were and, while the animals had dispersed, the car ahead was still blocking their way.

"Okay, let's do it."

As Mantizima threw the car into reverse, they heard a heart-stopping cry from an animal at the watering hole. A last hold on life, Ali thought. The cheetah had made his kill. His kill. Suddenly she was not uninvolved anymore. Just thinking the word sent a shiver through her whole body.

They made the turn and drove through the service entrance. The roads there were no better, but no worse than the Park's main artery of roadways. They were empty, however, and as the day wore on, the difference, they thought, would be even more apparent. They had to keep trying, keep believing.

Ali did worry about the unchartered nature of those roads. She wished they had thought to bring a compass. She had a naturally good sense of direction, however, and busied herself by sketching the roads they used and passed in on her map so they could backtrack if they had to. But while the move to the service roads gave them hope, it gave them nothing in the way of success.

After a while, however, a ranger's Rover approached and flagged them to stop. A white ranger this time, with a heavy Afrikaans accent, looked eager to speak to them. He was so quaint, so old-fashioned, Ali thought, as he tipped his bush hat to her. Then he addressed himself to Mantizima. With that accent, she thought, he was precisely the sort of person who should resent having to report to a black man, but he did not appear to. Not at all. She imagined that life in the ranger villages as not all that different from living anywhere else in South Africa, but maybe it was. Perhaps he had lived too long in that alien place, where life was justly reduced to its most primitive level, to put much stock in the convoluted designs South African civilization used to pervert the thinking of other men. But then again, she thought cynically, maybe he just knows the orders come from BOSS. For whatever reason, he seemed eager to help them.

"Are you Mantizima?" he asked.

Mantizima nodded.

"I was just going to radio you when I spotted your Rover. A car's been reported missing from the Malelane camp. A green Toyota. Don't know which model yet. I just got the word."

"Ali—" Mantizima started.

"Already on it," she said as she picked up the radio microphone to call in the helicopter.

"Don't know if it's the same one, but a green car was spotted on the service road up ahead. Too far and moving too fast for the ranger to reach it, but he radioed it in anyway."

"Thank you," Mantizima said gratefully. "You've been a great help."

"Just doing my job.... Oh, Mr. Mantizima," he said, stopping Mantizima from putting his Rover in gear. "Try not to get lost. With so many people in the Park, the only rangers you'll see will be those coming on or off

317

duty. And whatever you do, don't get out of your car for any reason."

Mantizima promised to remember the man's caution and, after waiting only for the man to tip his hat to Ali again, they were off.

8:30 a.m.—Durban

The hold was unloaded. Slowly. Painfully so. The crate with the red spot, it seemed, was determined to make its appearance fashionably late.

Logan still watched tensely from the sidelines, but the police officer who had been with him had joined in the search long ago. He watched in tight silence until the naval officer reported to him as ordered.

"Mr. Logan, I'm—"

"I know who you are, Commander. It's about time you showed up."

The Commander, an urbane, English-speaking man with a strong face and distinguished, steel-grey hair, generously attributed Logan's rudeness to strain and said none of the things he might have in response.

"What I want you to do is find two boats," Logan said. "You or one of your people."

"You mean ships, don't you? And we don't have to find them, Mr. Logan," the Commander said pleasantly. "We are the Navy."

"I mean boats, damn you. That's what I said, isn't it?" Logan exploded. "I want two small boats, motor-powered, not sail. If the Navy doesn't have what I need, get them from a local marina. Buy them from the owners. Pay anything they want. But do it now."

"May I ask what you plan to do with them. This is my area of expertise, after all."

"You can't ask anything. Just get on with it. Now. That's an order."

The Commander stiffly withdrew, promising the order would be carried out. Logan continued to wait, but the pressure was becoming too much for him. Finally, he threw his jacket on the dock and ran up the gangplank to help. He'd wanted to do it a lot sooner—those workers seemed to be going so slowly—but he'd suffered a severe loss of dignity already, and dirtying his hands did not seem like the proper way to get it back. Dignity weighed heavier for him most of that morning until the passing of time tipped the scales towards urgency.

He was not much help. He was more of a hindrance to the men who were good at that job, or who had become good at it in the last couple of hours. Fortunately, he was not at it long.

"We found it, Mr. Logan," came a voice from the hold. "We see the red spot."

"Well, get it out here, old chap," Logan said in a surprisingly pleasant tone brought about by relief. "Hurry it up now."

The crate was still wedged in, so it took a while to get it out, but soon it was resting on the dock. The Commander returned just then to tell Logan his men had commandeered two cabin cruisers that were just what he ordered. Then, using another crate as a table, Logan spread a nautical chart out for him and the Commander to see.

He wished he understood it better. He ought to, he'd spent enough time on the water. His parents had had a yacht and always encouraged him to learn more about running it. His father had loved to play captain, but Neil always thought that should be left to the crew. He wished now that he had paid more attention.

"This is where I want you to place your ships," he said, making a sweeping circle with his finger.

"Wouldn't it be better like this?" the Commander asked. He took a pencil out of his pocket and hastily sketched in his suggested positioning.

"Yes, that's fine," Logan said, wishing he could tell the difference. "but I want it to be a solid blockade. Absolute. No one is to be let through."

319

"There's a Soviet sub in the area. Always patrols this part of the Indian Ocean."

Logan asked whether the Commander could find out if the sub was in the designated area. The Commander said he could and ordered a man to radio the sub.

"If it's there, order it out," Logan shouted to the man, then turned back to the Commander.

"We can't really order it out, you know," the Commander said. "These are international waters. We can ask them to cooperate, but even that might cause an incident."

"Sod your incident!" Logan swore. "I told you, if it's in the area, get rid of it. I don't care how. And if it's not there but tries to enter, you are to consider it an act of war. Nothing less. Is that clear? If you have any doubts, you can check my authority with the Minister of Defense."

"No need for that," the Commander said, his eyes suddenly veiled for a moment.

Because you've already checked, you bastard, Logan thought. He would pay for that. A lot of people were going to be paying debts when this was over.

"Now this is my plan," Logan said, returning his attention to the chart. "I'm going to have that...." His voice trailed off. He didn't know what to call it.

"It's a bomb, isn't it, Mr. Logan? A rather powerful one, I'd estimate. I shudder to even think what kind, but there's only one kind that could create this much of a fuss, isn't there?"

Logan met the Commander's eyes and nodded. "Do the men know, do you think?" he asked.

"Some of them do, certainly. The brighter ones. Perhaps some of the others have been told."

Logan marveled that they had any seamen left at all. He was surprised there hadn't been a mass mutiny. If his life hadn't depended on seeing it through, he would have been long gone.

"I see. Well, to get back to the plan. I'll have the bomb put on one of the boats. The other boat will follow it to the drop-off point. I'll need two volunteers for that. Have someone get them."

The Commander gave that order to a subordinate and returned his attention to Logan.

"We'll leave the bomb out on one boat, and the other can take both men back to the nearest destroyer. I don't know how far out to place it. I'm not sure what its range is nor how much time we have."

"I think I can make an educated guess as to the first," the Commander offered. "As well as the placement of the destroyers, if you trust my judgment, that is. As to the second matter, how much time we have, well it's always a throw of the dice, isn't it?"

"Fine. It's all up to you. But remember one thing—most important—the blockade is not to be penetrated or broken for any reason. No one is to leave his ship, no one is to be let through, and no ship is to be moved out of position. Is that clear? Any sacrifices will be made for the greater good."

The Commander resisted telling Logan that he'd been in the South African Navy for over thirty years, that he'd understood all that before Logan was born, and simply assured him that his orders would be carried out.

The junior officer returned then with a pained look on his face. "I'm sorry, sir, I was only able to get one volunteer."

"One? That's not enough. I need two," Logan said to the officer, then turned to the Commander. "Order them if you have to, but—"

"Order them on an obvious death mission? I can't do that."

Logan did not think it was that obviously deadly. If it were, Mantizima's threats notwithstanding, he wouldn't be there.

"What are we going to do?"

"I'll take one of them out myself," the Commander said.

"Don't be so noble. I need you to set up the blockade."

His mind went blank. It was a void. It was holding out all thought in self-protection because he knew there was one thought fighting to get in that he did not want to think. The only possible solution.

"I'll take it out myself," he said at last.

He realized from the looks on their faces that in their world, by their code, that offer should have been made long ago.

Logan gave the final order and the men scattered with alacrity to their assigned duties, leaving him alone while he waited for the bomb to be loaded onto the boat. Mantizima's warning came back to him again with striking clarity, sending an icy chill through his whole body.

8:40 a.m.—Kruger National Park

Using the same logic, Kloff, too, had taken to the service roads. And, like the others, he found himself alone on them. It allowed him to make good time, but it also made him aware of how alone he was. He did not regret the decisions he had made, but he was now more aware of their full implications. Out in that wilderness, stripped of the sense of control he'd had in his office command post, he had to struggle to hold it all together.

He saw a ranger up ahead turning into the public area of the Park and honked to get his attention. He pressed on the accelerator until he had joined that Rover.

"I'm Kloff, with BOSS. I'm looking for two people, a black man named Mantizima—"

"You're in luck, Mr. Kloff. I just left them," said the ranger who had stopped Mantizima's rover. "Not ten miles up this road."

"Thank you."

322

"Good luck to you, Mr. Kloff. Oh, sir, I almost forgot. The car you're all looking for is probably in that direction, too. A green Toyota. A Corolla. I didn't know that when I spoke to Mr. Mantizima. Do you think I should radio him?"

Kloff assured the ranger that he would tell Mantizima and he pulled away. He pressed his accelerator to the floor, accepting the bouncing around that speed meant on those rough roads. He had to make it! He had to get there. He did not think much about the green Toyota; not aware of everything that had happened, he didn't even know who was driving it. A peculiar division of labor had evolved between them, of which only he was fully aware. That Toyota did not fall into his area of responsibility; he had other concerns.

9:10 a.m.—Kruger National Park

The heat was unbearable. It came off the earth in shimmering waves that were like a corrosive gas that ate into everything.

It was not supposed to be that hot in September, Ali thought bitterly. But none of this was supposed to happen.

The road was getting worse and the bush along the side of the road, while not lush, was greener and more dense than any they'd seen thus far. Excluding that one officer, it had been hours since they'd seen anyone. They had not yet seen the green Toyota, if it existed. The only comfort they took was in realizing Rahmire wouldn't dare to try to change cars here; it was too dangerous.

Mantizima's body was hunched forward, almost as if he thought that would make the car go faster. His fingers were molded to the steering wheel. The Rover hit a pothole and rocked badly, but he did not slow down. He couldn't.

Ali kept the radio mike with which they communicated to the helicopter gripped in front of her mouth. It was a connection, a lifeline to their only hope. The skin of her knuckles was blanched over the joints. Both of them were strained far beyond their physical endurance, but neither had enough feeling left to know it.

In passing, they noticed a herd of elephants romping and playing in a nearby river, but neither made any mention of it. They had not uttered even a single word to each other in the last hour. Nothing broke their intense concentration.

Then, suddenly, a huge male elephant stepped into the road ahead of them, roaring in outrage, his ears flapping wildly in anger.

"My God!" Ali shouted, shattering the silence.

The elephant broke into a forward trot, charging faster and faster in their direction. Ali was totally paralyzed by a fear more vivid than she believed herself capable of feeling. Mantizima, at the wheel, could not afford that luxury. He did not underestimate the elephant's seven tons of weight, but he decided to take a calculated risk. He slammed on the brakes, bringing the Rover to a quick halt. The elephant stopped, too.

Stalemate.

"The way I see it, we have only two choices. We wait him out till he realizes we're not threatening his family, which we really don't have time for, or we go around."

"Do it," Ali said.

He drove into the bush, faster than was safe for those conditions. Mantizima struggled to control the wheel, but it pulled out of his hand, leaving the speeding Rover momentarily without a driver. The Rover and the people in it were violently thrown about. The mike whipped out of Ali's hand, banging around until it landed on the floor. She feared it was damaged, but did not risk letting go to find out.

They made it back to the road. The elephant, left in a cloud of kicked-up dust, was too smart to do something as insane. His domain uninvaded once again, he slowly made his way back to his family. Ali and Mantizima couldn't believe it. They'd actually made it. They both talked at once, the relief and fear coming out at the same time.

Only when they were quiet did they realize there was a third voice in the car—the one coming from the radio. The helicopter pilot was trying to communicate with them.

Ali snatched the mike up from the floor, desperately hoping it was not damaged. It was not.

"Yes, come in."

"Your prey's dead ahead. Stopped, fortunately. You can't miss him if you keep going the way you're headed."

Mantizima slammed the accelerator to the floor, demanding all the overworked engine could give. Eventually they found the green Toyota—abandoned in bush too dense for even a Rover to penetrate.

There was the lush green she'd longed for. Obviously watered by some underground spring, they'd been seeing evidence of its existence for miles. Well, here's your tropical welcome, Ali thought acidly to herself. Make the most of it.

They sat in silence, in bitter defeat. There was no way the Rover could continue to follow him.

"I'm going after him," Mantizima said at last.

"You can't!"

"I have to."

"The copter could—" she started desperately, but she knew the helicopter could do nothing but direct them. "We could drive—" But they couldn't do that either.

"It's the only way."

"Terry...no...." Ali said. She knew there was no way to stop him, however, so there was only one choice left open to her. "I'm going with you."

"No, you're not, Ali. You're staying here."

"Don't give me any of this macho nonsense, Terry. I won't be protected. We've come this far together, and I won't be—"

"Leave me something to come back to."

She couldn't argue with him; she knew of nothing to say. She nodded her weary decision to let him go.

He opened the car door and walked out.

9:20 a.m.—Indian Ocean

The bomb had been left at the drop-off point, and Logan and the sailor who had volunteered were on their way back to the destroyer.

Logan never even glanced at the crate from the time he jumped from one boat to the other. He never looked back. But he knew his attention was still riveted to it, even though he was facing away. He was with it still, he would be until it was over.

He glanced at the seaman standing next to him, but said nothing. He thought stupidly that he was sorry that the man had a face, or at least that he had to see it. He needed for someone to do that job or something, but he didn't want to know that someone was doing it. He wondered why the man had volunteered, knowing, had he not been forced to, he never would. He felt a small, uncharacteristic, grudging sense of responsibility for the man and he did not like having to feel responsible for anything.

Time stood still. It did not pass, it did not move. Nothing, Logan was sure, could possibly be happening during that time anywhere in the world. Their boat moved, but only up and down, rising and falling on the choppy swells, never forward. Only the ships in the distance grew magnificently larger. Only that. Nothing else.

The closest destroyer was now within reach, not much more than a half-mile away.

I've made it! Logan thought, breathing, he was sure, for the first time.

Then, suddenly, the engine of the boat died. Logan and the sailor looked at each other in disbelief. It couldn't be happening. The seaman tried again and again to restart it, but it was hopelessly dead. It couldn't be happening, but it was. It had happened.

Logan felt light-headed, giddy. He felt a wave of hysteria sweep through him. "Buy cheap and you'll always get cheap," he heard his mother's voice saying in his mind as she had so many times. He had bought cheap with that boat, but never again, he giggled to himself. Next time he would come prepared.

No, he told himself, he couldn't let this happen to him. He had to take hold. He had to get a grip on things. He was responsible.

He forced the hysteria out of him. He was responsible, he repeated to himself. He was responsible. He forced it down. Forced all feeling out of him, leaving room for desperately needed thought. And when he'd succeeded, when there was only a receptive darkness with him, only one thought emerged.

He *was* responsible.

He alone.

For everything.

Not Mantizima, not Kloff, not Aykroyd, not any of the people he'd pushed out of or into his path as circumstances designated. He alone was responsible. Warrick was too, of course, but they were partners in crime. Logan made it all possible. Of all the people Warrick employed, Logan was the one he could not have done without.

He felt alone. Like a scared little boy. He learned what fear really was. There was no one he could go to for help, no one he could blame. Money could not buy him out of this and power couldn't push him. There was nothing between him and certain death but his own power to decide, the very power that had put him there.

He looked into the face of his companion and saw a confident belief in him. There was control and acceptance for you, he thought. With very few words, he could easily lead that man to his death. Control and acceptance. In that little boat he found everything he'd wanted all of his life.

The pill tasted bitter in his mouth.

"It's all right, sir," the sailor assured him. "I'll radio the destroyer. She'll pick us up."

"She can't move out of formation. None of them can."

"Can't move—What do we do?" the seaman asked, his confidence crumbling.

What did they do? He alone had to decide. He, the man responsible.

Logan tried to swallow, but his mouth was dry. His throat gulped hard in the effort.

"We swim," he said.

"It's close to a half-mile, maybe more. In this water we'll never—"

"We have no choice. Now swim!"

Logan pushed the man overboard. Then, with only a brief moment of closing his eyes, of trying to block out the truth of the hell he'd created, jumped in after him.

CHAPTER TWENTY-SEVEN

SEPTEMBER 22, 1979

9:25 a.m.—Kruger National Park

Sweat poured out of Ali's scalp and ran down her face. Her tongue flicked out occasionally to catch the salty beads when they reached her mouth, but other than that, she took no notice of them.

I must be dying, she thought calmly. That was the only explanation for the fact that her life was passing, as predicted in death, before her eyes. Not her whole life, only that part of it that happened since September 6th. That seemed to be all of it, or all that mattered.

With the scrupulous accuracy of someone closing the final books, she reviewed it all. But not with disinterest, as she had always expected. She judged herself every step of the way.

She reviewed her conversation with Trudi. She'd been right then. There was so much she was afraid of. But why? What was this need of hers to cover all bets?

She laughed bitterly as she glanced around. She didn't cover all bets; she hadn't covered that one.

No, she thought seriously, she'd never feared all of the risks, only the ones that mattered most, the ones that would have hurt the most if she lost. She thought about Trudi and the way she must have felt that day as she approached the moment of crisis. She looked so solemn. There was a real moment of human drama when she took that difficult first step.

Ali knew it wouldn't be difficult for her; it wouldn't be dramatic.

It wasn't. She knew it was already over.

It was so simple, this business of living, she thought, if you only let it be. You had to reach out and take what you wanted, to fight for your life as if it were all you had—because it was.

She licked more salty fluid away, but this time it wasn't sweat, it was tears. She was crying, soundlessly, probably for the first time in her adult life. They weren't tears of pain for time lost or joy for time won. They were tears of victory for having come home.

She had never wanted more from her life than she did at that moment. And all of it was embodied in the person of one man. He was everything she wanted, everything she'd wanted to reach for all the years of her life, but had been afraid of missing. She was not afraid now—but he was gone.

There was no choice, no drama; she knew what she had to do. The future she wanted to share with him had to begin at that moment.

She opened the door and stepped out.

Just then, another Rover screeched to a halt behind hers and a thin, sandy-haired man stepped out.

"Where is he?" the man asked.

She pointed. She accepted the man's presence there and only partially questioned his apparent understanding.

"Come on."

"Wait," she said. "Who are you?"

"A friend," Pieter Kloff said.

He held out his hand and, like a child, with an uncanny sense of friend and foe, she took it.

9:30 a.m.—Indian Ocean

Logan's arms ached with exhaustion. He couldn't take another stroke. He did. He took that stroke, then another, then another. He was reduced to living life by the moment, taking each second one at a time, getting through it, then moving on to the next. That's what it took to get by. He had no choice.

They were getting close now. He could make out the faces of the men on the deck of the destroyer. They were lowering a rope ladder into the sea. They wouldn't do that, he thought, if they didn't know the swimmers were close.

They'd made it. Almost. But he had thought that before.

He looked around for the seaman. He'd been near Logan most of the way, but he wasn't there now. Logan treaded water as he turned his body around, rising on some of the waves, being doused by others. He spotted the seaman several yards away. He was barely holding his own. Logan saw him take a mouthful of water and go down. He came up sputtering a moment later, only to be pushed under by the next roll of water.

Damn! Logan thought irritably. He's a sailor. Don't they teach them to swim?

"Can't make it," the man shouted to him when he reached the surface again. "Go on. Save yourself."

How he wanted to. He'd never wanted anything so much in his life. But he was responsible. He repeated that over and over again, like some mystical rite he dared not challenge. It was up to him. He was paying now for the life he'd chosen, he thought, but that life hadn't been worth this price.

Reluctantly, he made his way back to the man. His body hurt so badly he wanted to cry, so badly he wanted to stop, to give up right there. That he was backtracking, covering ground he'd already counted as done, made the swimming much harder than going forward.

He reached the man before he drowned, although not much before. He grabbed the seaman under his arms and tried to do with one arm what he had barely been able to do with two—to swim back to the ship.

Somehow—he didn't know how—he had to make it.

331

Mantizima did not consider himself a brave man. He wasn't unaware of the chance he was taking. It was just that he thought he must have come into life lacking a facility on which many people's lives seem to depend—the ability to evade. He saw too clearly the consequences of cowardice.

He made his way through dense growth, pausing occasionally to listen, like a tracker, for the sound of his prey. Rahmire, he knew, might have left the car ages ago. He might be anywhere by now. And even if he were near, Mantizima's city-trained hearing just might not be sensitive enough to know it. Still, he had to try. It was the only chance left.

He pressed on, moving as quietly as possible. He paused at a fork to try to decide which way Rahmire would have gone. How could he choose? He wiped the sweat from his dripping forehead and pressed his hand to the dirty leg of the pants he had worn for more than the last twenty-four hours.

Rahmire had traveled in an almost due north line all day. He'd hardly deviated at all. He would probably continue that way, Mantizima decided. If he walked that way at all, he would continue towards what must be his planned destination.

He walked on, moving as he believed Rahmire would. He'd taken a lot of chances since they'd started. He'd made rash predictions, first about Warrick's actions, and then Rahmire's. Ali was becoming irritated with his impression of an oracle, he thought. But he was sure he understood both men, even though he did not know them. And he'd been right most of the time. Yet his accuracy hadn't paid off.

Then it did. He spotted Rahmire at the end of a clearing just ahead. He did not know what to do. This was what they'd been working towards for days, and suddenly he had no idea what approach to take. Should he sneak up on him? Should he attack? Or should he try to gently coax him? Or better still, startle him to make him lose his concentration. Maybe they would all work, if he could only figure out what order to put them in.

"Jones!" Mantizima suddenly shouted.

Rahmire whipped around. He clutched the case in one hand and his knife in the other. Mantizima glanced at his eyes and saw the look of a man frightened beyond all reason. One slip, he knew, and it was all over.

New energy surged through both men, a result of a basic need for survival. They faced each other in tight silence, squaring off like two anxious fighters eager to get into the first round. But these men were not fighting for a title, they were fighting for their lives, in a contest that couldn't end in a draw.

In the quiet both men should have heard the soft, breathy sound of a cat hidden across the clearing. So intent on each other, however, neither did.

Mantizima's breath came quickly, in deep, hard drags of air. Rahmire's, however, was shallow. He was waiting, Mantizima thought. Rahmire didn't understand any of it. If only he could put him off-guard.

"Jones," he said softly. "I'm here to help you." In one fluid motion, he slowly extended his hand. "I'm a friend. A friend of...."

Of who's? he thought. Damn! He'd unthinkingly gone too far. Then the connection fell into place.

"Of Ali's," he said with sudden inspiration.

The slight easing of Rahmire's facial muscles confirmed his theory. Mantizima suddenly felt charged and struggled to restrain himself. Of the two of them, he now had an edge, however slight. He knew what he was dealing with. And he now knew the right approach. It wasn't guesswork anymore. He had to appear to be a friend to a man who desperately needed one.

Mantizima slowly took a step forward. Half a step. He eased one foot up but did not transfer his weight to it, just in case he had to jump back. If Rahmire allowed that....

He did.

"I come from Ali," Mantizima said as he completed that step.

Slowly, he took another step.

Rahmire seemed mesmerized, like an animal suddenly frozen in fright, desperate to believe the hand stretched out to him was not that of a hunter.

"I come from Ali. He sent me to help you. He's very proud of you...Rahmire."

Closer.

"Ali wanted me to help you, Rahmire. To help you get the case out of South Africa. I'm an African, I know this land. I can do it."

Closer.

Rahmire remained still, unaffected by Mantizima's approach. He was spellbound by Mantizima's slow, fluid motions and his gently persuasive voice. He understood little that was being said to him. The part of his mind responsible for processing it was virtually disconnected. But some of it filtered through, and it was what he desperately wanted to hear.

"Give me the case, Rahmire, and I'll help you."

Closer, closer.

"Give me the case."

Closer, closer, closer.

Almost there.

Mantizima was a cat. Sleek and strong, capable of flowing like liquid. But Rahmire was a snake, coiled and ready, his venom deadly.

Mantizima stretched his arm to its limit. Closer, closer. Close enough to take possession of the case. His fingers brushed the handle, they curved around.

"Give it to me, Rahmire. Give it to me."

His fingers touched Rahmire's hand. And in that touch something happened.

Rahmire felt the cage door swinging shut on him. He smelled a trap. His conscious mind did not put all the pieces together. He did not grasp that he had placed Mantizima. He'd been watching them all for so long. He had seen him with the Hayden woman and she was a friend of Warrick's. He didn't put all that together, however; he simply knew that the man trying to strip him of what he'd killed for was the enemy.

The snake struck, shooting out from his tight coil. The cat was not prepared.

Rahmire tossed the case gently on the ground and came at Mantizima with the knife. Mantizima reacted, but not soon enough. It happened so quickly, and his resources had been slowed to meet the needs of the occasion. He couldn't shift gears that rapidly. And his resources were drained.

They'd both been charged with a like amount of current when they faced off against each other the moments ago that seemed like an eternity. Rahmire's was unused, it was ready; whereas, Mantizima's was nearly spent.

Mantizima's liquidity abruptly turned to glass. His movements were stiff and jerky. He held Rahmire off, but could not overpower him. The knife came at him. Mantizima grasped Rahmire's arm. For an instant the knife was suspended in a contest of strength between them. Gradually, Rahmire's strength proved greater. The knife slowly cut through the air. At the last instant Mantizima knocked it out of its path, but he did not succeed in lessening the grip that seemed molded to the handle.

Then Mantizima lost his footing. His shoe slipped on some moist grass. He went down. The ground that was soft underfoot was hard on his head. It stunned him for a second, and in that instant Rahmire pounced. Rahmire was on him, fighting for all he had.

I'm done, Mantizima cried desperately. Finished. It was a good fight, but not good enough. He'd given it everything, yet it demanded more.

He knew he didn't have a chance.

9:47 a.m.—Indian Ocean

They made it. Logan and his companion reached the destroyer.

He wearily grasped the rope ladder, using all he had just to hold on. He saw anxious concern on the faces of the men on deck and wished they weren't so literal in their obedience. He would have paid any price for someone to climb down that ladder to help him. But he was the one who had ordered that measure; he, the man in charge.

He caught his breath and pulled the man who was practically dead weight to the ladder. He dove, or rather, let his body sink under the water, to hook the seaman's feet on the rungs. Then he pushed the man up, but he did not respond.

"Come on, man, climb!" Logan cried. "I can't do any more!"

His desperation must have reached something in the half-conscious man, for, slowly, the nearly inert body moved out of Logan's hands. The man slipped twice, both times back to where he started, but eventually he held his position and then slowly moved up.

Logan clung to the ropes, wearily waiting for his turn.

9:49 a.m.—Kruger National Park

No, he had one chance, Mantizima thought, rallying. Only one. To squeeze the life out of Rahmire before Rahmire could take his. Mantizima extended his hands and closed them around his opponent's throat.

Rahmire still had the obvious advantage. His position, despite the placement of Mantizima's hands, was one of strength, whereas, Mantizima's was of weakness. Rahmire was sure he could hold out the longest. If he were right, he had only to take offensive action—he did not need to defend himself—while Mantizima had to do both.

Mantizima attacked through the hands at Rahmire's throat, while trying to hold off the knife with his elbow.

He did not make it.

The knife slashed into his arm. The blood flowed freely. With the rapid reasoning unique to men in times of crisis, Mantizima quickly assessed his condition. The blood did not feel like it was coming fast enough for an artery to have been severed. He still had a chance.

But why wouldn't Rahmire die? What was keeping him going? The fingers squeezed tighter and tighter, but it was not enough. Mantizima's strength was gone, his account overdrawn. His only hope was to tap into some future vault of energy. If he did not use it now, he never would. But he did not know how to learn the combination.

Then, slowly, it came. His thumbs increased the pressure on Rahmire's windpipe. The younger man coughed and sputtered, but his own strength did not lessen.

Rahmire still had enough left to ease his body to the side, despite Mantizima's efforts to hold him where he was. He slowly pulled the knife back over his head. He grasped that the race was almost won, the tape merely inches from his chest. He wheezed a strangled gasp for air. He struggled to breathe, but could not. There was still enough life left in him, however, to poise the knife in a direct line with Mantizima's heart.

He started bringing it down, not swiftly, but surely. It held its line.

Then Kloff and Ali reached the clearing. Ali cried at the sight, as if it were her flesh that the knife was about to cut into. Kloff immediately raised his gun, but then he froze.

"Shoot!" Ali whispered tightly.

Nothing happened.

How could he do it? But for those occasional times at BOSS' firing range, he hadn't used that gun in years, never in a situation that critical. The men were too close. It would be too easy to hit the wrong man. If he failed, Mantizima was dead, but he grasped that if he failed the other way, from waiting, Mantizima was dead, too. He didn't have a choice.

He steadied the gun and squeezed the trigger.

Rahmire was hit in the leg, precisely where Kloff had aimed. He yelped in pain like a wounded animal and dropped the knife. but he still had more strength left than anyone would have believed. He was a dying animal in his last throes of life, gasping with his final breaths to hold onto that force. He staggered to his feet, struggling for air and balance and, before anyone could stop him, he grabbed the case.

He took off in a crooked line across the clearing. Kloff addressed himself to the problem. Should he shoot? Rahmire was an easy target. But should he risk damaging the case? Kloff did not know what was in it, but he could guess. How far could a wounded, half-strangled man get?

Before he reached an answer, however, the decision was made for him. The lioness who had been lying in the bush with her cubs, hiding from the warmth of the sun, had been lazily content to let the humans fight their war without any interference from her. But now one of them was coming too close to her young and, besides, her nose had been tickled by the smell of blood. Without warning, she took off after Rahmire, faster and faster, until she nailed him in a savage pounce.

The case flew out of his hand and struck a rock.

Logan clung wearily to the ladder. His exhausted companion had been pulled on deck. He would climb up himself in a moment when he regained a second's more strength.

Done! he thought. He'd done it. Let anyone dare to say he hadn't. Damn them all! He'd paid his debt.

Not quite.

It happened. Without warning. The explosion that threatened to rip the earth apart, which swelled into a fiery mushroom that promised to singe the sky.

Its force touched everyone, including the electronic nerves of that satellite circling miles above. But no one saw it. The sailors were fighting men, trained to know what to do in that eventuality. And they had been reminded of that training by their captains as their ships sailed to their assigned positions. That had been the Commander's decision. He couldn't do anything about possible fallout and accepted that danger as a part of their jobs. But they were his lads, he had to protect them as much as possible. He did not care what Logan would say about that breach of security.

But Logan would never say anything about it.

He had not looked at the blinding cloud, but was a victim of its might nonetheless. The force of the explosion sent mountainous waves rolling out in every direction. One of them picked Logan up and smashed him into the side of the ship. His head was crushed. The last thought he had, the braggart's dare to humanity, was the last thought he would ever have.

If a heaven existed, Neil Logan went to his maker to answer for a life that had been slightly offset, but not balanced, by the events of the last half-hour. If it did not, he just went to a grave at the bottom of the ocean.

It was deadly still in Kruger National Park. The only break in that quiet was that of the lioness and her family devouring their prey. It took time for sound to travel.

They all looked at the grisly sight of Rahmire's mangled body with unemotional calm. They did not worry about the close presence of the lioness; she was obviously content. They addressed themselves instead to the needs of the living. Ali slowly helped Mantizima to his feet and accepted Kloff's silent offer of his handkerchief to bind the wound.

They all moved, not quite in a stupor, but as if it did not concern them anymore. They had done all they could. It was now in other hands.

The sound of the blast when it hit was so fierce it knocked them all to the ground. Yet it, too, left them curiously unaffected. For better or worse, it was all over now. As Warrick had once said, all over but the shouting.

They said nothing to each other. There was nothing to say. Ali pulled herself up and slowly helped a badly battered Mantizima to his feet. She held him up as they slowly made their way back to their vehicle.

Kloff stood behind, watching them move off together. If he'd had it in him, he would have smiled. He was not shocked or disgusted, but rather warmed by the sight of them. Whatever happened in this sometimes sorry world, he thought, life and its joys were still the strongest force and the only one that really mattered.

Mantizima and Ali were lost in each other, but then she remembered the unknown friend who had offered her a hand when she needed it. She stopped and offered hers to him, a gesture of thanks to the man who had won the future back for her.

The unknown friend accepted it.

EPILOGUE

In the days that followed, the world clamored for an explanation of what happened that morning, but South Africa remained mute.

The passing time was gentle on the participants in the tragedy, giving them much needed, much deserved quiet time. The chance to heal. Things had to slow down to that level, however; they started out much more quickly.

Kloff had arranged for medical care for Mantizima before they even left Kruger National Park. Then they were airlifted to a waiting plane that was to bring them back to Johannesburg. Things were chaotic on the plane. Using the radio, Kloff tried to learn what had happened out in the Indian Ocean. But it had been such an unconnected operation from the start, and now the loose ends had been scattered to the four winds.

South Africa was stunned into silence.

Eventually, however, Kloff managed to reach the naval Commander, who gave him a sketchy outline of what had been their end of the mission. He ended on a reluctant note. In the mopping up it was discovered that Logan was missing, presumed dead.

Kloff turned to Mantizima for a fleshing out of those bare details, presenting him with a moral dilemma. Mantizima had been fully prepared to break his blackmail assurances to Logan. He had intended to bring the man to justice, somehow, someway. He owed that to Rune Aykroyd. But now Logan was dead. He *had* been brought to justice of a sort. Society could do no worse to him.

341

Could anything be gained by not allowing the story to die with Logan?

Then Mantizima remembered a memorized quote from a childhood lesson. "The evil that men do lives after them; the good is oft interred with their bones." If there had been any good in Logan's life, it had gone to rest with him. The effects of the evil were still with them, however. Justice had been served on the dead, but what of the living? Could Mantizima look Kloff, the man who had saved his life, in the eye and not tell him he had probably been scheduled to take the fall for Logan until Mantizima happened along, presenting a better choice for the part?

He told Kloff everything, starting back from that day in Boston when he first learned of Nora Brand's plans. He told him everything Ali knew and things she didn't. He told him everything that had happened in that hotel room between him and Logan.

"I guessed most of it," Kloff had said when he finished. "Probably not as fast as you, but I was fairly sure about him. Not about his having Rune killed, however. That I never imagined."

Never would, he implied. But he was glad to have that information, grateful for the chance to make a final notation before closing the book on a man he wished he'd never known.

They'd landed in Jo'burg and went their separate ways. Mantizima and Ali badly needed rest, but there were still things to do. They had to go back to the hospital where they had left Trudi, as he had promised.

The girl who had struggled through the night made it. Trudi still had a long, hard road of recovery ahead of her, but the worst of it was over. She had stabilized enough to be transferred to a White hospital in Johannesburg. Her doctor was sorry to see his unusual patient go.

Mantizima had told the doctor he would return to take the heat if he could, but there wasn't any. The police came to investigate the next morning as expected, but then dropped their investigation without a word of explanation. Kloff had seen to that.

"Mr. Mantizima," the doctor had said in amazement, "you must have friends in very high places."

"Yes, I do," Mantizima had answered, still not completely understanding how he had come to earn that friendship.

They took Trudi back with them, and then the time was their own. They did not hear from Kloff again. Ali had heard a rumor that he'd been promoted into Aykroyd's old job. Fast turnaround in that chair, she thought. But it was just a rumor. Their only touch with South African officialdom was a call they both received from Lukas Kroonhof, the Director of BOSS. He asked them to confirm a report Kloff had made. They did what he requested, asking nothing of him in exchange. They did not know what Kroonhof looked like, but in talking with him, both felt that he sounded like a very old man.

They shifted into a lower gear once they were settled again in Johannesburg, a quiet state that sometimes seemed like a daze, and sometimes like lethargy, but which was neither. They needed to move at that slower pace for a while. They needed time to recover, time to think about what had happened, to integrate the near past into the remainder of their lives, so they could finally put it to rest.

While Ali felt emotionally cut off from everything, she was surprised to find herself physically in the same condition. She was not reached by her paper in the days that followed September 22nd, yet she knew they had to be trying. They wouldn't pass up a chance to tap a reporter on the spot of one of the hotter stories circulating the world at that time. And her calls to San Francisco never went through either; the lines were always jammed, no matter what phone she used. She knew the South Africans were censoring her, she'd met that before, but she was surprised by the magnitude of the network in which they had draped her. In principle, she deplored that censorship, as she always had, but she felt personally unaffected by it. She could have circumvented their efforts, she knew. It would have been easy. While there was no official confirmation of anything, other reporters were sending out their speculations of the event. She could have had one of them send her story, even though that would have meant sharing it, or she could have asked the American Embassy to send it out in a diplomatic pouch. She did neither.

She spent a lot of her time, as much as the doctors would allow, with Trudi. Trudi had no plans for the immediate future other than to heal, but she knew the plans would come when she was ready, and was confident she would be strong enough to carry them out. They talked together for hour upon hour, but they never mentioned a word about what happened that morning or in the two days that preceded it. There wasn't any need to. Postmortems were no longer the order of the day. Yet they communicated freely, in the special way only people who have come through a common disaster can. They shared more than the particulars of having tried to stop a crime, however; they'd each been baptized anew by the flame of the same torch, and it bound them together for life.

She also spent considerable time with Mantizima. He found, much to his surprise, that he was suddenly allowed to move freely, anywhere he chose. He was given much more freedom than the average South African white man. There were two men assigned to him. They followed him everywhere, without making any attempt to hide their presence. But their manner was more like that of bodyguards, protectors, rather than policemen. They never knew what prompted that action, though they presumed it to be Kloff's work.

Mantizima took the freedom offered to him, which he intended to take anyway, but the presence of the guards made it so much easier. He was able to visit Ali openly in her hotel room. No more sneaking and hiding. He never knew if the hotel management was assaulted with cries of outrage because of his actions because those cries never reached him.

He and Ali had not been particularly aware of fearing the consequences if their relationship had been known. That fear might have existed, however. They noticed the change when it did not. Unbridled, their passions reached new heights. Their nights were glorious wonders, enhanced by the attainment of a level of feeling they wouldn't have believed possible. Maybe it wasn't that they were simply free to express things they'd always felt, maybe what they were feeling was new, a more vivid awareness of being alive as a result of having come so close to death.

For whatever reason, their nights were wonderful. Their days, however, were sadly lacking.

The sudden removal of terror left a void between them that was quickly filled by a seemingly insurmountable wall. When they talked, it was only about things that did not matter. They were awkward together, uncomfortable, worse than strangers.

He wanted desperately to share with her the thoughts he'd had about them in the hospital waiting room. He wanted to plan for the future. But he had offered that future once before and it had been rejected. She wanted to tell him about what she had experienced while waiting in the Rover in Kruger, that she was no longer afraid or ambivalent about commitment. He gave her no opening. Both wanted to speak, but neither did. He remained silent because she did and she did because he did. Each viewed the other's frustration about having to be silent as a fence around privacy.

They passed a few days in those quiet ways. Then they each received a call asking them to come to the office of the South African Minister of Defense.

Ali wore her rust silk dress for the appointment. She hadn't had it on since that night when she went out with Aykroyd. Poor Rune, she thought, but her grief was no longer fresh. He seemed to have died in the distant past, a lifetime ago. And she hadn't loved him. He had attracted her, she admitted, but that was all it would ever have been. Something might have happened, she knew, if it hadn't been for Mantizima. When she'd been offered the whole man, how could she have been content with the fraction? Because he became a man of similar stature, the man he should have been in the end, she knew she would never forget him. She would keep the memory of him as a precious piece of memorabilia. And it was in the name of that that she went one day to his grave and left a flower.

She and Mantizima walked down the corridor at the Ministry in silence. As they passed an elderly black man cleaning the hall, he stood at the wall and lowered his head to her. That standard procedure shocked her until she realized that while so much had happened in her life, nothing had changed in anyone else's. Still, the action concerned her. It had occurred once before in Mantizima's presence, in one of BOSS' corridors when they went to watch Wade Petri's interrogation. She tightened inside, knowing how he had cringed then. Now, however, he did not notice it.

The "old man" of the Defense Ministry, as he was affectionately known, one Johann Willem "Willi" Ruysdale, greeted them warmly.

"What can I say to you?" the Minister of Defense said. "I had wanted to express my gratitude to you both. But where do I start? I just thank God you're both still alive," he added in all sincerity.

He went on to tell them about some of what had happened in the past few days. The level of radiation was measured, and did not appear to be too threatening to the people of South Africa, although that couldn't be said with certainty for years to come. Kloff had indeed been promoted into Aykroyd's former position. Logan's parents had been told the truth about his death and, while saddened, they were not surprised.

Then the Minister turned uncomfortably to Ali. "I have a request to make of you, Miss Hayden. I'd like you to agree to forget what happened. As far as your paper is concerned, that is."

"You can't stop her from printing it," Mantizima said defiantly.

"No, I can't," the old man admitted. "I could threaten her, but I don't think that after what she's been through she'd be afraid of me. I could imprison her, but your Embassy would have her released in time. No, I can't stop her if she chooses to, I can only ask."

"Don't you think the world should know what happened?" Mantizima demanded.

"Perhaps, but I don't know any way to tell the people who would be justifiably outraged without also telling those to whom it would give unhealthy ideas. The world is in enough danger with these terrible weapons hanging over its head. But at least those are in the hands of governments. One hopes they will be responsible. What chance would we have, however, if they became the staple of every terrorist's private vendetta?"

"Have you told the Israelis?" Ali asked.

"No, why should I?"

"Don't you think it concerns them?"

"That hasn't been shown. Israel does seem to have been the most likely target, but remember that man who was run over was in Cairo. What was he doing there? Should we tell the Egyptians, too, that revenge for their having made peace offerings to their neighbors might have been planned for them? Should we tell Washington because Alan Warrick was an American? And should we tell Ottawa about Nora Brand? She's been picked up, incidentally—she'll be given a very quiet trial. But should we tell the Canadians because she was involved? Where would it stop?"

His look to Ali was a silent appeal. She hesitated for only a moment.

"All right," she said. "I promise you I won't print this story in a newspaper."

Mantizima was shocked. He thought she must be lying for some reason, but he realized she was not when he looked at her. He knew that face so well. She was telling the truth—she did not intend to print it in a newspaper.

Ruysdale was visibly relieved. With that threat out of the way, he addressed Mantizima.

"Mr. Mantizima, what can I say to you? Nothing can repay the debt we owe you. I've looked into your situation, however, and I think I can offer you something. I promise you that if you choose to stay with us, as I hope you will, things will be very different. You won't be given a passbook. You'll be classified as...." He hesitated, not really knowing what to call it.

"As an unofficial White?" Mantizima asked.

"Yes, something like that."

Ali studied Mantizima in tense silence, searching for some reaction. She saw none.

Poor fool, he thought of the Minister. He really believes his gesture is so magnanimous, but by what right should it be a gesture?

"Oh, I won't be staying," he answered easily. "I have a business to get back to. I've already been away too long."

Ali sighed in relief and grasped his hand. If the Minister was offended by that outward display of affection, he showed no sign of it. Mantizima couldn't understand her surprise until he realized he hadn't told her. The decision had never been consciously made. When the dust cleared, it just stood out as the only conclusion he could sanely have reached. He did not know the words that had come to Ali in her moment of crisis, but he felt their equivalent then. It all was so simple if you only let it be.

"I am so sorry," the Minister said. "I'm truly sorry to lose you."

"There is something you can give me instead," Mantizima said, starting to feel once again like the sharp, business horse-trader he had been.

"Anything."

"You can give my family exit visas. My sister and brother-in-law, Elizabeth and Entato Siqusno, and my mother, Deborah Mantizima, if she chooses to leave. I don't know whether she will. She's not a young woman any longer, her whole life has been lived here, but if her children are gone...."

The Minister demonstrated that he knew more than a little about Mantizima's background. "I'm sure you realize your mother is not the problem. Nor your sister. But Mr. Siqusno is another matter."

"Need I remind you, sir, that you promised me anything?"

"...No, you don't. I can't guarantee that another country will accept them. That will be your problem. But they are free to go whenever they choose. I'll see that the paperwork is done today. When are you planning to return to the States, if I may ask?"

"This afternoon, if I can make it."

Ali was shocked. He said nothing to her about going away, but neither, she remembered, had she mentioned her plans.

"Well then, God go with you."

The interview was over. They stood up to say good-by. Ruysdale shook Ali's hand, and suddenly felt a little unsure about the promise he'd extracted from her, but he said nothing. Then he gripped Mantizima's hand, holding it longer than convention required.

"Be patient with us, Mr. Mantizima. Please. Your people's time will come. I promise you that."

"Don't take too long, Mr. Minister. Every day, all over the world, we see oppression at work. We see it from governments, from terrorists, between private people. And we see the inevitable backlash of death and destruction, but somehow the oppressors never do. Here in South Africa we've just witnessed the effects of one terrifying countdown to destruction. Let me warn you, sir, another one is underway even as we speak. Another countdown is being marked off this very moment, one of an even greater magnitude, one with the force to tear this country apart, but one that is within the power of the people of South Africa to stop."

The Minister understood, but his only answer was to repeat the tired phrases he had already uttered. "Adapt or die," he meant. How often had those words been spoken in those Pretoria mausoleums where the Ministers dwelt? And to what end? With adaptation so slow, they must not have considered the threat of death to be real.

Mantizima knew he could say no more, however. His words would only fall on deaf ears.

Mantizima and Ali walked through the building in a silence unbroken until they reached the lobby, where it was clear there was not much time left for them. They were so strained in each other's presence. She felt so nervous, like an insecure schoolgirl trying to hold onto her first boyfriend.

"I'm glad you're going, Terry," she ventured hesitantly. "You don't belong here."

"No, I don't," he said quietly, wondering how he could ever have believed he did. "You know, you surprised me in there. When you told him you weren't planning to give the story to your paper."

"Oh, that," she said simply. "I decided not to days ago."

They stopped on the building steps and faced each other.

"I thought the story was what it was all about," he said. "At least, part of it. That's the way it started."

"It...changed...." she said inadequately.

She wanted to tell him about the thoughts that led up to that decision, but somehow the time never seemed right. Things *had* changed. She no longer thought of that story in terms of her career; there had been too much death and destruction for that. She now thought of it as her responsibility. She still thought that people had to know about it. They had to know that it happened and it could happen again. And she was really the only one who could tell them because she was the only one who knew it all who had a public voice. But how they learned it now seemed equally important to her. She couldn't allow herself to release the story in an irresponsible way, she couldn't unleash it in a circus, and she knew that's what it would become. The lure of the sensationalism of it would be too much for any newspaper publisher or TV producer to resist. She could just see it. The sidebars with graphic descriptions, perhaps even diagrams, of how the bomb must have been built. The interviews with Rahmire Jones' mother saying he was such a good boy. With Warrick's neighbors, who thought that, underneath it all, he was a great guy. Well, dammit, she thought, he wasn't a great guy, he was a truly evil man. But if people heard that often enough, eventually they would believe it. They would want to believe it to preserve their own feelings of security. All true perspective would be lost.... That was why she thought how she told it was so important. But that was not all of it. There's also another story there, a larger one, the one Mantizima warned Ruysdale about. Together, she thought, they would give a complete picture of the thing the world should dedicate itself to fighting.

She wanted to tell him all of that. Because it represented a turning point in her life and because he was the man who helped bring her to it. She wanted to tell him, but she didn't know how. The past, the things they had shared, however, demanded a better explanation than the one she had given him.

"Let's just say I finally found a story where the 'whys' are more important than the 'whats.'"

He did not understand immediately, but then the connection was made. "Your novel? You're going to write it as a novel?"

351

She flushed with pride for how far she'd come. He really did understand, she thought, and, more importantly, he seemed to care.

"Oh, Ali, I'm really happy for you," he said, a touch wistfully.

She waited, but he did not continue. She waited for him to offer again the place for her to write it. That den in the house by the ocean. She could see it in her mind. She belonged there. She wanted it more than she had ever wanted anything. But he did not offer.

What was happening to them? she cried inside. But she already knew. They were saying good-by. It had all the earmarks of la grande kiss-off. She had to have recognized it. She'd initiated it often enough. This time she didn't want it, however. She had to stop it. But she could not do it. Her life depended on it—and she couldn't do it.

Then a calm settled over her as it did in the Rover. She'd come too far to turn back in definite defeat now. She had to try.

"Is that light still burning in the window?" she asked.

"It always has been," he said in genuine relief. "I didn't think you wanted it."

"Not want it? Oh, Terry...."

"But listen to me, Ali," he said sternly. "I need a commitment. I know that's hard for you. I'll give you time if you need it. I won't pressure you. But I have to warn you I can't live in this day-to-day manner the way you can. I need a commitment."

"You've got it," she said effortlessly.

They laughed together. It was all so easy.

"But I can't come back with you immediately," Ali explained. She had responsibilities, she said, that she'd been avoiding too long. "Once they release the hold they've had on my calls," she explained, "Elliott's gonna pounce on me. By now he must be as anxious as a mother turkey before Thanksgiving. I'll have to scrape up

352

something for him. In a day or two I should be able to knock out those pieces he sent me to do. By the word, they'll probably be the most expensive stories he's ever assigned. And, somehow, I'm going to have to convince him I was in a coma last week."

She also said that she had to go back to Cairo until a suitable replacement could be found.

"But I'll be with you by Christmas," she promised.

"I'll be waiting."

Ali didn't know what to do then. They were in a public place, there were people everywhere. Mantizima did not let that concern him. He took hold of her arms and pulled her to him. He kissed her long and hard, knowing it would have to hold him until she was with him again. He paid no attention to the shock on the faces around them, to the fallen jaws. They did not matter. They never really had.

He released Ali, and she quickly ran off to an empty taxi waiting at the curb. He watched it drive off, then noticed the car that had been parked behind it and the man leaning against it, looking as if he'd been there for some time.

Pieter Kloff was waiting for him.

"Where is she going?" Kloff asked of Ali when Mantizima approached.

"Eventually...home."

"I'm happy for you both."

"Thank you. I understand congratulations are in order for you, too. The Minister told me you'd been promoted."

"Yes, but that's only temporary. Word obviously hasn't reached him. I handed in my resignation this morning."

"Why?"

Why? What could he say? Kloff thought. He was simply the wrong man for the job. He had sworn to uphold the law, but parts of it held things he no longer believed. He could not tell that to the man responsible for opening his eyes. He couldn't tell him how he felt. He

353

didn't know himself. He was not sure whether he felt grateful for Mantizima's unconscious role in stripping him of the bliss that ignorance had provided. That would take time to sort out. But he knew he was not sorry.

"It was just time for a change," Kloff said simply.

Mantizima nodded his understanding of more than the words.

"I'll never see you again," Kloff said. "I—I'm glad to have known you."

"Me, too."

They clasped hands for the first and final time.

"I talked to your mother this morning," Kloff said then, hastily covering his embarrassment. "She told me you were leaving today. I thought you might need a ride to the airport."

"I do. Thank you."

"Don't you have any luggage?" Kloff asked.

"It's already at the airport. I sent it on ahead this morning."

"Then there's nothing keeping us here."

"Nothing. Nothing at all."

Kloff held the front passenger door open and Mantizima climbed in.

As he rode to the airport and the changing panorama glided past the windows, he bid farewell to the land that had given him birth. Then he watched it recede into the background. He was not part of it, he knew, and it was not part of him.

He had found the answers that had brought him there and he was finished with them. He would not forget his brothers. He wouldn't forget South Africa's fight, and he would not avoid it or be silent about it ever again, as he had for too many years. He was not afraid of it. But he had come through an ordeal, not with the knowledge that he had won the right to live his own life as he wished, but that it had always been his. He had faced those two great imposters, triumph and disaster, and walked away his own man. He still wished the best for his brothers. He honored their desire to stay and fight for their place in the South African sun. He was glad to be leaving them ammunition for their battle—a shining image to hold up of what a man, any man, Black or White, could accomplish, what he could be—and he hoped that it served them well.

But it was not his fight any longer.

He parted from Kloff at the gate and made his way to the aircraft. He saw the stewardess at the door, her glossy, professional smile firmly in place. She glanced at his boarding pass.

"That's in the first cabin," she said. "Three rows down on your right, sir."

Sir. It had been a long time. It was good to know it still fit as well as it had before, perhaps even better. Sir. The address of a civilized world to which he was glad to return.

As he felt the plane lift off, leaving the land of his ancestors behind him, he knew that South Africa should mourn the loss of a citizen such as he, that she should cry out to her lost children, begging them to return, but because she did not, because he knew that she probably never would, he also knew he would never look back.